PASSION'S SONG

His arm wrapped around her waist, and she felt the reckless desire to want to stay thus, forever.

"Allesandra, my lady," he whispered. "Let me show you that I am not your enemy."

Her heart thundered against her chest, and she said nothing. Instead, she allowed him to slide his hand up her arm and hold her shoulder as he kissed her temple. Then his other arm slid about her and he held her in a warm embrace. Their kiss was natural, as if she'd known him forever. And she could not deny that she wanted him. How had he wormed his way into her heart and mind? Was he one of Lucifer's angels then? Tempting her beyond her control?

Her body throbbed with a desire stronger than any she had ever felt, and she knew she was not going to fight him anymore.

"Madam," he said in his sensuous tone, "I am no poet, and I do not waste time on words. I would show you my feelings. With actions, I would prove myself."

He led her to the bed and then knelt down to lift the hem of her garment as reverently as any troubadour would do. He kissed her ankles and then her calves, making her gasp as he pulled the garment upward and then over her head until she stood before him in her thin, form-revealing smock.

His lips found her ears and throat, while his hands flamed the desire in every part of her body. She pressed her lips eagerly against his; her hands could not help nesting in his thick black hair. They lowered themselves to the bed, and he stretched out beside her, exchanging her kisses with his, feeling the delight of her skin, as she touched and caressed his muscular torso.

There was no thought but for the pleasure of which the poets sang . . .

The Troubadour's Song

Patricia Werner

Zebra Books
Kensington Publishing Corp.
http://www.zebrabooks.com

ZEBRA BOOKS are published by

Kensington Publishing Corp.
850 Third Avenue
New York, NY 10022

First Printing: November, 1997
10 9 8 7 6 5 4 3 2

Printed in the United States of America

Acknowledgment

Thanks to Deborah Rochefort and *The Compleat Anachronist* for permission to quote her translation of the first stanza of Peire d'Auvergne's "Dejosta ls brues jorns e ls loncs sers."

One

12 September 1213 A.D.

"All of the heretics are on the march against us, it would seem," said Gaucelm Deluc to his general, Simon de Montfort, who was commander of the crusade against the heretics in the fertile southern lands of the Languedoc.

They stood at the battlements on top of the walls of the fortified town of Muret, which they had occupied only since yesterday. There had been no real resistance from the town militia when the French army had marched in. But now the heretics were attempting to take it back.

Indeed, on this morning the sun was so strong that the colors of the landscape were hot. Yellow fields, violent reds and oranges burnished the leaves on trees that huddled near the marshes on the upper bank of the Louge, an insignificant stream that trickled into the wider Garonne.

Where the two rivers joined, the town of Muret formed a triangular fortress of considerable strength, protected on two sides by water and the citadel that formed the northeast wall of the town. A curtain wall stretched along the quay where the Garonne glistened and then turned southwest to flank the lower plains stretching out toward rolling hills on the west.

Even though Gaucelm was a French noble, from a family of fine lineage, loyal to the Capetian kings of France, he could not help but be affected by the warm, rich lands of the South. Ever since he'd ridden out with the other Frenchmen who'd taken the cross on this crusade, Gaucelm had found these rolling plains and lush forests appealing. Enchanted was the word that came to mind, though as a warrior he did not believe in any kind of enchantment.

Beside Gaucelm, the wily Simon de Montfort watched the besieging army make camp. He was a slightly smaller man than the tall, broad-shouldered Gaucelm Deluc. Though smaller of stature, Baron de Montfort was nonetheless commanding in his leadership.

Gaucelm's bravery and intelligence had attracted Simon's attention, and in councils of war, he had come to depend on Gaucelm more and more. For his part, Gaucelm respected this man who had a genius for battle strategy and could build an effective army out of shifting groups of men from all parts of France and out of mercenaries of dubious reliability. The two had become friends as well as colleagues of war.

From boats moored on the Garonne, siege engines were being unloaded and rolled into position on the opposite bank of the Louge from where Gaucelm and Simon stood on the citadel wall. Since dawn, the machines already in place had begun to harass the priory situated inside the walls beside the north town gate. But Simon's own archers positioned along the top of the wall tried to discourage the heretics from loading their projectiles onto the machines of war.

Below them, the heavy wooden gates of the town thudded shut, then the envoys of the opposing camp clattered their mounts across the bridge spanning the Louge. Shouts were heard as the enemy envoy trotted onto the road and back into their camp.

"They outnumber us, my lord," said Gaucelm.

Across the meek Louge, the count of Toulouse, the count of Foix, and the count of Comminges had gathered the southern forces in a disorganized camp, protected on the east by the flowing Garonne. The heretics had a force of more than a thousand mounted knights and men-at-arms, supported by possibly ten thousand foot soldiers.

"Ten or eleven thousand to our sixteen hundred," answered

Simon, touching his dark mustache and short beard as he considered. "But our nine hundred horse matches their mounted men of about the same numbers."

"Hmmm, just so," said Gaucelm. He studied the melee of horsemen and foot, the gathering of three allied armies under three different Languedoc nobles. "I do not think they form an organized whole. Perhaps they cannot agree on how to retake their town."

"So it would appear," agreed Simon. "I do not understand why they do not build a barricade on their western flank. Nor do their archers form any line of defense."

Gaucelm could see that the heretics' camp lay open to attack from the west. Any sensible army would dig a trench and put up stakes, at least. For then they could retreat behind it. But the camp was unprotected on that side and what appeared to be a council of war was taking place on the meadow across the road from the camp. Sun glinted off helmets and chain mail while men-at-arms held upright lances with pennants drooping from the ends and painted shields bearing the colors of the various southern knights.

"Perhaps that is why."

Gaucelm nodded his head toward an army that suddenly poured over the crest of a hill nearly a mile west of the town. Simon narrowed his eyes and stared at this new host, his quick military mind estimating their number.

Gaucelm also counted the horsemen that moved in a ragged line to join the allies awaiting them. When they got nearer, he could see their battle standards flying from long poles.

"The king of Aragon," he said.

About eight hundred horse spilled down the slope to swell the ranks of the already huge army that was beginning to besiege the fortified town of Muret. But neither Simon nor Gaucelm panicked. As his most trusted lieutenant, Gaucelm knew how Simon de Montfort, the remarkable general of the king's army, worked. Though the forces against them were now eight to one

if all the foot soldiers were counted, Gaucelm waited and surveyed.

He had been watching the camp gather since dawn, for he was
the most help to the wily Simon when he could read the minds
of their opponents. Once Simon's mind was decided on a strategy,
the general relied on Gaucelm to quickly relay the orders to their
battle corps.

But now, even in their disarray, this new force under the banner
of the king of Aragon looked daunting.

"Do we sally forth to meet them?" asked Gaucelm.

Even with the best strategy, the odds were against them. Their
nine hundred horse could surely be swallowed up against a cavalry of two thousand allied horse, to say nothing of the ten thousand or so of the heretic forces on foot.

"Not yet," said Simon, glaring into the oncoming force. "We
wait to see how they will array themselves."

His own forces waited out of sight of the enemy in the market
square of the new town, which was below the old town at the
foot of the castle where Gaucelm and Simon stood. There, at a
moment's notice, they could form into battle array and carry out
his orders. "You say this Peter of Aragon is a hero?" asked Simon.

"A knight-errant," replied Gaucelm with a dismissive shrug.
"The winner of many tournaments and many raids against the
Moors in Spain, but no fit match against our discipline."

"And Count Raymond VI of Toulouse is no warrior either,"
said Simon with a sneer. "He promises the pope he will root out
heresy in his lands, pretends to be a good Catholic and loyal
subject to the king. But we know he does nothing but turn his
back while heretics flourish under his nose." Simon smoothed
his mustache, considering. "He is equally indecisive in battle,
from what I've seen."

Both men knew and agreed that this last point was how the
two opposing forces differed.

Gaucelm and Simon and the small garrison that held the town
of Muret were here because Pope Innocent III had finally con-

nived to make King Philip Augustus of France send an army to crush the heretics of the Cathar sect who flaunted orthodoxy.

The heretics were stubborn, independent people with their own language and character, distinct from that anywhere else in France. But the heretic counts could not agree, and Simon de Montfort had nipped away at the southern lands of the Languedoc, leaving many of the towns in the hands of French knights and barons who had conquered them.

Never had crusading been so easy. Pope Innocent III had offered more than spiritual blessings; he decreed that the northern barons could depose any southern lords who had protected or tolerated heresy. The chances for plunder were great—and they did not have to hazard a voyage to the Holy Lands to fulfill crusading vows.

"Peter of Aragon's troops do not even ride in formation," said Simon with disdain in his voice. "I've heard it said that he has taken on this enterprise to please his mistress, the wife of a baron of Languedoc."

Gaucelm uttered a sound of contempt. "True, my lord, if we are to believe his own handwriting in the letter we intercepted on its way to said lady."

"We need not fear to get the better of this light king," said the righteous Simon, "if he has declared war on God's cause to please one sinful woman."

Above them, on the battlements of the citadel, French crossbowmen in their hauberks of mail released their deadly bolts which sped with great accuracy at the enemy still trying to work the stone-throwing mangonels. Screams pierced the air where the besieging heretics had not seen the powerful crossbows raised and fired in unison. At the same time, longbowmen fired from narrow, vertical arrow loops, slots in the citadel tower walls from which hundreds of arrows produced a deadly rain on those unfortunate enough to be within their range.

But Gaucelm was no fool. The French held the town, but a long, wearisome siege was hardly the way to maintain their position of strength. They had only sixteen hundred men to command at the moment, and soon those men's forty days of service to the crusade would be up, and they would want to go home. No, they must act.

Gaucelm could almost hear the thoughts forming in Simon's mind as the two men watched the new army under the standard of the king of Aragon straggle onto the meadow where the other leaders of the allies met in their council of war.

Finally, Simon spoke. "We will lull them into thinking we have no choice but to hide behind these walls," he said. "And then we will appear to withdraw."

"To withdraw, my lord?"

"As you pointed out, we cannot hope to overcome them with numbers, and so we will depend on our training and on the element of surprise. If we cannot hope to meet them in a pitched battle, we will have to take them on one division at a time."

Gaucelm smiled. "Ah, you have a plan."

"You, my friend, will take all our foot soldiery and throw open the Louge gate. You will lure whichever of those foolish lords wishes to accept your challenge into an assault on the gap we will open for them."

"With seven hundred spears and crossbows, we can easily hold the passage," said Gaucelm. "The heretics can only march across the bridge three or four abreast at most."

"Just so. After they are distracted by this ploy, I will take the knights and ride out of the south gate."

"Ah, you will appear to withdraw, and then when their guard is down, you will circle northward and surprise them."

Though it was a daring plan, and the numbers were still against them, Gaucelm knew the wily general had carried out such strategies before.

"We will strike swiftly. Their own confusion will serve in our behalf," said Simon.

"Godspeed."

Gaucelm wasted not a moment taking long strides along the parapet walk. He issued quick orders to the sergeant-at-arms, and within seconds, his orders were passed all along the wall.

* * *

When Allesandra Valtin saw Peter of Aragon's forces ride over Perramon Hill, her decision was made. She, too, had been watching the allies make their camp on the opposite bank of the Louge from where she stood in the citadel. Trapped in the town when Simon de Montfort had taken it, she'd agonized while the siege outside had formed.

If Simon de Montfort knew that within his grasp was a baron's widow who now controlled substantial southern holdings and who was a close friend of the count of Toulouse, the evil de Montfort would take her hostage. She would be held for ransom or worse, should Simon become desperate. And Simon de Montfort had a reputation for cruelty.

"Count Simon is occupied in defending these walls he has taken," she said to her friend, Marguerite Borneil, in whose castle they were incarcerated. "We are fortunate that most of his army already turned homeward, and he is left with only a small garrison."

The dark-blond Marguerite looked over the taller Allesandra's shoulder into the sunlight where the confused sounds of the siege were reaching them. "You think he would massacre the town."

"I do." Allesandra clenched her jaw. "He has done so before. They say he once threw the lady of the castle down a well and heaped stones upon her until she died." It made Allesandra shudder to think of the horrible tale. "He goes beyond the usual rules of reprisal."

"A man much to be feared."

"That is why we must dislodge him. I will not stand by while the people of Muret are murdered."

"That is what our besieging army is supposed to prevent, my dear."

"But they will not," said Allesandra in a tone of aggravation, "unless they can act as one. See how our contingents mill about. They are not formed into any sort of battle array. Some do not even stay by their horses. Indeed, it looks as if none of the corps know what the other is doing."

"You sound as if you do not rely upon your friend Raymond to command his fellow counts."

"How can he when they have all had such quarrels recently? Only this threat from the north brings them together. I love Raymond as a friend and respect him as my overlord, but I fear his weakness."

"Which is?"

"Indecisiveness."

Marguerite sighed. "Raymond simply wishes to maintain peace by promising the pope he will do what he can to eliminate the heretics. But of course these are his people, he will not raise a hand against them."

"I do not question his character. He has protected us by not betraying us. I only question his generalship. But enough talk. I must go."

"Where?"

"There . . ." She nodded in the direction of the milling knights on the meadow beside the road to Toulouse.

Peter of Aragon was almost upon them, but Allesandra did not expect the king of Aragon to unify the southern lords any more than Count Raymond could. The counts of the Languedoc were all too independent, and they had never had to defend their principalities as one against the king of France before. She must help them.

"I'll go with you, then," said Marguerite.

"No, you might be needed here to try to ascertain what the devious Simon de Montfort will do. But you must get out of the clothing that will give you away as a noblewoman. You'll be less easily captured that way. Have your maid bring simple clothing. You must appear to be a townswoman. And I must look like a young man. Can that be managed?"

Marguerite gave orders to her maid, and sent a squire to saddle Allesandra's horse. Soon the ladies' sleeveless supertunics were cast aside, long-sleeved gowns and chemises tossed onto benches while the two ladies divested themselves of the marks of their stations. Allesandra donned the loose linen braies and hose drawn up over them and tied them to the breech-girdle that held the braies around the waist.

Marguerite could not resist teasing her friend even in the midst of such dire straits.

"You are certainly adept at male underclothing," she said as her own maid laced up a simple gown at her back and then combed Marguerite's long straw-colored hair over it, handing her a wimple.

Allesandra reached for the man's shirt and pulled it over her head. "I was married for many years, madam. I am no stranger to a man's wardrobe."

Over the shirt, she pulled a long-sleeved tunic, not unlike the dress she was used to wearing except for its length, which came only to her knees, revealing the hose beneath. The long slit at the neck of the tunic revealed the linen shirt and the curve of her breast. But the plain nut-brown cloak she drew about her shoulders and tied at her throat would disguise her feminine form to all but the most discerning eye. She loosened the pins that held her hair dressed in plaits and wound over the ears. Long, loose-flowing dark hair tucked under the cape would more resemble a young man's hair than the coils meant to be hidden by wimple and veil.

"Come," she said to Marguerite, who now appeared to be a housewife to one of the burghers in town.

Marguerite followed Allesandra through the outer chamber, and the maid was about to grasp the handle of the heavy door when a thunder of footsteps sounded on the spiral stairs beyond.

"Wait," said Allesandra. "Something has happened."

She pressed herself to the edge of the door and grasped the handle to pull it open only a crack. In the flicker of light from wall sconces that lit the inner staircase she saw the hated French foot-soldiers fly past, quivers of arrows on their backs, longbows tightly strung in their arms.

A tall knight in hauberk, the chain mail garment that covered his long-limbed body from chin to toe, clanked down the stone steps and stopped a few feet from where Allesandra peered out. He issued sharp commands to the archers in northern French, which Allesandra understood from a year spent in that region, and she closed the door tighter for fear of discovery.

"What is it?" whispered Marguerite, who had flattened her back to the door at the sound of the hurrying soldiers.

Allesandra opened the door a crack once more, but the knight in command of the infantry had not moved. She lifted a finger to her lips to indicate to Marguerite that they must be silent.

She could see little of his face, hidden by the helmet with nasal bar covering his nose and mail laced over chin and tied to the helmet with thongs. But his deep baritone voice brooked no argument, and the sleeveless surcoat covering the chain mail to the knee was of rich material, the panels yellow and blue.

The long sheath that hung from his belt was of finely tooled leather, and the sword hilt drew her attention. The cross-guard was inlaid with ivory and gold, and the round pommel carved in regal design. His long, triangular shield was divided into quarters of the same colors as his surcoat.

A knot formed in her abdomen as she watched the archers move past in hurried discipline. Sergeants-at-arms stood behind this commander. When he barked orders to them, they flew down the stairs to take up positions by the north gate. Her throat felt dry. The Frenchmen had planned something.

The archers were followed by more foot-soldiers, these carrying long, sharply pointed lances. The knight called out to a sergeant-at-arms who stopped beside him.

"Make a sharp fight at the gate," he ordered. "A distraction to lure the enemy inside. The crossbows remain above to make sure you will have no more on the bridge than you can manage."

The sergeant nodded and clattered downward to take charge of the challenge.

Oh, Raymond, Allesandra thought to herself desperately. *I must get to you and tell you what has happened within the castle and how many men are within the town.* She clenched her jaw, trying to still the nervousness and listen to the French knight. For in moments she hoped to be in Raymond's camp, and she could relay what she heard here.

The knight said no more, but as he turned, she caught sight of his blazing dark eyes, a formidable expression on what she could see of his well-defined face. Prominent cheekbones spoke of his noble birth, and determination and courage showed in the way he moved as he joined the flow of soldiers hurrying downward.

She waited only a few seconds to see if any more soldiers would come from above. Her breath came in quick, shallow gasps. She would have to take a chance. She was not armed and hoped to be taken for a mere squire. Surely they would not massacre the citizens yet. And mere soldiers would not be able to tell that she was in actuality a noblewoman worth interrogating.

"Now," she hissed at Marguerite, who took her place holding the door as Allesandra slipped through.

Her heart pounding, she took the stairs downward. Ahead of her the soldiers clanked. Every time she glanced backward over her shoulder she feared discovery, for all her bravado about her disguise. But she made it safely to the ground level in time to see the soldiers filing through the great hall. She hesitated. Her way to the stables lay in the opposite direction. Should she follow the soldiers and gain even more information to relay to Count Raymond on the field?

At the moment of her hesitation, the knight she had glimpsed upstairs burst through the passage at the opposite end of the great hall. Instinctively, she stepped behind a screen. Now, sword drawn, he glanced about the hall as if to ascertain if there was any danger from the rear of his guard. Since the Frenchmen were in a hostile citadel in a hostile town, there was always danger of treachery from within.

Two servants had been sweeping up the soiled rushes from the floor and had hidden behind the wall hangings as the soldiers passed. Now they crept out to continue their task, but froze at the sight of the tall, fierce Frenchman.

For a moment Allesandra held her breath as the knight's eyes swept over the screen behind which she hovered. But he must have decided it wasn't worth his investigation, for he turned and followed the rest of his men down the passage. Clearly they were on their way to the north gate.

She decided to follow them no farther. The stables lay in the opposite direction, and if she were to ride out of the south gate, through the old town and out the small door that led to the quay beside the river, she could tarry no longer.

She turned and wended her way through the castle, reaching out to offer reassurance to those she passed who worried for their fate. For with her hood thrown back, most of Marguerite's household recognized her.

"What will happen, my lady?" asked the wife of Marguerite's steward. "The bishop has left the priory and has taken refuge in the lord's bedchamber above." The woman's eyes lifted to the ceiling above which lay the master's sleeping chamber.

"Don't worry," said Allesandra. "Your mistress will direct the defense of the castle."

Marguerite's husband was in the field with Raymond. Simon de Montfort had taken the town of Muret in order to control communications between Toulouse and the Pyrenees. With her husband absent, the lady of the manor assumed full seigneurial duties, as in all households of this sort, and that included defending the castle when there was danger.

Allesandra hurried on to the stables and located her own steed, the chestnut mare she'd ridden here from her own castle, a day's ride to the southwest. She'd come here to meet with her friend Count Raymond and to take word of the latest danger back to the Cathar believers who met in her district. But it seemed she must assist in a battle before she could have her conversation with Raymond.

She left the stables none too soon. One of the squires dashed into the courtyard from the lower town just as she opened the side door leading to the quay. The water outside carried the sound of sudden cries and clashing metal. She grasped the squire's arm.

"What's happened?" she demanded.

"An assault," he answered, his eyes round with panic. "At the north gate." He pointed in the direction of the skirmish.

"Who is fighting?"

"The count of Foix leads the charge against the French garrison."

"On the bridge?" She frowned.

"Yes, madam."

A stupid place to fight, she thought, but held her tongue and let the squire dash on his way to be of help where he could

Now she wasted no time. Once on the quay, she mounted up and pulled her hood forward to shield her face. Then she kicked her heels into her horse's side and flew south along the quay, away from the battle beside the town wall. She passed the ancient Roman masonry of the old cité, and then the new wall of the lower town. Ahead was her goal, the south bridge over the Garonne that led to open country.

But as she turned onto the bridge, the south town gate creaked open behind her, and a contingent of horsemen poured through. Allesandra's heart leapt into her throat when she saw Simon de Montfort himself lead his men forth. But the frightening sight only spurred her on, and she bent over her horse and urged the mare to dash over the bridge. For one horrifying second she imagined all of de Montfort's corps coming after her and taking her prisoner, and she dared not look back.

Instead, she turned when she'd crossed the bridge and pressed the mare to the north, where even with her hair and the wind in her eyes, she knew that the allies' boats waited. She raced for her life. Only when the camp was within sight and she plunged her horse into the Garonne did she dare look back.

The French army had not followed. She could now see the enemy forces riding southeast on the road away from the town. The sight confused her. A withdrawal? With the infantry still fighting at the north gate? Some deep suspicion nagged, and while she paused, her horse breathing hard after the short burst of speed, she tried to grapple with the French strategy.

Then she urged the horse into the middle of the river. "Come on, Kastira," she addressed the horse. "Swim."

As she swam the horse through the middle of the river and came out on the bank at the edge of the allied camp, Allesandra had time to assess the chaos in front of her. In the distance by the north gate the count of Foix's colors showed that his men still engaged in mostly hand-to-hand combat with French soldiers, fighting for possession of the bridge. The gate was open and now several horsemen slashed their way in.

"My God," she breathed, riding through the camp, where the rest of the allied infantry still milled about, yelling and gesturing excitedly. "It's some sort of trap."

"Where is Count Raymond?" she yelled at a knot of soldiers she approached.

"There," one of them answered, and pointed to a tent in the middle of the camp.

She nudged her horse forward and then dismounted when she found her objective.

"Raymond," she shouted, her soft boots sliding on the damp grass.

Count Raymond VI of Toulouse turned from the group of men with whom he was speaking and looked at her in surprise. He was clad in chain mail and helmet, but even if she didn't know the slope of his squarish shoulders, his surcoat of red and white identified him, as did the pennant drooping from several lances held erect by his tent.

He stepped forward to meet her. "My lady Allesandra, what are you doing here?"

"Come to assist you," she said in tones that brooked no argument. "Simon de Montfort is up to something and you've no time to waste."

"Yes, yes, well, you see the skirmish at the gate. I had suggested building a barricade by the road in case the French do break out of the gate. But Foix and Comminges do not agree."

They were distracted by shouts and sergeants-at-arms running through the camp toward them.

"Sir, they withdraw," said a knight who spoke to the men-at-arms, and then turned to address Count Raymond.

"They withdraw?" he asked, lifting his thick eyebrows under his helmet.

"They've been seen on the road south in formation," said the knight.

"Well," said Raymond. "Perhaps they realize that we outnumber them and are giving up the fight."

An image of the French knight on the staircase in the tower came to mind, and Alessandra stepped between the men.

"It is a trick, my lord," she said, making Raymond look at her. "They would not withdraw their cavalry and leave their infantry in the middle of an assault on the other side of the town. Rouse your men, sir, Simon de Montfort is going to attack."

"My dear," said Raymond, "he will hardly attack us in the field. We outnumber him fifteen to one. It would be his suicide."

Exasperation overwhelmed her. "You are in charge of this army, Raymond. We haven't time to argue."

He shook his head helplessly. "I've been arguing all morning with Foix and Cumminges. Now King Peter is making camp across the road. Surely our forces are large enough to handle any sorties Simon de Montfort might make. But you heard the message. Simon withdraws. We will retake the town with little difficulty now. But you must get yourself out of danger, my dear. You could be injured by a misdirected missile."

"Where is Peter of Aragon?" she demanded, holding on to Raymond's mail-clad arm and not letting go until she had an answer. "If you will not form into battle array, perhaps he will."

"He makes camp on the right flank, but come into my tent, my lady. You must protect yourself."

Instead, she dropped Raymond's arm and rushed to her horse. A sergeant-at-arms saw her fly in his direction and assisted her to mount. Then she picked her way through the disorganized camp, staying behind the line of mangonels and balistas that haphazardly launched stones toward the crossbowmen who fired down on the count of Foix from the citadel parapets.

Getting free of Raymond's camp, she flew across the road toward Peter of Aragon. Some of the men were pitching tents, while others clumped in groups. Squires watered horses. Some of the knights even had their helmets off and were refreshing themselves at the edge of the Louge. She rode through the camp, asking her way to King Peter.

But when she reached the opposite side of the camp, she saw she was too late. For while she'd wasted time talking to Raymond, the French corps had evidently wheeled northward and crossed the Louge above the northward-bending loop where the land was marshy, but not impassable.

Suddenly a great cry went up as she stared in horror. Simon de Montfort's men, in tight battle formation, bore down upon the unsuspecting camp.

Two

All around her the complacent knights began to stir. She watched with horror as the tight French formation crossed the river at its lowest point. And then they were up the bank and upon Aragon's men. She wheeled her horse so as not to be caught in the midst of the battle.

"A sword!" she shouted at some men-at-arms still on foot. "I'm unarmed."

One sergeant-at-arms heard her cry and turned to respond. At that moment her hood flew back and the hair that loosened from the cape betrayed her.

"Madam, get back," the man said in surprise at seeing a woman mounted for war.

"Not without a weapon to defend myself," she demanded.

The force of her words persuaded him and he handed her a short sword.

The French corps had already penetrated the camp, which was taken entirely by surprise.

The knights attempted to get to horse. But they hadn't time to form into battle array. Now from the other side of the road, Raymond's own men mounted and tried to join the mêlée. Just what Allesandra had feared would happen seemed to be taking place. And the camp had no barricade behind which to fall back.

She struggled to skirt the men attempting to join the rush, for she was no soldier, and though she'd come to warn them and to try to talk the three armies into acting under one commander, she could not win the day herself. Now that battle was engaged, she would do best to get out of their way.

She passed back to the road and saw that the Count of Foix's men rushed in a tangle from the bridge, leaving the enemy holding it. Not having coordinated their orders, Foix's infantry rushed into the fight, while Count Raymond's infantry attempted instead to barricade their camps with wagons and carts. She saw the men forming ranks in front of the wagons, the bases of their pikes fixed into the ground, the lancelike heads of steel pointing forward to protect archers who took aim from the wagons.

But now the unprepared mounted knights began to scatter like the wind at the impact of the two front squadrons of the French army. As the knights of Foix and Comminges began to disperse, the foot-soldiery poured back toward the camp. King Peter's knights were finally assembled, and she could see his banner waving. But the surrounding French outnumbered them.

A French charge was led against the king of Aragon. For a moment, the small solid mass of Frenchmen were swallowed up by the less closely arrayed ranks of Aragonese. The mêlée swayed backward and forward, the din excruciating.

She watched as the knight she'd seen in the castle led a third group of Frenchmen across the river. He wheeled his small division westward and closed in upon the right flank of the Aragonese. She watched in astonishment as, riding at the head of his rank, he received a shower of blows. But he held his own, cut a space around him and plunged deep into the mêlée.

In a moment the cry went up, "The king is dead. Peter of Aragon is dead."

"Oh, my God," Allesandra whispered to herself, stunned at the carnage as more of Peter's knights fell.

The rest began to flee. But the French army did not stop at vanquishing the southern knights. They pushed forward, cutting down the infantry like so many trees in a forest. Those who could get away fled in all directions. The sight was too horrible to do anything but numb her.

But she realized that she, too, soon could be slashed to bits by the merciless French. She looked about for Raymond, saw his standards and rode toward them. But when she got behind the lines and approached his tent, he was nowhere to be seen. There was no more time. She could not risk being taken, for it was not merely her life that was at risk. She was responsible for her estates, and if she were captured, the French would claim her fief and all those who depended on her. The heretics she protected would be rounded up, interrogated, fined. If they did not recant, they would be imprisoned or burned at the stake. She could not stay here for this rout.

She dug in her heels and guided her horse back to the river, swam across, then flew along the way she had come. Fortunately de Montfort's men were busy securing the north gate, and she was still able to enter the town from the quay.

They had lost Muret because three counts could not stand together, and that brave fighter Peter of Aragon had arrived too late to save the day. Anger and tears kindled her determination to fight back at the French who had invaded these lovely lands in the name of the corrupt but powerful Catholic church. She must not allow her own lands to fall to the greedy enemy.

From the corner of his eye, Gaucelm saw a figure with long dark hair fleeing along the edges of the rout. A woman, from the way she sat the horse. And the urgency on the angular, pale face turned his way for one brief instant was unmistakably feminine.

Her dark eyes glared hatred, and then she was away, plunging into the river. He watched only long enough to see her horse clamber up the bank and turn to gallop beside the river. Then he turned his attention back to the field while his horse picked its way among the dead.

"The day is ours," said Gaucelm, riding up to his commander after having organized the collection of booty among the fallen. He was winded and perspiring, and he removed his helmet to let the breeze cool him. His surcoat was stained with blood. Fortunately little of it was his own.

Simon surveyed the carnage from his horse as his soldiers walked among the dead, picking up weapons and shields. He took some pride in the cleverness of his strategy, but he also believed it was a manifestation of the fact that their cause was righteous.

"God has thrust through His enemies with avenging swords," he declaimed, "and executed His wrath on the people who have offended Him by deserting the faith and associating with heretics. What of Raymond of Toulouse and his son?" Simon asked of Gaucelm.

"Escaped."

"Unfortunate," replied Simon. "We have defeated the combined forces of the princes of Languedoc, but it remains for us to enter the count's own city of Toulouse."

"Nevertheless," said Gaucelm as he surveyed the fallen, "the crusading season has been a success this year. We have taken much territory for the king of France in the name of the pope."

"We have," said Simon. "Come, our job here is not yet done. We must enter the town and see to it that the bishop is installed."

Simon wheeled and gathered his little entourage, which crossed the north bridge and entered the town. Inside the gate, they turned into the priory courtyard where Bishop Fulk awaited them, flanked by two deacons in church vestments. Bishop Fulk was a tall man, made to appear taller by the ornamented triangular-shaped mitre on his head, the points rising from the band in front and back. His pale cheeks flushed with excitement, and the satisfied curve at the corners of long, thin lips indicated his sense of righteousness at being part of the victorious party.

Gaucelm remained mounted while his commander dismounted and walked to where the bishop had positioned himself just outside the entrance to the chapel on steps that placed him above everyone else. Simon knelt to kiss the bishop's ring.

"Rise, my son," intoned the bishop to the humbled commander. "The heretics have asked for the judgment of God, and God has judged in our favor."

He frowned momentarily at the rest of Simon's contingent, who remained mounted, as if he expected them to also humble themselves before God's most holy representative.

Gaucelm nonetheless remained upright in his saddle. He was no fool. The French had just gained a victory where the fiercely independent lords of the Languedoc thought they could dislodge their enemy. If the French soldiers did not remain fully armed and on guard while order was being reestablished, they could easily be betrayed.

Seeing that the knights who accompanied Simon would not get down from their horses, the bishop was forced to raise his robed arm aloft to dispense his blessing. The embroidered threads of silver and gold glittered in the now-hot sun that glared down upon the scene of carnage and victory. From the distance, the wails of the bereaved carried to them. The bishop blessed the army of the pope, and then Simon stood.

"Will my lord bishop ride with us through the town? It is our duty to accept the keys to the city as a symbol that Muret and any lands dependent on it now pay homage to our spiritual leader, His Most Holy Eminence, Pope Innocent III, and to his majesty King Philip Augustus of France."

"Most assuredly," said the bishop in a voice used to preaching in vast cathedrals to humbled minions. He lifted his hand and allowed one long finger to signal the arrival of his litter for the procession through town.

Simon had no need to send word to the councilmen of the

town. They knew they were defeated, and though Muret had housed a French garrison for two days, town government had proceeded on its own course. Now a display of homage would be expected. After that, financial arrangements would be made for damages and tithes paid out of the citizens' pockets to their new overlords.

The ornate litter was carried out on the shoulders of the bishop's servants. His staff of deacons and other local priests had garbed themselves in their finest vestments for the display of victory. Still in battle garb, Gaucelm rode beside Simon ahead of the litter, and the other knights followed behind it, as the procession left the priory and made its way into the streets.

Glancing upward at the citadel above them, Gaucelm could see the French pennants being flown from poles on the ramparts as their men quickly took control of the town walls and the castle. Then they passed into the crowded, narrow streets, where wattle and daub and timber houses leaned irregularly two and three stories to steeply pitched roofs.

Since the battle had been outside the walls of the town, there were few signs of suffering here. Except that ordinary business in stalls and ground-floor shops that opened to the street had come to a halt. Gaucelm perceived the subtle difference and narrowed his eyes to study the housewives in gowns and mantles and merchants in fur-trimmed surcoats who broke off from hushed conversations to stand silently and acknowledge the victors.

No one cheered. Some of the women knelt and bowed their heads as the bishop's litter passed. But most of the citizens stood silently, staring straight ahead. Only the geese honked and fluttered from under the hooves of the horses. As Gaucelm looked from one face to another, he read the resentment there, pride, and yes, hatred. He felt the clutch of uneasiness at the eerie silence within the town.

The Catholic church was determined to root out heresy in these lands. How many of the citizens of Muret were either heretics themselves or sheltered them? Gaucelm was a fighting man, loyal to the king of France. He'd sworn his fealty and had engaged in many battles over territory. The king's enemies were his enemies. He had fought to take lands back from the English King John, and Gaucelm was proud of helping King Philip extend his empire.

But this long struggle in the South over religion was a different kind of war. He watched the citizens of Muret avert their faces from the knights who rode in victory, then drop their eyes before the bishop. These people were not going to be easy to subdue.

"What are your plans for the townspeople?" Gaucelm asked Simon as they made their way slowly.

"I shall spare them. A town without its artisans and merchants is a town without an economy. If there is no one to sell our armies supplies, we cannot support ourselves. If these burghers cooperate and give up the heretics we want, no harm will come to them."

"That is wise, my lord. And the estates we shall surely gain will work the better for the king of France and for his vassals if we leave them intact and reap their harvests for ourselves."

"True, my friend," replied Simon. "A show of power is necessary at times, but perhaps we have already made our point."

They followed the narrow streets of the old town to the old Roman wall and passed through into the lower new town. Here the packed streets were straighter, and they came at last to the market square where the contingent formed up around the bishop's litter. Opposite them on the steps of the Church of St. Denis waited the mayor and the town councilmen.

The rich colors of their mantles and hose, their fine soft leather boots, and the gold and jeweled clasps showed their wealth. They stood in a tight group, no doubt wondering if they would be alive or dead after they handed the keys to the city over to the bishop. None spoke. The cries and moans of those who had lost loved ones in the battle were farther away now, barely heard.

Bishop Fulk alighted from his litter, and his deacons made sure his vestments were straight. Simon and his knights dismounted while the sergeants-at-arms who had accompanied them held the standards behind them.

The bishop approached the church steps and the mayor came down and knelt on one knee in front of him. In the silence, a breeze ruffled through the market square and past the church. Everyone waited. But Bishop Fulk took his time surveying the scene, a satisfied smile on his face as he gave his blessing. Then Simon stepped forward. His narrow dark eyes glittered, and his tone brooked no argument.

"I, the victor of this day, Simon de Montfort, general of the French army, hereby claim this town and all its lands for his majesty, King Philip of France, who has taken up the sword in the name of God's holy Catholic Church. Until our august king decides how to dispense this town, I hand the keys to the city to His Holiness, Bishop Fulk, who stands as the pope's representative on this holy mission. You will cooperate with his court and answer any questions he may have in his quest to erase the evils of heresy from these lands."

Simon's eyes now rested on the faces of each of the town's representatives in turn. "Those of you who answer the questions put to you of the bishop's court will be spared. If you say you know nothing of heretics and are proven to be a liar, you will suffer the same fate as unrecanting heretics themselves." He paused while his words sank in.

Finally, the mayor, a substantial-looking man of medium height, got to his feet and spoke. "We hear you, my lord, and we abide by the king's overlordship and to any he may appoint to govern our fair town."

He lifted up the heavy, clattering keys to the city gates and to the count's palace.

Simon stepped forward and took them from the solid burgher, whose well-trimmed beard and the hair curled beneath his ears now ruffled in the breeze. Simon handed the keys to the bishop and then knelt for a blessing.

Gaucelm itched for the ceremonies to be over. There was still much to be done, and he stole a glance back at the town above them. A gentle slope rose from the market square up through the new town. Church spires, chimneys, and roofs rose toward the citadel at the top. He suddenly remembered the woman fleeing the battlefield, and something told him she was important. Gaucelm did not know himself to be prescient, but some sort of warning came to him.

As soon as the ceremonies were over and Simon mounted again, Gaucelm caught Simon's ear. "The citadel, my lord. Is it secure?"

"You saw our standards flying from its ramparts. The leaders we vanquished from the field surely will not take refuge there. I will not be so merciful if I find them in person."

"No, but there may be other persons there who we must not let slip away."

"Oh? And who might that be?"

"I'm not sure, my lord. But the counts' women may remain."

"Hmmm. You are right. I'm sure that my lieutenants will have arrested any nobility they have discovered there. We will question any such prisoners at once."

Gaucelm did not speak. But he knew the knights left to secure the castle could only arrest noblewomen if they knew them to be noble. He urged his horse a little faster, hoping Simon would keep up the pace.

When they entered the archway at the bottom of the citadel and dismounted in the courtyard, one of Simon's men came to report.

"We have secured the palace, my lord." The sergeant was a reliable enough man to Gaucelm's knowledge, plain thinking and honest, but not given to subtleties.

"Good. And who is in residence?" asked Simon.

"The count's wife, my lord, Marguerite Borneil. She awaits you in the great hall."

"Very good. Anyone else?"

The sergeant betrayed some puzzlement as he continued to

report. "She was with another lady when we found her, my lord. A friend who says she's from Rouen. She speaks French."

"I see. But you doubt her word?"

"It's not for me to judge, sir, but her accent is not northern."

"Ah, I see." Simon turned to Gaucelm. "Well now, this sounds interesting. We shall have to see who this French-speaking woman is. Come."

They followed the sergeant inside and up a circular staircase. Gaucelm blinked to accustom his eyes to the darkness of the tower, lit only by oil lamps in sconces placed at intervals along the curving stone wall. They came to a door guarded by several French soldiers who stood aside to let them pass.

As they passed through the small guard chamber beyond, Gaucelm began to pay closer attention. As Simon's chief advisor, Gaucelm made it his business to notice everything. One never knew when remembering some small fact would help them later. Whenever he moved through a palace such as this, he noted the passages, entries, and especially how many exits there were from a given place. And where enemies might hide. They'd been in and out of the citadel since yesterday, but Gaucelm was still aware of the dangers lurking in a place where they were not wanted.

The next door led them to the great hall, a large room now well lit by tall, pointed arched windows on one side of the room, green wooden shutters thrown outward on their iron hinges. The opposite wall was covered with painted wall hangings. The rushes on the floor had been freshened. Men-at-arms stood at attention at the edges of the room, guarding their prisoners, a small knot of women near one window.

Gaucelm walked the length of the room with Simon and then stopped before the women, some of whom were seated on stools. But two of them sat on the broad window seats. One stood at their approach, and the women on stools rose and walked a little distance off. While Simon addressed the lady of the castle, Gaucelm strove to see the other woman's face, which was in shadow.

A broad stripe of sunlight lay across her lap, and he would have taken her for a young man if he didn't know better. For the leggings and knee-length tunic she wore were the same as she'd worn on the battlefield. But a graceful hand lay atop the mantle that had been tossed aside and now trailed down the low steps leading to the window seat.

While Simon addressed Marguerite Borneil, whose simple clothing did nothing to hide her own nobility, Gaucelm continued to watch the face hidden in shadow in the recess of the window.

"Madam," said Simon. "I have word that you are the lady of the house."

"I am, my lord. And in my husband's absence I am castellan. While it is true that my husband is Count Raymond's man, he would wish me to be an honorable loser in this hateful war. I place my household in your hands, since I must. I give you my word we will prove reliable prisoners. I only beg mercy and not cruelty in your treatment of us."

"There will be no undue cruelty if you cooperate with us, madam. You are aware of my mission. I seek to assist the Holy Pope in eliminating heretics. You will be questioned and expected to hand over all heretics known to you, but I will leave it to the bishop and his court to conduct the investigations. I am here only to secure the castle."

Marguerite lifted a heavy ring of keys from the folds of her mantle. "Take these, my lord. We have nothing to hide."

Simon accepted the keys. "I thank you, my lady. I expect housing and food for my troops, and fodder for the horses. The town will give us supplies from the merchants as we need them."

Marguerite lifted a hand and the steward approached and bowed. "This is Pantier, my steward. He will see to all your needs. I will arrange a supper this evening in your honor."

While all this was going on a few paces from her, Allesandra watched warily from her seat by the window. Her jaws were still clenched in anger, for her plans had gone awry. No sooner had she ridden into the courtyard of the castle, than some of the French soldiers had commandeered her horse and marched her into the castle as a prisoner. There'd been no time to change her clothing. Recognizing her for a woman, they'd put her under house arrest with Marguerite until the commander could appear and decide what to do with them.

She admired Marguerite's coolness in addressing the iron-willed, sly Simon de Montfort. For though the French commander was only of medium height and build, she sensed the icy fire in his veins and the heartless cruelty that lay just beneath his hauteur. His dark mustache and short, pointed beard emphasized his angular, haughty face.

There was a different quality to the knight who stood with de Montfort quietly observing everything with his alert, dark eyes fringed with dark eyelashes in a clean-shaven face. He'd removed his helmet and arming cap to reveal thick dark wavy hair that was cut below his ears. His broad brow spoke of intelligence. Well-proportioned eyebrows and a long, straight nose spoke of nobility, and pleasing lips remained shut until his commander spoke to him. But she was distracted from her observations by de Montfort, who now glanced about the room.

"I understand there is another woman of class present. Who might that be?"

Allesandra tensed.

The tall, dark knight now spoke in a musical baritone voice. "Here, my lord," he said, and gestured toward where Allesandra sat.

How did he know? she wondered. For she did not miss the nuance of victory in his tone. She was so startled by his words that her mouth parted in surprise and she straightened. Seeing that she would be better off confronting the two Frenchmen with her hastily concocted story than appearing recalcitrant, she rose from her seat and stepped down to join them. Marguerite introduced her the way they had planned.

"My lords, this is my cousin by marriage from Rouen, wife of the master mason of the cathedral there. She has been visiting me at this most unfortunate time."

Allesandra was fortunate that she spoke French. Like Marguerite, she had been educated by a tutor who foresaw the day when the southerners, who spoke Provençal, might need to be conversant in French.

While the northern country had a name, France, the southern principalities had been too fragmented politically to call themselves any one regional name. However, the war had united the southern lords to a greater degree than before, and now they accepted the appellation Languedoc for convenience.

"Well, Gaucelm," said Simon, "a lady from Rouen. One of our own. A good Catholic no doubt."

She did not miss the challenge in his demanding voice, but she strained to appear unruffled. "Yes, my lord."

The knight called Gaucelm took a step nearer and spoke. "I have spent much time in Rouen. Perhaps I have seen the cathedral upon which this lady's husband works."

She felt her face warm. She had never set foot in Rouen, but called to mind drawings and illuminated pages of the cathedral that her tutor had shown her long ago.

"Perhaps, my lord."

The corners of his mouth lifted slightly and his eyes glimmered. But his challenge was not cruel like that of de Montfort.

"When I was there, the roof had not yet been raised, nor the spires completed. Tell me, is it finished now?"

"Not completely, my lord."

She had no idea, but she could lie about finishing touches even if this knight with the disconcerting presence attempted to trip her up.

Simon de Montfort interrupted. "And does this master mason have a name?"

Fortunately, Marguerite supplied a name, for Allesandra was too busy thinking up possible answers for the imposing Gaucelm, whose piercing eyes challenged her.

"My lord General, allow me to present Elisabeth Chavanne. Her husband is a cousin of my husband's," said Marguerite.

Gaucelm had not taken his eyes off Allesandra, who struggled to lower her gaze and curtsy to the French commander. The sooner she and Marguerite were left alone, the better. But she feared they would be kept under guard, and she would have no way to escape. Every moment she remained here placed her own demesne in more danger. For she was certain that once Muret was secured, the French army would waste no time laying claim to the lands farther south and west toward the Pyrenees, which bordered on the kingdom of Aragon.

"I am honored, sir," she said, eyes still lowered.

"Hmmm," uttered Simon. "If you are, as you say, no enemy of King Philip of France, then I have no reason to restrain you. It is odd, however, to find a French woman from the North residing here in the south at such a time. Such sympathizers with the southern nobility are rare. And in man's dress at that."

"She was mounted and on the field, my lord," said Gaucelm. "I saw her this morning."

Allesandra was startled. How could he have noticed her when he was busy directing an attack? But she did not deny it.

"I see." Simon de Montfort clasped his gloved hands behind his back. His boot scraped on the rush-covered plank floor as he came to stand more directly in front of her. "So, a northern lady who takes so much interest in a battle as to be present when our forces attacked. On which side was she fighting, Gaucelm?"

"She was riding for the river when I saw her, my lord."

Gaucelm had not precisely answered Simon's question, and Allesandra quickly took advantage of it.

"I can easily explain my ride this morning, my lord. I had been out helping a sick forester and his wife since yesterday. I had no knowledge of the attack until I came upon the armies by the river. When you saw me, I was no doubt engaged in trying to cross the river to get out of harm's way."

She allowed herself a glance at Gaucelm. When their eyes met, she thought she saw a challenge flicker there. Her story gave her more courage, but the heartless Simon de Montfort quickly threatened her again.

"How noble of you," he said, crossing in front of Gaucelm. "Then again, perhaps you were in the forest ministering to heretics."

Three

Allesandra lifted her chin. It was on the tip of her tongue to strike back with a venomous insult, for she did not like this Simon de Montfort. Under normal circumstances Marguerite would not stand for having one of her guests insulted thus. But they were prisoners of war. Already their tangle of lies might end up strangling them if they did not find a way for Allesandra to escape back to her own home. So she tempered her words with a false sweetness.

"My lord, if the people in the forest are heretics, it is their business, and they hardly shared their beliefs with me."

"Hmmm, perhaps. Well, I'm afraid I cannot remain here to discuss these matters. Gaucelm, these women are under house arrest. They may move about the castle freely, but they may not communicate with anyone outside until the bishop has seen them. I leave you to make arrangements with Lady Borneil for the garrisoning of our men here. I must give orders regarding booty."

Gaucelm nodded and Simon turned to bow to the ladies. "I accept your invitation to supper, my lady."

Then he turned on his heel and marched back through the hall. His guards held the doors for him to pass through.

"Does this inconvenience come as a surprise to madam?" Gaucelm asked Allesandra.

There was still that annoying challenge to his otherwise attractive voice.

"I—" Allesandra hesitated. Then with stronger words, she stated her true feelings. "Time was when a woman could travel safely with only a few retainers, and go on journeys and pilgrimages. Now armies march across the land, and one must fear for one's safety."

"Ah, I see. Then you were hoping to return home soon?"

She felt a slight flush creep into her cheeks. "Yes, I was. My . . . husband expects me."

"Hmmm. Then perhaps you can send word. If you would care to write a letter, I will see to it that it is carried to Rouen for you."

She nodded politely. "How kind. I will write this evening."

She hoped he would leave them alone, but instead Gaucelm paced a little way in front of his lady prisoners. Apparently their interrogation was not over just because the hateful commander had left.

"Tell me, Madam Chavanne, do you always dress thus when riding into the forest?"

She glanced down at the man's tunic and leggings she had not had time to discard. Then she met his piercing dark eyes once again.

"Yes, my lord. As I said, the roads are not safe anymore. Dressing as a man, I feel safer even in the nearby woods."

"Hmmm. I see." The corners of his distractingly sensual mouth turned up slightly. "Surely then, we can expect you to honor us with feminine attire for supper this evening."

She clamped her teeth together at this boldness. But she lifted her chin. "Of course, my lord."

Gaucelm now flicked his eyes to Marguerite. "And you, madam. There is no reason to hide in a simple housewife's gown. Even as a captive you may dress according to your station."

Marguerite's eyes widened, but she said nothing.

Allesandra's thoughts were in turmoil. She had hoped to escape tonight, but now she must make a show of being present at supper. The matter was now more than inconvenient; she had backed herself into a corner fraught with danger.

Gaucelm took a step backward. "You heard my lord de Montfort's orders. You are free to run your household, Lady Borneil.

My sergeants-at-arms will remain here with you. They will carry any communications you wish. If you have needs they cannot provide, I will attend upon you at your call."

He then bowed low, and for a moment Allesandra envisioned him as a French courtier, instead of a mail-clad knight. But she looked away, just as his head rose to eye level. She retreated to the window seat and leaned there until Gaucelm crossed the hall, gave orders to his men and disappeared through the heavy doors.

She took a deep breath. Marguerite turned to speak to her steward and the household staff who had waited for orders. When she was free, Marguerite returned to where Allesandra stared out the window. In the courtyard below, French knights cried orders and went about their business. Glancing upward, she saw the French men-at-arms standing guard on the walls above, and a tremor passed through her.

"Now that I have started this masquerade, I must finish it," she said to Marguerite in a hushed tone. "But I have placed you in more danger than I anticipated."

"Nonsense, my dear," said her friend in a lowered voice that would not carry farther than where they stood. "This is my house. It is my responsibility to aid and shelter you against our enemies."

Allesandra glanced nervously at the guards posted at intervals along the hall. "We must be careful. The men-at-arms might not know Provençal, or then again, they may only appear not to understand. They will carry any plotting they hear back to that knight called Gaucelm."

Marguerite studied her friend. "He unsettles you, does he not?"

"Who would not be unsettled in the face of such lies as I have just told?"

She shook her head, her already disheveled hair further trailing about her shoulders. "I was wrong to come here two days ago, for now I have left my own castle undefended except for the household guard."

Marguerite laid a comforting hand on her arm. "Your intentions were honorable. You sought only to help our friend Count Raymond in dealing with his allies. We had thought that Simon de Montfort's forces had dispersed. No one expected him to march in here yesterday."

Allesandra wrung her hands and paced before the window. "Raymond. Where has he gone, do you suppose?"

Marguerite's lips drew into a grim line. "There's no way to tell now. Better that we do not know his whereabouts until it is safe to contact him."

"You are right. We must struggle through this supper the mighty French general orders. But I will still attempt to slip away in the middle of the night. You will have to tell them in the morning that you knew nothing of my departure. I will leave a note saying that I was so homesick and frightened, I decided to set out at once for Rouen, despite the dangers. Do you think you can persuade them that I acted on my own without your help?"

"Of course, but I would feel better if you remained here where I can at least assure your safety."

Allesandra breathed deeply. "You know I cannot abandon my household. Neither would you in the same circumstances."

Marguerite looked worriedly at her friend. "Yes, you are right. Then I will help you prepare for your journey."

Allesandra glanced again at the guards who pretended not to watch them. "Very well, but we must be careful."

The meal that evening, held in one of Marguerite's rooms, was performed without mishap. A friendly fire flickered in the large fireplace. Servants brought tempting dishes, which the knights and the women ate with spoons and knives, sopping up the sauces with thick crusts of bread, washing it all down with cups of wine.

If the French knights knew the strain their female companions felt, they did not display any concern for it. Marguerite dressed in her finery, and Allesandra did as commanded, garbing herself in a long-sleeved turquoise tunic, embroidered at hem and wrists. Over this she wore a sleeveless dark-blue surcoat with deep armholes.

In keeping with her story of being a mason's wife, she avoided fine jewels, but fastened the surcoat at her left shoulder with an ivory brooch and adorned the chignon over her ears only with a few pearls. Her turquoise veil was held in place by a circlet of stiff linen across her brow, the veil falling gracefully down her back. Seated on the bench beside her at the trestle table, the knight Gaucelm seemed to approve.

Like de Montfort, Gaucelm was now divested of chain mail hauberk and appeared in a sleeveless forest-green surcoat, the deep armholes revealing a long-sleeved gray linen tunic that came to the ankles, embroidered with silver threads at the neck. On his feet he wore soft kid boots. Allesandra learned that he was of the house of Deluc from the Ile de France, the king's own demesne in the basin of the Seine, and that his family were close allies to the Capetian kings.

She had previously given little thought to the French king who had seemed so very far away in times past. He'd always been busy fighting King John of England over lands they contested. The southern lords recognized him as their overlord, but his authority existed in name only. King Philip had had no power in the independent south until he'd agreed to support the pope in this hateful conquest.

With half its territory already conquered, the Languedoc fought to hold its towns and castles and hoped to overthrow the French where they had gained a foothold. It was regarding this overthrow that Allesandra had hoped to aid her friend Count Raymond VI of Toulouse. But her ill-timed journey had ended in this house arrest.

The supper conversation put her French to the test, but she tried to hide behind feminine modesty in only answering questions put to her. Still, she was not unaware of the penetrating glances of the knight next to her, and when the last course was removed and everyone had wiped their hands and lips on the tablecloth that also served as napkin, she hoped that she would soon be released, for she had laid plans for tonight.

As a good hostess, Marguerite had had to plan some entertainment for her guests.

"My lords," she said, "we have at hand a very good jongleur. Perhaps you would like to hear some songs."

"Ah, songs of the famous troubadours of the South, no doubt," said Simon.

"Yes, my lord. He has a repertoire of well-known songs as well as some composed by the lesser known."

"Perhaps a few songs would not hurt," said Simon. "Let the jongleur come in."

Marguerite nodded to a servant who went to fetch the waiting musician.

"I have heard," said Gaucelm to his supper companion, "that not only knights, but also some women write poetry in the South."

Allesandra's heart missed a beat. Surely it was her own deception that made her feel as if every comment and every glance of Gaucelm's dark eyes saw through her lies to the truth, or perhaps he had coerced one of the servants into telling him of her true identity. Like a serpent, perhaps he waited with poison knowledge and would strike out with the truth when she was least expecting.

"I do not know, my lord." Allesandra fought to answer calmly as the musicians entered the chamber and formed a grouping a little distance away.

For one frightening moment, she was afraid that the jongleur would sing a song of her own composition and give her away. She could easily pretend not to be familiar with these songs of romance and sardonic parodies. And of course the jongleur would sing in Provençal, so she suspected Gaucelm and Simon de Montfort would understand few of the words and none of the subtlety.

Singer, harpist, and lute player, all dressed in parti-colored knee-length tunics and leggings that fit them like skin, bowed low to the table and then began their music. As Allesandra had predicted, Gaucelm soon leaned his head toward her and spoke.

"Very pretty, but of what does the young man sing? Love? War? Of the breath of spring?"

She allowed herself to breathe. The jongleur had begun with a very well-known song by one of the most famous troubadours who had died in the last century, a song about which she could speak safely.

"I have heard this song before," she began. "He sings of a prince who fell in love with the countess of Tripoli without ever having seen her."

Gaucelm allowed himself a chuckle. "And on what word did he fall in love with a woman he had never seen?"

Allesandra creased her brows in concentration, pretending to listen to the jongleur's words and to struggle to remember the tale as she had heard it. She dared not let Gaucelm know that as a patroness of the troubadours and a poet herself, she knew the song by heart.

"The prince heard the glowing descriptions of her beauty and charms from the pilgrims returning from Antioch. He made many verses in her honor, and finally, because of his desire to see her, he put to sea."

Gaucelm seemed entertained by the tale. His dark brows rose in interest. "A man would travel to the East merely to see a woman of whom he had heard?"

In spite of herself, Allesandra smiled. Even in the present danger, her love for troubadour poetry sustained her as it did others in this land. Gaucelm's interest in the song threatened to loosen her tongue into eloquence, and she pressed her lips shut for a moment to regain her composure.

Under her breath, she murmured the words the jongleur sang, giving herself time to translate to French.

"The nuances and much of the rhyme are lost," she commented. "But the story goes that on board the vessel to Tripoli, the prince took ill. At Tripoli they thought he was dead and carried him to an inn."

"Poor man," said Gaucelm, watching her carefully.

"Yes. But when it became known to the countess, she came to him and . . ." *And held him in her arms,* she kept herself from saying.

"And then?"

"He recovered his senses, and he praised God that He had sustained his life until he had seen her. Then he died in the countess's arms."

She expected Gaucelm to laugh or mock the story, but he did not. For a moment he only looked at her. Then he slowly raised his wine goblet to his lips and drank. When he finally took his eyes from Allesandra's face, he lifted his cup in a toast.

"Well then, to the poet, who wrote a very tragic song."

Her hand shaking softly, she lifted her goblet to join in the toast. "Indeed."

"Does it end there?" he asked after having drunk again.

Allesandra paused. "She did him the highest honors and buried him in the house of the Templars. On that day she became a nun because of the grief she felt at his death."

"Then it was a tragic loss on both sides. Unrequited love."

He looked away from her and watched the musicians, and she thought she caught a glimmer of emotion in his eyes. Eyes that until now had been searching, penetrating, watchful, but had shrouded their own expression.

Beware, she warned herself and resolutely put her wineglass down. She dared not converse with this man anymore; he was her enemy. He could not really be interested in poetry. He distracted her from her purpose, which was to end the meal as soon as possible and prepare for her night's journey, for she did not plan to sleep another night in this place.

Marguerite requested the next song, but Gaucelm sat silently beside Allesandra. She was no longer asked to translate. As soon as Simon de Montfort had had enough, he stood and thanked the hostess for her hospitality. For the first time since Allesandra had met the pope's relentless crusader, she heard him speak words that were somewhat human.

"I know this has been difficult for you, madam, since your husband is absent with the army I seek to destroy. As a wife you are duty bound by the Church to obey your husband's wishes. Therefore, I wish you to know that I hold no personal grudge toward yourself." He flicked a glance at Allesandra. "Or toward your cousin, who finds herself in such an inconvenient circumstance. If you are truly religious women as you say you are, you have nothing to fear from us. I thank you for this meal, and I wish you God's blessing."

Marguerite lowered her head, accepting his compliments as he bowed and made to leave. Gaucelm bowed also and took leave of Marguerite. But then he spoke to Allesandra, with whom he had shared the supper conversation.

"Thank you for telling me the story of which the jongleur sang, madam. I was much diverted by the evening's entertainment."

She said nothing, but stiffened her spine as he bowed to her.

The good nights said, both men took their leave. As soon as the door behind them shut, the musicians stopped. But Marguerite turned to them.

"Pray continue. Your music will soothe my . . . cousin and myself."

Since the French guards were just on the other side of the door, she and Allesandra still had to be careful. They retreated to stools by the fireplace to talk softly out of anyone's hearing. The music conveniently proved a distraction.

The two women clasped each other's hands and spoke urgently. Though all had been planned in the afternoon before they'd had to garb themselves for supper, there seemed so many words to exchange now that the night was upon them.

"Are you sure you will feel safe?" whispered Marguerite. "I have done everything I could think of. Your squire has readied the horses, and my steward has seen to extra food."

"Yes, yes, of course. I am only anxious to be on my way," answered Allesandra. "But we must pretend to go to bed."

Marguerite nodded, for she knew the plans.

"And you will send me word of Raymond?" said Allesandra.
"I will warn the believers, though we cannot expect the parfait
to do other than martyr himself if it comes to it."

Marguerite gave a deep sigh, lines of concern on her face, her
shoulders sloping forward as if releasing the weight she'd carried
all evening. "No, I suppose not."

Allesandra was not herself a Cathar, one of those heretics the
crusade sought to reveal and eliminate. But like most noblewomen in the South, she knew of groups of believers who gathered around a teacher, a parfait, who lived a life of self-denial
and preached doctrines abhorrent to the Catholic Church.

And southern Catholicism was considerably less strict than
their co-religionists in the North. By custom and way of life, the
people of Languedoc were a culture first and Catholics second.
Catholics and heretics lived side by side in complete harmony
and friendship here. But gone were the days when priests and
heretics debated in public, each side enjoying the intellectual
stimulation of the questions posed. All that had become dangerous. Now when heretics were identified by the bishop's courts,
they were imprisoned, their property confiscated.

Allesandra did not want to think of the horrors that had
plagued them since Pope Innocent III had taken up this crusade
more than two years ago. She dared not think of it because the
anger would prevent her from thinking clearly. And think clearly
she must if she were to evade the French guards this night.

She squeezed Marguerite's hand. "Do not fear for me. My
squire will see me safely back to my demesne."

"I will keep you in my prayers," said Marguerite.

"And you will be in mine," said Allesandra.

Then because she could not stand the apprehension, she gave
her friend an ironic smile. "You will have the worst of it, I fear.
For you will have to dine with Simon de Montfort day after day,
unless he tires of your hospitality."

Some of the grim expression left her friend's face, and Marguerite smiled. "I think he is a man who is easily bored with
feminine company. I have no doubt he will take to dining with

his men in the knights' hall. Especially if I make sure they get the best of victuals."

Above the hall, the great bedchamber had been turned over to Simon. Gaucelm warmed his hands in front of a fire that awaited them when they had retired there. A retainer followed them into the room, and at Simon's direction, deposited a rolled parchment on the wooden table in the center of the room. Above them, oil lamps flickered in a wrought-iron wheel suspended from the ceiling beams by heavy chains.

Simon divested himself of his fur-trimmed mantle and then stepped to the table and unrolled the parchment. The fact that the general had business on his mind did not surprise Gaucelm. He turned his attention away from the pleasant evening they had just spent and looked to see what Simon had to show him.

"Tomorrow," said Simon, without preamble, "you will lay claim to one of the substantial demesnes in this district."

Gaucelm's spirits picked up. One of the reasons he'd come on this crusade was for the reward of fiefs that could increase his wealth. It seemed that his general had found one for him as a result of their victory today.

"The Valtin lands lie fifteen leagues southwest of here," he said, pointing to an X on the parchment map. "In a bend of the Garonne where it turns northeasterly for some distance, the fortress castle commands one of the routes to the kingdom of Aragon."

"Hmmm," said Gaucelm with genuine pleasure. He smiled as he studied the castle's position. "Yes, I see. An important demesne. If the castle is well fortified, it would be a place to hold off the mountain counts, should they become unruly."

"Exactly," said Simon, straightening. "That is why I trust you to it."

The two men clasped each other's hands, and Gaucelm gripped Simon's forearm with his other hand. The reward he had just been given was greater than he expected, and the responsibility of watching the southeast border of Simon's newly conquered lands, one that he could relish.

"And the baron whose castle it is?"

"Dead. The castellan is the late baron's widow. Her household retainers should be easy to subdue, her knights a trifle for one of our disciplined corps. I'll need the other two corps here in case Count Raymond and his friends try again."

"And the widow?" Gaucelm asked. "Is she in residence now?

"Alas, the word I had from my sergeants who inquired was that she is nowhere to be found."

"Curious. Perhaps she has come to some harm. I will make plans to leave before dawn. We will search for the missing widow as soon as we set foot in the demesne."

Four

Allesandra was again dressed in masculine clothing for her escape that night, the better to conceal her identity should they be stopped on the road. Her late husband's squire, Jaufre de Vilela, who had accompanied her here, had managed to slip out of the castle and out of the city gates during the confusion earlier in the day when the French soldiers were securing the castle.

Not hoping to be able to get horses out from under French noses, Allesandra had instructed Jaufre to purchase horses from some of the villeins in the forest, or better yet to catch horses who had lost their riders during the battle and now wandered the countryside until the French soldiers could round them up.

She prayed that all had gone well, for there had been no way to get a message from her squire since her hasty conversation with him that morning. He was to wait for her at the forester's cottage where she had told Simon de Montfort she'd been that morning tending the sick.

All the exits from the castle were guarded, of course, and guards kept watch along the town walls. There was only one way out, a method Marguerite thought was far too risky. But it was a trick Allesandra had cultivated as a young girl at her father's castle when playing with her brothers, before they'd been sent away to train as squires elsewhere.

Now making their preparations in the women's solar, Allesandra carried a large bundle. Marguerite made sure she had flint and steel in the pouch tied to her girdle and then picked up a lantern that they would not light yet.

"It's been some time since these secret passages have been used," Marguerite whispered as they moved toward the door to the solar. "But I've had them kept in good repair."

Then Marguerite laid a finger to her lips, signaling that they should not talk again until later, when they would reach their destination on the castle walls.

They paused by the door and Allesandra strained her ears, but they heard nothing on the other side. Either the guard keeping watch on the other side had moved on, or he waited silently. Marguerite then moved to a woven wall hanging and reached behind it. Finding the lever, she pushed it in, and then gave a shove.

A door creaked, sending a spike of dread through Allesandra. But the steward must have kept the hinges oiled, for they gave only a slight whine and then were quiet enough. The warp of the door made it scrape against the floor, but with another shove it settled back, revealing a dark inner passage.

Allesandra slipped through and flattened her back against the cold stone wall, while Marguerite closed the door as quietly as she could. They were in pitch darkness until Marguerite struck flint to the steel, and a flame came to life. Quickly the horn lantern was lit. Holding the light to show the way, Marguerite started down a set of stairs.

As Allesandra well knew, any well-built castle had these secret passageways. For ever since the Moslems had encroached on their lands five centuries ago, the people of the Languedoc were prepared to fight treachery. Still, Allesandra's heart beat against her chest. They did not know what or who might await them at the other end. At the bottom of the stairs they passed along a level corridor and then came to another set of stairs.

"These lead to the servants' sleeping quarters," Marguerite whispered.

When they reached a solid door, Marguerite hesitated only a moment, as if girding herself in case it was not the steward but a French soldier who waited on the other side. Finally, she knocked.

To the two women's immense relief, the door moved inward quietly. The round, bearded face and balding pate of Marguerite's steward peered in at them.

"No trouble?" Marguerite whispered.

"The way seems clear, madam," he said.

Without more ado, they slipped through, and Pantier led them between the pallets where the male household servants' deep snores accompanied their dreams. On the opposite side of the circular tower room was yet another door.

Then the steward paused and glanced at Marguerite, who nodded. They were ready. For on the other side of this door lay the walkway atop the curtain wall, from whose crenelations the French bowmen had shot their arrows that morning.

From the other side, Marguerite had explained to Allesandra, the walkway appeared to end at the circular tower wall. But if one carefully inspected the lines of masonry blocks, it could be seen that a door had been carved. However, either the French had been too busy, or had taken the solid-looking tower for what it seemed. For so far, none had demanded entry there.

Now the steward eased the door open, and the night air floated in to bathe their faces. A torch lit the walkway halfway to the tower at the other end. French guards could be seen sitting or sleeping, their legs stretched before them, their backs against the wall under the torch.

Allesandra swallowed. Hers was a daring plan. For a glimmer of a second, she hesitated. What if she remained in the warmth of the castle and simply stayed under house arrest? But she summoned her resolve. She must go ahead with her plan.

The trio acted in well-rehearsed silence now. Pantier took the bundle Allesandra had been carrying and slipped outside. He knelt by an iron lever buried in the masonry that was normally used to hold a crossbow when loading. Around it he knotted one end of a sheet from the bundle. While he did this, Allesandra crept to the wall and peered over the parapet.

Below and to the left, torches were lit on the bridge. The occasional footstep and murmurs of guards came to her from there. But directly below was a straight drop to the Louge, slowly emptying into the swifter Garonne to their right. Only a small lip of bank edged up to the castle wall, and then the wet sand and water.

Now Marguerite risked a whisper into Allesandra's ear. "Try to stay away from the open windows in the tower rooms." She pointed downward to one such narrow slit, just wide enough for an archer to aim an arrow. "No light will come from this tower, but you can't be sure someone won't be awake."

Allesandra nodded. The French soldiers were garrisoned in the opposite tower. The near one housed Marguerite's own retainers. But if one of them could not sleep and was surprised by an apparition gliding down the castle wall, he might give a cry. She turned and gave Marguerite a brief hug and then nodded to Pantier.

He picked up the bundle of sheets now tied to the iron lever and hoisted it to the edge of the battlements. Then he carefully unfurled it. Their calculations had been correct, the bottom sheet just brushed the bank like a white wraith. With trepidation, Allesandra glanced along the walk, but their business had not roused the French soldiers. Nor was there any disturbance from the bridge. No shout greeted her ears as she clambered to the edge of the parapet, swung her legs over, and grasped the sheets between her hands.

Pantier and Marguerite knelt to hold the taut sheet, helping to secure it as if not quite trusting the ancient crossbow lever. Then, without allowing herself to think further about what she was doing, Allesandra clamped the soft leather of her boots about the sheet and eased herself down the wall.

She grasped the sheets with a death grip, but then as soon as she felt herself truly over the great drop, her shoulder touching a wall that now offered no support, she loosened her grip and began to slide gradually downward. She hung on as the sheet rope began to twist, spinning her around. She touched the wall with her foot for balance and continued downward. Fear clutched at her heart, but she tried to concentrate on what she must do. Any moment could bring a shout from the soldiers, an arrow, death in the water below.

Out of the corner of her eye, she could see the lights and the soldiers on the bridge. But the night was moonless, and no light reflected up from the stream below. The last time she'd tried this trick, she'd been a decade younger, and perhaps the height not so great. She tried to look only at the rough stones of the curtain wall, for when she looked down, the stream seemed to taunt her with its distance.

Faster now, she slid along, passing one tower window, then another. Finally the ground seemed closer, and then with another movement, she was down, and breathed at last. She stepped free of the sheets and then looked up, unsure if she saw Pantier and Marguerite lean over to see her on her way, or if it were imagination. She daren't even wave in case it was neither but a guard, so she eased herself onto her knees, sat back on her heels on the bank, and caught her breath. In a moment the sheet began to crawl upward and away from her.

Fortunately it was still late summer, and the Louge only waist deep. For now she unbelted her short man's tunic and lifted it over her head. Then she took off her boots and wrapped them in the tunic. With her eyes adjusted to the darkness, she found a place where the bank was not too steep. She must be careful of disturbing loose rocks that would give her away. But she managed to make her way down the sandy bank to the water, drifting slowly along.

Even here, she must not make any more noise than the stream

itself, or she'd be done for. From the wall above, she'd seen that the stream was covered in darkness, but now as she stepped into the mud, she felt that the entire citadel must be watching her.

She struggled to concentrate on what she was about, and eased into the water. Halfway across, she took courage and moved more quickly, her own movement hidden by the gurgles of the stream. And then the water receded, so she drew herself up, found footing on the bank, and clawed upward in the darkness.

As she stood dripping on the other side, a sickening vision overtook her. She had to make her away alone in the darkness across what this morning had been the allied camp. Of course from the castle she'd seen and heard both the French and the local townspeople come to claim their dead. But what if the soldiers had not yet removed all of the dead for burial and she tripped over a body? Worse yet, what if she came upon some unfortunate Provençal who lay mortally wounded but not yet dead.

"Stop it," she commanded herself. She would never get to the woods and make her escape if she allowed such thoughts to tarnish her resolve.

She began her walk across the trampled meadow, going carefully, avoiding the refuse of the camp. Valuable weapons had been looted, but broken pieces, wagon wheels, and piles of rocks used as missiles in the siege machines remained. And the stench of death was all about. Fortunately, the odors had been diminished by the wind that carried them southward.

She stubbed her toe on a hard object protruding from the ground, and as she paused to favor her foot, she touched it again. Leaning down to make out its shape, she grasped it and tugged. A long dagger came away whole, missed no doubt by the French because it had been plunged into the soft earth. She wiped it on the grass and tucked it into her belt. A little farther on, she found a leather scabbard that she took also. It had no metals or gems upon it and so must have come from a humble man-at-arms, but it would do nicely for the dagger she'd found.

Moving faster once she'd crossed the erstwhile camp, she came to more open land. And as she hurried across, she could now make out the line of trees. Only desperation would make her enter the dark woods alone at night. And before she got there, she paused, straining her eyes to watch for Jaufre's signal.

Behind her the lights from the castle were small pinpoints now. Nevertheless, any light shown here could be seen at the castle, so she still had to be careful.

"Jaufre," she called in a soft voice.

Of course there was the danger that he had been found out, arrested, and that in his place French soldiers waited to ambush her. Her voice shook as she called out again. But then she heard his answer, and relief swept through her.

"Lady Valtin" came a high-pitched voice she recognized. Then footsteps, and a figure emerged from the edge of the woods. Still she held her breath until he got near and she saw it was him indeed. His short brown tunic and dark hose merged him to the night.

So relieved was she that she grasped his arms.

"Is everything as planned?" she asked, still feeling shaky.

"Very well, madam, and you had no trouble?"

Now the magnitude of what she had done made a wave of hysteria rush through her and she stifled a nervous laugh. She'd swung by a sheet, slid down a wall, crossed a river and a battle-field. But it had been no trouble.

Her breathing came in gasps as she gulped in air to steady herself. "All went well."

"You are damp, my lady. Come, the forester's wife has dry clothes ready and waiting."

"And horses?"

"No great difficulty. I caught two chargers, wandering after the battle, and I secreted them deep in the woods. The French soldiers did not have time to penetrate that far."

"Well done, Jaufre." For the first time since she'd crept out onto the castle wall, she began to feel that they might succeed.

"The horses are too big for my lady to ride comfortably, but they are well-trained and sure-footed chargers. They'll carry us back home swiftly. Come, here is the path to the forester's."

The forester's cottage was located some distance in the forest on cleared land with a stockade fence around it. A small gate in the fence was unlatched, and Jaufre led his mistress inward.

"The hounds are kenneled and muzzled," he said. "No need to fear their teeth or their bark to give us away."

As an officer of the count of Toulouse, the forester held a responsible and often hated job: With his greyhounds, he pursued and arrested poachers.

They crossed the yard to the wattle and daub house and climbed wooden stairs to the doorway on the upper level. Below in the byre where the animals were kept, she indeed heard the whining of hounds, straining to identify an intruder. Allesandra gave a shiver, for if the French soldiers were on her trail, the dogs would be their allies.

But the forester's wife hustled them into a cozy hall, warmed by a fire blazing in her stone fireplace. She shooed Jaufre into another room to wait with her husband while she got Allesandra out of her wet clothes by the crackling fire.

"You are very kind," said Allesandra as the woman took her boots and tunic and set them aside.

"Ah, 'tis nothing. When we heard your plight, we were only too glad to help. My husband had seen the horses scatter after the battle and was able to help your man get a few of them. You're a brave lady to be wanting to ride home in the dark and with the pope's soldiers everywhere. I fear for you if you're caught."

Allesandra had the wet leggings and shirt off and accepted the towel the woman handed her to dry her clammy skin.

"There, stand close to the fire and warm up, then put these on."

In moments, Allesandra felt dry and warm again and was dressed in clothing she was beginning to feel belonged to her. For it was still safest to ride garbed as a man in case they were stopped.

"How far is your castle, my lady?" asked the forester's wife.

"Fifteen leagues," she answered. "I should never have left there for all the good I did at Muret."

The woman shook her head and said bitterly, " 'Twas a terrible day. Even this far we heard our lads being cut down like so many trees in a forest. Wolves, those French, tearing open the throats of the sheep, lapping up their blood. The county of Toulouse will not forget or forgive."

Allesandra paused in brushing out her tangled hair so as to twist it under a hood. She grasped the woman's arm and held her plump hands, while looking her in the eye.

"Nor will I forget or forgive. I have taken a vow to help overthrow the French in these lands."

The woman's soft gray eyes looked hopefully into Allesandra's violet ones, taking courage from the brave young woman.

"I believe you, my lady. Those French have no right to disturb our way of life here." She tightened her jaw before she spoke again. "We don't need those rich bishops to tell us how to pray."

Allesandra trembled as she dropped the woman's hands. No doubt the forester and his wife were Cathars, but she asked no more. The less she knew, the better.

"I thank you for your help. Please accept these coins to help repay your kindness."

The woman shook her head. "Kind of you, but I want no money. We must help each other here."

But Allesandra pressed the coins into the woman's hand and closed her fingers over it. "For the believers, then."

The woman looked at her hand and then up at Allesandra, saying no more. Allesandra knew that the money would go to support the Cathar believers and their parfait, most likely now in hiding since they could no longer meet openly.

She and the woman exchanged a meaningful look and then she turned and fastened the dagger by its scabbard to her girdle, covering it with her short tunic. "Jaufre," she called softly. "I am ready."

Her retainer came into the room followed by the brawny forester. She thanked the man for his help, and then he wasted no time leading them outside and behind the byre where the horses were waiting.

Jaufre had not lied when he'd told her the horses he'd caught were tall, big-boned chargers, the sort men rode into battle. Her roan had a thick mane, massive chest and withers. But Allesandra did not hesitate to step onto the mounting block and then into the saddle, her thighs stretched over the awesome horse.

"He's bigger than your mares," said Jaufre as he mounted a dapple gray of the same great size. "But gentle enough. Do you think you can handle him?"

She patted the horse and spoke to it, and its ears pricked. She was a good horsewoman, and felt confident that she could master the war horse.

"We've fifteen leagues to get acquainted," she said. "He seems a good steed."

The forester led them to the gate and made them wait until he walked out a ways to make sure they were alone. Allesandra and Jaufre waited on their horses, ears straining to catch the sounds that came to them on the night breeze. She might have been missed at the castle now. Or Marguerite and Pantier might have been stopped with the tied sheets as damning evidence. She could only pray that her escape had not endangered her friends.

The gate creaked, and the forester reappeared.

"The way seems clear. You'll do best to stay in the forest. This path leads due west. When you come out you'll be well past Perramon hill and into the countryside beyond."

Allesandra well knew the lush, hilly countryside between Muret and her lands by day. Riding by night would be a greater challenge.

"Thank you, kind sir, for all you've done."

Then she and Jaufre rode through the gate, their horses snorting and shaking their heads, ears forward to catch the sounds in their path. They moved very slowly, not risking a light. The moon had risen, but its pale light could not penetrate the thick forest.

"I think I'd better dismount and walk," said Jaufre after they'd made only a little distance. "These woods are too unfamiliar to risk a wrong turning."

With Jaufre on foot leading his mount and Allesandra's mount following, they fared better. How long she was in the saddle she did not know, for she bent all her effort to peering into the woods or at Jaufre's shadowy figure ahead. At last the trees thinned and they came out of the woods, so used to darkness by now that the glimmering starlight, and the light from the large, yellow moon, seemed bright. They could plainly see every feature of hilly country ahead.

Jaufre mounted again and they began to make their way in the open, braver now that they were away from the garrison in the town.

"We'll make better time by the road, my lady. But we'll be more likely to meet someone. We could cut over the hills and stay out of the way of any soldiers, but the horses will be harder worked. What is your choice?"

She only considered a moment. "The road. I've a grave feeling that all is not well in our demesne. Every moment it costs us to get there is ill spent."

"Very well. We'll come to the road just past those trees, I think."

Once on the beaten road they made better time. But it was eerie to ride along in the depths of night. The soft rolling hills dipped away to the cover of trees near tributaries that flowed into the mighty Garonne, which tumbled down from the Pyrenees. Coverts of underbrush and woods where bands of outlaws or soldiers, for that matter, might be waiting. More than once, she felt for the dagger she had tied to her girdle. And she knew that Jaufre was well armed. But she daren't dwell on such possibilities.

Instead, she spoke to her horse, finding that indeed a little pressure from knee or rein communicated a subtle order for the horse to change his speed or adjust his gait. He was a good steed, and she thought they would do well together.

"I wonder what his name is," she said while she and Jaufre rode together past a rocky hillside.

The ridge above rose to be outlined in a faint change of color in the night sky. Beyond them gnarled grapevines clutched clusters of their fruit, soon to be harvested. Even in the predawn light, they could see bushes of broom bordering the vineyard, with branching stems, long used to sweep cottage floors.

"The horse? Hard to say? Perhaps, my lady, you should name him yourself, for he's yours now."

Riding a big, heavy-boned charger was bone-jarring even at a walk. And she understood why knights only used these war-horses for battle. For everyday travel they rode lighter palfreys, the heavier horse carrying packs until a battle. The horse slammed his massive foot down with every shattering step until her spine began to ache. But it was a minor inconvenience when she considered the progress they were making. She tried leaning forward and shifting her weight.

"I think I'll call him Roussillon, after my lord the count's favorite wine."

The big horse whickered at the name, and she took that to mean he did not mind.

The sun came up on a dewy morning. Now the greens of the hillsides they passed turned into blue ridges in the distance. They passed a walled abbey, its gardens spiked with cypress trees. But they dared not stop to take a meal yet, and so pressed on into the hills, winding upward and downward, sometimes keeping to the road, sometimes striking off on a cart track that passed through small villages where the peasants busy with early-morning chores stopped to watch them.

Allesandra inhaled the great solitude of the hills as they rode on, stopping occasionally to water the horses and take a drink themselves. They still had more than a day and a half's ride ahead, when they paused to breakfast on bread and cheese.

They began to question peasants they encountered. "Have you seen any French soldiers?" Allesandra asked a woodland farmer who stopped with his load of chopped logs.

He shook his head. "Heard they were in the towns north of here, but none come this way. Not that they're welcome."

"Thank you."

But as the day waned, they tended to be more alert. When they came to a straggle of houses built along the road, they paused well in the distance to scout for any sign of soldiers. They stopped to dine at a simple tavern, but gained no more news.

Roussillon nuzzled her when she came out of the tavern, and she offered him pieces of an apple. Her heart warmed to the big horse and she declined to trade him for a smaller palfrey when she had the opportunity.

Allesandra was bone weary. And even though the thought of home urged her onward, she knew they had to rest. So when darkness fell, they asked for rooms at an abbey that took in guests. They left again early next morning.

Jaufre helped her mount again for the last stretch.

A mist seemed to hover over the mountains in the distance, but they pressed on. By late that day, the sun glinted on rocks and soil, turning everything to flame. Allesandra must have dozed in the saddle, for she was jerked awake when they stopped on the crest of a low hill on her own lands and looked across the narrow valley that spread upward to her own château. A feeling of welcome should have pervaded her sore body. But instead a tremor of fear paralyzed her as she stared upward.

From the cylindrical keep and the two square towers that topped the yellow sandstone walls flew pennants with fields of blue and drops of gold—not the colors of Toulouse, but the fleur-de-lis of the Capetian kings of France.

Five

She was too late. The sting of grief grew to a simmering anger and then one of despair. Her home had been taken by the French already, but how?

"Come, Roussillon," she said, and kicked his sides, leaning

forward. Nothing was to be gained by hanging back. It was her duty now to find out what devastation had been wrought by the French and who had commanded it.

Jaufre flew with her through the meadow and then up the slope toward the bridge over the dry moat that surrounded the castle. Castle Valtin rose on a rocky hillside to command a long valley that twisted through the mountains and eventually led to the passes through the Pyrenees. To their right, the summer's harvest stretched in rows along a gentle slope, waiting to be gathered in. She saw no evidence of carnage such as there had been at Muret, but . . . dear God, were any of her household knights dead, servants ill treated? Her heart twisted inside her as she conjured up the worst.

They drew up to the gatehouse where French guards stood with lances crossed barring the way.

"Let me in!" she shouted, Roussillon rearing on his hind legs as she jerked him to a stop.

A sergeant-at-arms stepped forward. "This castle has been taken in the name of the king of France. Who wishes to enter?"

"Lady Allesandra Valtin," she shouted. "Get out of my way. This is my castle."

And she turned her charger preparing to run them down, for the way across the drawbridge behind them was open.

But their lances parted as she charged across the bridge, her retainer behind her. And then she was under the upraised portcullis and into the cobbled inner courtyard. While she waited for Jaufre to dismount and come to help her down from the great horse, she glanced around anxiously. To her immense relief several of her own grooms and other of the household servants stopped their work to stand and stare at her. Normally they would nod or call out greetings, but the presence of the French soldiers muted them.

Once on the ground, she turned to find her steward, Julian Farrell, having come down the steps from the hall to greet her. He was a middle-aged man of thin build, but tall. Even in such a crisis, he possessed a bearing of competence and honest demeanor. His gray eyes were anxious, and his mouth pressed into a straight line beneath his long, arched nose. She rushed to him.

"Oh, my God, Julian, what has happened?"

The lines of regret and worry in his face seemed to have aged him ten years.

"I'm sorry to inform you, my lady, that our castle has been overtaken by the French. It happened just this morning."

She struggled to quell her anger. "It is my fault. I should not have rushed to the aid of Count Raymond, for all was lost at Muret as well. If I had been here to defend my home . . ."

Her eyes lifted to the wall walk where more guards were posted and the hated French pennants on long poles flew above the towers.

"Do not blame yourself, my lady. Your household guard fought bravely. They were simply taken by surprise and outnumbered. The French penetrated the gatehouse by stealth before we could get the portcullis down and the drawbridge lifted."

True, she had sent as many knights as she could to help Raymond in the field, leaving only a small corps to defend this place. She thought her men were needed in the field. How wrong she had been. Rage and humiliation overwhelmed her, but she kept a dignified demeanor before all those watching her.

She inhaled a long, steadying breath. "And who is it led this attack?"

"The knight Gaucelm Deluc, a vassal of Simon de Montfort."

Her eyes opened wider. The same man! New humiliation filled her. How he would gloat that he had outfoxed her. How he would laugh at her feeble lies! Standing in the growing shadows of the end of day, she came to realize the terrible truth. She was his prisoner.

In the next moment, worse fears plagued her. "My men-at-arms, were they all . . . ?"

"Two died bravely," reported Julian. "The wounded are being attended. The rest are taken prisoner in the tower."

"There have been no vengeful atrocities committed, then?"

"No, madam. The victor has been most reasonable."

"Thank God for that."

Julian cleared his throat, the creases in his proud face deepening. "I am to bring you to him as soon as you arrive."

She straightened. "Where is he?"

"In the great chamber, my lady."

Again she fought the despair that swept over her. Gaucelm Deluc had wasted no time installing himself in the chamber that had been hers and her husband's before he had died in battle two years ago. She was undermined at every turn. But she summoned some pride.

"I will see him when I have changed into proper clothing and refreshed myself."

Julian would say nothing to counter his mistress, but she could see from the unhappy look on his face that he'd been ordered precisely to bring her before the conquering Gaucelm immediately. Still, she made a show of her own authority. She was still a noblewoman in a place that had been her home since her marriage.

She turned and started for the entrance to the keep. With Julian following her, they mounted the steep stone stairs. The guards at the heavy nail-studded door stood aside to let them enter. Passing through the antechamber, she swept across the large hall, but she was stopped on the other side where she would have taken the circular stairway in the tower that led to the solar.

"Let me pass," she ordered through clenched teeth to the implacable man-at-arms with short-cropped brown hair who barred her way to the tower.

He did not move, his fixed gaze staring straight ahead at nothing. Then she made the same command in French so he could understand, but still he did not move. To her left was an arched passage that led to the few steps that would take her to the great chamber above the hall. Light glimmered from oil lamps in sconces and she could imagine a fire flickering in the great chamber, beyond.

They were going to force her to confront the rude, unscrupulous, greedy Gaucelm Deluc who had the nerve to ensconce himself as lord of this castle, her castle. Very well then, she would see him now, inflamed by her anger and humiliation, but she would hold nothing back. If she were forced to surrender the keys to this place, she would accompany them with words of hatred and vows of vengeance. She hurried up the steps and through the door into the great chamber.

Gaucelm Deluc stood garbed in a tunic of dark blue and surcoat of reddish brown, hardly appearing as if he'd just fought two battles in three days with a hard ride between. He turned from gazing into the fire licking at great logs in the fireplace. His sun-bronzed face held a slight frown, but as he watched her approach, a change came over it. She saw the muscles in his jaw twitch, but if he was surprised, he did not betray it except for the flicker in his dark, intent eyes.

"Madam Chavanne, I did not know I would have the pleasure again so soon. But pray, this is not the way to Rouen. Perhaps you are lost."

His toying made her all the angrier and she spat out her words. "I am not lost, and you have already no doubt realized that I am not the wife of a master mason at Rouen, but the lady of this castle."

An ironic smile tinged his lips. But then he became sober again and bowed to her as was her due.

"I see. I am sorry then that our acquaintance should be so awkward."

He straightened and stepped toward the fire, all business now. "I have claimed this castle and all its lands in the name of the king of France."

She took a step toward him, her hair disheveled after the many hours in the saddle, dust smudging her face. "You have no right."

He lifted a brow slightly. "I have every right. Or have you not noticed that Count Simon de Montfort leads an army to claim the county of Toulouse for France. And you, Madam Valtin, are a vassal of Count Raymond of Toulouse."

Her voice rose in fury. "You descend on our rich and favored land with fire and sword. Is it religious fervor or greed that makes your ruffians want to lay hands on these territories? Do you stop to discover who is Catholic and who is not before you seize castle and domain? I think not."

She was aware of his challenge as he glared at her. "And you, madam? Are you a heretic?"

His gaze made her tremble, but she lifted her chin. "I am not."

Neither spoke for a moment, and she forced herself to remain standing close to him, meeting his gaze. He searched her face and she felt a warm flush creep up her flesh. He had no right to question her, and yet in that moment she realized how much more uncomfortable it would be to be questioned by the bishop's court.

Resentment of Gaucelm Deluc's invasion of her privacy flared, and her heart pounded in her chest. She clamped her jaws shut in the face of whatever questions he might ask next. And yet even without his asking them, she felt as if he looked into her mind and soul.

His hardened face relaxed a trace, as his eyes swept over her face, sank to her lips, her male attire, and then moved away again to study the fire.

"This is a war, madam."

Her words were low, filled with bitterness. "A war to destroy a way of life."

"What way of life?"

"You know very well what I mean. Your king wants access to ports on the Mediterranean. You want to exploit our rich soil, our vineyards. Your intolerant bishops wish to strangle freedom of thought and punish those who wish nothing but to read the Bible, which the Catholic Church does not allow for anyone but a priest."

He watched her now, and she knew she was treading dangerously, but her passion made her continue.

"Poetry and song flourish here, trade with the eastern ports makes our towns rich. But the mighty Church and your barbaric mercenaries wish to take that all away."

He waited, knowing he would gain more by allowing her to pour out her emotions than if he silenced her. He well knew it was in this way that traitors trapped themselves. But she paused to catch her breath and leaned a hand on the octagonal table where lay a few books and rolled-up maps. She shut her eyes a moment, and the blood drained from her face.

"Madam, you are tired from a strenuous ride," he said, somewhat concerned. "Perhaps we should continue this discussion at a later time."

She forced her eyes open, but his figure blurred in the light from lamps and fire. Indeed, the strength seemed to go out of her. She'd eaten little in her hurry to get here, and her body was bruised from the jarring gait of the war-horse. Dizziness suddenly overtook her and she staggered.

She took a step, trying to shake the dullness from her head. Her hand went up, and at that moment Gaucelm moved toward her. She gave a small cry and then felt herself fall, as everything dimmed.

Gaucelm reached her as she fell and caught her in his arms. He knew that the effort she'd expended on trying to race him here had cost her. He brushed the hair from her face as her head lolled into his shoulder, and then he picked her up in both his arms and strode toward the great bed.

He took the step up to the canopied platform and lowered her onto the fur coverings. As he laid her down, he sat on the edge, feeling the springy softness beneath him. He arranged a feather pillow beneath her head and took a moment to smooth her tangled hair, surprised by its richness. He put off summoning assistance for a reason he could not name. But looking at her face, the long lashes lowered over her eyes, he felt a twist of emotion. She was an avowed enemy of France. She had lied to him. But he could not help but admire her bravery and her courage. He had not met many women who would fight so hard in a soldier's world.

His finger drifted across her cheek. He thought he saw color returning to her face and felt relief that she must not be seriously ill. However, he ought not delay getting help for her any longer.

He stepped down from the bed and crossed toward the door, opening it. His trusted sergeant-at-arms stood there, a square-bodied, loyal vassal, a man who had seen much of life and had a family in Ile de France, but who had trained Gaucelm in arms and then served him when he had achieved knighthood.

"Enselm," he said. "The lady has taken ill. Send for the doctor and her female attendants."

"Yes, sire."

While help was being summoned, Gaucelm returned to the bed to watch her. She was breathing deeply, which was good. Sleep and a nourishing meal were likely all she needed. He shook his head slowly from side to side. Whether she was a heretic or not, he could tell she had information of them and would have to be questioned, for she had hotly defended a way of life repugnant to the Church. He suddenly hoped that she would give the bishops the information they needed and not cause herself undue difficulty.

His hand rested against the carved bedpost, its fine grain smooth against his hand.

Gaucelm was a good Catholic, but he did not give it undue thought. He was too busy to read the Bible. He was a soldier of France, loyal to a king who had extended his realm from the small region of the Ile de France to include the formerly English fiefs of Normandy, Anjou, and other lands.

King Philip Augustus ruled efficiently. He brought prosperity to France, relieving the reclaimed provinces of the heavy taxation that had ruined them under their English kings, Richard and John. He'd rebuilt towns, conceded new privileges and confirmed old privileges to towns and abbeys. And he would do so in the south of France. It was his way.

Gaucelm turned away from the bed to let his eyes circle the richly laid-out room. This castle was his reward for his loyal service to Count Simon, and it was well deserved. France needed to be made stronger still, and the conquest of the Languedoc would achieve that. The Church had made a crusade against heresy profitable.

There was a knock on the door. "Enter!" he called.

Enselm showed in a man of bronze far-eastern coloring and aged features. "The doctor, sire."

Gaucelm motioned to the bed, and the doctor went to examine Allesandra. In another moment, two women entered the room. The younger one of pale coloring and quick, frightened movements stifled a squeal by covering her mouth with her hand. The older, more solid matron frowned at the bed, but then evidently seeing that the doctor was making his examination, grasped the younger woman's other hand and guided her to the other side of the bed, where they waited. The older woman frowned in concern at her mistress, whose eyes were still closed, while the younger one looked as if at any moment she would join the lady of the castle in a faint.

Enselm joined Gaucelm near the fireplace and the two men exchanged hushed words.

"Fainted," said Gaucelm. "Overcome by her efforts. No doubt she'll recover. Is your search proceeding in orderly fashion?"

"Yes, sire," said the sergeant. "I've done as you instructed. The men understand there's to be no looting."

"That's good. I will reward them later."

Gaucelm continued thinking aloud to his trusted vassal. "I see no reason to destroy castle and lands that are now ours. This southern wealth will strengthen France. Make sure that if there are any infringements, no matter how minor, they are brought to my attention."

Behind them on the bed, Allesandra was beginning to stir. The doctor stood back and put his smelling salts into his cloth bag. He turned to address them.

From campaigning these two years in the south, Gaucelm now understood some Provençal. Although the dark-skinned doctor's speech was touched with an Arabic accent, his meaning was clear enough.

"The lady needs rest and nourishment, my lord. I'll prepare a sleeping draught for her woman to give her. She should not exert herself until she regains some strength."

"Very well," said Gaucelm. Then to the women, "Have her

bed made ready in the women's quarters. I'll bring her to you there."

The women scurried off to prepare, and Enselm escorted the doctor out. When the door closed, Gaucelm returned to Allesandra's side. She gazed up at him with heavy eyelids and moved one arm as if preparing to get up. He reached out and touched her shoulder, gently holding her back.

"Rest easy, my lady. The doctor has instructed that you are not to exert yourself. You need to rest."

She opened her mouth to speak, but then closed it again, allowing her eyelids to fall shut. She was not asleep, he could tell, only resting, regaining her strength. The glow from oil lamps and firelight cast a honey-colored halo about her. Even thus clad, he thought her beautiful. He resisted the impulse to touch her face again, but remembered its texture and the way the soft, thick hair curled about his fingers.

For an instant . . . but then he pushed the thought away. They were enemies. In the morning she would be forced to turn over to him records, keys, acquaint him with the running of this estate. She would not like it, but he dearly hoped she would be cooperative. He did not want to use extreme measures. If he forced her, she would be harder to control later. And such was not his way.

But business could wait until tomorrow. At the moment he gazed at her lovely face. Then her eyes opened again.

Allesandra looked up to see the dark, handsome face staring down at her. His broad shoulders, clad now in tunic and loose-sleeved surcoat, looked nonetheless more powerful than when she'd first seen him in mail hauberk and brightly colored sleeveless surcoat. Thick, dark hair framed his brow and fell below his ears. By virtue of conquering her house guard, this man was now her lord, but she would never let those words rise to her lips.

"My soldiers," she croaked.

He straightened, relief that she had spoken now replaced with businesslike fierceness.

"Two were killed. There were some injuries. But your Arabic

doctor and his minions have been busy seeing to them. They are under house arrest in the tower but shall have provisions."

She felt the emotions twist inside her. How could it have happened so easily? All that she held of the Count of Toulouse, a good and just feudal overlord who was also a friend, now slipped from her grasp into the hands of these enemies! She shut her eyes again. Right now she was powerless, but she would wait and plot, send word to Raymond. They would overthrow the French. But she struggled to present a calm expression. Gaucelm Deluc must not see any of this.

"And the bishop's inquisitors, when will they come?"

He glanced at her quickly. "Are you so anxious to be questioned?"

She closed her lips, a muscle twitching in her cheek. Gaucelm gazed at her face and then lifted himself off the bed and stepped down.

"Let us not consider such matters tonight. I will take you to your chambers where your women will help you to bed. Rest well tonight, madam. Tomorrow is time enough to discuss the future."

Her eyes flew around the chamber that had been hers until now, but she said nothing. She was too proud for petty argument; she would spend her breath only where it mattered.

"If you are ready, I will take you now."

She attempted to rise, but he put out a hand.

"You are still weak. I will carry you."

She opened her mouth to protest, but his strong arms had already slid under her and she could not help but grasp his shoulder for support. She had not been in a man's arms since her husband had died, and the sudden feel of muscular flesh affected her.

She blamed it on the dizziness of her faint. But when she lifted her left arm to clasp her own hand about his neck, her fingers brushed his hair. His face was dangerously near hers, and she felt her heart turn over in her chest. A sudden grief penetrated her heart, and the weakness of her state overcame her. She bit her lips and hid her face in his shoulder, giving up the struggle.

Gaucelm, too, responded to the feel of the woman he carried in his arms. As he'd gazed at her lying so helplessly on the bed, his body had told him that he found her desirable. He knew he should not consider her feelings in any way. She was his captive, her property was now his. But Gaucelm was a courtier and found the seduction of a woman more pleasant if done in a civilized manner.

He entered the women's quarters and carried Allesandra to a bed they had made ready. Nearby, a brazier filled with coals warmed the room. As he placed her there, he laid her head on a tapestried pillow, and her eyelids fluttered weakly.

"She is awake," he said to her female attendants, "but weak. See that she gets rest and nourishment."

Then he turned on his heel and retreated.

Allesandra was beginning to revive, but waited until the door shut before she roused herself.

"My lady," said the young blond Marcia Pruniaux, "are you all right?" She flung herself to her knees, grasping the bed covers.

Allesandra raised herself to lean on pillows they tucked under her back and shoulders. She was feeling better now, and when the matronly Isabelle Beguinot handed her a cup of warm broth, she sipped it. How comforting to know that her old friends were here to aid her.

"I will be well," Allesandra answered, trying to smile reassuringly at the two women who leaned over her and who surely had much to tell her. Marcia frowned in concern as she knelt beside the bed.

"But tell me how the castle was taken," said Allesandra as she took a sip from the goblet of wine with the doctor's sleeping powder in it. "I must know."

Isabelle sat down on the edge of the bed, concerned first that her mistress would be well. Her tale was a matter-of-fact one, told in a tone that could repeat harsh facts when the need was upon her.

"A single rider appeared at the gate this morning. He called to the gatekeeper that he had a message from you. The drawbridge was let down, and he was admitted. But he killed the gatekeeper before the watch knew what was happening. His companions had been hiding in the moat and came across the bridge to fight the other guards. In the confusion, the rest of Sir Gaucelm's men appeared out of the woods and flew across the meadow and drawbridge and into the courtyard."

Allesandra closed her eyes. "And then what happened?"

"There was a brief skirmish, but our men were outnumbered. Sir Gaucelm's men quickly ascended the towers and the walls, and when they were in his control, our guards had no choice but to surrender."

"They would have fought to the death," Marcia quickly put in in her high, young voice. "But this Sir Gaucelm ordered the fighting stopped and for our soldiers to throw down their weapons. Seeing as how it would accomplish nothing to keep on fighting, they finally did so."

"At least there was no slaughter," Allesandra said after a long sigh. "Still, I should have been here."

Isabelle patted her hand. "I doubt you could have done anything, my lady. It was a surprise attack, and we were outnumbered. Besides, you had gone to help Count Raymond."

Allesandra pressed her lips together grimly before replying, "I failed in that mission as well. The allies fled in disarray. At least Raymond and his son got away. Peter of Aragon was killed."

The other two women looked glum. Marcia went to the window and pulled the shutters against the chill of evening.

"They will have us all then, will they not?" she said.

Allesandra sat up a little straighter. "They will try to have us. But there is still hope."

Isabelle spoke. "They've already taken Béziers, Carcassonne, Lavaur. With Muret taken, they will threaten Toulouse next."

"They will not take Toulouse," said Allesandra fiercely. "It is near the end of the campaigning season. They cannot hope to surround a city of twenty-five thousand people. And there can be no shortage of water in a city bordered by the Garonne. The only chance for Simon de Montfort's besiegers is that the Catholic citizens would open the gates for them. But he will find out that the people of Languedoc pay little attention to religious differences. Toulouse has struggled for a century to obtain independence. It will never accept the rule of an authoritarian bishop or a French count."

"But the fiefs of Toulouse are great," said Isabelle. "I am not sure the French will give up so easily."

"No," Allesandra conceded, "not easily."

"And what will you do now, my lady?" asked Marcia.

Allesandra clenched her fists. "I must act as this Gaucelm Deluc expects me to. If I cooperate with him, he will not execute me."

"What do you think he will want of you?" asked Marcia.

"My profits will go to his king, for one," said Allesandra. "But that is not the worst part."

"No," said Isabelle. "We will be descended upon by the bishop's inquisitors, no doubt. They will ask us if we are Cathar. If we say no, they will ask us who is. And if we lie, it will go very badly for us."

Allesandra's face burned. She lowered her voice as the coals in the brazier seemed to flicker. "That is true. We must act very quickly and cleverly if we are to protect those who need protecting. Perhaps we can help the believers find a safer place to meet if they insist on meeting."

"And how will you do this under the nose of the man who now rules your lands?" asked Marcia.

Allesandra gazed at her companions for a moment. "I will have to find a distraction."

"A distraction?" queried Marcia.

"We cannot expose our friends the Cathars, but there is something else our captor knows us to be famous for."

The women gazed at her doubtfully, but she gave them a sly smile.

"Our poetry. We will introduce Gaucelm Deluc to the ways of the troubadours."

Six

Allesandra was not disturbed with word from Gaucelm until late next morning, when a messenger appeared to say that Sir Gaucelm requested her presence at dinner that day. A normal meal should be served in the hall, and the lady of the castle must appear beside Gaucelm, acknowledging his overlordship.

Allesandra gave Gaucelm's messenger a stony look but answered that she would comply. When he left again, she turned to her friends.

"He wishes to humiliate you before your own household," said Marcia, looking as if she might cry.

"He wishes to make a point," snapped Allesandra. But then she gathered her temper in. "We will concede his point, but we will work behind his back. You must all help me by appearing docile."

"What do you plan to do?" asked Isabelle from where she sat on a bench, keeping her hands busy doing some mending.

"I will find a way to go to the believers and warn them. It will be best if they do not meet so near the castle as they are used to. One of them can carry a message to Count Raymond. I must meet with him so we can lay a plan to overthrow these French."

"But that will be dangerous. The guards will be watching," said Marcia in a hushed tone. One never knew when one of the guards in the passageways outside might lean his ear against the thick wooden door to catch the women's words.

She gave a secretive smile. "I will appear at dinner this noon resolved to my fate. I will hand over the keys to our lord and master, and then I will ask permission to hold musical entertainments and poetic competitions as we are used to do."

"Do you think he will grant it?" said Isabelle, not looking up from her sewing.

"I don't see why not. When he isn't out fighting, he enjoys music and poetry," answered Allesandra.

"How do you know that?"

Her expression was ironic as she replied, "I had the pleasure of dining with Sir Gaucelm and Count de Montfort, or rather the *dis*pleasure, especially in the latter case. They housed themselves in the Lady Borneil's castle at Muret and before I could get away, we were placed under house arrest. As hostess, Marguerite entertained them."

Marcia's eyes widened. "Did he tell you then what he planned to do here?"

"No, he didn't even know who I was then. I claimed to be a northern woman. I thought I had him fooled." She allowed herself a little shrug. "Perhaps not."

She arose and went to the small writing desk and lifted the lid to retrieve parchment and quill.

"Come," she said. "We must make plans."

As was the custom, the household assembled in the great hall at noon. The steward Julian stood by the pantry door directing the servants in carrying the dishes in from the kitchen. Although nothing was said, the glance he exchanged with his mistress assured her that although he was doing his duty by serving their new overlord, in his heart he remained loyal to her. She was grateful for such loyalties. There might come a moment when she would desperately need them. Quietly that morning, she had instructed Julian to let it be known among the staff that an appearance of submission must be made.

When Allesandra entered the room, silence gradually fell over those assembled. She stepped up to the dais to take her place at the high table. Gaucelm was already there and turned to meet her. She began her act of cooperative submission without losing her dignity. And as Gaucelm bowed to her, she looked out over the strange household, her own people huddled together in knots, Gaucelm's retainers lined up next to the benches set before trestle tables stretching down the hall.

It galled her to have to do what she must do. But she prepared herself to hand over the heritage that was hers, to symbolically relinquish lives into the hands of the man who towered beside her. A man whose kindness or cruelty she had no notion of. But she must live through this meal. She turned to face the enemy who seemed to mock her with his handsome looks, waiting, watching her with stealth, she thought.

"My lord," she began in a voice that could be heard to the corners of the hall. "I surrender my house and my lands, hitherto held from the count of Toulouse, into your hands. For my vassals' sakes, we beg mercy and restraint in all your dealings. We pray that the profits you will reap from these lands go to a just and good king who will see the good in treating his people well. We hope that in time we may show you a way of life that you can respect."

She rattled a huge ring of keys that she had tied to her girdle, which she now untied. "Rather than cause more bloodshed, I humbly submit to you, Gaucelm Deluc of the Ile de France. As your vassal, it is my obligation to serve you. For God has judged in your favor." *Temporarily,* she thought to herself.

An uneasiness could be felt between the two cultures that stood separated in the room. And again Allesandra felt a cold hand tighten around her heart. How could they expect to live in peace when their ways were so foreign? They did not even speak the same language. Beliefs and culture were different. But she handed Gaucelm the keys and made a deep curtsy.

He, in turn, behaved courteously, accepting the keys with one hand and offering her his other hand to lift her up. She accepted his hand, felt its strength, and then reclaimed her hand as quickly as she could, while she lifted her head to hear what he would say.

"People of Toulouse," he said in a booming voice. "I accept the surrender of this castle and all its lands in the name of the king of France. It is my hope as well that we can live in peace until the conclusion of this holy war. We come as the army of God. As I am vassal to the king and have sworn to fight for France and Holy Church, so I accept this fief and the service of this noblewoman, Allesandra Valtin. Let us dine today in symbolic unity, and tomorrow you will see our justice where there is no cause for retribution."

His men hailed him in a cry that struck Allesandra as that which must have come from Germanic tribes of old. As if enacting their warrior heritage, the corps of soldiers grasped drinking cups and downed the wine in them while her people stood mute.

The formalities over, Gaucelm gestured for a servant to pull back the carved, high-backed chair on the dais. He waited until Allesandra had been seated, and then he, too, took his seat.

This was the signal for the rest of the diners to sit on the benches along the side of the trestle tables, and the servants began to bring in the meats. The silence was punctuated with low words here and there, the scraping of benches, and then the sound of wine being poured into cups. When the din covered private conversation, and the high table had been served, Gaucelm surveyed Allesandra.

"I see you are much better this morning."

She lifted her spoon to take a sip of the fish soup in the bowl she shared with her dinner partner. "I am better," she said, not looking at him.

"I am glad."

Was he? If so, only because having her coöperation would make his assumption of overlordship easier. She kept her face blank, pushed away the soup and accepted a trencher of meat set before her while Gaucelm sampled the soup.

When she glanced sidelong at him, she was disconcerted to feel a tremor of awareness dart through her. How empty the high table had been since her husband had died. Grown used to widowhood, Allesandra had been in no hurry to remarry, and her overlord Count Raymond had not pressed her. But she'd never expected the master's seat at the high table to be filled in this manner. She'd always expected that in due time it would be filled by a man Count Raymond would find for her, a man worthy of her estates and of herself.

There was no denying that Gaucelm Deluc emanated authority. Worse for her, that courteous manners accompanied handsome, aristocratic looks. She ate slowly, adjusting herself to their strained situation when he washed his meat down with wine and then turned his gaze upon her.

"Have you been widowed long, madam?" he asked her.

She took her time answering. "Two years. My husband died fighting the Moors in Spain."

"I see. He was a hero then."

"Yes."

She preferred not to discuss it. She rarely thought of the man she'd called her lord and master. A kind man, the marriage had been arranged by their families, and they had been companionable enough. It was on the tip of her tongue to tell Gaucelm that her husband had been fifteen years her senior, but then she held her words. It was none of his business.

Gaucelm let the matter drop and turned to business. "Perhaps after dinner, you will have your steward show me your records. I need to acquaint myself with the demesne."

She adopted a pleasant look. "Why make it difficult? As you say, if you are taking no reprisals, I see no reason not to show you the demesne myself." And keep him away from parts of it she didn't wish him to see.

His left arm rested on the table as the servants brought another course. She found it difficult to meet his gaze evenly, for her heart pounded skittishly and her skin felt clammy. Truly, his searching gaze was going to make dissembling the more difficult.

Gaucelm's other hand rested on the carved arm of his chair near her. She saw him grip the arm as if restraining some emotion within himself, and her awareness of his power increased. For a moment she wished fervently for a conqueror more like her late husband, a man of ordinary looks, genial and conservative, if lacking in fiery spirit. Gaucelm was a hardened warrior who was also sensual, but a man who brooked no argument. Something about him overwhelmed her. She grasped her wine goblet and took a sip to steady herself.

Looking straight ahead, she said, "My steward Julian will show you what records and household accounts you wish to see. I am at your service whenever you would like to see the lands and meet your tenants."

"Very good."

Then taking a breath, she remembered her plans to distract him and turned a pleasant expression upon him. "I do have one question, my lord."

"And what is that?"

"In times that were more gay, our evenings were spent in song. Many notable troubadours visited this court. Now they are away. But if it would please you, my messengers could let it be known that you would find it interesting if the troubadours and their jongleurs again visited this court and performed and composed as in days before the war."

He narrowed his eyes slightly as he searched her face, suspicious of her offer. There had to be a reason she was so anxious to entertain him.

"Diversions for my men are always welcome," he said. "I would learn of these troubadours."

"I am glad," she said. "I think you will find it pleasing. We will do our best to acquaint you with our ways."

He smiled and took a piece of fruit.

"Tell me, where the troubadours gather, I have heard it called a court of love. Is that not so?"

She gave him a sly smile. "That is so. There are many rules a courtier must follow if he is to be accepted in a court of love."

Gaucelm lifted a dark brow, curious about the southern passions he'd heard sung of in flowery phrases.

"I have heard that these poets who are famed for their verses are also fighting knights. How can a man trained to arms and combat also know music and verse?"

"That is not difficult for a people steeped in Latin literature. And some of the love themes have perhaps come back to our shores from the eastern lands."

"Hmmm. Then I suggest you assemble your court, madam, as long as they know into whose demesne they are being invited. And they must come accompanied only by musicians. A half-dozen troubadours at most. They may keep their arms if they give their word not to draw them. They will be given safe escort here."

"Of course."

Assembling so many knight poets in one place might offer them a chance to retake the castle, but Gaucelm was not foolish enough for that. No, her entertainment would work in other ways.

They finished the cheese course and washed it down with wine. Then Gaucelm rose and held his hand to escort Allesandra from the dais. She accepted Gaucelm's hand only as far as the edge of the dais. She took her hand from his firm, warm grip to hold her train as she descended the steps to the rush-strewn floor.

"It is a fine day," he said, forcing her to turn again and face him at the entrance to the hall. The din of the meal inside was still in the background. "If you would still like to accompany me in my inspection of the demesne, I would be glad for the company."

"As you wish. I can be ready in half an hour."

He smiled in amusement. "And do you have a horse to ride that would be more suitable than that charger you brought from Muret?"

"Roussillon is a very good mount," she said defensively.

He chuckled. "Oh, indeed, good for a strong soldier, but hardly for a lady. Don't worry, I do not wish to take him from you unless I need him," he said, seeing the ire rise in her lovely face. "I simply inquire as to a horse on which you would find more comfort."

She forced herself not to argue about Roussillon, to whom

she'd grown very attached. But of course on familiar lands, riding at leisure, she would be better off on one of her mares. She started to issue an order and then remembered their positions. How vexing it was to have to be submissive, and for a moment she wondered how long she would be capable of it. However, she took a breath and then spoke calmly.

"If you would be so kind as to have one of the grooms saddle my bay, I would appreciate it."

He nodded in deference. "Then I will meet you in the stables in one half hour from now."

She dropped a small curtsy and turned, her blood pounding in her veins. This was going to be more difficult than she had expected. It was a full two years since she'd been beholden to any man. Her widowhood had left her well fixed. She could not put her finger on all the conflicting emotions that coursed through her as she hurried to the women's chambers to have her companions help her dress in loose gown and mantle appropriate for riding.

Allesandra had hoped to slip away to have a word with those whose lives were in danger, but there was no chance. If Gaucelm insisted in galloping over the demesne, it was better that she be with him. By now word would have reached the believers that the castle had been overtaken. The bishop's court would soon follow. She must make it look as if no Cathars inhabited this neighborhood, though she doubted the bishop would believe that for a moment.

A half hour later, they rode out through the gatehouse, her own guards now replaced by French men-at-arms. An eerie shiver raced down her spine. She felt almost guilty that her captor allowed her freedom, while her own house guard were shut up in the towers. Julian had assured her they were being well treated, but it furthered her resolve to reverse the situation as soon as plans were laid.

From the upthrust natural escarpment that formed the foundations of the castle, they rode down into the fertile valley. Blue sky, fleecy clouds, and yellow grain splashed the early-autumn afternoon with color. Once past the fields, they began a gradual rise up a terraced slope where villeins tended the Valtin vineyards. Allesandra refused to think of them as the Deluc vineyards. They'd been in her husband's family for too long.

Gaucelm gazed at the undulating horizon in the distance, beyond which the snow-capped peaks of the Pyrenees bordered the kingdom of Aragon. The clear air made the distance seem negligible.

Allesandra pointed in a southwesterly direction. "The river narrows between those two peaks. That is our border."

"I see. It is interesting to translate what I have seen on maps to the reality of rocks and hills."

Borders and passes, more likely, she thought. From the way he squinted into the distances, she could see his military mind working. He would no doubt get a firm fix on his new lands in a very short time. But now that Peter of Aragon was dead, what enemy could he expect to ride from that direction?

Gaucelm got down to inspect the grapes. She followed him, her own eyes scanning the fields. But the villeins kept well away, finding work to do at the far end of the fields. By now all would know that they had a new overlord. And they would come to pay their respects when it was time. For now, Allesandra tried to discern who among them might see who she was with and pass the word along as warning.

"They say that wine has a memory," he said, dropping to one knee and letting the vine trail across his gloved hand. "That wines are deeply unsettled at the time of the harvest. Do you believe that?"

His look sent a searing sensation across her, and she looked away, her expression neutral.

"The natural world is in some way part of us," she answered. "If we abuse it, we cannot expect it to be so generous with us in return."

"An interesting belief," he said, dropping the vine and regaining his height, "if perhaps somewhat pagan."

She took his meaning and squared her shoulders. "If you are

suggesting it is a Cathar belief, I doubt it. You must understand all the influences that have played a part in our land, my lord. The Arabs have left their traces. The Genoese and Venetians have traded here. Languedoc is a mixed culture. You will find many ideas unfamiliar to you; not necessarily all of them are Cathar."

"Not necessarily."

He took a step toward her between the vines, and she resisted her impulse to move back. She must not let him think she feared him. At the same time, his nearness affected her, and she began to see that it was not the enemy in him, but the man that he was that caused her such discomfort.

Her heart rattled, and she touched a stake in the vines to help keep her balance. For Gaucelm was so near she could almost feel the warmth from his face. His eyes danced across her face, and she looked down as his gaze dropped to her lips.

A sudden rush of sensual longing filled her, and her lips parted as she took in a quick breath. How traitorous of her to find her enemy desirable. How traitorous of Simon de Montfort to send a man here capable of reminding her of her widowhood, to remind her of pleasures that had once been her right, but that she'd lived without and hardly missed these two years.

Gaucelm said nothing, but did not take his eyes away. As she flicked a glance his way, she thought that he took in her figure before returning his dark eyes, tinged with hunger, to her face.

She turned away, breathing quickly, moistening dry lips. An attractive man he might be, but she must not let him know she found him so.

She returned to the horses, and the dry grass crunched under his leather boots behind her. Without a word he laced his strong fingers together for her to step into briefly as she mounted, her long, loose skirt sweeping behind her.

Still trembling from what had just passed between them, Allesandra turned her horse and trotted along beside the pale-barked plane trees shading the edges of the vineyards. Ahead, a grassy meadow beckoned. From the top, flat-toned bells made a faint tintinnabulation where a large flock of sheep grazed. The shepherds kept their distance from the lord and lady flying along in their direction.

Allesandra circled before they reached the flock, leading Gaucelm off toward the more open lands beside the river. Here she could safely point out cottages that belonged to a hamlet of working peasants, his subjects now, and lead him away from the forested folds in the hills behind them.

They slowed to a walk beside the sparkling waters, ducking to avoid overhanging branches. At the small collection of thatched cottages, craftsmen and farmers stood up from their work before their cottages, the women with eyes downcast and the men with caps in hand.

"This is your new master," she said to the people of the village. "His steward will collect your revenues. I have sworn the oath of fealty to him. You will all come to the castle tomorrow beginning in the morning to do the same."

The peasants looked at their new overlord with a mixture of curiosity and reserve. Gaucelm, used to such situations, maintained a stance of authority, but looked each man in the eye and nodded formally.

"I think you'll find my justice fair," he said in a voice that carried. "I wish to see the region increase and bloom for the glory of the king of France. You've no reason to fear anything from me. When the king prospers, you will prosper."

Eyes suddenly shifted. Glances among the villagers were exchanged, and Gaucelm watched them carefully. No reason to fear him, no. But perhaps there was much to fear from the religious courts that would come in his wake. Ahead of him Allesandra rode on, leaning down to say a few words to those she knew. From their smiles and greetings, he could see that they respected her and held affection for her.

They rode out of the village, and Allesandra led him along a path beside a stream. No need to dig canals here. The rivulets and brooks that brought the melting snows down from the mountains watered the fertile lands. Gaucelm could not help but feel pleased at what Simon had awarded him. But his satisfaction was tinged with an ill wind of what was surely to come. For he had to remember the conditions under which he'd won these lands. And the purpose of the crusade. He knew that many of the people he'd seen today would suffer. For even though the Lady Valtin strove to convince him that no Cathars lived here, he knew otherwise.

Allesandra slowed her horse and turned to him. "Have you seen enough for today?" She asked it with respect and no malice.

"Perhaps. Let us stop here and refresh the horses and ourselves."

He got down and led his horse to the stream for a drink. Then he took Allesandra's bridle and brought her horse to a tree stump where she could dismount. She got down with agility, and he again noticed the freshness of her face. Pride lurked under her submissive actions. But it was a pride he could understand.

Then he removed a wineskin from his saddle and unstoppered the top.

"Wine?" he offered.

Thirsty from the warm September sun, she accepted, the sweet liquid moistening throat and lips before she handed it back to him. Then he led the horses to where they could graze and leaned himself against the smooth bark of a plane tree, whose branches shielded them from the glare of sun.

"Rest a while, my lady," he said, and removed his gloves.

She came to the spot where he stood, but she did not sit on the convenient log that had fallen. Nor did she lean beside him against the tree.

They were silent for a moment, listening to the gurgle of the brook, the occasional breeze carrying the sound of the sheep bells from far above them. It was a peaceful land, belying the carnage she had witnessed when two cultures clashed. Gaucelm Deluc might be a fair conqueror, but she must remember what he represented.

"Tell me," said Gaucelm, picking up a twig to smooth between his long fingers. "Why has not Count Raymond found you another husband? Surely there were many suitors for your lands."

The question startled her and she glanced at him, resenting the way he had put it. She was careful not to reveal too much in her answer. "I had no need to remarry. I had the ability to run the demesne. And the right to my own life."

"Hmmm. While it is clear that the count of Toulouse profited from your holdings, you could not perform the required military service for him. It surprises me that as your guardian, he did not wed you to an ally of his own."

His eyes gave away nothing as he looked into the distance.

"My lord Raymond was wise enough to see that he could profit from my lands without my remarriage. And of course I paid a fee in lieu of giving military service."

She trembled as she spoke and then waited for his answer. A woman possessed neither physical power, political clout, nor personal freedom. Her intelligence was her only weapon, that and her gift for song. Perhaps he had brought her here to inform her that he was choosing a husband for her. One of his vassals, no doubt, who would take control of her life and curtail the freedom she'd experienced these past two years.

But Gaucelm was wrestling with emotions of his own. He was her overlord now and he could dispose of her as he pleased. He could marry her himself if he wished; Simon would give him leave. But he was not anxious to marry a heretic. As to the pleasures she might offer him in bed, he'd no doubt that her body would be delectable. But her icy stares and the temper that she struggled so to hide made him think twice about either proposition. She was a formidable woman, not easily molded in a man's hands. Ah, but there were mysteries about her he wished to unveil. He would let things move in that direction slowly. He had business to conduct with her first.

For now, her lands were his, he mused. He must see to it that she helped him profit from them. He roused himself from his reveries.

"This evening," he said, pushing himself away from the tree, "I would like your company for supper in my chamber. We can continue going over matters of the demesne."

She tried to keep a level look. This evening she had other plans, but evidently, they would have to wait.

"Very well, my lord."

They remounted and rode back through the hills and valleys until the castle was within view. Gaucelm let his mind roam over the many responsibilities that were now his. And yet the woman at his side distracted his thoughts. They would dine alone in his chambers this night. He dared not allow himself to think that an evening of business might also be one of pleasure.

But one thing was clear in his mind. Allesandra Valtin was a woman he would be wise to keep near him. For she was keeping many secrets from her enemies, and he needed to learn what they were.

Seven

Gaucelm had the accounts brought to him before supper so that he could verse himself in the running of the household. So when Allesandra arrived, dressed now in a flowing tight-sleeved gown of light green, he was prepared to discuss business.

Allesandra stepped into the lamp-lit chamber. Her hair had been dressed in coils about her head and held in place with white netting as became a widow. But at first glance of her, he had the impulse to reach for the coif and release the tresses that had flowed down her back in disarray when she'd first confronted him at the castle. He preferred to see the fire in her than this tight, controlled lady of the castle, who was not used to taking orders from anyone.

Gaucelm turned to greet her. "Good evening, my lady. I hope you have an appetite, for your cooks have prepared a delicious meal."

A trestle table next to the fireplace had been draped with a clean white tablecloth. A servant she did not recognize set a blown glass carafe of dark-red wine on the table and stepped back for Gaucelm to inspect the platters of fish, steaming bowls of stew, and fresh-smelling loaves of bread. He dismissed the servant, who slid out noiselessly.

Pan lamps suspended from wrought-iron brackets in the carved oak paneling cast an eerie light. Float lamps in green glass holders flickered on the table. The corners of the room remained in dimness except for a wall sconce near the door.

Gaucelm was dressed in a tunic of gray with silver threads and sleeveless crimson surcoat. Sandal leather crisscrossed feet and ankles and rose up muscular calves. Even as she stepped into the yellow lamplight encircling the table, Allesandra felt a weakening of her resolve to keep her distance from this man.

Already his presence seemed to draw her into the room. She watched his browned hands pour wine and hand her a goblet, and when she glanced into his eyes, she was undone, as she had been at the vineyard.

She sipped the wine quickly and turned her gaze to the table. If she must acknowledge the undeniable masculinity Gaucelm Deluc possessed, then she must find a way to use it to her advantage. For even though her pulse now quickened at the intimate scene he had set, her mind worked quickly for ways to turn her acquaintance with her captor to good use for her own purposes.

Gaucelm watched her for a long while, and after a second sip of the rich, full-bodied wine, he knew that his plans to discuss business this night were lost. He had only intended to have this lady in his chamber so that he could learn more of the running of the household and try to fathom what plots were hatching in her mind. But looking at her in the pale light with door closed on the rest of the castle, and only the balmy night air coming in the narrow unshuttered windows, he knew now that he wanted something else.

The woman before him had been dispossessed by him. Perhaps the power he felt as a conqueror now released desire into his loins. The idea of bedding her in order to seal and savor his victory tempted him. But he did not want to possess her cruelly. He wanted her submission.

All this passed through his mind in the blink of an eye, and he forced his mind to other matters. He thought he saw in Alle-sandra a faint struggle of her own. But not being privy to a woman's mind, he could not guess at what it was. She found words before he did.

"My lord," she began. "What do you intend to do with the prisoners locked up in the tower? They are no good to you there."

He set his goblet on the table, glad for a topic he had already considered.

"I will ransom them. My sergeants are sending out word to their families now. If any among them choose to swear an oath of fealty to me, they may stay here. But only in numbers less than my own men. I will not risk an uprising. Those who are ransomed will go, but without arms or mounts, which I claim as spoils. It is still a time of war, as I am sure you can understand."

"Yes, quite," she replied. "It is only my duty to do what I can for their welfare."

"Agreed."

There was another knock on the door, and the servant entered again, this time with a tray of sauces for the fish and cooked greens, which he set on the table and then left.

"Let us dine, madam, before our food gets cold."

She took a seat in the high-backed carved chair opposite Gaucelm and picked up the spoon to taste the stew. She found her appetite increased, and had no difficulty doing justice to the food.

After eating in silence for a while, Gaucelm leaned back and began a conversation about the native wines and crops such as any well-bred courtier would. She could not get over the illusion that instead of bitter enemies, they were intimate acquaintances enjoying a pleasurable meal. That after dinner perhaps she would sing to him.

The tingling of her spine when he addressed her, and the gentle ache she felt in her chest awakened feelings she had relegated to another place. Perhaps he read her mind, for he again brought the conversation around to her late husband.

"Tell me, my lady. Was your late lord one of these poets of whom you speak so highly?"

She suppressed a secret smile. "No, he was not. Though he was a great patron of the courts of love."

"Ah, yes, the court of love. You must instruct me in how it works. You said there were many rules."

"That is true, as you will see when the troubadours arrive. I have sent word since you gave permission."

His eyes gleamed. He smiled and sat back while the servant removed trenchers and platters, then came back again with bowls of fresh strawberries and a pitcher of cream.

Gaucelm rose from his chair and walked to the tall, ornately carved cabinet that stood against the wall at the foot of the curtained bed. It was not locked, for Allesandra remembered that there had been nothing of great value in it. Only things of a private nature, and she felt a rush of apprehension that he so casually reached inside a place that had been privately hers for the last two years.

He extracted several loose sheets of vellum as well as a collection of songs she herself had bound between boards covered with soft kidskin and sewn into the binding with stiff threads. He brought the collection to the table.

"I have not spent all my time reading documents to administer the estate. These, if I am not mistaken, are works of a more literary bent."

She exhaled a breath. "You are right, my lord. They are."

"As I thought. But you can help me here. My Provençal is not fluent. I do not think I can appreciate the poetry as well by reading it to myself. Perhaps on your tongue, the words might flow better."

Her cheeks warmed. "You wish me to read aloud?"

He lifted a shoulder and dropped it. "It is a suitable pastime for an evening, would you not agree?"

She met his gaze steadily as she took the vellum sheets and

then the book he handed her. A knock on the door signaled the entry of the servant waiting on them. And together with two more servants they removed the remains of the meal, gathered the crumbs in the tablecloth, and then folded up the trestle table and leaned it against the wall.

The high-backed chairs were moved nearer the fire and Gaucelm threw himself in his, placing his feet on a low stool. Indeed he had every appearance of a lord in his own castle. *Her* castle, she reminded herself. But she sat demurely on the other chair and opened the book. If he must hear a song, let him hear something fine, but not too provocative.

"Perhaps you would like to hear the work of Peire d'Auvergne, who was a canon in the Church before he became a jongleur. He served the Spanish monarchs before he died some thirty years ago."

"Please," said Gaucelm, and gestured with a hand that she should begin.

To Allesandra it seemed that Gaucelm was settled in for an evening of entertainment. She had an hour yet before she must attend to her other errand, so why not lull him into a less watchful state that would serve her purposes?

"Near the time of brief days and long nights," she began reading in lilting tones, "when the clear air grows darker, I want my thoughts to grow, branch forth with new joy to bear fruit and blossom, for I see the oaks being cleared of leaves, and the jay, thrush, nightingale, and woodpecker withdraw from discomfort and cold."

She read it in Provençal, and then paused to ask if he desired a translation into French.

"No," he said with a shake of the head as he gazed with a half-smile at the fire. "On your tongue, the words are clear enough. Pray continue."

She read the vision of distant, far-off love, hoping that Gaucelm's ear was attuned to the interwoven text with its alliteration, related rhymes, and nuances of meaning. And from his response, it seemed clear that he mostly understood.

"Very nice," he said when she had finished. "There is a secretive quality to the words. He seems to speak in paradoxes, or perhaps the language is too obscure for a Frenchman to grasp."

"You are right," she said, lowering the book to her lap like a good instructor. But also because with the book on her lap he was less likely to see the shaking of her hands. "Troubadour songs always feature hidden meanings and inner rhymes."

"And unrequited love. Is this a constant theme as well?"

She did not meet his inquiring look as she said, "It is the custom of troubadour knights to sing the praises of the ladies that dispense hospitality toward them."

"Hmmm. I have even read in your literature that a nobleman cannot be a perfect knight unless he loves a lady. Is this true?"

She still did not look at him. "It is believed among our knights that all chivalric qualities are strengthened by worship of a lady."

Allesandra had repeated these principles many times in discussions with both men and women. But telling Gaucelm about the rules of courtly love unnerved her. Perhaps because he seemed to be such a willing student. But sly. If she were not careful, he would do something to trip her up.

"Ah, I see. And does the lady return the favor? Or is this courtly love merely a gesture?"

She gave a subdued smile. "Troubadour love is not necessarily mutual. The knight loves. The lady does not have to reward him."

"Then the ladies in these poems are passive goddesses who are adored whether they wish to be or not." His tone sounded doubtful.

"That is so, my lord."

He gave a chuckle and uncrossed his legs. "And you, my lady, have you many poems written in praise of your own virtues?"

She lifted her shoulders and dropped them. "I would not know, for the lady of the poem is never identified."

Gaucelm dropped his bantering tone and got up from the chair. He stepped toward the fire and placed his hand on the carved mantel above.

"If I loved a woman, I would not be satisfied with worship from afar."

Her heartbeat quickened, but she could not stop her words of explanation. "It is the longing that gives our poetry its appeal. His desire increases the knight's prowess."

Gaucelm seized the andiron and poked the logs, sending up sparks. "And so the knight fights the harder because he thinks of his lady's charms. But never to be rewarded with them for himself?"

She could not stand the throbbing of her pulse at so dangerous a conversation and stood up, setting the book in the chair.

"How can he be, when the lady is most often the wife of another man?"

"And when she is not?"

His words caught her by surprise. He replaced the andiron, then turned to gaze at her face. They stood near each other, and Allesandra knew that she should leave. But her lips opened to draw a quick breath, and she was lost to the moment.

In one step he reached her, his arm coming around her waist, his breath fanning her hair.

"Yourself, for example," he said in a low, sensual voice. "You do not seem the ice-cold goddess of whom these poems speak. You are flesh and blood, my lady. Am I not right in guessing that you have loved? That your heart now desires to be unlocked? If not your heart, then surely your body misses a man's caress?"

He did not even know where he found the words, they only poured forth from him expressing something of what he felt, not all of which he could understand himself. Her breast curved against his chest and his hand pressed her against him of its own accord.

She did not struggle to get away, but gasped and trembled in his arms. He smiled into her hair, lightly kissed her temple. Her quick breathing only stimulated him all the more.

"My lady," he said in a hungry voice.

Then he tilted her chin with his other hand and found her lips with his own. Delicious lips, soft, sensual, that moved against his. He pulled her into him, drowning in her beauty and softness. This was his reward.

Allesandra's mind spun. Her blood throbbed in her ears, and she was powerless to move. Had he not supported her with both his arms, she knew her knees would give way. She could only part her lips more to taste of the wine on his lips. To be in a man's arms again was awakening a need far greater than any she had felt with her husband. Gaucelm seemed to overpower her, to swallow her in strong limbs and set her blood on fire.

He murmured softly, words of desire that matched her own, and all thought fled as he kissed her ear, her throat, his light embrace supporting her waning strength. From where had this hunger arisen, she wondered helplessly just before she began to summon strength again.

"Allesandra," he whispered into her ear as his hand came up to brush cheek, shoulder, and lightly touch her breast. "If you are as you say you are, then we are not enemies. Perhaps a better resolution awaits us than captor and captive."

She steadied herself against the swoon that tempted her and turned her face to the side. Gasping for a deep, steadying breath, she forced the words out.

"If we are not enemies, then you would perforce return my lands."

"It is too late for that. You were a vassal of Raymond of Toulouse, who leads the southern allies. You've already sworn the oath of fealty to me. Let me become your lover. I will protect you."

She wrenched herself from his grasp and braced one hand above the fireplace.

"I swore the oath because you dispossessed me," she cried. "It is not becoming to so quickly succumb to you, my lord. My . . . people would lose all respect for me."

With the blood pounding in his ears and his loins ready to experience the pleasures that Provençal poetry only alluded to, Gaucelm found it hard to keep from grasping her once more. The tear that ran down her cheek and glistened in the yellow light moved him, and he managed to control his lust. When he held out his hand to her, it was slow and gentle.

"I will not force you, madam. Such is not my way. It only seems to me that you need a man to show you the ways of love again. I give pleasure as well as take it. Who would know, behind this closed door? They would expect that we have much business together."

He had drawn near, and his voice had a soothing effect on her raging emotions. What he said tempted her, and her lips longed to be kissed again. Her breasts ached to be touched. She had felt his desire through the soft folds of their clothing, and it had aroused her. But she would be a traitor to give herself to him.

"What is between us is of the flesh only," she said with a shaking voice. "It is not my way to satisfy flesh without being loyal to heart and mind."

"I understand," he said simply, with no demand in his tone. Still, he touched her burning cheek with his finger and then brushed it across her lips.

"If you change your mind . . . come to me in the night."

Then he lowered his head to kiss her lips softly, gently. He broke off the kiss, giving her room to gasp, moisten her lips and turn to cross the room.

She did not look at him again, but paused before the door. "Good night, my lord," she said in a low voice.

Then she pulled on the wrought-iron handle and passed through the door. Beyond her, torches lit the passage. A sergeant-at-arms shuffled up to close the door.

"Does my lord want anything?" asked the sergeant behind her.

She heard Gaucelm answer in a distant voice, deep in thought, "No, nothing. I will sit up a while. Wake me at dawn."

Allesandra hurried to the chambers she now shared with her female companions, hoping that they would interpret her flushed appearance as apprehension before attempting a dangerous outing.

"My lady," said Marcia as she entered. "We just returned from the hall. The Frenchmen had many questions for us, and we worried that we would be too late."

"I only now got away myself," said Allesandra, divesting herself of her overtunic and then sitting on the bed to exchange her slippers for sturdy leather half boots. She would not take the time to change into her by-now-familiar male attire, for the distance she had to go tonight was not far, and she would go on foot.

"We will go with you," said Isabelle.

"No, I would prefer not," said Allesandra in hushed tones. "It will be hard enough for one to slip out. You must remain here, and if any of the Frenchmen knock, you can answer that I am asleep."

Isabelle lifted down a plain dark woolen mantle from its wooden peg and handed it to her. "You'll need this once you get outside. You'll be less noticeable in it than in your fur-lined mantle."

"And where is the package I am to take?"

Isabelle wrinkled her brows. "Are you sure it is not better to leave it hidden where it is?"

Allesandra shook her head. "We've been lucky that these French soldiers have not searched our quarters. When the bishop's inquisitors come, as I know they must, no place within the castle will be safe. I must take it now."

Isabelle turned to the writing desk, upon which were spread several sheets of parchment, quills, and ink jars. Marcia helped her remove the items, and then they lifted the top to reveal the compartment beneath. From its depths they removed a squarish object, wrapped in several folds of dark cloth. Allesandra tucked it into the folds of the mantle she held over one arm.

"It will be safer with our parfait, for if Sir Gaucelm knew that the women in this castle read the scriptures on their own, as is forbidden by the Catholic Church, he would surely turn us in as heretics."

Marcia and Isabelle returned her apprehensive look, but she squeezed the older woman's hand.

"With this bound copy of the scriptures out of our hands, they can prove nothing."

"As long as you are not caught going out," whispered Marcia anxiously.

"If I am stopped, I will say I am going to the garderobe, or to visit a servant who is ill. Sir Gaucelm did not say I could not move about the household."

After assuring the two women that she would be all right, Allesandra took the circular staircase to the level of the court-yard. Then she pushed open the door and walked out into the courtyard, heading purposefully, but in no great hurry, for the kitchens. Several guards watched her progress, but did not stop her.

Once within the large central kitchen, she crossed toward the large hearth beside which several of her own kitchen staff sat. They murmured and rose at her approach, but she put a finger to her lips. Her longtime cook, Ivetta, glanced at the cloak across her arm.

"Quickly," said Allesandra. "I do not know if I am followed. I must use the tunnel. They have not discovered it yet?"

"No, my lady," said Ivetta.

The cook and a scullery maid took down the pots that hung from wooden pegs buried in the plastered wall. "You will need a light." And she reached for an outdoor lantern and some flint and steel.

"The wick is trimmed. You should have no trouble lighting it."

They pushed the panel inward, and Allesandra stepped into a passage she had not visited for many years. She saw Ivetta's plump face just before she heard men's voices and the scrape of boots coming into the kitchen, but Ivetta did not show any fear.

Allesandra held her breath as the darkness enfolded her. She could barely hear the voices on the other side of the panel now and felt as if her heart stopped beating.

But in a moment she heard muffled laughter, then the women's voices. Perhaps the soldiers simply wanted a midnight supper. There seemed to be no panic, and Allesandra groped her way down a few steps before she knelt to strike flint and steel. Feeling in the darkness, she slid up the thin plate of horn to light the wick, and the lantern cast its dim glow.

Not waiting to find out anything more about the soldiers in the kitchen, she quickly descended to where steps gave onto hard, damp dirt. She lifted the lantern high to reveal cut rock. Now the twists and turns of the tunnel came back to her and she hurried along. When the ground began to rise, she allowed herself a breath of hope.

She came to a steeper slope and then some wooden steps embedded in the earth and climbed upward. Here she must be careful, and when she felt the cool air of night ahead, she slowed her pace. She paused where the rock of the tunnel stopped and felt the thorny branches woven into a door that hid the opening to the forest. It wasn't far to where she had to go, and it wasn't beasts of the forest she feared. Rather, she had no way of knowing if any French soldiers might be out roaming the woods at night. But why should they be?

She issued a silent prayer and then pushed the hawthorn screen open. In the moonlight, the path at her feet was clear. She pulled the mantle close about her and stepped out into the night, listening for any human sounds. A nightingale gave forth its song.

She made out a pinpoint of light ahead that one would miss unless one were looking for it. Now she hurried along the path and soon reached a clearing. In the center stood a tenant's holding with timbered manor house surrounded by a palisade. A figure came out of the shadows.

"Who goes there?" asked a young man's voice.

She pulled back her hood. "Lady Valtin," she responded. "I've come to warn the believers of danger from the castle."

"My lady," said the boy, now recognizing her. "They are within."

He opened the gate, and they passed into the yard. As she crossed to the steep wooden stairs leading to the hall above the undercroft, she caught the low murmur of prayer. The boy led the way up the stairs, giving two knocks before he opened the hall door for her.

Filling the room between the thick oaken pillars that supported the vaulted roof, thirty or so men and women stood, their heads bowed in prayer. Near the blazing hearth at one end, a man with long straw-colored hair dressed in plain muslin gown delivered a blessing, his hand raised. Beside him a blond woman was similarly garbed. There were no crosses or other icons to be seen anywhere in the room, for Cathars abhorred the gaudy opulence of Catholicism.

When the blessing was over, the congregation lifted their heads. Those who had been on their knees arose. The parfait, Bertram de Gide by name, smiled.

"My lady Valtin," he said in a welcoming voice. "We had heard that you'd returned."

She knelt to receive the parfait's blessing, and then he took her hand to raise her up again.

"I've come to tell you of more danger. Sir Gaucelm Deluc and his French soldiers are now in possession of the castle."

With a twinge in her heart, she turned to face the men and women who moved forward to better hear her words, some taking seats on the benches around the room. "He is not a cruel man, though loyal to his liege lord, Simon de Montfort, and to the king of France. However, Bishop Fulk is in Muret now, and make no mistake, his court will descend on us within weeks. I've come to warn you not to meet again, for the French soldiers will report whatever they see and hear to the inquisitors."

At the mention of the hated inquisitors a murmur of concern passed through the room.

"My lady," said Emice de Laurac, the woman also dressed in the plain garb of one who has pledged oneself to poverty and chastity, "we heed your warning and knew that something like this was coming. We have met tonight to gain strength from our numbers. Our parfait has blessed us and sends us on our way. It will be up to individual consciences to recant or not as they must."

She and Bertram exchanged glances, and then he laid a firm hand on Allesandra's shoulder.

"Emice and I must preach wherever we may be heard. But we would not endanger our flock. In order to preserve our beliefs, we advise our followers to live quietly, not drawing attention to themselves."

"That is good," said Allesandra. "I fear you should not meet together in large numbers anywhere within the county again."

"A sad decision, but perhaps wise. Does this Sir Gaucelm say when the bishop or his inquisitors will arrive?"

She shook her head. "Only when their business in Muret is concluded. I would beware. They may arrive at any time."

She lifted the wrapped Bible from her cloak and handed it to him.

"It is no longer safe to keep the holy scriptures about the castle. We would be accused of heresy for certain if it became known that the women in the castle read it for themselves."

The parfait took it in his hands and unwrapped it. "We will keep it safe for you."

A trace of bitterness passed over his otherwise open and generous countenance. "It is one of the many evils of the Catholic church that says only priests must read and that Christians must be kept in ignorance."

The Cathars believed that only a personal experience with God was valid and refused to accept the ecclesiastical hierarchy that stood between the individual and God in the Catholic Church.

Then his kind blue eyes gazed at hers. "And you, madam. Will you remain at the castle? I am sure there are many here who would gladly help you out of the county should you wish to leave."

She shook her head resolutely. "No, I must stay and act as if nothing out of the ordinary has happened. The French rulers know that we are used to a way of life wherein Catholics and Cathars have lived peaceably side by side for many years. It is that tolerance that they cannot understand. I, myself, cannot understand the pope's wish to control the thinking of every man, woman, and child. We seek a different path here. But for myself, I believe I can convince them of my innocence."

She felt a surge of guilt as a vision of Gaucelm's arms about her passed through her mind. But she dared not ponder it now.

"Do not worry for my sake, Father."

"Very well. Then we shall pray for our torn land and for the return of a way of life that once blessed us all."

She steadied her voice as she said resolutely, "The only way that way of life can return is by the expulsion of the French. And to that end, I pledge my efforts on your behalf. Even if it costs my life."

Eight

By word of mouth and in the way that news travels across a countryside in a land where feeling is high and the people close knit, the troubadours received Allesandra's call. Those former vassals of Allesandra's who promised to swear the oath of fealty to Gaucelm were released from their imprisonment. The rest were ransomed by their families.

So a week after Gaucelm returned to what was now his castle on the Garonne, the preparations for a banquet and several days of entertainment were under way.

Once again the household was readied for guests. Wine casks were brought up, fresh rushes were strewn, and wicks were trimmed. Wall hangings were cleaned to bring out their bright colors. Even the servants were garbed in new clothing. Goblets and lamps were polished, pots were scrubbed. Fresh herbs were gathered and tied in bouquets so that their scents would freshen the air.

On this day, Allesandra sat on the dais beside Gaucelm for the ceremony at which her former vassals would swear the oath of fealty. Gaucelm appeared in a new tunic of turquoise and a loose-sleeved surcoat of darkest blue with silver threads. His noble face wore an expression that spoke to all that this was his due. He was lord and master here, but he would be fair as long as there were no infringements to his rule.

Sitting beside him, Allesandra trembled to think how close she was to falling under his spell. Even without looking at her, he seemed to emanate possessiveness, and she feared that one false move on her part might betray a dangerous intimacy between them to those watching.

In consequence, she sat stiffly, dressed in crimson finery embroidered with gold threads. A crimson-and-gold veil, held in place with a cloth band about her forehead, flowed over hair coiled in refined chignon as befitted her submissive status. Her hands clasped the carved chair arms and she faced straight ahead as Gaucelm carried out the ceremonies. As each man approached, Allesandra said his name so that Gaucelm might know what to call him. She knew her household staff and guard personally, but Julian stood at her left shoulder to give her the name if she had forgotten it.

The men-at-arms were free men, defeated in battle, but offered the choice between following him and returning unarmed and unhorsed to their families. Their mistress had already offered her oath, so there was no need for those who chose to do so as well to feel traitor. Service to a lord was freely entered into, and this freedom of choice was jealously guarded by all concerned.

With heavy hearts they watched the French swallow up the southern counties.

The steward, Julian Farrell, now took his turn to walk to the edge of the dais and kneel on the top step. As he shifted his middle-aged body to one knee, Allesandra caught the flicker of his gray eyes before he lowered his gaze. Her heart went out to the man who had served her and whose father had served this castle before him.

"Julian Farrell," said Allesandra, without looking at either man.

Julian put his bony hands between those of his new lord.

"Do you wish without reserve to become my man?" asked Gaucelm.

"I so wish," Julian replied. His tone was firm, but without joy. "I promise by my faith that from this time forward I will be faithful to Sir Gaucelm Deluc and will maintain toward him my homage entirely against every man in good faith without any deception, and that I will keep good faith with King Philip Augustus the second, of France."

All this was sworn next to a jewel-encrusted, finely illuminated copy of the Bible, which sat on an ornately carved stand to Gaucelm's right. He picked up a gold cross and touched it to Julian's forehead.

"I accept your fealty, Julian Farrell. Defend the true faith." Then he leaned forward to seal the alliance with a kiss on both cheeks.

Julian stood and resumed his place on the dais, so that the next man could approach. Allesandra barely moved a muscle throughout. Only her eyes held silent messages to her old servants and tenants. In those looks were conveyed secret thoughts and feelings that could not be revealed to the man who swore the vassals in.

After all the vassals were so sworn, Gaucelm stood up and spoke to them in a solemn and commanding voice. His eyes traveled over each face as if not fooled by their benign expressions.

"I accept these oaths and promise in my turn to protect each man here and his family and his property. My justice will be dispensed fairly, my interest in your affairs will be great. For if you and your lands profit, so will I and so will my lord, the king of France. Let us drink now to a new unity in France."

The assembly retrieved their drinking cups from the trestle

tables, and as Gaucelm raised his jeweled goblet, so did they lift their vessels. They swallowed and then gave a shout.

The formalities over, Gaucelm set down his goblet and turned to Allesandra, offering her his hand.

"My lady, let the entertainments begin."

She stood up stiffly, and stepped down from the dais. The vassals sought out their friends, letting servants move the benches from around the wall. Gaucelm led Allesandra to the side, out of the way of tablecloths being spread and trenchers being laid.

"All has gone well so far, my lady," he said, glancing around at his new household. "I look forward to the more amusing aspects of this evening's fete. And I am most eager to see this court of courtesy you have described."

Allesandra forced a smile onto her granitelike face. "I hope it pleases my lord."

His eyes slid to the men who had just sworn their oaths to him, now joined by wives, sisters, mothers who had also been invited.

"There are many modest young women here, it appears," he said. "Blooming youth to tempt soldiers who have been away from their homes for long and men who have been cooped up in the tower."

"Do not worry, my lord. The court of courtesy is one of manners and genteel behavior."

A gong was sounded for the evening supper. Allesandra and Gaucelm took their places at the high table while festive platters of roast pig and lamb were brought in. They turned their attention to the fine meal as the company before them began hushed conversation. The kitchen staff had done their very best with fine sauces, expensive spices, the best cuts of meat from a recent slaughter. The bread was hot and moist, the feast delectable to the palate and filling to the stomach. And Allesandra could read the pleasure in Gaucelm's countenance whenever she glanced his way.

He leaned his head toward her during the second course.

"You have a fine cuisine here in the South, one I look forward to acquainting myself with. It seems each day the cooks think of new things."

"I am glad you enjoy the food, my lord."

"No less than the wine and the other comforts of these fair lands."

He sipped from his glass and gave her a look of pleasure, a look that made her pulse race. She was careful to sip her wine slowly.

After the meal, the tables were folded down and removed, the benches moved back to leave room for the musicians.

Julian approached and informed Allesandra that Lucius Hersend and Jean de Batute had just arrived, escorted by the French soldiers from the borders.

At the mention of the names of two of her best friends who were also among her favorite troubadours, a smile warmed her cool countenance. Welcome came to her lips, and she turned expectantly to look for her friends to enter when she caught Gaucelm's gaze. His eyes flickered. One eyebrow seemed to lift in curiosity, and as he followed her gaze to the entrance to the hall, she imagined that his look became even more intent.

She dared to think that her pleasant anticipation of the arrival of two of the featured guests caused Gaucelm a qualm of consternation. And then her smile widened, relief flooded an otherwise troubled heart. She left Gaucelm behind and moved forward through the gathering to greet the two troubadours.

"Lucius! Jean!" she cried just as they entered and looked around the festive hall.

Then they saw their hostess and came forward to take her outstretched hands.

Lucius Hersend was a broad-shouldered ruddy knight with curly hair of reddish gold. His blue eyes, which had been guarded and wary when he'd first come into the room, now danced with merriment, his face open to all that was about him. He went down gracefully on one knee, his lute still strapped to his back. As he spoke, he glanced from Allesandra to the right and left, as if trying to assess the circumstances.

"My lady, my heart has been dead these many months in my absence from this place, but now it beats again. My eyes can see again, now that your beauty shines upon them."

"Enough, Lucius," said Jean, grasping his friend's hand and pulling him back to his feet. "My lady, do not believe these false words of his. I myself heard him praise another lady just as highly only because she offered him a banquet and a rich mantle."

Allesandra laughed in delight at the hyperbole so common to troubadour praise and poetry. She'd been so long buried with war and heavy concerns that just to see these two sprites from more peaceful days did her poor heart good.

In contrast to Lucius's flaming hair, blue eyes, and fair coloring, Jean was slight, tan, with plain features and dark hair clipped long over his brow and short about the ears and back of his neck. He spread his arms wide, his open, fun-loving face full of mock sadness.

"It is I who have suffered. While Lucius secluded himself in a tower to write love poetry to his newest patroness, I was tending my old mother in the village, for she is ready to leave us for heaven. While Lucius feasted at his lady's table, I was living on stale bread and water because the armies ate up all the food in our demesne. While Lucius laid his head on tapestried pillows, I slept in a tent, for I did my forty days' service to my overlord just before I received your summons."

"Never mind," said Allesandra, still amused. "You are both welcome. And since the contest is not until tomorrow, you need not vie to bestow the greatest compliments."

Jean dropped his doleful pose and leaned his head closer to Allesandra. He flicked his eyes about them and spoke in a low, cautious tone.

"I was afraid this was a trick. I thought it suicide to ride into an enemy-held castle. But then I thought perhaps you needed rescue."

Lucius, too, became serious and closed their circle.

"Indeed, this is a dangerous undertaking, is it not? Can it be true that your new overlord requests the diversion of a court of courtesy? I think he serves the stern Simon de Montfort."

"So he does," whispered Allesandra. "And he is very clever. His mission is to find heretics."

"Hmmm," said Lucius. "I begin to see the picture. We must play our songs and act gay. For as you say, what do we know of any heretics?"

He opened his eyes wide and shrugged, palms up. Allesandra felt secure that these two would know how to behave.

"Good," she said. "Now let me introduce you to the man to whom I was forced to surrender this castle."

Jean paused before following her, forcing her to turn back toward him.

"Surely you do not intend to let him keep it, my lady?"

She gave a lift of a brow. "You are right. I do not intend to let him keep it for long."

Then she turned, finding that Gaucelm watched them from near the dais where he spoke to his sergeant-at-arms, Enselm, a man of undoubted loyalty and one who would be suspicious of her every move. She could see in the way the sergeant moved his gaze about the crowd that he would watch for any danger to his master and warn him of any treachery.

The jongleurs began to arrange their instruments in the musicians' gallery above the doors. By the time she reached Gaucelm, Allesandra's face again wore a demure expression.

"My lord, may I present these two most excellent troubadours. Lucius Hersend is known far and wide for his *pastorelas,* our dawn songs, as well as for his love songs."

Lucius gave a quick doubtful look, but he flourished a hand and gave a deep bow. "My lord, I am honored."

"Welcome, Lucius Hersend," said Gaucelm, assessing the other man. "I am much interested to hear these songs of which Lady Valtin speaks so highly."

"And Jean de Batute," Allesandra continued. "Jean's *sirventes,* which are very satiric, are the most amusing in the land. I hope you will appreciate them."

Jean's face held a slight expression of arrogance, but he bowed in deep humility until his host addressed him.

"Welcome to you as well, Jean de Batute. I am not so fluent in your language that I am sure to understand your humor, but one can always learn."

"I will strive to entertain as well as to enlighten, in that case," replied Jean.

"My lord," said Allesandra when the introductions were over, "the company is assembled. We will begin at your pleasure."

Gaucelm noted the pink flush to her cheek but could not tell if it was because of her delight at having her friends near her or whether she was anxious that her court of love might please him. He preferred to think she cared enough to impress him, but already felt twinges of jealousy and wondered if he had made a mistake in appearing so lenient as to invite these troubadours.

Gaucelm stepped onto the dais and raised a hand until the crowd quieted.

"You are all welcome," said Gaucelm. "Since a court of courtesy is presided over by the highest ranking lady present, I humbly turn over this court to my lady Allesandra Valtin." He paused to look upward at the expectant musicians in their gallery. Then, taking his time to survey the mixed gathering in the hall, he commanded, "Let the entertainment begin."

Trumpets blared, and ladies took their seats on the benches while Allesandra mounted the dais. A surge of the old joy crept into her veins, though not without the tempered caution that had come from a time of war.

"Welcome all," she said. Tears came to her eyes to see a gathering again so colorful and gay in this hall, as it was meant to be.

"A song, please." It took another moment before she could speak without trembling. "Who here has composed something new for my lord's pleasure?"

Lucius stepped forward. "I have, my lady, if I may offer so humble a piece."

A stool was brought for him to place his foot while he

strummed the lute. The crowd grew quiet. Behind him from the gallery, the jongleurs strummed accompaniment, for the musicians knew which piece Lucius would sing first.

The song of spring and new love gradually brought smiles to the cautious gathering. Allesandra glanced at Gaucelm only once, but could not read his expression. He lounged in the carved-back chair with fingertips together beneath his chin. When Lucius finished to polite applause, Jean stepped forward to claim the center of attention. He had changed from traveling clothes into a knee-length white tunic belted over midnight-blue hose. He surveyed the people and waited until the applause died.

"My lady," he finally said and gave a bow. "I am in great need of advice from one knowledgeable in the rules of love, for I am abused."

The court murmured, and Allesandra smiled, for this was the way a court of love was conducted. The Provençals present all knew the thirty-one Laws of Love. These laws were accepted by common consent of all the courts of courtesy, and all decisions were based on them.

"What is your predicament?" She descended the steps to place herself on the same level as the others.

Jean turned to include the audience in his tale of woe and gestured expansively as was his way when he expressed himself.

"My lady-love had accorded me the last favors in her power. But I requested her permission to bestow my homage on another lady. She granted my request."

He paused a little and crossed the floor. "But after a month I returned to my old love and declared that I had never besought any indulgences or desired any favors of affection from the new lady whom I had courted."

The audience whispered and hummed at this turn of events, but quieted to listen to what else the troubadour had to say.

One hand on hip, the other lifted to his side, he exclaimed, "My sole thought was to put to the proof the constancy of my best beloved and first-loved friend."

"And how did your first love receive you?" queried Allesandra.

Jean placed a hand on his chest as if feeling the pain in his heart.

"On my coming to her with this tale, she deprived me of her love, declaring that I had rendered myself unworthy of it by the mere act of soliciting and accepting permission to leave her."

Now the crowd chattered among themselves, for the case was a knotty one. Allesandra walked among the court.

"Let us now debate this issue. Ladies, what say you?"

A woman of fair countenance and russet hair, a friend Allesandra knew from a neighboring castle, stood up. "My lady, I have an opinion on this case. For it so happens that I am the second lady in question."

Mirthful chuckles came from those entertained at this. Jean turned to the redhead and flourished a bow, getting down on one knee to listen to her testimony.

The young woman came forward and spoke to Allesandra in arched tones.

"The troubadour Jean de Balute, who pleads the misuse of his mistress, misused me as well with his ruse. He came to me promising to demonstrate his love. But after that first meeting, he did nothing. He never came to see me again. After a month, I heard he had gone back to his former mistress."

Other witnesses spoke, vouching for this lady's testimony. One by one others gave their views, in declamatory tones. Some sided with Jean, others sided with the lady who rejected his love. After due deliberation, Allesandra mounted the dais again and gave her verdict.

"I render the lady who rejected the returning lover to be guilty," she said.

Jean spread his arms, palms up, and bowed.

Allesandra continued with her indictment. Her eyes slid sideways to Gaucelm, then back again to her court. "Such is the nature of love. Frequently lovers pretend that they desire the affection of someone to whom they are not attached. This, in order to assure themselves of the constancy and devotion of their beloved. It is an offense against the rights of lovers to refuse any tenderness or favor to the lover who desires it again, unless that lover can clearly be proven to have broken faith or proved disloyal in his duties."

The court erupted in good-natured congratulations to the pleader, who picked up his lute and began to strum. Viols and harps joined in from the gallery. Allesandra recognized the melody and threw an embarrassed glance toward Gaucelm, who lounged in his great chair, one finger stroking his chin as he watched the proceedings.

Jean began the first lines of a *tenso*—a discussion in poetry of the various points of courtly behavior—he had exchanged with Allesandra last year. He began his stanza. She would have to reply with hers.

"My lady is a *bel cavalier*," he gaily sang. "I had returned from the chase and paid her a chaste visit and accidentally left my sword in her apartment. When I returned to fetch it, I saw my lady without her seeing me. She had divested herself of all but her smock, and had buckled on the sword by a baldric across her chest."

To the amusement of the court, Allesandra was now forced to sing her stanza. "No doubt the lady you saw felt freedom in such habiliment, and delighting at the sight of the weapon, donned it to resemble a man."

"She drew sword from scabbard," sang Jean, pantomiming the actions for the audience, "and tossed it into the air. She caught it again and wheeled it glittering from side to side. I gazed in amazement through a crevice in the door. Vouchsafe, madam, to give me your advice. I love a lady of superlative charms. Tell me, ought I die of love without revealing my feelings to her?"

"Declare your love," sang Allesandra, "and request that she retain you as her lover and her troubadour. You yourself are noble and will honor her with your declaration. There is no one who would not receive you as her knight."

The tambourine and stringed instruments crescendoed to the climax as Jean spread his arms wide and sang from his heart. "You are my lady, madam."

"Then, Jean de Batute," she replied in the song. "You are my knight."

The court applauded and laughter filled the hall as the tambourines crashed three final beats. Flushed with the stylized performance, Allesandra returned to the dais. Her pulse fluttered with all the excitement, and when she stole a glance at Gaucelm, she saw his disapproving stare. She managed to turn and take her seat while the revelers formed a circle for a dance. When the din covered their conversation, Allesandra summoned the courage to ask after Gaucelm's pleasure.

"Most revealing," he answered somewhat sharply. "To exaggerate the importance of love beyond all limits. According to this poetry, love seems to the lover to be more rewarding than heaven."

She smiled at his understanding of what their poetry was all about.

"It is that, my lord, according to these dictates. Because of being in love with his perfect lady, a knight attains both skill and honor, becomes valiant and brave." She spoke with some feeling.

"I see. Then it is doubtful whether a knight without a lady-love can ever attain such heights of honor, since the lady is his source of inspiration."

"That is true, my lord."

"Ah, then, whether or not the lady reciprocates, the knight's worship produces a state of ecstasy."

"You have understood well, my lord." She caught her breath, waiting for the beating of her heart to slow down.

He had leaned closer as they exchanged these words, causing Allesandra to tremble with the buddings of desire that his nearness did not fail to awaken in her. Indeed, his hand rested on the arm of her chair, and his face was very close to hers as his dark eyes shone into her soul.

"I would be careful of those words, my lady," he said with a note of warning in his sensual voice. "There are those who would perceive this ceremonious worship of a woman of the flesh to be misplaced. Some might call it heresy."

Nine

Allesandra stared at the face hovering near hers and pressed a hand against her damp brow. But Gaucelm continued to speak in a tone meant only for her ears.

"I merely warn you, madam, that when the bishop's inquisitors come to this court, as soon they must, it will be an easy matter to draw attention to such things."

She faced forward angrily, refusing to look at him. "You purposely twist my words, my lord. I supposed you were enjoying the music."

Now he closed his hand easily about her forearm. "So I was. I merely wish to warn you."

His tone was convincing, and she spoke in a low, urgent voice. "You mean to say you are familiar with an inquisitor's methods."

He gazed at the frolicking company before them, their brightly colored costumes mingling against the gray stones and painted wall hangings of the hall. To anyone watching, it would merely seem that they were talking about the festivities at hand. But he answered her question. "I have seen them work."

She sat back in her chair. While still uncertain whether she could trust him, she took his warning to heart. She would have to be more careful in her speech when danger was near.

Gaucelm made no more mention of inquisitors but stood up and offered his hand. "Perhaps you would like to join the dancing while I talk with my men," he said.

She acquiesced and stepped down to join the circle now forming to dance in formalized patterns to the flute, stringed instruments, and tambourine. She forced her mind away from her fright and conversed with her friends. When she turned to execute a step, she saw that Gaucelm had joined a group of his men drinking by the hearth. His profile was illuminated by the flickering fire, and by oil lamps suspended from brackets on the wall. Therein lay the real danger, and she knew it. Not danger from an inquisitor's court, but danger from a man who was waging a private war against her heart. And who would be the loser?

She must be wary even while she enjoyed herself among her friends. By the third dance, her throat was dry and she sought refreshment. Gaucelm broke off from his group at the same time, and they walked together toward a table laden with dried fruits where a servant dispensed wine.

Handing her a silver goblet full of locally harvested wine, Gaucelm smiled. "Perhaps you would care for a breath of fresh air after your exertions."

She nodded, unsure if this were wise, but she followed him to a door leading out of the hall. They took a stairway that led upward and out onto the ramparts. The fresh night air cooled her brow, and the sounds of revelry were now replaced by the soft night breeze.

The land below and forest beyond were still visible in faint outlines. The countryside to the north and east rolled away in dips and folds. Tiny lights burned in nearby cottages and on the westward hills where shepherds roasted their supper. Nearer, the occasional footstep of a guard on duty could be heard from the drawbridge below.

When Gaucelm finally broke the silence, it was to comment on the troubadours and their ways.

"I fail to see how these rules of artificial etiquette can actually lead to feelings of devotion between the lovers in these songs," he said.

Allesandra tried to explain. "It rests with the suitor to convince the lady of his sincerity."

Gaucelm chuckled softly. "But only by a number of artificial signs. And if the lover takes a misstep, his behavior is reproached in one of these courts of love."

"That does not mean his affections are not sincere."

He chuckled. "Take the case of the gentleman who loved a lady, but had not the opportunity of speaking with her. He arranged that by his steward he and his lady-love could communicate."

"You have been reading our literature," she said, surprised, but still suspicious.

"I must practice my Provençal if I am to live here and hold these lands for France. If I am to dispense justice, I must do so in the native language. How better to understand the southern people than by reading their literature?"

"That is so, my lord."

It was on the tip of her tongue to ask if other Frenchmen were so willing to educate themselves in the ways of the Provençals. But she withheld her comment.

Gaucelm went on. "The gentleman's and the lady's love was thus concealed in perfect secrecy. But it seems that the steward, forgetting his duty to his master, pleaded his own suit with the lady, and she gave him her affection."

"Ah, yes, I know the case," replied Allesandra.

Gaucelm described the story just as poetically as if he'd been a troubadour himself. But he needed neither music nor instrument to weave the tale about her, his voice low and beckoning.

"The gentleman was naturally indignant with the steward, so the story goes, and denounced the intrigue to a court of love."

"And do you recall the verdict?" asked Allesandra as they strolled farther along the ramparts.

"According to the story I studied in your books, the crafty knave was allowed to enjoy his stolen pleasure. But the court of love decreed that both of them be excluded from the love of everyone in future. That the lady never be invited to an assembly of ladies since she violated the precepts of womanly modesty in stooping to love one so low. And the steward be forbidden to be seen near an assembly of gentlemen since he broke the laws of honor."

All this talk of love and Gaucelm's nearness quickened Allesandra's heartbeat in a most disquieting way. He moved to lift a hand to her cheek, and her face tingled at his touch.

"I would not want any harm to come to you, my lady, should the wrong ears interpret your love games. There is still much in your friends' poetry that sounds like heresy." His voice was very low, almost a whisper. "Take heed."

She felt her throat go dry and the blood rush through her limbs. "Is it inevitable that there will be an inquisition here?"

His hand slid round her head and along her back, and he gently pressed her toward him in a protective gesture. "I am afraid that cannot be stopped. It might be better to tell me the truth about your friends than to wait for the bishop's court."

Her feelings teetered between remembering what Gaucelm stood for and gratefulness for the mercy he had shown thus far.

He tucked her shoulders against his chest and gazed outward at the land that was the bone of contention between the king of France and the nobles of the South.

"I fight for the unity of France," he reminded her. "And the king fights for the pope. One needs to take care in these dangerous times."

"We are in your hands now, my lord," she said, trembling against him. "You are our protector."

He reached to turn her in his arms, his voice and look suddenly intent. "Would you have me as your protector? I believe we do not have to be enemies, if you would be truthful with me."

She opened her mouth to speak, but the words choked in her throat. Gaucelm did not resist the temptation of lowering his lips for a kiss.

The joy at having a man's strong arms about her swallowed Allesandra, and she could not help but respond to his embrace. In her confusion, she tried to think of how he might be right. If he were on their side, he would be able to protect them from the evils of the French inquisition. But there was no time for plotting, for Gaucelm's embrace became more urgent.

She trembled as they stood close. His arm wrapped around her waist, and she felt the reckless desire to want to stay thus, forever.

"Allesandra, my lady," he whispered in a hushed voice. "Come with me now. Let not this night keep us apart. Let me show you that I am not your enemy."

Her heart thundered against her chest, and she said nothing. Instead, she allowed him to slide his hand up her arm and hold her shoulder as he kissed her temple. Then his other arm slid about her and he held her in a warm embrace. Their kiss was natural, as if she'd known him forever. And she could not deny that she wanted more of him. How had he wormed himself into her heart and mind thus? Was he one of Lucifer's angels then? Tempting her beyond her own control?

Somehow her feet moved as he wrapped one arm about her waist and led her the short distance to a doorway. He escorted her down the steps to the door to the great chamber.

The evening of celebration and the intimate discussion of the ways of love had drawn them undeniably together. Alone now in his chamber, the effects of the evening fanned their desire. The look of passion he had thrown her way now feasted on her own flushed face as he gathered her into his arms again. Her body throbbed with a desire stronger than any she had ever felt, as strong as the sinful ones sung about in the poems. And she knew she was not going to fight him anymore.

"Madam," he said in his sensuous tone. "I am no poet, and I do not waste time on words. I would show you my feelings. With my actions, I would prove myself."

All thought was gone now, except for those of this man. She pressed her lips eagerly against him, and her hands could not help nesting in his thick, black hair. Only the light from the fire in the fireplace cast the burnished outlines of his chiseled face. She caught a breath as his hands began to caress her through the folds of her robes.

Then he pushed aside her surcoat, threw off his own and deftly untied the girdle at her waist. His lips found her ears and throat, while his hands flamed the desire in every part of her body and her own hands eagerly explored the muscular prowess of his powerful frame, traitorous as it was. She was hungry for this man and no longer cared to resist him.

It did not seem to matter that only hours ago she had told her friends that Gaucelm Deluc was her enemy. That she vowed to work to overthrow him and reclaim her castle. For now all she wanted was for him to claim her for his own. The need her body had felt ever since she'd been thrown together with him in this castle now cried out for fulfillment.

He led her to the bed and then knelt to lift the hem of her garment as reverently as any troubadour would do. He kissed her ankles and then her calves, making her gasp as he pulled the garment upward and then over her head until she stood before him in her thin, form-revealing smock, slit up the sides to reveal calf and thigh as she trembled where she stood.

Now he relished gazing at her feminine form, only temptingly covered by the flimsy smock.

And she could only stand and gasp in wonderment as he removed his own tunic and shirt, untied girdle to drop braies and hose, and stood at last before her in naked masculine magnificence.

She was no virgin and did not turn in shyness, but gazed in heated passion at the male display before her. She could barely breathe, so great was her excitement as he stepped up to her, gently grasped her shoulders with his hands and then lowered his mouth for a kiss. She opened her mouth, drinking in the pleasure of his hunger. His hands found their way under her smock, while his hard organ brushed her thighs.

The craving between her legs tingled with unbearable need, and then his mouth found her breasts, kissing, teasing, prodding through the material until she thought she would faint. Then he removed the smock, and they embraced each other, flesh to flesh. They lowered themselves to the bed, and he stretched out beside her, exchanging her kisses with his, feeling the delight of her skin, as she touched and caressed his male firmness and muscular torso.

All was passion and ecstasy. There was no thought but for the pleasure of which the poets sang and the ultimate with which a lady could reward her suitor. She raised her knees when he lifted himself to mount her, and arched her back, crying out when he joined his flesh to hers. His own excitement was such that she heard his ragged breathing, and his voice was fraught with passion as he whispered, "This is the ecstasy of which I've dreamed these many nights." He bent over her, cupping her face in his hands.

She clasped his shoulders, giving herself completely to the thrusts of pleasure, building and building in mutual exaltation until the pinnacle of fire exploded within. How long had this been unremembered in her years of widowhood and how much greater was this cry of rapture. She wrapped herself around him in the moment of intense, deep passion that threatened to carry her away.

He kissed her again as he held her damp body to his, and then they lay entangled, his face against her flowing hair, her limbs clasping his.

She did not want to let him go, until finally they moved to lie next to each other in more ease. Still, he caressed her hair, and she lay a hand against his hip. She wanted him to be forever thus with her, their bed a safe haven in a time of war, the enemy subdued.

It was the dawn breaking that awoke her. A great serenity washed over her, and she snuggled deeper into the bedclothes, her hair spread across the pillows.

Then she sat up, pulling the covers with her, embarrassment flooding her. She remembered the pleasures of the night before, but now feared the consequences. Gaucelm was not in the room, but her garments had been thoughtfully laid across the foot of the bed. No maid came to help her, but surely her women would know she did not spend the night in the women's quarters. She would have to make some excuse.

She rose and dressed quickly, but took time to braid her hair and cool her flushed cheeks. When she made her morning appearance, she must not look as if she'd just risen from her master's bed.

Then she borrowed a mantle, hanging on a peg. Her thought was to make it look as if she'd just come in from the forest. Why not go outside first, make her way to the house where she'd been a few nights ago? She could have a few words with her friends and then return, no harm done, and tell Isabelle and Marcia that she'd been away all night.

It was the hour when most of the household would be breaking their fast, so she made her way to the tunnel entrance without difficulty. When she came to the end, and pushed aside the hawthorn branches that hid it, she paused to make sure there were no Frenchmen about. Then she hurried along to the holding. To her surprise a great many people gathered in the yard, including Jean de Batute and Lucius Hersend. She was through the gate and into the yard before anyone noticed her.

"My lady," said Jean, breaking off. "There's news."

"What's happened?" she asked as faces turned toward her.

"Count Raymond and his son have landed at Marseilles. The southern provinces are rising up to join his army. Lucius and I are planning to go join the uprising."

"Do we still hold Toulouse?" she asked urgently.

"We do, and the walls are being strengthened every day."

The fear that she had kept at bay while distracting Gaucelm with a court of courtesy returned. She regarded her friends, the people for whom she was responsible, or had been as chatelaine of the castle.

"It is dangerous. Our captor, Gaucelm Deluc, speaks every day of the threat of an inquisition. I've told you all to disperse. Any gathering such as this will be suspect."

One of the women spoke up. "Our parfait is within. There is

a consolamentum. Do not worry, my lady. We have guards posted to let us know of anyone coming."

Allesandra drew in breath. The parfait conducting the Cathar sacrament so close to the castle? She broke away from the group and went up the steps to the house.

There the lady Cecelia Fontanta, dressed in a pure white gown with white veil, was kneeling before the parfait Bertram de Gide, who was just ending his sermon with a prayer.

Then Cecelia lifted her head and promised to devote herself to God alone. Allesandra was deeply surprised to see her friend take this drastic step. Whereas the believers were allowed to marry and to go on living in a world which the pure eschewed, one accepting the consolamentum renounced the world entirely.

Cecelia spoke in a firm, joyful voice. "I promise never to lie, never to take an oath, never to kill or to eat of an animal, and to abstain from all contact with a husband."

Bertram imposed his hands on her head and then bent to give the chaste kiss of peace on her forehead. She arose and exchanged the kiss of peace with those in the circle around her. Thereupon the rest of the believers dropped to their knees, for one who had taken the consolamentum was an object of veneration for ordinary believers who had not yet been consoled.

When Cecelia saw Allesandra, she beamed upon her friend and came to take her hands and then exchanged the kiss of peace with her.

"My dear Allesandra, I am blessed that you could share this moment with me."

"Cecelia, are you sure you are ready to do this?"

The other woman's eyes shone as with inner peace. "Why not? My husband is dead, my lands are confiscated. If I am to suffer at the hands of the inquisitors at least my soul can have its reward. There is nothing left for me here on earth, but many joys in heaven. I will take to the road with Bertram and Emice and preach to the other believers."

Allesandra would not argue with her friend's choice, she only cared for the danger they all might bring to themselves.

"I'm afraid we cannot deceive the French who hold my castle if we continue to meet this way," she said. "I am suspected myself, but I have led Sir Gaucelm to believe that I am as orthodox as he. We have an uneasy truce."

"Have you, my dear?"

Guilt flooded her veins, and for a moment Allesandra wondered if the newly blessed initiate had been granted the power to read her heart. She tried to blink away the traces of her deception. But Cecelia went on to other matters in a practical way.

"Do not worry for us. We will be gone from here ere you are asked to betray us."

"I would never do that."

Jean entered the hall and broke into their conversation. "Quickly. There are soldiers approaching through the woods. We must leave by the back entrance."

The crowd scattered. "This way, my lady." Jean escorted Allesandra out a door and down a ladder behind the animal pen.

When she glanced back, she saw that the men about the house were now engaged in splitting wood and doing other normal chores. She could only hope that Cecelia and Bertram would find a way to secrete themselves if the French soldiers became too curious.

She and Jean stepped quickly along a path into the woods behind the house. In the distance she heard shouts, and then the sound of horses' hooves breaking through dried branches on the forest floor.

"Quickly. Sit there," ordered Jean, pointing to a fallen log.

No sooner had she taken a seat and Jean brought forth a flute, which he put to his lips, than three horsemen broke into the small clearing and splashed across the brook.

Jean's back was to the men entering the clearing, and for a moment he held Allesandra's eyes, conveying a warning to her. Her heart sank as she saw that Gaucelm rode with Enselm and a squire. There was nowhere to hide. And when the riders saw them, Gaucelm raised a hand for the others to halt.

Setting eyes on him after their night of passion caused her

heart to crash against her chest and her palms to sweat. Yet her face must give no hint of either the seduction of which she had been a part or the ceremony she had just witnessed. But there was a flicker of annoyance on Gaucelm's face, which darkened into a cloud of displeasure as he walked his mount toward her. She stood up, as Jean lowered his flute and turned to bow to Gaucelm.

"My lord Deluc," said Jean quickly. "You have surprised us. My lady Allesandra and I had sought this place to compose our tenson for this afternoon's competition. As you can imagine, it was important for us to get away from that sneaky Lucius who would foil us by satirizing our song if he could."

"Is that so?" asked Gaucelm, as his mount snorted and heaved its sides after the short run across the meadow. "I find it curious that you would roam so far."

His eyes glanced suspiciously about the trees and clearing, and Allesandra felt her cheeks warm. He seemed to insinuate that he'd caught them at activities other than what they professed. His look of accusation inflamed her. Surely he could not believe that she would rise from his bed only to run off with another man the very next morning. She looked for words that would allay his suspicions without giving anything away. Jean was quicker with a defense.

"It was necessary, my lord. In these competitions, one cannot risk a spy. It is the greatest embarrassment to perform one's song only to hear the lines twisted and mocked by a clown who comes afterward. But perhaps my lord would like to hear what we've accomplished so far."

Gaucelm's eyes only glanced at Jean but bored into Allesandra. He paused, taking his time to assess the situation. The lines of concentration creased in his cheek and at the corners of his eyes as he made up his mind. Allesandra read the displeasure still in his eyes.

"I think not. Such hard work deserves a better audience for its showing. We are on the trail of a deer. I would caution you to take better cover. For had we not come upon you thus, one of our arrows might have caused you great harm."

"We will take your advice now that we know hunters are about. If my lady would be willing to retire now that the greatest work on the tenson is done . . . ?"

"I would be so inclined," she finally said.

She and Gaucelm exchanged a long look, and then Gaucelm lifted his chin and spoke to his companions, who had stopped a little way off.

"Come, let us not waste the day." And he trotted off with the other two.

Allesandra trembled and sat down again on the log. "That was a narrow escape."

Jean glanced back in the direction of the house they had just left.

"Evidently their suspicions were not aroused, for they did not seem interested in any kind of search, so intent were they upon their game."

She dared not mention just what suspicions she had read in Gaucelm's eyes, but gathered her strength again.

"Come," she said. "We must make our way back to the castle in ease, as if we have been doing nothing here but playing music. It is fortunate we did not have to prove our point by a demonstration."

Jean smiled. "Perhaps my cleverness would have indeed been put to the test. But then, they are not familiar with our songs and would not have recognized it had I sung an old one."

"Do not underestimate our overlord," she cautioned. "He is more knowledgeable of our ways than you would suspect. He has not been idle since he took over the great chamber in the castle where all my writings are kept. He is lettered and has made a great study of the Cathar religion and the songs of the troubadours."

Jean's thoughts turned pensive. "In that case I wonder how much he understands the symbolism in the songs. Does he take the literal meaning or the mystical one?"

"It is hard to say. For the moment, I believe he thinks that troubadours praise and adore only a fleshly lady. But he did warn me last night that the praise and ecstasy we sing of might suggest heresy."

" 'My verse must confuse fools who cannot understand it in two ways'," Jean paraphrased the troubadour Alegret.

"Let us hope," said Allesandra, "that Gaucelm Deluc is such a fool."

Ten

A squall had blown up, and with the howling wind and sudden rain, the bishop's coach and entourage of horsemen, dressed for riding in long black cloaks, made their way over the crest of the hill and wound along the road up to the castle.

"Who goes there?" shouted the guards at the gatehouse from their portal.

"The bishop of Toulouse" came the answering cry. "With legates from the apostolic see." The coach was allowed entrance and clattered over the drawbridge and into the courtyard.

The word was carried to Gaucelm, who had retired to his chamber. Annoyance filled him when Enselm roused him.

"So," he said, throwing aside bed curtains to put on a tunic. "It has come so soon. And in inclement weather, no less."

By the time he was dressed and in the hall to greet his midnight visitors, he had assumed a respectful demeanor. But he did not go any farther in showing reverence to the bishop and his party than he must.

Outside, the storm howled, and the lights that had been lit for the guests flickered from the drafts coming in through shuttered windows.

"Reverend Bishop," Gaucelm said. "I did not expect a visit from you this night."

"No doubt," said Bishop Fulk. He had taken a seat in a high-backed chair by the fire, which was being stoked. His companions still wore their traveling cloaks, hoods thrown back to drip on the rushes.

"My holy brothers have just joined me from Rome with instructions to make a list of heretics in this vicinity. We traced some names to this demesne. Perhaps now that you have been in residence here you can help us."

Gaucelm kept his features neutral. "I see. And have you this list now?"

The bishop waved a hand. "In the morning there will be time. We know the whereabouts of those we seek to question. They will not try to run, for that would only prove their guilt."

"Very well. Then may I have the steward show you to chambers? They may be Spartan, for we are ill prepared to host so noble and holy a party as yourselves. Had you sent word ahead . . ."

The smaller of the two legates with Bishop Fulk now spoke in a thick, nasal tone. "Christ did not fuss over simple accommodations. Neither shall we."

Gaucelm did not have a taste for the self-righteous, but he only nodded and turned to issue orders to a servant to awaken the steward and find rooms for the guests. Wine was served, and because of the late hour the bishop and the two legates followed the sleepy steward, Julian, to quarters.

Gaucelm was curious indeed as to who it was they sought to interrogate, but he would not find out this night. He was tempted to seek out Allesandra and warn her. But he tried to tell himself that was not necessary. She had assured him she was not a heretic. As to her friends, they would have to look out for themselves.

The news was brought to Allesandra next morning as she, Isabella, and Marcia were brushing their hair and dressing for the day. Julian had not wanted to wake them in the middle of the night, he explained.

Allesandra sent Julian with word for Jean de Batute and Lucius. "Tell them I will meet them in the musician's gallery as soon as I can."

Then she turned to gather her thoughts as she opened the shutters and looked out upon the damp courtyard. Marcia joined her at the window, wringing her hands.

"Dire news, my lady. Do you think the others got away in time yesterday?"

"Let us hope so. But it bodes ill that they have come here. Sir Gaucelm did warn me. I just did not think it would be so soon." She pondered his words of yesterday, and felt a tremor.

But she stiffened her spine and took upon herself that mantle of confidence and calm that she had always worn as chatelaine. Just because she did not possess the demesne anymore was no reason to show fear. Her own people still looked to her for guidance.

She met Jean and Lucius in the musician's gallery where they gathered to speak in hushed tones behind a screen. She noticed that Lucius was unusually silent, and his face was pale.

"There is a way to escape this," she said. "I can send you through the tunnel to the woods . . ."

"No," said Lucius, turning back from the small window that looked down over the stables where he had been watching grooms come and go. "They will know who is in residence here. Did not Sir Gaucelm's own men-at-arms escort us here? They know we will not run, for that would prove our guilt."

Jean sank onto a bench, looking glum. "Yes, I suppose that is true. We don't know what they want, but we had better be prepared to answer questions. There aren't enough of us to put up a fight."

"Let us hope that our friends have gotten safely away." She did not say it, but she did not want to stand and watch the parfaits being interrogated. For they would never recant. She forced herself to state the case as she saw it.

"The court will only mete out extreme punishments to those they know are heretics and who refuse to recant. They will ask us to name friends, that is true. I have persuaded Sir Gaucelm that I know no such heretics."

Lucius stared at her. "That is noble of you, madam. But what will happen to you if it is found out that you lie?"

Her heart trembled with apprehension. "I will take care of myself. You both must act as you think best. I cannot tell you what to do. The Church wants converts. It is not in their interest to punish heavily those who have in their eyes simply erred."

For a long moment she and Lucius exchanged gazes. Then she took his hands and kissed him on both cheeks as a friend. No more was said, for noises below made them step back and watch silently through the screen as the bishop and his entourage entered the hall, followed by Gaucelm and Julian.

Tables, benches, and chairs were arranged as the bishop, dressed in white tunic and dalmatica of silver and gold threads, indicated with the flick of a long, thin finger what he wished. And then his clerk handed him one of a roll of parchments. He sat down in the high-backed arm chair and Gaucelm's men-at-arms slipped into the hall, staying near the edges of the room. More of the household had drifted into the hall to see what was going to happen, but they hovered at the back of the hall.

When all was arranged to his liking, the bishop spoke. His eyes glinted as he cast them about the room, and when his gaze passed over the screen, Allesandra felt a chill crawl down her spine.

"I am here on the authority of the Apostolic See to question those here about a number of persons suspected of heresy, living or dead. My authority comes from His Holiness in Rome as is delivered here in these documents, brought to me by these legates."

"And who on this list is present that you wish to see, my lord Bishop?" asked Gaucelm.

Bishop Fulk narrowed eyes and lifted chin so that his mitre tilted backward slightly. "The Catholic leaders in Muret have provided me with the first name on the list. Baron Georges Valtin."

From where she watched in the musician's gallery, Allesandra's hand flew to her chest and she drew in a breath. Her late husband. She staggered forward a step and had to brace herself against the screen. Jean's hand at her elbow steadied her.

Below in the hall, Gaucelm spoke calmly. "The Baron Valtin is deceased, my lord."

The mitre rocked forward and the chin lowered once. "So I understand. However, if he is proven to have been a heretic, then his lands are forfeit to the church." A thin smile followed.

A murmur traveled the length of the hall.

A muscle twitched in Gaucelm's cheek. Bishop Fulk must know very well that the lands he referred to now lay in Gaucelm's own hands, hard won by his campaign with Simon de Montfort. However, now was not the time to point that out.

"Have you proof?" he queried.

The bishop waved a sheaf of statements. "These were taken in Muret, where this court began. Many we questioned were reluctant at first to name heretics."

He glanced benevolently at the gathering of household members cowering on benches and standing at the back of the hall. His voice began to drone in patronizing kindness as he explained the generous view the Church was willing to take with those who had strayed, through no fault of their own.

"It is best to define what heresy is. In case there has been any misunderstanding through ignorance rather than evil, let me say that only one reading of the Holy Scriptures can be true. The Mother Church interprets the scriptures for the lesser educated in order to preserve and protect the fabric of Christian society. Therefore any deviation from orthodoxy is heresy." His voice boomed on the last word and then softened again. "But only if pertinaciously defended."

He paused to smile benevolently at the gathering. "Legally, one must first be instructed that his beliefs are not orthodox. Only after this, if one insists on defending them, may he be branded a heretic. Otherwise those beliefs are simply an error."

Behind Allesandra, Jean muttered an epithet. With a gesture she cautioned him to silence.

"For those who see their errors and recant," the bishop continued in a singsong voice, "a light penance is imposed. Especially if the saved one gives us names of others who have equally been led astray."

Allesandra's heart thudded in her chest. Jean whispered thoughts similar to her own into her ear. "He wants to trap us into condemning our friends," he hissed. "These elite churchmen care nothing for souls, but rather for those whose property is worth confiscating. They are the devils."

"And?" inquired Gaucelm below. "So that those present understand the consequences, if one is convicted for following the heresy and continues to do so? What then?"

Fulk folded his hands in his lap and looked pleased to explain. "Isolation in order to give them time to reconsider. And fines of varying degrees."

"I see," said Gaucelm. "And in the most extreme cases?"

"Property is seized, of course."

The room was quiet, and Allesandra was aware of the tension felt all around. She put a hand on Lucius's shoulder to give it a squeeze. He covered her hand in response, but did not turn from staring through the screen.

"Lucius," she said, looking up at him. "You must do what you think best."

Only then did he turn his head and gaze down at her with a worried look. "Do not concern yourself about me," he said softly but firmly.

Then she swept down the stairs and entered at the back of the hall as Bishop Fulk again raised the issue of her late husband. Allesandra only took a moment to take a breath and steady her nerves. Then she moved forward slowly. Those she approached parted until she stood in the hall. Gaucelm turned from the bishop and strode toward her. His face was hardened, and she could read no expression there.

"Here is the lady Allesandra Valtin," he said, offering a hand to lead her forward.

She kept her back straight and walked forward until she was a small distance from the bishop. "You wished to question me, my lord bishop?"

Bishop Fulk gave her a long, intimidating look and then slowly lifted the parchment to read from it. She knew he was doing it to irritate her. He already knew what lay therein. However, she waited patiently, determined to show no emotion. Finally he dropped the parchment to his lap.

"Was your husband a Cathar, my lady?"

She heard small gasps coming from women in knots in the recesses of the room. She willed them all to keep silent.

"I don't know what you mean, my lord."

"Oh? One would think a husband discussed his religious beliefs with his wife. Or was your marriage one of no intimacy at all, not even verbal?"

"My lord," said Gaucelm stepping forward. "I am as interested to ferret out the straying lambs in your flock as you are. But surely you'll allow this lady the dignity—"

"Silence!" Bishop Fulk's hand went up. "You have no experience interrogating, and this is not your business."

Then in slightly softer, more oily tones, "I will forgive the interruption since you have not had these dealings in your household before. But I advise you to keep silent, sir. Otherwise your interjections will look oddly as if you are in defense of those I question. I must ask this lady about her husband's behavior even including intimate details of their marital life, for the very reason that these reveal much about what a man believes."

Gaucelm's jaws clenched, but he said no more. Allesandra looked back into the bishop's face. "My husband spoke to me of religion," she answered evenly. "That is true. He was no Cathar."

"Is that so?"

"It is so."

She marked Bishop Fulk for what he was and stared into the

conniving eyes. She saw the malicious glee he took in making her speak of her relations with her husband. But she was not so proud as to risk punishment for mere prudery. She would not let this greedy churchman who sought control to succeed in humiliating her. She knew what he wanted to know and she said what he wanted to hear. A Cathar parfait who had taken the rite of consolamentum pledged a life of chastity. Her anger fortified her.

"My husband and I had proper conjugal relations."

"But you did not conceive?"

"No, I did not. He was away much of the time."

"Then he did not abstain?"

"As I said, my lord. When my husband was home, I served him as is a wife's responsibility. We took joy in it. He ate meat as well."

The listeners gasped and murmured, but still she faced the bishop staunchly. She felt Gaucelm's burning gaze. She shook inwardly, but she was mentally prepared for whatever might be thrown at her.

"Hmmm." He turned to another line of questioning. "I have testimony by your husband's friends saying what they heard the baron your husband utter as to his faith. Shall I read it to you?"

"If you like, my lord." She managed a pleasant smile as if whatever he was about to reveal was new to her.

He picked up the parchment again. "Several deacons were secreted nearby to overhear the following conversation between Baron Georges Valtin and his kinsman Castronovo of Muret. Castronovo showed the baron his hand and asked if the flesh will rise again; the baron said that the flesh will not rise again. Only a spirit. If it is to be saved, it will pass into another body to be born again and complete the penance."

"I never heard him say thus to me," she said to the bishop with conviction.

"Is that so? And did he not condemn the practices of the Roman Church, the unintelligible chanting, alms for the dead?"

Suddenly her husband's voice echoed in her head, telling her how all the singing in Latin deceived the simple people. She could not help but shut her eyes for a moment, but she opened them again quickly. "No, my lord. I cannot recall him ever saying so."

"Do you swear it?"

"I swear it."

A hush fell over the court. A Cathar would not swear, for oath taking was prohibited in the Gospel. And if she swore to whatever the bishop wanted her to say, this above all else would convince him.

He studied her. Then with a flick of the wrist, he gestured that his clerk should carry forward a heavy, bound copy of the scriptures, which he placed on a lectern.

"Approach then," Fulk challenged her. "Place your hand on the scriptures and swear in the name of Jesus Christ, the Son of God, that these things are true."

A thin sheen of perspiration broke out over her skin, but she stepped forward and placed a hand on the leather book binding. Her voice was low, but firm. She swore. And then she turned and walked slowly to the back of the hall. Around her, voices conversed, whispered. Bishop Fulk exchanged words with the legates, and then just as Allesandra was drawing breath, he boomed out the name of the next person he wished to interrogate.

"Lucius Hersend, if you are present, as we believe you are, come forward to answer to the Apostolic See."

Her heart clenched as Lucius and Jean appeared together in the arched doorway. Jean came to assist her to a seat before she fainted, but Lucius strode purposely forward.

"Well done, my lady," whispered Jean.

"I lied," she whispered, her words covered by the buzz of conversation as Lucius made his way forward.

"It does not matter," Jean reassured her. "God will understand."

She placed her head in her hands as Jean stood to get a better view. But even seated behind onlookers, she could hear what the bishop said to Lucius, who now stood to reply to the barbed questions.

"Lucius Hersend, you stand before us accused by those who know you as a follower of the Cathar belief. Is this true?"

"I am no Cathar, my lord, though I was raised among them."

"And when the count of Toulouse agreed to expel heretics, why did you not do anything about it on your lands?"

Allesandra peeked through an opening in the crowd and saw Lucius straighten his shoulders. "We cannot expel all those who deviate in the way they believe, my lord. Many do not care for dogma, but they speak out against clergy who wear gleaming rings and raiment. Such display can hardly be expected to persuade poor villagers back into the fold."

The crowd rumbled and gasped.

Allesandra stared as Lucius's voice rose. "It is hypocrisy that the people in my town decry."

What followed surprised her. The bishop posed a question in Latin, and Lucius answered. She had enough Latin to follow it herself, though she knew that many present did not. Fulk questioned Lucius on many points of Christian doctrine, and to her relief, his answers were orthodox.

Finally, one of the legates brought forth a reliquary containing bits of bones of the saints. "And will you swear to your orthodox faith on these relics?" asked Fulk.

Whereupon Lucius's face turned ashen. "I will not swear."

A gasp went up and many of the women covered their mouths with their hands.

"Aha," accused Fulk. "You are repelled by the relics."

"I did not say that," Lucius argued. "But you yourself know that we are forbidden from taking oath. The scripture itself prohibits it."

Fulk had come here to make an example, and he was going to make an example of Lucius. The bishop rose and extended his draped arm, pointing a long finger at the knight before him.

"You will not swear on the relics. You criticize the clergy. You preach that personal experience of God is enough and that you reject ecclesiastical hierarchy. You are a heretic, Lucius Hersend. I have sworn statements saying that you have been heard to preach that Christ was not of the flesh."

"He was not of the flesh," thundered Lucius, beyond all caution. He was lost; his conscience would not let him continue the lie. But he would have his say. He took two steps forward.

"For nothing of this world is good. This world is evil. Good is pure spirit unbound by worldly existence, a being of pure and perfect love. An evil god created this world to imprison unfettered souls that they might serve his will. He is called *Rex Mundi,* and all of earthly existence is under his domain."

Fulk pounced on his victim, his eyes flashing his victory and his face ringed purple in his rage. "Dualist!" he shouted. "Dualist!" again and again.

Allesandra was on her feet now and pressed forward.

"Oh, Lucius," she breathed his name. But hadn't she known he would do this? For Lucius took the Cathar faith very seriously and he did preach. Many had heard him. There was not a chance that he could lie his way out of it, even if he so desired.

But Jean had followed her and tugged on her sleeve. "Caution, my lady," he whispered. "A display of emotion will only undo what you have done."

He checked her display of feeling and she clamped her mouth shut and stood to the side as the bishop pronounced excommunication in thundering tones.

"By the judgment of the Father, and of the Son, and of the Holy Spirit, by virtue of the power granted the Apostles and their successors, we unanimously decree that Lucius Hersend, the sower of scandalous beliefs, false denouncer of priests and bishops, shall henceforth be excluded from all Christian communion, both in this life and in the life to come.

"Let no Christian give him greeting nor the kiss of peace. Let no priest celebrate mass for him, nor administer to him the Holy Communion. Let no man keep him company, nor receive him into his house, nor drink, nor eat, nor converse with him, unless it be to urge him to repent."

Fulk's voice rose to shake the rafters. "May he be accursed of God the Father, who created man; may he be accursed of God the Son who suffered for man's sake; may he be accursed of all the saints, who since the beginning of the world have found favor in the sight of God. May he be accursed wherever he may be, in the house or in the fields, on the highway or in the footpath. May he be accursed living and dying, waking and sleeping, at work and at rest. Depart from us. As fire is quenched with water, so may his light be extinguished forever, except he repent and make amends."

At the final words, the voices around Allesandra mumbled, "Amen, so be it, so be it. Let him be anathema. Amen, amen."

But her lips did not move, nor did Jean's beside her. She watched in horror as Lucius was outlawed from the kingdom. She trembled with emotion, but she could do nothing to help him.

He passed out of the hall, and she started to follow, but heard Jean's caution in her ear. "Wait. He will head for the stables. If you wish to speak to him there, we must make our way carefully."

She clenched her fists, and the moistness of perspiration clung to her, but she waited as the court reshuffled itself. She caught a glimpse of Gaucelm. He looked stern, displeasure across his brow, but for what cause, she could not ascertain.

A spurt of anger caused her to blame him for allowing this to happen in her household. *His* household now. In reality there was nothing he could do, but it brought back to her the dire circumstance she was in and the power he held over her by being who he was and on the side of the king and of the Almighty Church.

Then she slipped out of the hall with Jean, being careful they were not noticed unduly.

"The grooms will see us," said Jean. "But if we are questioned we can say we were urging Lucius to repent."

She was grateful for Jean's reasoning. Her own mind was too tormented to lay strategies just now.

They found Lucius saddling his mount. He'd had time to gather his personal belongings and was in the final stages of loading his packhorse. Jean stood guard by the door while she flew to her dear friend.

"Lucius," she breathed as he turned and took her hands briefly.

"Do not trouble yourself, madam. I could not pretend."

After brushing away a tear of grief, she steeled herself again. "Do not let this hateful anathema ruin your life, Lucius. You know that your friends still love you."

He bent to kiss her brow. "I know it is true. And yet you will all be brought down unless you play their game. I leave now so as not to endanger you."

"We will fight back," she said with determination. "Toulouse stands firm. When Raymond has regathered his forces, we will mount another fight. If God wills it, we will repel the French and win back our lands and our way of life again."

He smiled sadly. "Whereas we were once left to think for ourselves, tolerance seems to be a thing of the past. Beware. The Roman Church is powerful. They need to persecute. It reinforces their claim to power."

"Oh, Lucius. I'm so sorry things have come to this pass."

He wasted no more time, but led his two horses to the door. There, he quickly embraced his comrade, Jean.

"Go in peace," said Jean.

"And you likewise." And then he mounted up, gave them both a final salute and rode out into the stable yard. Jean made Allesandra wait until the way was clear. Then they went forward.

"I will retire to my chambers," she said sadly. "I have no more wish to watch those the bishop chooses to intimidate."

"Then I will go and stand at the back of the hateful hearing and report to you what happens," he said.

It was on the tip of her tongue to ask how Jean perceived Gaucelm was managing the court that had landed in his lap. But then she thought better of it. Gaucelm appeared to have little choice in the matter. Though in her heart she wished that he would stand and defend her, she knew bitterly that he would not draw sword against the very churchmen he had tried to warn her would come.

Eleven

For two more days, the bishop's court went on. On the third day, Enselm informed Gaucelm that a letter from Simon de Montfort had come. He went immediately to his chamber to read it. Simon was moving against Toulouse at last and needed Gaucelm if his newly acquired domain was secure. If he could not come in person, Simon needed as many of his men as he could spare and still leave the Valtin lands safely guarded.

"I must go myself," he told Enselm.

"As you wish, my lord. The garrison here is in complete control. If my lord wishes my services in Toulouse, have no fear that the sergeants here will have no trouble holding this place."

Gaucelm considered. "These southerners seem docile enough with no one to rouse them to rebel, but I do not trust them. My lady Valtin thinks I am blind to the conversations she holds with her friends the troubadours. Bishop Fulk has finished his hearings for now, but I've no doubt he will return. I am aware that the humility and acceptance of French rule lies only on the surface. I would prefer that you remain here to keep order. Should there be a conspiracy or a threat, I can trust you to handle it."

"Count Raymond has gathered an army and rides for Toulouse, my lady," said Marcia. "We just heard from Peire Bellot and Christian Bernet." Two more troubadours came in response to the invitation. They had prudently waited until Bishop Fulk and his legates had moved on. Naturally, they would bring news of the movements of the French.

"They're here, then? I must see them at once."

"You'll no doubt find them with the others in the musicians' gallery," said Marcia.

As Allesandra hurried to greet two more of her friends, her mind was turning over plans. An army riding for Toulouse. The citizens there were strengthening the walls. No doubt Simon de Montfort was planning an attack. She must do what she could to help Raymond fend off the wily Simon, who had outgeneraled the southern allies at Muret. If Toulouse fell, Raymond would be completely usurped. All of the counties of Toulouse would fall to the French. An outcome that frightened Allesandra greatly.

The sound of instruments playing bits of music greeted her ears as she entered the hall. Gaucelm had instructed that the fête should continue in spite of being interrupted by the bishop's hearing.

Jongleurs with their instruments were gathered in small knots in every corner of the hall. But from the subdued tone of the gathering, she could tell their minds were more on the events of the crusade than on the music they'd been summoned to perform. She turned and ascended the staircase leading to the musicians' gallery. There the two new arrivals were exchanging hurried words with Jean. They broke off as she approached.

"My lady," said Peire Bellot. "We have news."

A large, stocky man, ten years older than the others, with short, straight light-brown hair, graying at the temples, he took her hand and kissed it, but wasted no time with frivolities.

"My friend," said Allesandra. "I am very glad to see you. Welcome."

Christian Bernet joined them and also bowed over her hand. But his young, angular face was fraught with worry. "We've just learned about Lucius."

"It was unfortunate, but I trust he'll make his way for now," she said. "You both had a safe journey?"

Peire spoke for them both. "Yes, my lady, though we thought

twice about venturing here with the French soldiers." He exchanged glances with Christian.

The younger man spoke up. "It might well have been a trap. But we knew your handwriting and came, thinking you might have need of us. For this festival could have been a disguise. Then we heard that the Apostolic See had sent its hounds. Glad we are to see you safe."

"Safe, yes, but at the mercy of our captor, Gaucelm Deluc and his men."

Peire lowered his voice even further. "He is Simon de Montfort's man, I've heard of him. We must be very careful."

"He rules here for the moment," she answered warily. "He speaks often of heretics, using the church as justification for seizing these lands. I've persuaded him that we are all cooperative with the bishop's wishes. That we shelter no heretics here."

"Hmmm, and you say he believes that?"

"For the moment, at least. But tell me of Raymond and his son. I am anxious for their news."

"Both well," reported Peire. "They escaped from the debacle at Muret when they could do no more. Their vassals knew they'd be more good alive to inspire the people than dead on the field. And so they were spirited away to refuge in Marseilles where they raised an army. Now they have regrouped and return to Toulouse."

Christian and Jean listened intently to Peire's exchange with Allesandra.

"And what of enemy forces?" she asked.

"Simon de Montfort moved from Muret yesterday. He no doubt plans to surround Toulouse, for they'll never let him in."

"We cannot let Toulouse fall."

"No, madam, we cannot."

The three troubadours looked at her with solemn faces. Christian spoke. "What do you wish us to do?"

"To behave as if you know nothing, for the moment. We must carry out the competition as planned. But I must think of a way to help Raymond."

"Surely that is too dangerous," said Jean. "You must stay here."

"Why?" she asked bitterly. She thought of the joy she had experienced with Gaucelm, but she knew she must push that aside in the light of responsibility.

"I am not in control of this demesne now. I have nothing to defend. As long as Raymond and his son are free, there is a chance that he will oust Simon and I will be able to reclaim my lands. I cannot sit on my hands and do nothing. I cannot sit by and watch Toulouse fall. I must help them defend it."

"Gaucelm Deluc will not like to discover you missing, should you go to Raymond," said Jean.

"No, but there will be no one to blame. If I do not tell you my plans, he cannot accuse any of you of being conspirators."

"But you'll need one of us to escort you," said Christian. He glanced about to make sure no one else was listening to their hushed conversation.

"That's right," added Jean.

"Or all of us," said the crafty and more mature Peire. "For if one of us goes with you, Sir Gaucelm will not believe that those who waited behind did not know. I say we all go when you go."

She could see the wisdom in that and would not wish to risk having her friends punished for her own escape. She looked at the grim faces standing around her.

"Very well. I'll lay the plans and we'll leave together for the good of Toulouse. But until I tell you, go on as if you know nothing. Distract these French with your witty songs."

"As you wish, madam," said Christian.

She took each of their hands again and accepted chaste kisses on cheek and wrist, binding them in purpose and friendship.

At dinner, Allesandra again took her place beside Gaucelm, who greeted her civilly but with no hint of the intimacy they had shared. She allowed her eyes to glance across his face as seldom as possible, for when she did, she suffered double pain.

Three nights ago she had given way to passion, had recklessly cast aside all thought except for the pleasure he gave her. Her heart still pounded with a yearning that she could not master, weak as she was. And yet she knew her duty. If her feelings were torn from her grasp, so be it. Even Gaucelm had the good sense to know that they could not betray to others what they had done. For both of them would be seen as traitors.

Passion aside, Allesandra was still loyal to her cause. And now she plotted to leave and go to Raymond's side. They must defend Toulouse at all costs. The disaster at Muret must not be repeated. The survival of Languedoc was at stake. If she must live with a maddening desire for a man who was an enemy, so be it.

After the meal, she rose to begin the entertainments. Gaucelm was civil to the troubadours and bade them play. Allesandra had cautioned them to sing the least dangerous of their songs, songs of spring and of forlorn love. Keep Gaucelm and his soldiers guessing for whom each lovesick troubadour made his verses.

But when she returned to the dais and risked a glance at Gaucelm's handsome face, deep in thought, she could tell his mind was not on the entertainment. Fearing the worst, she smiled nervously at him and took her seat while the minstrels played and clapped.

Gaucelm's long fingers lay along his chair arm, his sinewy arm half covered with the folds of his robe. His body was nonetheless taut for being garbed in linen tunic and silver-embroidered surcoat, and even to sit next to him in a straight-backed chair made her aware of her need. If she shut her eyes for one brief moment, she could envision being next to him between linen sheets, their skin drinking in each other's. She opened her eyes, the throbbing in her veins a threat to what she must do. Her voice shook as she ventured a question.

"My lord seems distracted," she said. "Does the music not please you?"

His eyes grazed her face, and for a moment the veil lifted. "It is pleasing. Forgive me if I do not seem attentive."

Her breath was shallow, but she forced herself to meet his gaze. "On what does my lord ponder?" she risked asking.

His eyes cleared, opened wider, and then a spasm of bitterness crossed his face. He glanced briefly at her mouth, the body that had lain beside him, and then armored his expression with determination, gazing back at the musical frolic below. His words pierced her heart, so sharply did he utter them.

"On treachery, loyalty, risk, danger. All the elements of war."

She swallowed and waited until she could speak steadily. "Are such things a threat now, my lord?"

His grip on the carved wooden chair arm tightened, and his mouth tensed. "That depends."

She should say no more and so fell silent. Neither did she trust herself to stand. If she was thus affected, how could she carry out what she intended to do? And yet she must tear herself from his side as quickly as possible. When she did not see him, it was a little easier to remember who she was and what he represented.

Somehow the day passed. To their credit, the troubadours carried off their part well, challenging each other to improve upon their songs. But to the practiced ear, the music lacked warmth, the instruments were played without inspiration. The performance distracted but did not uplift. Too much wine was consumed in hopes of masking their failings. Only Allesandra noticed that Gaucelm did not drink anything but water.

By evening the hall was cleared. Guests and soldiers alike retired to rest or stretch their limbs outside before the fires would be lit and supper laid. Allesandra sought out her friends, for she'd had all day to make her plans.

"We must not give the appearance of going," she said. "Therefore, you must leave your mounts here. There is another way outside, but we must carry arms and supplies with us. Be ready after supper. I will come to the guest chambers. They will not be watched, since the Frenchmen believe you to be working on your songs."

"We will be ready," said Jean, to which his companions nodded. "And we will be armed."

There remained one problem. When Gaucelm had taken over the great chamber, he had not given Allesandra time to remove any personal belongings she kept there. Once he'd learned of her poetry, she had taken some of the writings to the women's chamber for their amusement. But of other valuables that would come in useful now, he had not given leave for them to be removed.

His guards would keep her out of the great chamber when he was not in it. There was only one way to gain access when he was there. She approached the sergeant-at-arms, standing with arms crossed beside the door.

"I wish to see your lord," she said.

The man knocked on the door, and after being bid to enter, opened it to step in and announce her. There was no delay. Gaucelm looked up from where he was writing on a sheet of parchment at the round table in the center of the room. His retainer was just finishing lighting the oil lamps since the light from outside was fading.

"I'm sorry, my lord. I interrupt."

"I have just finished. Please enter."

When he laid the quill aside, he seemed also to lay aside whatever care it was he was writing about. He leaned back in the chair and gave her his full attention.

"What did you wish to see me about?" he asked.

"I . . ." she hesitated. "I simply wished to see you."

Her cheeks burned as she turned to walk slowly toward the tall window, with shutters pulled back to admit the fading twilight. She heard the chair scrape, and then he was beside her. He was not touching her, but she could hear his breathing. His voice was less strained and was tinged with a touch of emotion when he spoke.

"And I you, madam."

He reached slowly for her hand and lifted it to his lips. When he rested his mouth there, he did not hurry. Her heart twisted inside her as he kissed the hand and then turned it over to kiss her wrist, then her forearm.

She gasped a quick shallow breath as he put his other hand

on her shoulder and then moved closer to her. When he spoke, he seemed to utter her own thoughts.

"My lady, I rue the circumstances that brought us together. I rue the duty that will take me from your side. If these were peaceful times, we might enjoy each other publicly. As it is, we cannot even trust each other."

She trembled at the truth of his words. Why deny them? Still, she had enough presence of mind left to perceive that he seemed to be talking about going away, and she tensed. Was he going to join his general? Perhaps she could learn something that would help Raymond.

But his kisses put her mind on other things, and then she was in his embrace, kissing his face, her fingers running through his hair as she indulged in his affections.

"Allesandra, my love. I want you desperately."

She hardly had to answer, for her own responses were showing him. She had known when she'd walked into this room what would happen, but she had perhaps been fooling herself about the intensity of their mutual need.

She did not resist when he led her to the bed. She responded willingly when he threw off his tunic and then disrobed her. If this had not been her purpose in coming here, still she had not expected to keep from him once she was here.

He held nothing back and yet was just as gentle as before. Wild urges were not restrained, and when he touched her, she yielded, her body an instrument upon which he played. She tasted of him, relishing the salty, masculine sensation of him. And she thrilled as his lips and tongue taunted, teased, aroused her. The intimacy was maddeningly ecstatic, the feel of his hard muscles fulfilling her in every way. The hunger for a man's love that she'd kept within herself these years poured forth, as they both gave voice to their need and their pleasure.

He lay beneath her so that her hair formed a curtain around their faces. Her breasts grazed his chest. Their kisses set them both on fire. Then he set her on her knees above him so he could feast his eyes on her body.

He made love as a man possessed, holding her fast against

him long after their climax was complete, as if not wanting to be torn from her. Then he lay her on her back and kissed her possessively as if wanting to imprint his claim on her. When at last he raised himself on his elbow, he let his finger drift along her brow and through her hair spread on the pillow.

"Stay and sup with me," he said finally, a wistful smile upon his face. "We've worked up an appetite."

"Gladly," she replied, looking into the eyes that seemed to devour her, while her own heart beat with the knowledge that she was truly his prisoner in more ways than one.

He ordered that supper be brought and then they took their time draping themselves in their tunics once again.

"My lord, I used to keep a brush and some things here. Will you give me leave to collect them? The better to improve my appearance for you."

His hand drifted to her face, and then his finger lifted her chin.

"You are lovely as you are, your hair all disarranged. But of course you may have your belongings. Where are they?"

She glanced over her shoulder. "There, in the chest. And in a jewel case with the books in the cabinet."

He smiled indulgently as a man who loves, and she tried to hide the guilt she felt. Still, as he started to walk away, she grasped his arm. "Gaucelm . . ."

He paused, looked back, the love still in his eyes. "What is it?" His words were soft, kind.

"I . . ." but she broke off, turned away. "I do not know . . . Nothing."

He reached for her and turned her in his arms. They faced each other, passion and hopelessness mingling in the muted lamplight.

"I know," he said softly, bending to brush his lips ever so lightly across hers. "I know."

A knock sounded, they broke apart, and then a retainer brought a wooden tray. A second man cleared the table, spread a tablecloth on it, and set the food down. Carafes and goblets were brought in. While the meal was being laid, Allesandra opened the trunk to find brush, scarves, other feminine items.

But while Gaucelm was occupied in talking with his sergeant-at-arms outside, she had time to find what she was really looking for. A jeweled dagger in its sheath and gold coins in a satin purse. She stepped behind the bed curtain and tied both to her waist beneath her tunic.

When Gaucelm again turned his attention to her, she was brushing her hair. He stopped to gaze at her, one foot on the step beside the bed. Then he held out a hand.

"Come. The food awaits."

Dinner was subdued, as each reflected on private thoughts, weighted and wary of that which kept them apart. Gaucelm seemed as reluctant to talk as she. Belatedly, she remembered her role as spy and made an attempt to learn his plans, deciding that the best approach was a bold one.

"They say Simon de Montfort is on the move. Will you go to join him?"

Gaucelm leaned back and regarded her. "And how is it you learn of this?"

His question did not threaten her. "Gossip travels, my lord. Have you not noticed the way word seems to spread on the very wind, faster than a messenger can deliver it? Such is the way of news."

"Hmmm. Then no doubt your sources are as reliable as mine. I have not yet decided upon my plans."

She heard the note of irony in his voice, even if his words were serious. Again her heart felt heavy. If they had met under other circumstances, perhaps this would have been the man who would put his suit to her. But she had to remind herself that they would not have met had he not come south with the conquering army.

After the meal, she feigned a yawn. "I fear the festivities have undone me. I hope you will excuse me early tonight."

He lifted a dark brow. "Indeed, these activities have tired me as well."

She did not miss his meaning and felt the color in her cheeks.

"However," he added, "I have demands on my time, and so do not mind ending the evening early. It has been most satisfying."

He scraped his chair back across the wooden floor and came

to escort her to the door after she'd gathered her belongings. The dagger and coins still rode safely at the girdle beneath her tunic. As she lifted her face to his, she saw the lines of responsibility drawn across his brow again. As he touched her cheek, there was a trace of wistfulness about his eyes. Unspoken knowledge passed between them, and she knew she would have to force herself through the heavy door. For once on the other side, she would again wear the coat of enemy.

"Good night, my lord," she said.

He kissed her brow. "Sleep well."

She passed through and did not look back as she took the passage and then the stairs to the women's quarters. Isabelle and Marcia looked up from their work as she hurried across to the niche that was now hers. She motioned to them to follow her and then put a finger to her lips to caution them.

"Here, help me undress."

They saw the dagger and the money pouch and looked at her with questions in their faces.

"If you do not know what I am about," she told them, "then you will not be lying when you tell the soldiers tomorrow that you do not know where I've gone."

Isabelle drew her mouth into a line of concern. "You are dressing for traveling and you take with you a weapon and money. We can guess where you are going."

"Yes," she said. "You can guess, but you will not know."

As she threw her mantle about her shoulders, Marcia voiced her concern. "Pray, you are not going alone."

"No, but you will find out soon enough who accompanies me."

She made her way to the guests' chamber without hindrance. When she entered the room, Jean turned and crossed to her.

"My lady, you've come."

The genial troubadours were now fierce-looking knights, garbed in mail hauberks over which they wore their brightly colored surcoats. Swords and daggers were fastened at girdles at their waists, and she'd no doubt that other knives were secreted in boots. Plain brown mantles with hoods were tied at the throat to drape across their shoulders.

"You'll have to leave your musical instruments here," she said. "Where we are going, you will not need them."

Christian turned and gazed sadly at his lute. Then he crossed to it and lifted it up to kiss its long neck. "It is a fine instrument, I hope to see it again."

But after that one show of sentiment, he joined the others in picking up their helmets. For these men were knights as well as troubadours and never hesitated to help a lady.

When she judged that it was safe, she led them as quietly as possible along the passage to the stairs. They huddled at the top to listen for any guards. But most of the garrison was still in the hall, enjoying their wine to the music of the jongleurs who had stayed behind to play. The group hurried down a staircase to the kitchens and waited until Allesandra judged that it was safe. The cooks and servants in the kitchen were all loyal servants of hers.

After she whispered a few words, the kitchen maids stood at the door to the pantry to make sure no one came, while the three troubadours crossed the kitchen to the door Allesandra had opened for them. She slipped in after them, and the trusted, matronly Ivetta wished them Godspeed and closed the door upon them.

Allesandra struck flint and lit the lamp Jean held. Then the men glanced about them, their hands on sword hilts, not trusting where the French soldiers might have gone before them.

"Come," she said, taking the light from Jean. "It is not far."

She led her friends through the tunnel and out to the forest. There, they crouched to get used to the forest sounds and to listen carefully. Peire went ahead to scout and returned before long.

"No one here about that I can tell," he whispered.

Then they flew along the path, the moon visible between the trees. At the manor, four horses were waiting.

"Julian Farrell told us of your need," said the steward as he opened the gate in the stockaded fence. "These horses will get you to Toulouse. Many from these parts have ridden off to join Count Raymond."

"And so do we," she said. "Thank you for the horses."

"Go now. If anyone comes to ask, we'll say we've seen nothing. There will be enough horse tracks in the forest from a hunt today that they won't be able to follow you."

When they were all mounted, they rode off through the forest, staying to the trees until they were well away from the castle.

"We'll have to risk riding in the moonlight when we crest the hill," said Jean, coming up to Allesandra as they stopped before riding out into the open.

"So we will," observed Peire. "But after that we can make a gallop across the plain until the hills fold again."

"Come, friends," said Christian. "For Toulouse."

They urged their mounts forward and climbed up the top of the hill. The moonlight caught them as they crested it. They did not look behind as they made for the valley on the other side. And then they kicked their horses into a gallop, their mantles flying behind them, as they thundered across, making for their destination.

Gaucelm assembled his men-at-arms in the courtyard well before dawn. They crossed the drawbridge and rode into the chilly morning, the morning star still glittering in the heavens. The sky had turned a pale blue by the time they crested the hill. And they were well across the plain before the sun climbed the hills to the east to touch the sky.

Twelve

Allesandra and her escort ferried across the broad, swiftly flowing Garonne when they reached the first crossing, and they kept well clear of Muret. They rode east and crossed open country, for they could not risk running into de Montfort's army on the main highways. They had to ferry again across the Ariège to circle all the way to the east of Toulouse. But at each crossing they gained more news. Yes, the French army was on the move, but it had been sighted moving across the plain to the west.

At nightfall of the second day of travel, Allesandra and her friends rode toward the flickering torchlight on the eastern walls of Toulouse. They drew forward in darkness, keeping their distance until they made sure the town was still in the hands of the Provençals.

"Listen," said Jean as they drew up in a line on the dark plain.

They all strained to hear, then Allesandra smiled. "It's singing."

"A work song," said Peire, "such as the peasants sing during harvest."

"They would hardly be harvesting at night," said Christian.

"No," answered Peire, "but they are working, building fortifications, perhaps?"

"Yes," said Jean. "That must be it. They are rebuilding the walls."

They moved closer until they could be sure that the calls of men-at-arms changing guards were in Provençal, and the voices at the gatehouse had no French.

Allesandra sighed in relief. "Then we are not too late."

They rode at a walk to the fortified stone gatehouse on the eastern bridge. Soldiers kept watch without, their bows strung, quivers of arrows at their backs. A sergeant-at-arms came forward, peering at the strangers.

"Who goes there?"

"The lady Allesandra Valtin to see Count Raymond."

Not being too quick to admit a band of knights, he strolled forward to inspect them.

"These are three trusted knights of Languedoc," she said. "Send word to the count that Lady Valtin is here with an escort."

He did not bid them enter, but nodded to a sergeant, who left to take the message.

While they waited, their eyes scanned the walls. A contingent of people worked by torchlight where the wall needed repair.

Heavy granite blocks were being hoisted into place by windlasses and mortared into place by masons above. It would not be completely dry by tomorrow, but it would give the appearance of strength.

A messenger hurried out from the gatehouse at last. "Count Raymond bids the lady Valtin and her friends join him at the castle," he said.

The sergeant did not need any further proof but ordered the portcullis raised, and the troubadours and Allesandra walked their horses across the bridge that spanned the moat.

Once inside the city, they could see the beehive of activity going on. The count of Toulouse's banners hung everywhere, the symbol of Languedoc patriotism.

In the torchlight, knights, burgesses, ladies, squires, and children pushed wheelbarrows of hewn stones to the windlasses that lifted them into place. Between the double thickness of stone blocks, the mixture of mortar and small stones was poured in.

"We are not too late," said Jean, as they rode in pairs down the cobbled main street.

Soon they had to go single file through the street, crowded as it was with carts, donkeys, citizens, horses, and dogs, as if it were the middle of day. Some of the shop owners even had their shutters open and their hinged tables in place to sell food and supplies to the busy crowd. It warmed Allesandra to see the determination of the citizens to withstand the threat from the French. And now that she was here, she was ever so anxious to see her old friend, the count.

They wound through the hilly streets, the troubadours behind her shouting greetings and encouragement to those working through the night. They passed the cathedral and came finally to the count's palace, where grooms came out to take their horses.

The entourage climbed the wide steps to the entrance, and since they were expected, they were shown at once into the vaulted hall. Raymond VI of Toulouse came out from behind a table surrounded by his advisors and crossed to greet them. Allesandra hurried forward to place her hands in his. It was the first time they had seen each other since the fatal day of the battle of Muret.

"My lord, how good it is to see you."

His broad, round face broke into a smile. He was a man of about fifty, and even without armor, he looked solidly built, with graying hair cut in bangs across his forehead and below his ears. Beneath his thick brows, his blue eyes shined in delight at seeing Allesandra, who had been his ward since the death of her husband and therefore very much like a daughter to him. He kissed her on both cheeks.

"My dear, I did not think to lay eyes on you so soon since the French vanquished us at Muret. I was saddened to hear that your lands have been taken over by one of de Montfort's vassals."

"Gaucelm Deluc, though I have to admit he has not been a cruel victor."

"Thank God for that."

He gazed pleasantly at her and then turned to motion his son, young Raymond, forward. "Look who has arrived."

Allesandra was also well acquainted with the son Raymond, who would be Raymond VII when the title passed on to him, providing they held on to the title in these present difficulties. The younger Raymond was a handsome youth, slender but strong, with long brown hair flowing in curls past his shoulders. His looks were almost feminine, but those who took that to mean that he was weak or had irregular sexual tastes were quite mistaken. Allesandra herself knew several young ladies who had capitulated to the young Raymond's charms, for he was one of the foremost troubadours of their times.

"Welcome, my lady," said the younger man. "I am glad to see you safe, as well as your friends."

He turned to eye his old comrades. "What brings this party together? I had thought you scattered to the four winds after the disaster at Muret."

"And so we were," answered Peire, "until we were summoned by the lady here.

"Were you in distress then?"

She colored slightly. "None other than submission to Gaucelm Deluc. But he was willing to learn of the music of the troubadours and so had me send for these gentlemen to entertain him."

Young Raymond barked out a laugh. "Don't tell me there's hope? That some among the French seek refinement?"

His father spoke. "Even if it were true, there is the more serious matter of the strictures of the Catholic Church. I still work to negotiate. But their demands are greater every day. But come, you will want to rest after your journey. Have you supped?"

"No, my lord. We paused only long enough to water the horses and eat fruit and dried meat on the ride."

"That at least we can take care of. My son will show you to quarters. When you have refreshed yourselves, meet back here. I will have something hot brought up from the kitchen. There's a pig roasting on the spit."

Glad to be out of the saddle, Allesandra followed the younger Raymond out. He led the way up stairs to a gallery encircling the two-story vaulted hall and directed the men to their quarters. He then offered his arm to escort her to a guest chamber.

"Did you hear any news on the road?" he asked her.

"Only that de Montfort was marching here, but not when or with how many."

"I've heard he has reinforcements from the North." He gave a long sigh. "Ah, me, perhaps we are in for a siege. But we are ready. You saw the work on the walls."

"Yes, we did."

"And de Montfort must know that even if he musters enough forces to surround our city, the Garonne flows past on one side so that there will be no shortage of water or of supplies brought in by boat."

"True." She smiled. "Toulouse is the very symbol of resistance to French domination, and you and your father the chosen leaders of the people."

He stopped in front of a large arched door set into the stone walls.

"You should have seen it as we marched up from Narbonne.

When the people of the towns saw our banners, they rushed toward us as if my father had risen from the dead. And when he entered Toulouse, the people fell on their knees, barons, ladies, merchants, all received him with joy and happiness. When we got down they kissed our clothing, our feet, our hands and arms. The sound of bells filled the city."

She gave a deep sigh. Only now did she realize what oppression she had been living under. The unlikely attraction to Gaucelm had distracted her. Perhaps he had fooled her with his kindness and with his love. But now in the center of things, she was reminded of the great cause.

"I must not keep you," said young Raymond. "Refresh yourself here. I will send a woman to help you. My father will be wanting to tell you of these things himself."

He left her, and she found herself in a comfortable chamber. A woman brought ewer, bowl, water, and towels. And she put on a clean gown provided for her. With hair brushed and coiled, she felt ready to meet her friends again.

Indeed, at the meal laid for just the six of them in front of a blazing fire, a great deal was exchanged. From outside the shuttered windows, they could hear the sounds of the work on the city walls being carried on into night.

Young Raymond was arguing with his father about the count's latest plan.

"You think you can bow to the storm," said young Raymond, his cheeks flaming with his passionate beliefs. "But I tell you it will never work."

As usual, Count Raymond refused to get excited.

"We must give it a chance to work. I have already sent a message to the archbishop, offering to persecute the heretics in my realm. We'll persecute just a few, enough to satisfy the church that my rule here can protect the Catholic faith. Thus, they will have no further reason for conquest. If the southern lords join the crusade, there can be nothing to confiscate, nothing to attack, and the northerners will have to go home. You see?"

He partook of the roast turkey and lamb while the troubadours spoke at once, adding their arguments. Jean, especially, was critical of any plan to strike a compromise with the hated French. It seemed to Allesandra that he was itching for another fight.

"The Church will hardly accept the promises of men who have already promised much and delivered little," said Jean. "It's true that Pope Innocent III might go along with you, but his legates don't trust you. I think they mean to finish the job this time."

"Then we must finish them," said Christian, brandishing a drumstick. "When they attack, we must drive them back from Toulouse and chase them north. Then we will regain all the properties they've laid their hands on."

"The Church is corrupt," said Peire. "We mock the clergy in our songs, if they but understood our words. Priests keeping mistresses, wasting the wealth of their churches, and neglecting their duties. While in the South, Catholic and nonbeliever live in harmony. But the bishops insist that all must conform to their way. Who can think of making a compromise with such men?"

"Was it not at Paris," said Christian, "that priests refused to bury the dead until heavy fees were paid? And at Rouen, a deposed bishop stabbed his successor to death. They are hypocrites, ravening wolves in sheep's clothing."

"Many of the priests are illiterate," agreed Jean. "Some of them scarcely know enough Latin to say the mass."

"How can they expect to be literate?" asked the count, lifting his wine cup. "There are no universities in which to train them. I, myself, have offered to the bishop that if we can reach an agreement, I will build a university here in Toulouse."

"A noble suggestion in any case," said Christian.

"I can excuse illiteracy when they are named to their posts by feudal lords who hold the parish," argued Jean. "But I cannot condone drunkenness. In some dioceses, the priests even indulge in gambling."

"And what of the king?" broke in Allesandra. "All of this talk of the church is very well and good, but it is the soldiers of the king that you fight on the field. Will you be able to overcome them this time?" She looked hopefully at Raymond, wishing she could feel more confidence in his ability as a general.

"This Simon de Montfort is a brilliant military man," she said, turning to look all her friends in the eye, one by one. "You have to admit that, after what he did at Muret. And he has other leaders who are just as clever."

"You mean Gaucelm Deluc, who wrested your castle out from under you while you were in Muret."

Her cheeks warmed. She was not sure that one or all of them did not know of her folly. If she were forced to explain, she would be at a loss. She hoped her burning cheeks only demonstrated her passion for the discussion and her embarrassment at having been away when her castle was seized.

"He was clever enough to trick my guards into letting him into the gatehouse. At Muret we suffered from lack of cooperation. How can you all sit here and talk about throwing back the enemy when the count of Foix and the count of Comminges go their own way? Tell me, my lord, have you spoken to them of your idea of compromise?"

Count Raymond gave a slight shrug, but instead of looking her in the eye, he tore off a piece of meat with his knife. "I have."

"And do they agree with your plan to persecute their own men?"

Young Raymond answered for his father. "They do not. They are for one more concerted effort."

"Well," said Christian, "it seems we will have that chance. It looks as if the walls of the city will be ready. What of the corps?"

"They are drilled, their weapons readied," said young Raymond, eager for the fight. "As soon as we have first knowledge of the enemy's approach, we will assemble within the walls. Let them come. Just as they expect to settle down for the siege, we'll ride out to attack."

Allesandra could not banish the image of being in Gaucelm's arms from her mind. Yet she knew that her duty and loyalty lay here. The French intended to destroy the southerners' country and their way of life. That must not happen. She must help them fight.

"How can I assist?" she asked. "Surely with the soldiers fighting, the women will operate the siege machines. I have experience there."

"Excellent idea," said young Raymond. "I will make sure you command one of the most important machines."

"Good," she said.

Suddenly she was not hungry. She would fight the French, for they did not belong in the Languedoc. She only hoped that she would not be forced to fire a weapon at Gaucelm. For that she did not think she could do.

It seemed that she had only just fallen asleep on the feather mattress in her chamber. Now the calls and songs of the night before had crescendoed to war cries. She sat up in haste, momentarily confused, and then she reached for her clothing. These cries and shouts were no building of the walls. This was the sound of battle.

She dressed quickly and then flung open the shutters. Her window faced into the town and gave a view of the southern town wall as well. Indeed, a battle was in progress, for now crossbowmen lined the crenelated battlement. Their steel-tipped bolts flew through the air toward attackers below. The projectile-throwing engines had been drawn into place within the town walls, and crews of men and women loaded and fired them. Stones flew high over the walls to no doubt harry the enemy forces outside.

She hurried from the room and to the spiral staircase within the turret. There, she hesitated. Having no idea what Raymond would wish her to do, she tried to decide where she would be most useful. On the ground she could assist in loading the projectile engines. There had been no time for Raymond to assign her to one. But from above she would have a view of the field and could better see what was taking place.

She decided on the wall walk and hurried upward. There on the top of the walls, the crossbowmen spelled each other in firing from the notches in the crenelated battlement. They had to alternate in taking shelter behind the protective wall to load their wooden shaft bolts by means of a mechanical windlass. From the top of the turrets above her, longbowmen aimed their feather-flighted arrows at the enemy camp.

She gasped as she peered over the shoulder of a bowman at the camp assembled below. Frenchmen were everywhere, returning fire with their own weapons and dragging siege machines into place. A small corps assaulted the gatehouse off to the right. She looked anxiously for colors to identify who the leaders were. The fleur-de-lis and de Montfort's pennants were firmly planted in the fields, and the besieging army encircled the town from the river to the curve in the wall, as far as she could see.

"Woman," shouted a sergeant-at-arms, "you're needed there." He pointed to a smaller version of the projectile throwing engines, mounted some distance along the wall.

She nodded and started forward. "Keep below the battlement," he ordered.

And she hunched down, keeping well behind the bowmen while arrows, bolts, javelins, and stones were flung above her head.

She got to the mangonella that had been rolled into a position where it could command the gatehouse below. The mangonella's long arm of wood was lengthened by a sling, which two women were filling with stones. Allesandra reached the pile of stones and assisted in the loading. A soldier inspected the heavy weight that would actuate the beam.

"Ready!" he called, and the women stood back.

He let go the weight, which caused the beam to describe a quarter of a circle. The sling flew upward, discharging the missiles. Below, the stones fell onto a knot of soldiers, causing them to draw back. The women lost no time in reloading the missile.

Suddenly there was a thundering on the bridge, the portcullis was drawn upward, and she glanced down to see young Raymond lead a charge outward. A war cry went up, and the southerners rushed into the fray. Allesandra saw Simon de Montfort, in the field, turn from where he was leading a group of soldiers and charge to meet the fight.

Metal rang out, cries went up, the mangonella fired once again on the confused enemy. This time the southerners did not disperse as they had at Muret, but stayed tightly together and pushed the Frenchmen back. But Allesandra turned her attention to the soldier commanding their war machine.

"Aim there," he pointed at the enemy. "I cannot tell which one is their leader."

"That one," she shouted above the din, "in the black-and-silver surcoat."

He nodded, and they pivoted their machine on its wheels. At the sight of their own soldiers in the field, those on the walls redoubled their efforts to drive the Frenchmen outward. Allesandra loaded stones furiously, her heart thundering from the exertion and excitement. She looked again to make sure Simon was still within their range. She gave the sergeant a nod. He reached for the weight and was almost ready to drop it when an arrow caught him in the shoulder. His face twisted, he gave a scream, and fell back.

Allesandra ran to him as he sank against the wall. The arrow had nipped his shoulder. But it cut through the cloth and made blood flow before it clattered to the walkway behind him. He touched his blood and looked at her blankly, more stunned than hurt.

"You're wounded," she said. "Here, I'll bind it quickly."

She got his sleeve off him, then she ripped away a piece of her linen chemise to tie the wound. "Hold that tight to staunch the bleeding."

"I'm all right, go back to the fight," he finally told her, grimacing with the pain.

She rose, perspiration dampening her temples, grime from the rocks on her tunic. She took his place at the mangonella and reached for the weight. Then she waited until she had Simon de

Montfort in view again. Truly, the southerners were pushing the French away all along their lines. The siege machines before the town walls had been abandoned as those operating them turned to flee. Some attempted to defend themselves in hand-to-hand combat against the men of Toulouse who'd rushed out to fight behind Raymond's forces.

"Put the heaviest stone in the sling," she shouted to her female companions-at-arms, who at once picked up a large stone between them and set it in the sling.

Allesandra aimed once more, dropped the weight and stood back. The mangonella pivoted. With a crack, the sling released its missile. Allesandra turned to stare with breath drawn as the heavy stone arched high in the air, over the moat and gatehouse. And as if flung down by God's own hand, it shot toward the knot of men surrounding Simon de Montfort.

For one horrifying moment Allesandra strained to see where Gaucelm might be. She spotted him in the rear guard just as the stone turned over in the air. She heard the crack as it hit Simon de Montfort squarely on his helmet, saw his arms fling up, his sword drop, as he fell from his horse.

Stunned at her aim, she forgot the mangonella, but leaned on the edge of the wall to watch. Now came cries that Simon de Montfort was down. She saw his loyal corps fight their way to him. They lifted him up and flung him over a horse to lead it from the field.

Then the cries went along the wall where she stood.

"De Montfort has fallen."

The word was passed down from the walls into the town, and cheers sounded. That the leader of the opposing side was wounded gave even more impetus to the men of Toulouse. They were determined not only to hold on to their city, but to chase the enemy from the field and extract vengeance from them. All of this was shouted jubilantly, even as the archers continued to take aim and pick off fleeing Frenchmen.

Allesandra glanced down at the soldier who sat against the wall staunching the wound that she had bound. Knowing that he

Take advantage of this offer to enjoy Zebra's newest line of historical romance novels....Splendor Romances (formerly Lovegrams Historical Romances)- Take our introductory shipment of 4 romance novels -Absolutely Free! (a $19.96 value)

Now you'll be able to savor today's best romance novels without even leaving your home with our convenient and inexpensive home subscription service. Here's what you get for joining:

- 4 BRAND NEW bestselling Splendor Romances delivered to your doorstep every month

- 20% off every title (or almost $4.00 off) with your home subscription

- FREE home delivery

- A FREE monthly newsletter, *Zebra/Pinnacle Romance News* filled with author interviews, member benefits, book previews and more!

- No risks or obligations…you're free to cancel whenever you wish…no questions asked

To get started with your own home subscription, simply complete and return the card provided. You'll receive your FREE introductory shipment of 4 Splendor Romances and then you'll begin to receive monthly shipments of new Zebra Splendor titles. Each shipment will be yours to examine for 10 days and then if you decide to keep the books, you'll pay the preferred home subscriber's price of just $4.00 per title. That's $16 for all 4 books with FREE home delivery! And if you want us to stop sending books, just say the word…it's that simple.

4 Free BOOKS are waiting for you!
Just mail in the certificate below!

If the certificate is missing below, write to: Splendor Romances, Zebra Home Subscription Service, Inc., P.O. Box 5214, Clifton, New Jersey 07015-5214

FREE BOOK CERTIFICATE

Yes! Please send me 4 Splendor Romances (formerly Zebra Lovegram Historical Romances). ABSOLUTELY FREE! After my introductory shipment, I will be able to preview 4 new Splendor Romances each month FREE for 10 days. Then if I decide to keep them, I will pay the money-saving preferred publisher's price of just $4.00 each... a total of $16.00. That's 20% off the regular publisher's price and there's never any additional charge for shipping and handling. I may return any shipment within 10 days and owe nothing, and I may cancel my subscription at any time. The 4 FREE books will be mine to keep in any case.

Name _____

Address _____ Apt. _____

City _____ State _____ Zip _____

Telephone ( ) _____

Signature _____
(If under 18, parent or guardian must sign.)

SP1097

Terms and prices subject to change. Orders subject to acceptance by Zebra Home Subscription Service, Inc. . Zebra Home Subscription Service, Inc. reserves the right to reject or cancel any subscription.

could not have seen what had happened on the other side of the wall, she told him, "Simon de Montfort has fallen. He's being taken away by his men."

The soldier gave her a look of admiration and awe.

"I know it, madam," he said. "I pulled myself up to my feet to see just after you dropped the weight. Simon de Montfort was hit, and it was you who fired the shot."

They had won the day. The French were flung back. From her position on the wall, Allesandra saw Gaucelm take de Montfort's pennant and carry it, leading the men in retreat. The siege was lifted. Toulouse was saved.

Just how badly de Montfort was hurt, they did not know, but now other men-at-arms came along to where Allesandra stood. A bowman who'd been firing above her on the turret shouted as he descended the outer stairway.

"There she is!" he cried, pointing to Allesandra. "That's her. She fired the shot that took de Montfort from the field."

Jean de Batute appeared in the crowd and lifted off his helmet. He was grimy and covered with blood, but little of his own.

"My lady, is this true? Were you operating this mangonella? For surely it was a great stone that hit the enemy general and turned the sortie into a rout. You are the heroine of the day."

She was at once lifted onto their shoulders and carried down the spiral stairs and out into the courtyard before the walls. There the word had spread that this was the woman who fired the shot that took down the great French general. She stared at the crowd waving and cheering her.

"I was unhorsed," Jean said, when they at last set her down. "But I saw the Raymonds chasing after the French. How far they will chase them and what vengeance they will take we cannot know until they return. But it is a great day. My lady, you will be remembered in history for your actions." And he knelt before her.

Allesandra was too stunned to find words. Everything since she'd bound the soldier's wound had passed around her as if unreal. She remembered being determined to do her part to throw off the French, to prove herself a worthy vassal of her lord, the count. She had no idea just how great would be the consequences.

"I cannot believe it," she finally said. "Let us pray that Count Raymond and his son have continued good luck."

As the wounded were attended, and the dead carried to their families, Allesandra went among the people to help with the wounded. The townspeople worked into the evening. Torches lit the streets and market square by the time she retired to her chamber to wash the grime and blood from her limbs. She replaced the torn chemise, put on a clean gown, and dressed her hair.

When she went down to the hall, Christian and Jean gave her the news at once.

"Madam," said Jean. "We've just heard. Simon de Montfort is dead. He died instantly from the blow of the stone you fired from the mangonella on the wall. You fired the shot that killed him."

Thirteen

Allesandra stared at them, her lips parted to speak, but she found no words. Jean had been among those who'd ridden out with young Raymond to vanquish the French. He'd lost his horse but fought hand-to-hand at the gate. Peire and Christian had helped chase the French soldiers across the plains with the Raymonds and Christian had brought back the news.

"We ran into unexpected reinforcements," he said. "The count of Foix was just coming to our aid, and when his men saw the French fleeing, he closed in on their flanks. More of the French army went down. The knights we captured to be ransomed told us that de Montfort is dead."

At the mention of knights captured for ransom, her heart fluttered uneasily in her chest. And she still had not fully absorbed the fact that she herself had killed the general of the crusading army.

"Don't you see what this means?" said Christian. "We have broken the back of the crusade. The men with de Montfort had completed their obligatory forty days of service, and at the news that their general is dead, they will make for their homes."

"Surely they will not just all leave," said Allesandra. "There are other worthy leaders among them." She tried not to show her own guilt in regard to the one she knew.

"That may be true," replied Christian. "But none with the passion and greed for the crusade that de Montfort had."

Passion and greed, she reflected. Perhaps that was true. Gaucelm was proud to have won his lands, but would he stay and fight to hold them now that his general was dead? She remembered how he had spoken of loyalty. He would gladly do what the king of France and what Simon de Montfort asked of him. But did he care to lead a crusade? If she knew him at all, she thought he would weigh the possibilities of any move he made before he committed more men to his plans. She would have to wait and see. But first she must find out his whereabouts.

"Gaucelm Deluc," she said, deciding that her companions would find it logical that she should ask of him, since he had been in control of her demesne. "What of him?"

"Not among those captured, which is too bad," said Christian. "For he comes from very good family, close to the French king. Surely he would be worth a fine ransom."

"Yes, a pity," she said, trying to hide her mixed feelings. "If he is not captured, then where is he? Will he circle round to take refuge in my castle, I wonder?"

"There is that chance," said Jean, "which is why we must ride at once to see you safely reinstalled there. Your old garrison can be gathered from among the forces here. If Gaucelm Deluc returns, we will be there to give him a good fight."

She agreed that they must ride as soon as feasible. If there was a chance for her to regain her lands, she must not waste a moment. "How soon can we be off?"

"We must let men and horses rest. But we can rise two hours before the bells of the churches ring prime and be a good way along the road by dawn. Deluc's forces will have to rest as well."

"Very well. I will make the preparations."

Then she reached out to take each of them by the arm and look gratefully into their loyal faces. "My friends," she said with much emotion, "I thank you for this."

"My lady," Jean said with a smile upon his battle-stained face. "It is nothing. A good troubadour never refuses aid to a damsel in distress."

She smiled at his words. "I suppose one could say that I am in distress."

"Indeed," replied Jean. "Until we regain your lands for you, one could say so."

She exchanged kisses with them both, cheek-to-cheek. Their devotion touched her. She was the traitor, for even now Gaucelm's fate concerned her as much as her own life. Even for that, she would never back down from attempting to regain her lands. That much was bred into her. But as she left her two heroes to go and pack for the journey, she sent up a small prayer for Gaucelm's safety, hoping her thoughts would reach him, wherever he was.

After a rest, Allesandra and her little band of men-at-arms rode through the next day and into the night. When they crested the hill for their first view of the castle the following evening, Allesandra held her breath. No French pennant hung from the battlements.

The gatehouse stood open to their entrance where they found many of her household guard back on their posts.

"What has happened?" she asked her steward Julian, who hurried out to greet them in the courtyard. He explained the circumstances as grooms came to care for the horses.

"After you left, my lady, Gaucelm Deluc took a corps of men to answer de Montfort's call, leaving only a small garrison here.

When news reached us of Toulouse, your own men who had sworn fealty to Deluc at a time when it was expedient, arose to overthrow the French sergeants who were in charge. They surrendered immediately on the condition that they be allowed to retreat and join their general in the field. We let them go because Deluc had not been unduly cruel to us."

"Then the demesne is once again in our hands. Oh, thank you, Julian. Send the men to me in the morning. I want to personally thank every one of them who arose on my behalf."

"As you wish, madam."

"Oh, Jean, Christian, I can hardly believe it."

"The tides of fortune have turned then," said Jean. "The French are retreating—at least, so it seems."

He glanced about the walls at the towers as if suspicious that some of the treacherous Frenchmen might still be lying in ambush for them.

"We must learn what has happened elsewhere tomorrow," she said. "It is too much to hope that this hateful crusade is over. Do you really believe that the death of one man can mean so much?"

"Simon de Montfort was a great general," said Christian. "France will be lost without him. Few other men accomplished as much as he with such small forces. Few other men had his eye for enemy weakness and his ability to make quick decisions, his courage, and his tenacity. He was the reason our people have struggled and lost ground these two years."

She thought, but did not say, that those decisions had been aided by his comrade Gaucelm Deluc. But as to whether Gaucelm would take up the staff of the crusade himself, she thought not. He was a leader, respected by his men. He was an adventurer, yes. But he did not have the ruthless quality of a de Montfort.

"Perhaps you are right," she agreed at last. "We are free of them . . . for now."

"And the other counts surely will drive away the French on their doorstep," added Jean. "The only man strong enough to bring another crusade south is King Philip himself, and rumor has it he has spent his treasury on his wars with England. It is doubtful he can come south without funds from somewhere. Yes, I think we are safe for now."

"Safe," said Allesandra, full of relief and touched by the loyalty of her knights.

And yet of her beloved enemy, she wondered. Even now her traitorous heart pined for him. Her body yearned for a touch that once known, she would never be able to forget.

She trembled to think that her victory had cost her his love. Could life really be so cruel?

"I wish to be alone now," she said to her good friends. "I am very tired."

"Rest well, my lady," said Jean. "You have earned a good sleep."

She left them and climbed the stairs. Tonight she would sleep in the great chamber as was her right. And there she found Isabelle and Marcia making the room ready with fresh linens. Herbs scented the room, and the oil lamps had freshly trimmed wicks, which gave a soft glow to the room. Marcia dropped another log onto the fire.

"My lady," said Isabelle, coming to curtsy before her. Marcia did likewise. Both of them smiled in great relief.

"We are glad to see you safe at home at last," said Marcia.

She kissed them both and let them help her out of her clothing. They brought ewer, basin, and towels, and when she had bathed, they dressed her in a comfortable gown for lounging. She had to admit it felt good to be pampered again after the battle and the hard ride.

"I am anxious to tell you all the news," she said to her companions, "but tomorrow. I am very tired now."

"That is to be expected, my lady," said Marcia. "But we have heard that you are a heroine."

"And the French soldiers vanquished from here," added Isabelle. "Our guard here was very quick thinking to act in concert."

"I am very glad for that," said Allesandra.

"Now we will leave you. Sleep well." Isabelle gave a great

sigh and shook her head as if giving expression to these trying times.

After they left her, Allesandra sat down before the fire to contemplate. So much had happened. She stared at the fire a long time, reliving the events of the past few days in her mind. She finally dozed where she sat in the chair, but was awakened by the clatter of horses into the courtyard and got up to open the shutters.

Below two horsemen were dismounting. With their mantles about them, she could not tell who they were. However, after they'd exchanged words with sleepy grooms and headed toward the tower entrance, she thought she recognized Peire Bellot from the bulk of him. But the other horseman was still hooded when they went in the door.

She moved toward the bed, still drowsy, and turned back the covers. Not thinking that the two men would want to speak with her tonight, she was surprised when there was a light knock, and a voice called out, "My lady, are you awake?"

Befuddled, she walked to the door. "Peire? Is that you. I saw you . . ."

She opened the door and then stood, mouth agape. Peire and Christian did indeed enter, but in their wake was none other than Gaucelm, himself. She came instantly awake, while he looked around the room as if to ascertain that they were alone. Then he pointed to the open shutters, and Christian went to close them.

She stared at them. "How is this possible?"

"He ambushed me, my lady," said Peire, though none too loud in case any curious guards stood outside the door. "We had chased the French from the field with Count Raymond. I was pursuing a few knights through the forest. The growth got too thick to move quickly, so I had to slow down. This man dropped from the trees and pulled me from my horse, holding a knife to my throat. I have to say it would have been impossible, but that he surprised me."

The big knight looked sheepish that he had been bested by the clever Frenchman.

"I did not harm your friend," said Gaucelm. "I needed him for a hostage. I knew the instant the general was dead that our cause was lost. We had to retreat. But not before I came to see you, my lady. I owed you that much."

He moved near to her but then clenched his gauntleted fist. She saw at once that he had not revealed to the troubadours just what their relationship was. Fortunately, she was too stunned to give anything away. She managed to find her voice.

"I am surprised, but I thank you for not harming your . . . hostage."

"Your men at the gatehouse knew my name and my voice," said Peire. "And so we were admitted. Glad I was to see the castle was back in our hands, anyway."

She glanced at her two friends, who stood frowning. She knew that they were not about to leave her alone with Gaucelm Deluc until she ordered them away. The situation brought a smile to her lips, which she managed to turn to an expression of relief that all were safe.

"You did well. I respect the risk my lord Deluc has taken and will guarantee him safe conduct when he leaves. You may leave us, my friends, so that I may speak to him privately."

"We'll wait outside your door, should you need us," said Christian, chin thrusting forward.

But Peire, older and wiser and no doubt beginning to perceive the nuances of the situation, corrected his friend. "I think not, lad. These two may talk late into the night. No harm will come to her, she's already given her word of safe conduct. Come, let us to our well-deserved beds."

Christian glanced at Allesandra for confirmation, and she nodded. "I will be quite safe. I thank you for your gallant concern."

"Then we will take our leave," said Peire. He bowed and then ushered his younger friend out.

When she had closed the door behind them, she turned and floated across the room into Gaucelm's arms. Hard and strong they felt as they wrapped around her. She leaned back her head to look at his face, and he cradled her head in his hand.

"My lord," she said, as he kissed her ear, her throat, her cheeks. "I am so glad you are safe. I was so worried, even though I fought for my people as was my duty. You are my enemy, my beloved enemy, Gaucelm."

He stopped her words with his mouth, and then they held each other tight, their hands roaming as if to make sure that their beloved was safe and whole.

"I must leave," he said between kisses. "Now that Simon is dead, I must ride north with my army."

At the mention of Simon, she turned her head and lay it on his shoulder so he could not see her face.

"Yes, the general. A victory for us, a loss for you I am sure. In that he was your friend, I am sorry. I cannot be sorry that we have banished the French from these lands." Her heart tore in two at their dilemma as she knew it would.

He silenced her. "Let us not think of that now. We have a few hours, then I must leave. I must be far from here ere the sun rises. Allesandra, I do not intend to forget you. I promise I will come back. I love you." He looked fervently into her eyes as if willing her to believe him.

"Oh, Gaucelm," she said, fast in his embrace, lifting her head to kiss his cheeks as he began caressing her hungrily. She thought her heart would break with love and desperation. "I do not want you to go. Make love to me."

A flicker of guilt crossed her mind as she realized that he must not know who fired the shot that killed Simon de Montfort. She knew that she should tell him, and she would tell him. Only his hands on her body, his lips against her burning skin were too delicious to break away from now. Let him make love to her, let them share these few hours of passion. She would tell him afterward.

Then thought was lost as he threw off his clothing and released her from the loose gown that covered her and unbound her hair. They lay together between the bed clothes, reaching for each other eagerly. Moist, hungry kisses grew in demand. Hands touched lovingly everywhere. Passion throbbed, her body was on fire. If this was the last night she could be with him, then she would hold nothing back, nothing.

And he took everything, like a man desperate to remember every inch of her, a man determined to imprint every part of her body on his mind so that he would never forget. And for her part, she kissed and caressed every part of him from his sleek, thick hair to his sinewy calves and feet. Though they breathed heavily with desire, they did not rush their love. Until finally he pulled her to him, touching every part of her body with his at once, and entered her, claimed her, made her his alone. Their souls flew up into the night skies together as they found love once more, a love that she had never known before and would never know again.

So powerful was the ecstasy that she thought she would not return to her body if it lasted, and so they descended together, whirling through the clouds, down again into soft, gentle fulfillment, their moans witness to what they had shared.

"Gaucelm," she whispered, turning her head, her hair splayed upon the pillow. How noble his profile looked. His eyes were closed, his thick eyelashes gracing his cheekbone, his nose, proud, his lips, full and sensitive, his chin firm. How she loved him. It hurt her more than she could describe.

"Gaucelm, my love."

But she had killed Simon de Montfort, his friend and leader. And if she did not tell him, it would be a wedge between them, the beginnings of the kind of secrets that keep lovers apart. It would turn them away from each other in the end. But if she did tell him, he would hate her. He would turn all that passion into rage, would rise, dress, be gone, and never see her again. Which was worse?

She held her peace, unable to move from savoring his passion, from having him beside her. All that would end soon enough. Give her an hour, and then she would tell him, hoping that he would understand. She thought it better that he hear it from her lips than from another. For an hour of peace, she kept her silence, drowsing in his arms.

But the consoling night drew her deeper and deeper. Their breathing blended, they went heavenward again in a peaceful sleep that was all too short. She dreamed and dreamed, turned in her sleep, slept deeply. She stirred at last as the sky turned a flinty gray. She reached an arm across to him, but he was not there.

She stirred, awake now, looking at the indentation where he had been.

"Gaucelm?" she whispered to herself. But there was no answer. She sat up, reached for her smock. He was gone.

He would not be in the hall, for he had said he needed to be far away ere the dawn. Only Christian and Peire knew that he'd been here at all. He would not let his presence be known for fear of vengeance.

"Oh, my lord," she said, sinking onto the bed again. "What have I done?"

And yet her fear and her hurt were tempered by the passion they'd shared last night. Surely he, too, would remember that when he learned the worst of her. She gave a sob. She could not even write him a letter, for it might be intercepted. The crusade might be lifted for now, but they were still enemies. One did not know what the French would do next. If they found another general to lead them, they would be back. The king might even entrust a new crusade to Gaucelm.

She sobbed, swaying against her hands, picturing Gaucelm at the head of an army with fire and sword laying waste to all of Languedoc, come to take revenge and to punish them all? It did not seem the sort of thing he would do, and yet . . . if he were angry enough, he might take on the charge laid down to him by his king.

She found the strength to rise, bathe her face with a warm cloth, and dress. She braided her own hair and coiled it under a wimple, not wanting to have to talk with Isabelle and Marcia just yet. She needed solitude, time to think, time to gain strength.

She made her appearance in the hall after the household had broken their fast. Julian was waiting for her at a table by the fireplace with the keys he had retrieved from Gaucelm's lieutenant at their surrender and with inventories prepared of all their supplies and staples. There were also letters from neighboring demesnes saying that the defections from other de Montfort holdings had begun. It seemed the French were slipping away with no further fight.

"That is good," she said to Julian as she finished reading one scroll.

"Indeed."

A soldier at arms posted at the arched entrance came forward and bowed. "Madam," he said. "Pardon the interruption. But we have just had a messenger announcing that Count Raymond and his son are on their way here."

She rose from her seat. "Happy news! We must make ready for them. Julian, see that a chamber in the tower is prepared. Let us have clean rushes in the hall. Wash down the courtyard, and slaughter a pig to roast for tonight. Set every servant about restocking supplies, and give me a list of what is needed. If the French did not seize all the goods from the villages, we will buy staples. Fresh bread will need to be baked. I must welcome my friends with all due show of respect."

Julian left to issue orders to the cooks, the butler, the pantler, and the chamberlain. With the household busy making ready for guests, Allesandra retired again to her chamber to pace and fret.

What was done was done, there was no undoing it. She could not write to her lover while she would be considered by her own people as a traitor for doing it. There was too much damage done for France and the Languedoc to enjoy any sort of real peace.

But neither could she go mad with worry. She was again the chatelaine of this demesne. She must find a reason to hold on. She informed Julian that she would be praying in the chapel, but to find her there as soon as Count Raymond arrived.

In the simple chapel, she lit lamps to reflect off the plain gold crosses. With a heavy heart, she prayed to her God, knowing in her mind that one God looked over all, rueing the petty arguments of his flock. Her arguments were not with the Lord, but with the

Church that claimed there was only one way to worship him. She prayed for Gaucelm's safety, drawing strength in simply meditating quietly and letting her thoughts float upward.

When at last she heard footsteps scrape on the stone floor behind her, she arose and turned with some less degree of turmoil in her heart. Young Raymond came forward to bow very low.

"My lady, I interrupt your prayers."

"No, Raymond. I was finished praying and simply resting my thoughts away from the world."

He arose and they looked into each other's faces, seeing there what the war had cost them as well as so many others.

Finally, he spoke softly and in a consoling tone. "Indeed, much has happened. But you seem unduly sad, my lady. Now is a time for rejoicing."

"So it is." She squeezed his hand warmly. "Come, let us go into the hall, and you can tell us all the news."

The entire household gathered in the great hall to hear the tale of the vanquishing of the French. Voices chattered excitedly as everyone found a place on a bench or stool. In their fashion as great storytellers, the troubadours did most of the narrating, beginning with the sortie out of Toulouse, for the benefit of those who had not been there.

"De Montfort was dead," said young Raymond, "though we did not know it then. They carried him northward across the plain, and we followed, thinking they might yet turn to fight. But it was not to be so. Finally, on the crest of a hill, one of their men awaited us with the white flag of truce. When we drew up to him, he announced that their leader was dead. They begged a truce so that they could fashion a litter for him and carry him home properly. The day was ours."

Christian picked up the narrative. In the background, just as Allesandra knew would happen, Peire plucked his stringed gittern. This heroic battle would find its way into a war song. More than once her name was mentioned as having fired the shot from the mangonella that killed Simon de Montfort. She blushed and bowed her head. Like it or not she would be memorialized for that. Her role was growing with each retelling of the events, and she spoke up several times pleading that she had done nothing but her duty.

"It was the brave men who rode forth from the gates of the town that claimed the day for us," she insisted.

"So they did," said Jean de Batute. "But you must claim your part, too, my lady."

And so Allesandra Valtin became the heroine of all Langue-doc. And lived with her guilt for the love she bore a powerful enemy.

Gaucelm rode east with his army, his heart heavy, his soul numb. They marched with a white flag flying, the symbol of truce. Villagers stayed within their cottages and crofts as they passed. They skirted large towns, sending emissaries to pay for what foodstuffs they needed. But in three days' time they crossed to the eastern side of the River Baise, and thereafter were in friendly territory.

Here the folks came out to cheer them and to pay tribute to Count Simon, who lay in state on his litter. Simon's eldest son Amaury succeeded him as count and as commander of the cru-sading army. But unlike his father, Amaury did not solicit advice from Gaucelm but from other knights as to which route was best, where supplies would be most readily available. And so Gaucelm was left mercifully alone with his black thoughts.

At night his squire pitched his tent. After strolling the camp in idle observation to see that all was well, Gaucelm shunned the firelight, the boasts and stories, the roll of the dice, and the com-pany of camp followers. Instead, he walked along the line of horses, found a lonely outcropping where he could be away from everyone and watch the night skies. Nor did he return to his tent before the evening star had set.

His friend and leader was dead. Of course that was the way of war, but it was a great loss to Church and France both, for they did not have another leader like him. Now who would lead the crusade?

King Philip was too busy keeping hold of his eastern lands, newly won from England. And in his bitter and morose mood, Gaucelm himself had no desire to ride at the head of an army. He was not the same man who had come on crusade two years ago, eager to fight for God and king. He was not bloodthirsty enough to walk before troops at the beginning of every battle and rouse them into a rage to kill.

Gaucelm turned even more inward now. He'd lost lands, friend, and more. He knew he would not be able to forget her. When he finally lay a weary head on his pallet in his tent, he saw her face before his eyes. He felt her creamy skin on the tips of his fingers. He remembered her ecstasy and knew that no matter if he never saw her again, he would not lie with another woman for a long, long time.

When the camp prostitutes crossed his path, he pushed them away so brusquely they often stumbled. None could understand what blackness had gotten hold of the handsome Gaucelm Deluc's heart. The soldiers counted it as his grief for Simon de Montfort, for the two men had been close.

But Gaucelm longed for Allesandra with every step his horse took, with every league he put between them. How was it that she had so captured his heart? How might he ever be able to return to her?

The army plodded northward. Already spirits were lifted. They spoke of the king gathering a new army in the next year, and they composed songs about Simon de Montfort's heroism. As they traveled, news began to catch up to them. In the way that gossip seems to float on the winds and across the grasses, it came to the camp followers, then to the soldiers, and then to the squires, who told their knights.

Gaucelm's new squire, William, was polishing his boots. His former squire had been killed in the fight outside Toulouse.

Gaucelm was inspecting his sword and scabbard. Tomorrow they would enter Ile de France.

"They say it was a woman operating the mangonella. The one that flung the fatal stone that killed the general," said William.

"Is that so?" replied Gaucelm idly, turning the sword hilt this way and that in the light from the flickering flame in his pan lamp.

"They've made songs about her in the South."

"Hmmm. Not surprising."

"She is one of those great ladies the troubadours sing about."

"Oh, is that so?" Only now did the squire succeed in capturing his attention.

"Yes, sire. The lady Allesandra Valtin."

Fourteen

Gaucelm did not look up to betray an expression; rather he continued to study his sword hilt. After a moment, he grunted, "Is that so?"

" 'Tis what they say." William scrubbed away at the boots. "Her mangonella was situated on the town wall above the gate-house." He shook his head. "To have such a sure aim, I wonder if she is a witch."

"No witch," Gaucelm said with more volume and irritation in his voice than he meant. Then he steeled his feelings. "But very fortunate for her side."

"Do you think the king will mount another crusade, sire?"

"I don't know."

He frowned, slid the sword into its scabbard and picked up his shield to inspect the splinters and gouges he'd accumulated on the field. He didn't add that his feelings about another mounted crusade to the south were mixed. And now to learn that Allesandra herself had killed his general!

His stomach turned in nausea, but he refused to show any

reaction. Instead, he said carefully, "I don't see how King Philip can afford to mount another crusade. He's stretched thin with his battles against England. And many of his barons are still in the Holy Lands."

He laid the shield on its side, anxious now to get to Paris and get the formalities over with. Then what? He had no inclination to go to the East. He would go to see his mother and his brother's family at their manor. But his presence was not needed there. Perhaps there would be some work King Philip would put him to. Gaucelm chafed at lacking a purpose. For all he really wanted was to see the woman he had loved in Languedoc. But if he wanted to do that, it seemed he would have to fight his way back to her on a new crusade.

And did he love her any less to learn that she had killed Simon? He closed his eyes and lay back, while his emotions roiled inside him.

He stretched out on his pallet, leaning on one elbow. He wished he had the gift of poetry that the southern troubadours did. For if he could not see her, perhaps it would ease his heart if he could write songs about her. And he could not risk a letter, for it would be treason.

"Allesandra," he said out loud, just to taste her name on his lips.

His squire must have thought he was referring to the song about the heroine of the South. "Did you ever see the woman?" asked William. "While you were there?"

"Oh, yes, I know her," answered Gaucelm, opening his eyes and looking up at the tent roof. "I have seen her."

William stopped his work for a moment to look with interest at the man he served. "Then you would know what manner of woman she is. Is she in league with the devil, do you think? They say the nobility in the South are all heretical in their views."

Gaucelm chuckled. "I do not know what is in her mind," he said.

He shut his eyes, resting and remembering while the squire

worked on silently until he finished his tasks, knowing enough not to disturb his master further.

The crusading army proceeded in formation beside the River Seine as they approached the Royal Palace. The body of Simon de Montfort was covered with a newly embroidered cloth of his colors, and his litter was carried by his most loyal knights, Gaucelm among them. The general's riderless horse was caparisoned in newly sewn cloth with brightly colored embroidery. Citizens lined the streets. And as they approached the massive palace, courtiers waved from parapets of the thick stone walls. The king's palace not only served as living quarters, but also as the depository for the king's treasures, and as an armory as well.

They carried Simon's litter to the foot of the broad stone steps in front of the gatehouse, where the palace guard waited, colorful pennants atop their poles. After the crusading army formed up behind them, the knights lowered the litter onto a bier that had been prepared for the body. At the sound of the clarion, the shouts died down and the king emerged with his entourage.

The king was not a tall man, nor muscular in appearance. But he had a sort of shrewd wisdom about him, and his sharp turquoise eyes missed nothing. His hair was a mixture of brown and gray, and the beard on his firm, determined chin, the same.

Gaucelm knew his practical intelligence to be tempered with sentiment. He was a man of shrewd caution and prudent courage. His quick temper was overruled by patient perseverance that had expanded his empire from a strip of land along the Seine to a formidable power. He was what his country needed at a time when, between England and Germany, France might have ceased to exist.

The king was garbed for the solemn occasion in a long red tunic and gold-threaded sleeveless overtunic, and white-and-gold mantle. His crown of gold and jewels glittered in the perfect sunlight, as did the jewels of his girdle, sword-hilt, and gloves. He presented a regal but concerned countenance and stood for a moment in silence gazing at the covered form of Count Simon de Montfort.

With the king was the pope's legate, the bishop Frosbier, dressed in ecclesiastical robes. Gaucelm and the other knights knelt as the royal party and the pope's legate came across the flagstones. Bishop Frosbier took a position a little behind and to the right of the king.

The breeze carried only the sounds of soft lapping from the Seine, rustlings of clothing, and stirring of leaves from the gardens beyond, as the crowd waited respectfully. At last, King Philip lifted a hand and spoke to the waiting crowd so all could hear.

"Rise, my loyal knights. We are here to pay respect to this great general, our loyal vassal and defender of the true faith. We mourn his loss and offer condolences to his loved ones. He will lie in state at our great cathedral Notre-Dame de Paris, so that all may mourn him. He will not be forgotten."

Amaury stepped forward and knelt before the king. "My lord, as the inheritor of my father's title and command, I thank you for the respect you pay us. It will be my great honor to continue in your service."

Gaucelm watched the king raise the young man to his feet and continue with the speeches. The papal legate, a tall, thin man with strong lines of nobility showing in his bronze-complected face, blessed the bier and then gave his blessing to Simon's family. While these proceedings were going on, Gaucelm allowed his eyes to flicker over the familiar surroundings from which he had been away so long.

He had a view of the gray stone walls of the palace on his left, the river beside which they had marched, the formal gardens behind him, and the spires of the churches rising over the timber and stone edifices that Philip had built.

The speeches were finished and the knights who carried the litter moved forward once more. To a funeral dirge played on clarion and pipes they took up their burden and wound through the gardens and along the street by the river as citizens paid their respects. Then they crossed the stone bridge over one arm of the Seine to the stone-paved streets of the Ile de la Cité. It was some distance to the cathedral.

The buttresses of Notre-Dame de Paris sprawled before them. The magnificent cathedral was as yet unfinished, but it was already renowned throughout the kingdom. Pilgrims came from far and wide to admire and to worship.

They carried Simon's litter inside the cool stone walls, and Gaucelm blinked in the dimness of the vaulted nave. The colored glass of the rose windows admitted muted sunlight from outdoors, and the rising pillars and ribbed vaults offered an awe-inspiring setting for Simon to rest in state before his burial.

The task finished, prayers and benediction were given by Bishop Frosbier, who had led the procession. Finally, Gaucelm arose from bended knee, free to go about his business.

His morose mood was still on him outside the cathedral when he jerked his head up and squinted in the sunlight as he heard his name called. He saw André Peloquin striding across the paved square. A man of equal height with sandy coloring, he was garbed in olive-green tunic and dark hose. His fur-lined mantle was richly embroidered, fitting for such a festive day and creating a prosperous look. His old friend was a welcome sight, and surely if anyone could ease his soul, André could.

"Gaucelm, my friend," said André as he embraced his friend. "I saw you in the procession and waited here for you."

"Glad I am to see you, my old comrade. I'm in need of a proper welcome. It's so long since I've been in these parts, I feel a stranger here myself. And much in need of news. I'd heard you were back from the Holy Lands, but my news is old. You must fill me in."

André laughed his sunny laugh, his tanned countenance alive with confidence and zest, making his blue eyes sparkle.

"Then join me at the tavern and we shall share some wine and perhaps dine if you've an appetite. But your mother and your brother and sister will be waiting to see you. Would you rather not see your family first and sup with me later?"

"I've a need for good company now," Gaucelm replied with certainty. "Then I'll see my family and sup with them this night."

He turned to look for his squire, who he knew would be waiting for instructions. Spying the young man, he issued orders for his horse to be left for him at the palace stables but that his belongings should be taken to his family's manor outside Paris.

"Be sure and relay to them that I am well but that I am with my old friend André Peloquin, with whom I have business. I send my affections, and I will attend on them this evening."

The squire nodded and went off to do his master's bidding. Gaucelm and André turned away from the cathedral square. They headed for the narrow winding street that led between shops where artisans worked and merchants displayed their wares at the front of tall, narrow houses.

"I heard the Provençals are no fighters," said André as they made their way to the tavern. "How was Simon defeated after two years of success?"

Gaucelm sighed, some of his bleak mood returning. "It's true that the lesser strongholds were easy to take. And in a pitched battle, the southern alliance lacked leadership. But the towns are strong. Much more independent and tenacious than any we have in the North. They govern themselves and behave independently. They've no love for us, that is sure."

"Hmmm. And so you were routed before the walls of Toulouse?"

"That is true."

They entered the tavern house and found a trestle table to one side of the room, near a stout oaken pillar supporting crossbeams above. The tavern keeper filled a carafe of wine from the spigot of one of his barrels and set it before them. There was enough conversation among other customers that Gaucelm and André could speak without worry of others eavesdropping on their conversation.

Gaucelm took a long draw of wine and then set his wine cup on the rough-hewn wood planks of the table. He let go a long sigh. "I tell you, André, I am weary of war. And yet I know nothing else."

"Ah, that is because you have seen defeat. What you need is the thrill of glory to revive you."

"Glory. Is there any? Is it really our duty to rid the world of all but those whom the Holy Church decrees are inheritors of the earth?"

André regarded his friend with affection and sympathy. "Ah, weary you are indeed. But much of what you say is true—though I would not have it heard that I said as much. Many times as I sweated and bled in the East, I wondered how the Lord could have allowed the Saracens to retake the land won with so much Christian blood, if the enterprise of the crusades is pleasing to Him."

"And how of our king's hard-won lands from the English?" asked Gaucelm, bringing the conversation back closer to home.

"He continues to grow strong and dominates all the dukes, counts, and seigneurs of the realm. The treasury grows from the money his vassals render instead of feudal service. Trade is encouraged. Truly he has strengthened the monarchy and weakened feudalism in France, while at the same time, he has left the English king weakened, subject to his feudal barons there. The same in Germany. He has accomplished much."

"And the Church? What of his relations there?"

Andre grunted so as to infer that things were not so harmonious between the king and the Church. "The king replaces ecclesiastics in council and administration with men from the rising lawyer class. He is not a man to let religion countermand his politics."

"What do you think he'll do about the South?"

Andre shook his head. "That, my friend, we shall just have to wait and see."

Gaucelm paid a dutiful visit to his family at their château outside Paris. The shell keep rose squarely on a mound above fair meadows and commanded the royal forest behind it. As Gaucelm entered his family's lands, he observed the vines being harvested. Most of the laborers took him to be just another knight traveling on the king's business. But as he neared the village, his father's overseer, Hercule, stopped his work and came across the field to salute him. He came through a gate in the fence and waited until Gaucelm reined in by the side of the road.

"My lord," said the overseer. "We had news that you were safely returned. Your family will be pleased."

"Thank you, Hercule. I see the harvest has not suffered."

Hercule looked proudly at the villeins gathering grapes, those in the distance singing while they worked. "Your family treats their villagers well. In return, they are more than willing to do the extra required of them at harvest time. It will be a good wine this year."

"Excellent." Gaucelm saluted the man and rode on.

The village was a straggle of timber-framed wattle and daub houses and thatched farm buildings along the road. A stone church dominated the scene. As he rode through, the villagers stopped their gossip and their work to turn and bow, the women to curtsy. For they recognized the younger son of the house of Deluc, back from fighting in the South.

After riding through the gatehouse of the fortified château and handing over his mount to a groom, he was received with honor and warmth by his mother, still lovely in her middle age, who waited for him by the large stone fireplace in the hall.

"My son, our prayers have been answered and you have returned safely to us." She beamed affection at him.

"Thank you, Mother," he said, kissing her hands. "And are you well?"

"Quite well, my son. We prosper. Your brother's wife is with child again, they are so blessed."

"That is good."

His pregnant sister-in-law, Marie, entered the hall and came across to hold out her hands to him. Gaucelm kissed her cheeks.

"You are radiant with good health, sister," he said, smiling down at his brother's bride.

"I'm pleased that you think so. And we are glad of your return. René will be glad to see you. But he is today at the manor near Amiens, and will not return for a week."

"Then you must tell me all the news," said Gaucelm, accepting a goblet of wine brought by a servant.

He knew his mother and sister-in-law would pamper him until he could stand no more. But he owed them his attention for a few days at least.

"Then you must rest and refresh yourself," said his mother, laying a fond hand on his arm. "We will prepare a banquet and some entertainment."

He could not help smiling at these women who welcomed him with open arms. Truly, it nourished a man to be so loved. But as he looked at them, he felt a tug in his heart. They loved him, but only in second place to the heir to the estate, his older brother. René would allow Gaucelm all the time he needed to stay here until he could decide his course. But a younger son was merely a guest in his family's demesne. Such was the way of the world. Even now Gaucelm felt that he had his own fate, and he would find it.

He was plagued with thoughts of the beautiful Allesandra, the traitorous enemy who loved him passionately. But how two such foes could join in love and harmony for a life together seemed at the moment impossible. So Gaucelm pushed away those thoughts, which caused in him an indescribable longing, took the seat by the fire, and turned his attention to the women's news about their lands.

Later that evening, Gaucelm's squire lit a fire for him in the chamber that would be his as long as he stayed in this household. His favorite dog found him not long after his arrival, and now the hound stretched out in front of the fire, head on paws, eyes on his master. The squire lit lamps suspended by chains from iron hooks in the paneled walls and left his master alone. Gaucelm picked up the bundle his squire had left rolled up after unloading his saddlebags.

He carefully unrolled it, revealing a small volume of vellum sheets, bound with thongs between leather-covered boards. He smiled to himself as he brought the book to the comfortable chair by the fire and opened it. No expensive illuminated work this, but simple, flowing handwriting floating across the page.

Gaucelm had picked up enough Provençal to be able to read it, though he knew that the more hidden meanings would escape him. But he formed the words softly as he began to read the somber, mournful poem. He held the book so the light fell across the page, and he gave a strong voice to the poems. The dog lifted his head and perked floppy ears, listening.

"You'll do as an audience, I think," said Gaucelm to his pet, breaking off and allowing a smile to curve his sensual lips. "Tell me what you think this means."

The dog whined, but Gaucelm continued reading. "Bitter, bitter my anguish be, and never, never, must I give up hope/ Great and overwhelming grief is life/ Dare I give heed to passing joy?" He lowered the book. "Dare I think that she speaks of me?" he whispered softly to the dog, who got up to come and put his head on Gaucelm's lap to comfort his master.

"Good boy," he said. "Yes, I miss my lady Allesandra. It seems hopeless, eh? That I will ever see her again. And now Simon's death stands between us."

Gaucelm felt no guilt over having stolen the collection of poetry she had admitted to writing. It was his one memento of her. And if she discovered the theft, perhaps she would realize it was small payment for his friend's life. She might be angry that the poems were gone, but perhaps she would hope that one day he would be able to restore them to her.

"And what of this one?" he said to the dog, then quoted another poem written by her. "No troubadour will sing for me, for I have raven hair." He smiled to himself, remembering how all the songs written by the poets who went from court to court praised flaxen-haired beauties.

He lowered the book, envisioning Allesandra's body stretched out on the bed, her raven hair fanned out over the pillow, and felt a powerful surge of desire.

With winter, campaigns were over for the season. Gaucelm was sent to help the king patrol counties newly won from England. Then everyone turned their attention to the Christmas feasts. Gaucelm returned to his family. To keep fit, there was hunting on fine winter days. When things were too quiet, he and André and other French knights jousted in tournaments. Gaucelm wore the favor of a lady no one knew. But for all that, the winter months passed slowly.

And yet, Gaucelm was aware that King Philip had not entirely forgotten Languedoc, for the king was reminded of it on a regular basis by letters from the pope. Noblemen in Gaucelm's position itched to march south again, to expand their fledgling demesnes gained by the wars against England. And so Gaucelm was present at a council convened by King Philip and attended by the papal legate Frosbier.

Gaucelm and André were both dressed in new tunics, surcoats, and fur-lined mantles. The royal guards stood with lances upright as the invited knights and ecclesiastics passed from gatehouse to inner ward, across cobbled courtyard and then up a wide set of stone steps to the arched entrance to the great hall. They waited in groups until the doors at the far end of the room opened and the king entered, robed in white and blue with gold fringe about his mantle, and a large ruby gleaming from his ring. He took a seat on the dais, and the council began.

"My lords," he said with a sweep of his hand to include them all. "You are here to advise me on this matter of a further crusade in the South, which I can ill afford. At the request of the Holy Pope of the Mother Church, we have crusaded there for two years in order to eradicate heresy. And yet those of you who have been there can attest how tenacious and slippery the southerners are. Conquer one county and what do they claim? 'There are no heretics here. We know no heretics.' Conquer the next county and it is the same. Why? Because the southerners protect each other. Their culture is what binds them, not their religion. I do not see the sense in further crusading if we cannot at least extend our territories to the south. But even in this, the southerners have presently foiled us."

He put his finger beside his cheek, his elbow resting on the chair arm as an indication that he was finished speaking. The turquoise eyes were alert and penetrating, making each man feel as if he looked directly at him.

"Your Majesty," said the tall, aristocratic legate, Frosbier, stepping before the king. "May I speak?"

"Go ahead, Reverend Bishop. I am aware that you speak for the pope. I do not wish to hide His Holiness's wishes from this assembly." And he gestured that the bishop should take the floor.

The bishop Frosbier, garbed in white robes with gold and silver threads, and his tall mitre on his head, nodded and then turned so he could also face the men assembled in the hall.

"My lords," he began in a reasonable voice. "A political solution that has left the heretics untroubled is unacceptable to His Holiness, the Pope. The count of Toulouse and the other southern lords have told us in the past that they would make a serious effort to eradicate heresy, and yet they do nothing." His voice had risen in irritation, and he paused to bring it under control. Nevertheless, his speech was insistent. "We have ceased to trust them. Therefore, His Holiness encourages those of you who wish to fight for truth to take up the cross again in the spring when the ground is thawed."

The king's chamberlain stepped forward. "Reverend Bishop, I am sure that His Majesty will agree with me. It is not that we disagree that the heretics should be banished. It is that there is no money left in the treasury to support another crusade."

He stretched out his hands, long fingers spread apart as if to emphasize his point. "Our feudal levies command only a certain number of men for forty days' service. After that, they will again go home. A sustained crusade must have paid mercenaries to sustain sieges and remain in the field. Where are we to get this money?"

The king knew what his chamberlain had planned to say, and now he lifted his black-and-gray brows with interest to see how the papal legate would respond. But Frosbier very smoothly ignored the issue of money.

"If a new crusade were undertaken to eradicate heresy once and for all in the South," said Frosbier, "I am also aware that there is the matter of who would lead it."

"Indeed," agreed Philip. "Our best general is dead. I myself am in ill health and cannot think of taking on such a venture."

"There is your son, Your Majesty," suggested Frosbier.

There was a stir in the hall, and Gaucelm and André exchanged glances. Yes, Louis might be just the man to take on a new crusade.

"A good suggestion," agreed Philip. "What do my knights say to that? Would you have Louis lead you in the coming season?"

André stepped forward and spoke. "Your Majesty, if I may speak. Your knights would follow Louis gladly, but he is busy in Poitou. It has taken a very firm hand to establish French royal authority in that county. Louis has broken the rebels' resistance, but the border zones are uncertain and the king's authority unsure."

"Precisely the reason for finding such an expedition desirable," suggested another baron. "For the border zones run into Languedoc."

For some moments Gaucelm had been aware that the king's intelligent eyes had been on him; now Philip singled him out.

"Gaucelm Deluc, you have been last season in those parts. What say you to the idea of a new crusade?"

Gaucelm uncrossed his arms and stepped forward with a nod to his sovereign. "I am torn, my lord. The lands are very desirable, but the people resent us deeply. As to the rooting out of heretics, that is not my business." He glanced at Frosbier.

"But from those I knew in the South I would say it will not be easily done."

The king rubbed his cheek with his finger, considering. Then he turned again to the papal legate. "You must ask His Holiness then, my lord bishop, just how much the Church would be willing to pay to meet the expenses of a fully mounted crusade. I am not saying that Louis will go. But if he is to take up the cross, then the Church must be the sponsor. I can see no other way."

Bishop Frosbier bowed. His expression showed that he was not completely pleased but that he would hold his opinions to himself. "I will ask His Holiness, then, if the church coffers can fulfill such a request."

The assembly broke into individual groups of murmuring knights and barons, and Philip made no move to silence them for some moments.

André said sidelong to Gaucelm, "A clever move by our sovereign. He is setting a precedent that if the Church wants us to defend Christendom, then she must pay for it. Clever indeed."

"Furthermore," the king finally interrupted, and the crowd quieted down. "We must be free to annex any lands overrun by our army."

Frosbier angled his mitred head in a nod. But Gaucelm did not miss the look of consternation that crossed the legate's face. He could well imagine that the pope did not really want a strong ruler in Languedoc. The pope must dream of a prince in Toulouse who would be a dutiful vassal of the Holy See. Therein did the Church maintain her power.

Whatever the legate was thinking, he said only, "We have learned that the southern counts will not persecute their own subjects; therefore a strong French presence is necessary to punish and expel heretics from the lands and to preserve the rights of the churches. I will see that His Holiness the Pope hears your offer to raise an army provided the Church will outfit her and pay to keep mercenaries in the field. As to the matter of annexing the lands that you overrun, I will see if His Holiness is in agreement. With all due haste I will take these negotiations to Rome. Do I understand your requests completely, Your Majesty?"

"I believe you do," answered Philip.

"Then I will take this message back to Rome."

The council concluded, and Gaucelm followed André out of the hall and into the sunlit wintry day. They pulled their fur-lined mantles tighter around them and went in the direction of the tavern where young knights like themselves met whenever in the Ile de la Cité on the king's business.

There, they could toast themselves by a fire and speculate about what would happen come spring. In the tavern, scholars fresh from their debates in university cloister and lecture room drank heartily and continued their arguments in French and Latin.

André led his friend to a bench at the end of a trestle table. When the buxom tavernkeeper's daughter came to bring them refreshment, André gave her a suggestive wink and grasped her hand in flirtation, forcing her to stay with them for a few moments.

"Mademoiselle," said André to the dark-eyed wench with full, sensual lips and a flirtatious look in her eye, "where have you been? I have longed for you all this month."

"I've been right here, monsieur," she responded. "It is you who have been absent."

André turned her hand over to kiss her wrist and ran his fingers along her inner arm.

"Ah, how foolish of me. For a man without feminine company is not living."

He pulled her down on the knee he thrust outward from the end of the table, so that he could nuzzle her throat.

"What say you to some time together, eh?" Her bosom was temptingly close to his hand, but she gave him no chance to fondle her. She thrust his head away and jumped up to the floor again.

"Monsieur, have a care. I have business to attend to, and you are not my only customer."

André gave her a lewd grin. "Ah, but perhaps I could pay to become your only customer."

She hesitated, and he saw the greed flicker in her dark eyes. Then she gave a toss of the head. "What makes you think I am for sale?"

André gave a look of mock horror. "Mademoiselle, I did not say that you were. It is just that my desire for your company has overcome me, and I would hire a private hall for us to dine in and be left alone. A palace, if I could afford it." Then he sighed sadly. "But alas, I am a poor knight and I cannot afford such things, even for my lady."

She laughed then, completely won over by his charm. She bent to murmur in his ear, her hair tickling his face, the neckline of the smock that peeked over her gown sinking to offer a tempting view of flesh. "Perhaps if you order us supper this evening, I can find a room where we can enjoy it," she said. "Come back then."

André felt his loins tingle in anticipation. And he held her there for one kiss on her plump cheek. "How fortunate for me, mademoiselle." Then he slapped her rump. "Now, bring us wine. I must do something to liven up my friend's spirits."

Gaucelm had watched the seduction with minor amusement. He knew that if they asked, the girl could find a friend for him. Not that his body wouldn't find release in a woman's flesh. But there was still only one woman that he craved. And she was hopelessly far away. He knew he was a fool to save himself for her. For the only way he could hope to claim her again was to arrive at her castle at the head of an army.

The girl brought wine, and the two men drank deeply. Then André brought up the matter of negotiations between king and pope.

"If Louis is already in command of Poitou, perhaps the Languedoc will be more easily subdued this time. What do you say, my friend? You were there."

Gaucelm lifted the corner of his mouth in irony. "I agree that

Prince Louis is a good man in the field. Though I have never fought with him, I have heard of his exploits."

Andre nodded. "He is a good leader, from what I have seen. If anyone can subdue the South, he will be the one."

"Yes," replied Gaucelm, "if anyone can. But it will not happen soon. You heard the negotiations. You know how slowly these things move. The legate must travel to Rome, and then the pope will have to consider the king's requests. It is a very large undertaking."

André did not miss the discouragement in his friend's tone. "Gaucelm, my man, all this winter you have been melancholy. I understand your bitterness at having secured lands in Languedoc, only to have the rebels rise up and snatch them from you. But if Louis mounts a new crusade, surely this will be your chance to reclaim them. Does this not give you hope?"

Gaucelm gave a grunt, but smiled wearily at his friend. "Indeed, it does. And you are right, the winter months hang heavy on my hands."

"You did the king's bidding along the new borders, did you not?"

"All well and good," answered Gaucelm, "but I did not find the borders to my liking. It had been a long while since I had to speak English to gain information for the king."

"Hmmm, but you do speak Provençal now . . ." André raised sandy brows in speculation, with more meaning behind his words than he spelled out.

"Yes," said Gaucelm, lifting his wine cup. "I do speak Provençal. And many of the southern nobility have learned French if only to defend themselves from us."

"Yes," said André. "I take it you became acquainted with a few among this nobility."

Gaucelm swallowed his sip of wine and shifted his body to lean one elbow on the table and gaze at the fire. "A few."

André gave a long sigh. "Ah, as I have been suspecting, you have been mourning these last months because of a woman."

Gaucelm did not try to hide his response. He smiled ironically. "And what if I have?"

"Hmmm," said André with a sad shake of the head. "The worst type of malaise. I myself love women, as you know. But there has never been one who would make me forget all else. Tell me, is this woman that you pine for of a love so great?"

Gaucelm dropped his tone of irony and knit his brows seriously. "I promised her I would return to her."

He did not add that he had done thus before he learned of her treachery regarding Simon de Montfort.

"And so you will."

"Ha!" Gaucelm exclaimed. "With an army at my back, you mean."

André smiled and tossed back another swallow of wine. "I see your dilemma. Perhaps she fell in love with you, but she will not forgive you if you destroy all that is hers. Something like that, hmmm?"

"You have it, my friend." Then he shook his head and lowered his voice. "But worse, even if I am again in the South and we are victorious, I am afraid she will be persecuted for her beliefs."

"Ah, you mean she is a heretic. Did she admit as much?"

"No. These southerners are very secretive about such things. To all appearances she could be a good Catholic. But I think she may have sheltered heretics nonetheless. At least that is all I suspected at the time."

His troubled frown led André to delve deeper. "Since you have not seen her since you marched northward, what has made you doubt her further?"

"I stole something from her, took it to remember her by, something for my comfort."

"Oh?"

His look softened and he stared into his empty cup. "Her poetry." He glanced up at André. "She is a patron of the troubadours. But more, she writes poetry herself."

"Yes? And what is it about this poetry? Love songs, battle songs, are they not?"

Gaucelm shrugged. "I thought so at first. But as I sit by my fire and reread them, I now see meanings I did not see before."

André gave a quick glance over his shoulder. "Then you must keep the poetry out of the hands of our bishops. Perhaps you would be better off to burn it."

Gaucelm nodded. "It would be safer so."

The two men drank silently, the noise around them filling the background with the sounds of levity. Gaucelm knew that negotiations for another crusade could take many months. He must find something else to do in that time or go mad.

Surely his friend was right. He should burn the book of Allesandra's poems, lest they be stolen or fall into the wrong hands.

Fifteen

King Philip Augustus was dying. Negotiations with the pope reached a standstill as France waited to see just how soon they would have a new king. In the meantime, the kingdoms so hard won in the Holy Lands needed protecting. And Jerusalem was still in Muslim hands. And so rather than remain in Ile de France with nothing to do, Gaucelm took himself off as part of a badly needed contingent of Christian forces.

They rendezvoused in Cyprus and spent the next months fighting small-scale operations against the Muslims. He was part of the great invasion of Egypt and helped to capture a defensive tower on the Nile. They dredged a canal, and in November, they took Damietta. But the Christians were paralyzed by a leadership argument.

When the Egyptians blocked the supply lines from Damietta and broke the dykes to flood the surrounding land, the crusaders were doomed. They left Egypt. Once more, Gaucelm sailed home to Ile de France for another winter.

* * *

When Louis VIII was finally crowned, he turned to his negotiations with the pope. And so it was that the trusted knights and
barons of the royal counties were again summoned to council.
Gaucelm and André rode into the Ile de la Cité on a fine spring
day, with a clear, azure sky and the fragrance from the royal
gardens assaulting their senses.

André had seen the changes in his friend. Gaucelm had tough-
ened and hardened from fighting in the East. His eyes lacked
luster, and what he felt, he kept to himself. André could see the
impatience in his friend. As if he were waiting for something,
dissatisfied, biding his time.

Now they were summoned to the palace once again. Perhaps
what Gaucelm had awaited more than a year would happen.

"Surely we are not summoned to hear bad news," speculated
André. "With the weather so fine, the king will want to expand
his borders."

"Hmmm," said Gaucelm. "Let us hope so."

The knights joined others of their class in the great hall. An
entourage of ecclesiastics hovered beside the dais. Then the doors
opened, and the men parted for King Louis.

He was a muscular warrior with thick blond hair and beard
and sharp, intelligent eyes like his father's. He wasted no time,
but after greeting the assembly and the pope's emissaries, he
addressed them all.

"My lords and holy fathers, I welcome you here to discuss
the matter that my late father, the king, was engaged upon before
he passed away. It has been my purpose to continue what my
father began, and in these last months I have turned all my attention to securing the borders of Poitou."

He stepped down from the dais to walk among the men, looking each in the eye, giving them the reassuring feeling that he
knew them. "As it turns out, the Mother Church also has business
in the South. Many of you were here when this issue was discussed with my father."

Murmurs answered him. He took his time surveying all present as if getting a sense of agreement. Then he returned to the dais, but did not mount it. "His Holiness the Pope still desires our help in routing out heresy in the South. To this end taxes imposed on the clergy have been raised to pay for such a venture."

Now the room erupted in a greater murmur and Gaucelm exchanged glances with André. Louis raised a hand for silence.

"We have word from the bishops in Languedoc, who still do not trust the count of Toulouse or his rebel friends. Count Raymond VI is too ill to fight, but his son Raymond VII is devoted to his father's cause. He is their leader in the field now. We could not trust the father, and we will not trust the son. Our late general, Simon de Montfort, fought well for us and died for his trouble. We will mount an expedition to the South in May this year to right that situation."

The assembly knew that the king wasn't finished speaking so withheld their cheers, but excitement passed through the room and looks of speculation and interest were exchanged.

The king now accepted a rolled parchment handed to him by the tall, confident papal legate Frosbier. Gaucelm studied him and decided he had not changed in the year and more since he'd seen him. He looked quite pleased with himself, and if anything, more ambitious. The king untied the cords that bound the scroll and then unrolled it to read the terms from it, summarizing for the assembly before him.

"To finance this crusade, beginning in the spring of this year, the king receives a tenth of ecclesiastical revenues of the French clergy for five years."

André whispered in Gaucelm's ear, "A large sum, eh?"

Louis continued. "We have the right to quit the crusade whenever we choose. We acquire all lands we overrun. All who participate in the crusade receive indulgences for their sins to the full extreme."

Gaucelm's mind wandered as the king went over the finer details. They were going to ride south. Already his blood began to move again in his veins. He could feel the fatigue of travel from the Holy Lands recede from his bones and the warm winds of the South call to him. For these many months he had tried to forget Allesandra. Her face had grown vague, only a shape that still glowed in his mind. But he remembered her body in every detail. And he still recited her poetry in his mind. In the hot, arid climate of the Nile, her poetry had kept him sane when he'd despaired of life. He could not even any longer dredge up the old resentment that she had killed Simon in battle.

He did not allow himself to think that if he rode south with a crusading army that Allesandra Valtin would hate him for coming as her enemy. He had no doubt of her loyalty to her southern friends. They were enemies still. But if he came so near, surely he would at least see her. What had the year wrought for her? Would she have changed? Perhaps she was beautiful no longer, burdened as she must be by running a castle.

But no, of course her purpose would have kept her beautiful and determined. But he knew she would see him. She would not refuse such a meeting. He dared not think he might hold her in his arms again. Too much time had passed for her to yield.

He turned his mind from personal thoughts as the knights and barons mingled and talked of war. Then he left the hall and retrieved his palfrey from the king's stables. He parted from André once they had crossed the stone bridge.

"So," said André, as his horse shook out its mane. "We ride south again in two weeks. For you, my friend, I am glad. I believe that since you set eyes on those lands, you have not been the same."

Gaucelm met his friend's look with one of acknowledgment. "Indeed, now we will do Louis justice and expand his claims. I will be ready."

"Hmmm," said André. He knew better than to mention a certain widow of Languedoc. Besides, it was best not to test fate. If God willed it, the lady would be in Gaucelm's arms again before the fighting season was over.

"Adieu, then, until we gather on the field to march, two weeks hence," said André.

Gaucelm lifted a hand in parting and then gave his palfrey his head to trot north and then west into the oak and beech forest and onto his family's lands. He passed through the gatehouse and into the courtyard and was calling out for his squire before he'd dismounted. When squire William hurried out of the stables, Gaucelm clapped him on the shoulder.

"We ride south in two weeks. All must be ready."

"Very well, my lord. We shall see that your weapons are sharpened until they may split a hair."

Gaucelm gave a laugh, something he had not done in quite some time. The fine weather and a march ahead fired his blood. He followed the grooms into the stables to examine the horses. He would personally make sure that his charger, his packhorses, and palfreys would be properly shod for travel.

Allesandra sat with her friend Raymond VII in his citadel in Toulouse. His father was gravely ill, though still with greatness of spirit. She knew that the sorrow the son felt was beyond words. She, too, sorrowed at the prospect of the loss of the man so loved by all of Toulouse. However, Raymond VII shouldered the responsibility of carrying on as she knew he would.

It was late in the evening, and the log in the hearth fire fell into the ashes. They sat alone on stools. On her lap was a book of poetry, which she had thought to read aloud to try and comfort Raymond. But instead, they had whiled away the hour talking, speculating, laying plans.

"My informants tell me that King Louis has concluded negotiations with the pope. They will come again, just as we knew they would."

She was silent for a moment. "Why could they not leave us alone?"

The younger Raymond regarded her. Such a lovely woman, and yet with a trace of sadness about her. Not the sadness of grief, but rather a melancholy. She wore her hair in a braid wrapped around her head under a wimple. She had lost some weight and her cheekbones looked sharper of late.

His own father was gravely ill, and perhaps he took comfort in her solemn mood. He felt he had grown closer to Allesandra. Among fine ladies and patrons of the troubadours, he knew none so noble as she. He had often praised her in his own poetry, sung love songs at her feet. They had exchanged tensos, and yet not until now had he seriously considered the notion that theirs might indeed be a suitable match.

He gazed at her somber countenance, her tightly bound hair under fillet and veil, her desirable figure in fitted green gown with surcoat draped as if an artist had arranged its folds. Her long legs were folded to the side, her graceful hands clasped about her knee. There was a strain all about her, but underneath that, still her loveliness shone.

Having lost the thread of their conversation, he began a new one. "Allesandra, dear friend, I have been thinking."

She lifted her eyes slowly and smiled sadly at him. "What have you been thinking?"

He curved his sensuous lips into a smile. "That you have been a widow for too long."

Her open, warm expression altered. Her lids lowered, and she transferred her gaze to the fire. He noticed how the skin about her high cheekbones drew tighter still. Her mouth straightened out into a firm line.

"Do you think so?" she replied.

Feeling his heart begin to beat in his chest, he moved forward onto his knees. "I do."

She gave the slightest shake of her head. "There has been much to do as chatelaine of my own demesne. I have not missed having a husband."

He risked raising his hand and placing it on hers. "But in days to come it would give you strength to have a husband. If we must fight again, you would be better off joining your lands to those of another strong and noble family."

Small lines about her mouth creased as she allowed herself an ironic smile. She lifted her heavy lids, her great violet eyes meeting his. "And whose house might that be?"

Raymond smiled back, undone by her frankness. Still, he lifted her hand to his lips and kissed it, then pressed the hem of her sleeve and the chilled skin of her hand to his cheek. "My own, of course."

"Aha, so I thought." She let her hand drift through his thick, brown hair, curling down to his shoulders. But the caress was one of friendship, not of passion.

He nuzzled his head against her hand. "My father would be pleased," he said. "Wouldn't you like to grant him a dying wish?"

Her hand stopped for a moment. "Has he said this himself?"

Raymond could not lie. "Not in so many words, but we have spoken of it in the past, I'm quite sure."

She pinched his ear. "Ow!" he exclaimed.

"Your father never suggested the idea to me. Not even a hint."

"Hmmm. I suppose it was because he didn't think I was good enough for you."

She gazed at him fondly. "You are still very young. Perhaps your father thought you needed to have your amorous adventures before you married."

He grimaced. "Allesandra, you know very well marriage is for the uniting of lands and titles. Amorous adventures occur because oftentimes bride and bridegroom cannot stand the sight of each other."

"Yes, I know. And of that was born our poetry." She gave a long sigh. "Love as perpetual torment, as an ennobling force, making its way around the obstacles of distance, class, marriage."

He let the back of his finger drift across her cheek. "You speak as if you have felt such a torment."

She gave him a regretful smile. "Perhaps I have. How could I write about it if I had not experienced it?"

"Yes, your poetry of late has been filled with sadness, it is true. Then tell me, if you do not love me, who do you love?"

She shook her head. "I cannot tell you. Such things must remain a secret always."

"You exasperate me, Allesandra dear." He thought a moment, picked up the poker and stirred sparks from the fire. "You know, when my father passes on, though I hope that is not for a very long time, I will be your overlord. I might not be so patient in letting you remain in your widowed state."

She sat up straight, her shoulders erect. "You would not make me marry against my wishes, surely. Our friendship is too great, is it not?"

He noticed that her last words were not as confidently spoken as the first of her phrases. Perhaps it would be wise to press his point, so that she would not take him for granted as her future overlord.

He shrugged. "I am not a cruel man, you know that. But an overlord is well served when a ward marries. You will better be able to provide knights when we need them, as surely we must, now that Louis is king."

Allesandra guided the conversation back to where they had begun. "We must make plans. Our people are loyal, but they are broken. Some of our cities cannot stand devastation again. We have not had enough time to recover. They remember too well what Simon de Montfort was like."

"But he is dead."

"Yes, but with King Louis at the head of an army, and the pope paying for it . . ." She shivered and did not finish. A feeling of dread passed over her, and she clutched at Raymond's hand. This time their grasp was one of mutual desperation. Her words were rasping as she half whispered, "Are we doomed, Raymond? Is our way of life fading away before our eyes? Are these forces too strong to withstand?"

Raymond pressed his lips together before he answered. His courageous heart wanted nothing better than to reassure her. They would fight to the death to defend Languedoc, of course. But he, too, saw the bitter winds of change, the evil of the hated word inquisition. And he did not want to place it on his tongue.

"Be of good heart, madam. We do not yet know the outcome. I have spies who will keep me informed of Louis's movements. He gathers his army now, and it is a very great one, of that I am certain."

Allesandra trembled, but would not show her fear. "I will help you. But we must have firsthand knowledge. I fear that some of our cities will indeed fall. We must find out which route Louis plans to take and do what we can to prepare our forces." Then her noble speech done, she squeezed his bony fingers between her own and gave a little gasp. "Oh, Raymond, I am afraid. Afraid for us, for our land, for what we fought so hard to win."

He got to his feet, angered to see this brave, able noblewoman shaking in fear of an army that was forming far to the north.

"We will take action. Action banishes fear. As soon as I know where Louis is going, I will tell you."

She rose as well and uttered her pledge. "And then we will do as we must."

That said, there seemed nothing else to do than to bid her good night. "May I escort you to your chamber?"

"No, I think I'll sit a while. We did not read from the book as we had planned to."

"Then stay, read by the firelight. My hounds will keep you company. Perhaps a few words of love and poetry will take your mind off these times we speak of."

"Perhaps."

After he was gone, she stared at the dying flames for some time. Her heart was heavy and there seemed no choice for her but a bitter course. She shut her eyes, leaning her head against the stone hearth. It had been eighteen months. She still saw his face, if more clearly in dreams than in the day. But she still trembled to remember what it had been like. It was her secret, and likewise her secret longing. For no one knew what had happened to her, and why the last year had added a harshness to her features.

She used to wear a widow's calm serenity, but now she heard herself turn shrewish when things did not happen to her liking. She had lost patience. Though the threat had been lifted when

Simon de Montfort had died, and all Languedoc had celebrated, she knew in her heart it would not last. How she knew it, she was not sure. Something on the wind told her.

But then there was her longing for Gaucelm Deluc, the man who had claimed her. For days and weeks she would tell herself that she was foolish to hope to ever see him again. She could not wish for him to come, for if he did, he would come to fight her people again. And she could not wish that, did not wish it. She spent many foolish hours imagining that he would sweep down from the North by himself and take her away somewhere, but where? He had told her he had no lands, no fortune. Only his skills as a knight. He wasn't even a poet. No great nobleman of another country would house them in exchange for his songs, for he had none.

But she did. Poetry was her one consolation. From winter to winter and now into spring again, she had scratched away in her chamber, filling sheets of parchment and vellum with her paltry lines. Scratching the vellum clean and starting again. If she wrote of a strong warrior in whose arms she had found ecstasy, she let no one see those songs.

But even when she wrote lighter songs for her friends, and let the jongleurs sing them in public, still there were hints of her long, lost love. And then she would catch the troubadours gazing pensively at her. They pondered which one of them she was writing about, no doubt, and set the gossips speculating. Let them speculate. Only Peire knew she'd seen Gaucelm the night he'd sneaked into the castle, and Peire kept silent. Surely no one would guess that the lady Allesandra Valtin was hopelessly in love with one of their hated erstwhile conquerors. She sometimes feared that they could read her thoughts. And then she tried not to think of him. For if they guessed the truth, or if someone of her household knew and spoke of it, she would not be able to face them for the shame of being called a traitor.

On some days, she did not think of love. There was much to do in such a busy household. And when their own demesne was prospering, she took servants and strong men to help rebuild the towns and the other castles that had been destroyed by Simon's forces. Crops were sown, a harvest brought in. And then the winter feasts had been seen to. The courts of love even flourished again for a time. And now it was spring and the herds were giving birth. The cycle of life seemed almost pleasant again. And yet the people had not forgotten. She could see it in their eyes. When one spoke to her, it wasn't long before there was a shifting of the eyes to look about to see if the threat of the enemy lurked.

No, it was not over yet. She no longer hoped for or expected happiness. She knew now that the best that could happen would be for her to be able to forget. Raymond VII would be her overlord one day. And she did not let their friendship fool her. He would insist that she marry if he found a match that would benefit his kingdom. Or he would marry her himself.

She supposed she could put up with him as a husband as well as anyone else. Unless—and here was where she doubted her resolve. Unless she ever saw Gaucelm Deluc again. And then, if he wanted her, if he came to her . . .

She shook her head, blotting out the vision, placing a hand to her beating heart. She could not bear to relive the fantasy again. For that was all it was, a fantasy with only the substance of a dream.

Sixteen

Gaucelm and André met the assembling army in mid-May. As they surveyed the troops encamped on the rolling plain from an observation point on a hill, Gaucelm remarked on the army's size.

"The king has demanded full military service from his vassals," said André, "and they have come. It is a war to recover what Simon de Montfort lost as much as it is a crusade."

"That is true," agreed Gaucelm. "The war chest swells with fines paid by those who could not serve. This is surely the largest force sent against the southerners."

"Indeed," said André. "Its mere size will terrify them. I would not be surprised if many should submit as we advance down the Rhône."

"We will see," said Gaucelm. "We will put your theory to the test."

The army moved the next day, slowly following the Loire southeast for more than a week before leaving it to take the Rhône southward. As they advanced, André's theory proved right. Promises of obedience to the king greeted them. The mere size of the army seemed to terrify the Provençals. The towns that had defied Simon de Montfort feared to oppose Louis VIII. One by one, as they heard of the march, the towns abandoned Raymond VII and asked for Louis's clemency and protection.

Allesandra and Raymond VII journeyed east in secret. They had spent the last night at the castle of one of the noble southern lords always generous with hospitality to his countrymen. Now they started out on a fine spring morning, the kind of day that would make a troubadour want to compose songs.

"One can hardly believe we are on a mission of war," Raymond said as they walked their horses along a busy road beside merchants making their way with heavily laden wagons to a fair. "Look about us. The flowers bloom, bees carry pollen. Does not the blue sky above make you think of other things than those which demand our attention?"

Allesandra drew nourishment from the calm surroundings, and yet in the back of her mind, her worries had not left her. "It is deceptive, my lord. The very reason for our journey is to find a way to preserve this peace."

"Yes."

His gay expression turned to one of pensive thought. For Raymond was really more than the gay troubadour he seemed to all and sundry. Strategy and intrigue were part of his duties to protect his people, and he would do his part.

A group of men-at-arms appeared in the distance, and Raymond narrowed his eyes. Then he held out his hand for Allesandra to rein in.

"Who are they?" she asked, peering at the three galloping horses, their armed riders hugging their horses' necks.

"Messengers," he said after a moment. "Never fear, they are our own men, come to inform me of any news between here and our destination."

She lifted her brows, heartened by Raymond's cleverness. To have informers know their route and ride to warn them of any dangers showed great forethought.

They pulled to the side and waited until the riders slowed. Then a sergeant-at-arms, hailing Raymond, rode up.

"King Louis has turned down the Rhône," he said without preamble.

"And?"

"The towns have all surrendered to the French. They fear reprisals. When word came of the size of the French army, they at once asked clemency and the protection of the king. They cannot withstand these forces and do not wish to be razed to the ground."

Allesandra saw Raymond's face tighten, his lips pulled into a grim line. "Any more?"

"We do have word that many in the king's army do not wish to fight the count of Toulouse. There will be a number of the disaffected among them."

This gave Raymond a momentary look of satisfaction. "But we cannot count on that. It is the size of the army that will frighten our countrymen, even if the soldiers are less than enthusiastic for their work. How far is the army from Avignon?"

"One week's march. He does not force march them, but makes sure they have rest and nourishment along the way."

"I see. Then we will be there before them." He glanced at Allesandra meaningfully, then spoke to the soldiers again. "Well done. Ride on to Toulouse. Tell my father, but assure him that we will stand firm. I go to assist Avignon. He knows that city will be less easily bowed to the king."

The soldiers lifted their hands in salute and then turned back to the road to ride at a less frantic pace with their news. Allesandra could see that Raymond would not show discouragement. She struggled to find words that would encourage him while at the same time truthfully assess their situation.

Her jaw tightened in sudden anger. Somewhere to the north a huge army marched south to squash her land under their heel. And with that army was a man she once loved. In that moment, sitting in the sun on her fine mount, she blamed Gaucelm. Reasonable or not, she thought, surely he could have kept the king away.

"Come," said Raymond at last. "We must hasten to Avignon. It is important we reach that city before Louis does."

The city of Avignon was neither part of the kingdom of France, nor of Languedoc. It was a city of the Holy Roman Empire and wished to remain so, though it lay on the east side of the Rhône, in the county of Provence.

"The Holy Roman Emperor has no authority in Provence," said Raymond, voicing these thoughts.

"Yes," said Allesandra. "Avignon is more like one of the Italian city-states than a French municipality."

"And yet the presence of a large French army near this independent republic is bound to cause fear."

"But the idea of letting that army march through its streets will be repugnant to the Avignonese, do you not think?"

"I do so think. We must get there as quickly as we can and assist them in seeing it that way."

They urged their horses to a faster pace, though they were too far from their destination to spend the horses thoughtlessly. They stopped to dine and rest in separate chambers at an inn. Louis's army was marching slowly. They would have time.

Raymond and Allesandra approached the city of Avignon three days later to see much construction going on outside the city walls. Raymond approached a workman and inquired what was being built.

"A new wooden bridge," replied the man with the grime of work on his face but a determined countenance. "It crosses the river as you can see, but goes outside the walls of our city."

"Ahhh," replied Raymond, at once comprehending. For the great stone bridge led across the river and into the heart of the city and through it. They rode forward.

"Why do they build a new bridge?" inquired Allesandra.

"For the crusading army, no doubt. They must have promised Louis access, but just as you said, they do not wish the army to come within the walls of their town."

They made their way around the construction and over the stone bridge. Along the quay, bales of supplies were being unloaded from barges and carted into the city. Inside the walls, commerce hustled and bustled, and they asked their way to the city governors. They were directed to a fine three-story stone house belonging to the head councilman, Thomas Wykes. At the house they were told that Master Wykes was at the guildhall, engaged in very important matters.

They found the guildhall at a very busy intersection of two narrow streets in the heart of the shops. When it was made known that an important personage was here, Master Wykes broke off from his conversation at a large trestle table and came to greet them. But Raymond stopped him from inquiring as to exactly who he was until they were guaranteed privacy. They were led to an upper chamber and the door shut before Raymond threw off his hood.

"My lord," Master Wykes began upon recognizing the son of the count and the marquis of Provence. He made a reverence, though not so great as to imply that Raymond's status was so very much above his own. "What brings you to our troubled city? Ah, but before you answer that question, may I offer you some of our local wine?"

"You may. The lady Allesandra Valtin and I have come all the way from Toulouse on the same business I believe that causes you to construct a bridge outside your town. But do let us begin with refreshment. That will make whatever follows that much easier."

Master Wykes bowed to Allesandra and bade his guests be seated at a stout trestle table. Flagons were brought, and the local wine tasted and commented upon. Then the business at hand was addressed.

"As you know," Master Wykes began, "we are not subject to the king of France, but we do not mind showing him respect. Our feudal lord is Frederick II of Germany. However, if the French king wishes to pass by our town, we have no reason to resist him as long as he makes no move to interfere with our government. We reached an agreement with him that allows him free passage."

"But you do not want him within your city walls," said Raymond. He respected these independent burghers, and if the situation were not so dire, he would look forward to watching them face off a huge army led by the king of France. Avignon was one of the great cities of the South, as proud as Marseilles, and as confident of its strength as Toulouse. But alas, he did not have the luxury of relishing the event. Too much depended on it.

Master Wykes's gaze turned to Allesandra. "And you, my lady. Have you also been subject to French rule in your lands?"

"I have, sir. Before we finally repelled them more than a year ago."

"Hmmm. And do you also have an interest in Avignon?"

His question made her careful of her reply, but surely this complete stranger knew nothing of her personal history. "Only as a spy and as advisor and friend to Sir Raymond and his father, the count. I am their ward."

Wykes's eyes became more assessing. "Ahh, I see. The king's army will arrive in a few days. By then the wooden bridge will be ready. We will send out an emissary to receive them. Beyond that, I cannot say."

"It will be to your advantage not to make it known that I am here to gain information. You could easily sell me to the king, of course. But I take you to be a man of honor and not in need of profit so slyly gained. If you would guarantee our safety within your walls, we can advise and help you should any negotiations become needed."

"A fair assessment," said Wykes, "and one I accept. You are right. While I know no such man who would stoop so low as to sell your presence to the king, I cannot speak for all the foreign merchants and their servants who come and go. While most of them flourish from our present economy, there may be the one black heart that would be so traitorous. I will say only that a nobleman from the West is visiting with his ward. Would that be acceptable to you, madam?"

"Yes, quite. My identity . . ." She hesitated, wanting to phrase her words so that they would be taken in the right light. "My identity would also be recognized by some of the leaders of this crusade, if those who fought beside Simon de Montfort return now with the king."

"Ahh, I see. So we will keep your name a secret as well."

"That would be best." Politically, of course it was. And yet, Allesandra could not help thinking . . . and yet if *he* knew she was here, what might he do?

She pushed such thoughts aside. She was here to help defend her land. They needed to learn where the king would strike next, after he marched around Avignon.

The meeting concluded, they were taken to Master Wykes's own house where they were introduced to his wife as a lord and lady of the West. The good woman understood the need for secrecy and showed them to comfortable rooms. Allesandra's room looked over a small alley. But beyond the corner of the house opposite, she glimpsed the city walls and could feel the breezes off the river.

Left alone, she leaned against the shutter and allowed herself to think of Gaucelm. In three days he would be on the other side of those walls, passing so near. And yet she could not reach him. He would not even know she was here.

* * *

Mounted on a white horse, Gaucelm was among the vanguard of crusaders that approached Avignon and saw how their path was laid out to veer off to the right. Lances were set in the ground with pennants flying, and citizens had turned out to greet them and cheer. The way across the stone bridge into the town was blocked by the crowd and the lances, and more citizens and a few men-at-arms lined the path to what appeared to be a wooden structure that crossed the river and led beside the town walls.

"Well," said André, who rode beside Gaucelm, "what do you think of this? They've built us our own bridge. Pray it is sturdy enough to hold our army."

"There come the gentlemen we may ask," said Gaucelm, watching a party of richly dressed burghers approach from where they stood near the foot of the new bridge. When they were within hailing distance, Gaucelm raised a hand for the troops behind him to halt.

"Greetings," said the leading burgher, a substantial man with wide face and neatly trimmed beard. His green satin cap matched a surcoat flowing over his round build. He came forward. "As mayor of the fair city of Avignon, I, Thomas Wykes, do hereby stand ready to greet King Louis of France in friendship and execute the agreement that he may pass freely by." He gestured to the new bridge. "We have here constructed a bridge for your use, thinking it more efficient than forcing so large an army to ride through such a crowded city as ours."

He looked up at Gaucelm, who was clearly the king's lieutenant. It was obvious from the caparison of the horse he rode, the polished lance, and sword hilt, but most of all from the bearing of the man himself, who sat his horse so proudly. Beside him, a fairer knight mounted on a dun horse gazed at him, and both men assessed the new bridge, the crowds turned out to greet them, and Master Wykes's contingent of councilmen and masters of the guilds arrayed on either side of the freshly built road.

The crowds stilled, watching. The troops rustled slightly, as further behind them the rest of the guard halted. Pennants lifted as faint breezes teased them up from their lances. No one spoke.

Finally, Gaucelm spoke to André, though he looked at Master Wykes. "Well, André. These people have built a bridge for us. Shall we cross it?"

André gave a shrug. He knew as well as Gaucelm what had been in the agreement between King Louis and the city of Avignon. But he was not interested in a confrontation. He was interested in moving the men across, making camp and then seeing what delights Avignon might have for knights like himself to sample for a price. "It is up to the king," he said.

"Just so," said Gaucelm, still meeting Master Wykes's gaze. Clever man. Clever enough to please the king? That remained to be seen. But for himself, he was not interested in fine details. Their goal was to cross the river.

"As long as the bridge is sound, I see no difficulty," Gaucelm finally said. "We will make camp for the night a mile from here, as agreed."

Master Wykes visibly relaxed. "We have merchants who will do business with you after you have settled in your camp. I will send them to the king's steward."

Gaucelm gave a curt nod and pressed his heels into his steed to lead the vanguard forward. At the river's edge, he got down to inspect the bridge himself, to see that it was sound. Satisfied, he remounted.

"Go and tell Louis about this," he said to André. "I will lead the vanguard to our camp."

"Very well," said André with his usual good humor. "Then I will look forward to a well-made camp and a well-deserved rest this evening."

André saluted and rode back while Gaucelm led the contingent across. Gaucelm only glanced up once and saw that more townspeople watched from the walls above them. There was a moment—but no, that could not be.

Allesandra was among the crowd of bystanders near the old stone bridge. But she was plainly dressed, a wimple and veil covering her hair and much of her face. It was not difficult to stand unnoticed beside Raymond, who was also disguised as a man of little means, and watch the soldiers approach.

Then she saw him. Gaucelm led the vanguard; there was no mistaking the colors of the surcoat covering his mail. And even though his face was partially hidden by his chin covering, she saw his face.

She nearly forgot herself and lifted her head to see him better, but then remembered their purpose was to spy, and she hid herself behind a merchant and his wife, whose shoulders she could peer over. But as Gaucelm began to exchange words with the mayor, her heart beat harder and the blood flowed more quickly in her veins.

She could not help her response and glanced quickly at Raymond, who would surely notice. So she whispered her recognition to him.

"That is the knight who ruled my lands under Simon de Montfort," she hissed in his ear.

"Ahhhh," he mouthed, and then returned his attention to studying the forces Gaucelm led.

When Gaucelm turned to look over the crowd, she ducked behind the merchant again. How desperately she wanted to let him know she was here. And yet how equally desperately she feared to.

Now he dismounted, and she could not help a surge of joy and relief. He looked strong. He moved with confidence. He was well. And then her heart contracted and she took a small breath to steady herself. It was wrong for a widow of her position to react like a silly young girl. She was infected with the love that her brother troubadours wrote of. And it was truly a sickness. A sickness and a curse.

She turned to speak again to Raymond. "I will slip into the town and up to the walls to better see them as they cross."

He nodded. "I, too, need to better assess the size of this great army."

They moved across the stone bridge, now blockaded from the

king's army, and took the stairs to find a place among the crowd lining the wall walk. The mood was tense. These people were proud; they wished to avoid confrontation. And yet there was also that air of excitement that always accompanied the unusual. But she was less aware of any of that than of her own conflicting feelings.

Below was a man who had watched her be interrogated for heresy, and yet a man with whom she shared an intimate secret. Their love had been a long time ago, and it was hopeless to nurse a flame she had tried without success to extinguish. And yet here she was, as he marched his guard across a newly constructed bridge.

Then Gaucelm glanced up once and she froze. It seemed as if he looked right at her. But of course the distance was great, and unless he knew to look for her, he could not possibly see her clearly. But her heart stopped, and somehow the certainty came to her that what was between them still lived.

"Oh, dear God," she murmured, and then looked quickly at those to either side. But Raymond could assume she was exclaiming over the fearsome army.

"Their ploy has worked," commented Raymond, standing just behind her right shoulder. "If the king follows, then Avignon is safe. They will camp a mile from here. We must wait and see for ourselves the number of their forces. It is a very large army indeed."

She turned to see the determination on his face and touched his arm. She had been daydreaming when their very lives were in the balance.

"Do not lose hope, my lord," she said.

King Louis rode toward Avignon, a glare on his otherwise fair countenance. There was no doubt as to who was king, for he rode with an escort that carried his pennants on long lances. The king's guard was arrayed in fine colors with the fleur-de-lis on their shields and on the horses' caparisons. He did not take kindly to the news that he was not to be allowed inside the bourgeois town.

"Who are these upstarts to tell the heir of Charlemagne where I may and may not go! If one town can bar its gates to us, then so can others. And if the army cannot enter the towns, then the whole expedition is useless."

"Your point is well taken, sire," said André, who had the unfortunate responsibility of relaying the news about the wooden bridge.

The papal legate Frosbier rode with the army to make sure ecclesiastical requirements were met in those places that submitted to the king. Now, at this mark of disrespect, he fueled Louis's stubbornness. "These Avignonese have not obeyed the pope in the past, Your Majesty. This bodes ill for our crusade. I advise you to assert your authority where it is already agreed that you shall pass freely."

"Indeed," barked the king in a louder voice. "Where are these burghers who will not admit the king?"

André stifled a weary sigh. These petty arguments were a waste of time to a man of adventure such as he. "They await you at the foot of the bridge, sire."

"The wooden bridge, you mean to say, not the stone bridge?"

"Yes, sire. At the wooden bridge."

King Louis rode forward, back straight, head erect. His glance stung all in his way. It could be said, André thought, that the air vibrated with his displeasure. Rather than await the results of the encounter, he rode forward again to find Gaucelm and tell him what was about to happen. The vanguard might cross the wooden bridge, but it would be a waste of time to proceed the agreed mile to pitch their camp. They might very well be pitching camp surrounding the walls of the town until they were let in.

As it turned out, the king ordered his tent erected at the place where the way across the stone bridge and into town was blocked. The Avignonese and the army alike watched as this was done and the king went within to await the arrival of the mayor and his council. When forced to seek audience with the king, Master

Wykes and his fellows lost whatever relief they had felt at the knight Gaucelm's taking the French vanguard across.

The burghers came. The king demanded. They negotiated. For the rest of that afternoon the matter was discussed. The burghers withdrew, discussed among themselves. The king listened to his advisors, which now included Gaucelm, who had returned to wait on the king.

"I do not want to fight at Avignon," said Louis. "But there is a principle involved." He repeated all his arguments. There seemed to be an impasse.

"The towns are where the resistance lies," Louis reasserted. "We must have a show of respect here or else all is lost."

At last it appeared that he had succeeded in persuading the burghers to admit him. Not the whole army, just his own royal party. But when they prepared to go forward at last to enter the town, the way was barred. Gaucelm and André rode back again with the news that the gates remained shut with no orders to open them.

By that time it was evening. Torches lit the scene. Louis ranted and paced in his tent. He clenched his fist and uttered his ultimatums to lieutenants and messengers awaiting his orders. In the corner stood the ever-present and influential Frosbier.

Finally, Louis walked to the stout table in the middle of his tent and brought his fist down on it. "I will not leave this camp until Avignon is taken. That is my final word."

"A siege, my lord?" said Gaucelm.

Louis leveled his blue eyes and looked straight into those of Gaucelm. "A siege."

A murmur passed through the tent, slowly, and then Louis issued orders, which were relayed by the lieutenants to the others. Gaucelm stifled a sigh and then went out with André to survey the scene. The army began the task of moving from where they had stopped to surround the strong walls.

André glanced at his friend with a shake of the head. "Direct assaults will be impossible. There is no weakness in those walls. The ground is hard; mining will be all that much more difficult."

"Indeed," commented Gaucelm. "So we wait. Our army is so strong they won't attempt sorties to run us off. We can patrol the Rhône as well as block land approaches, but I doubt we can cut them off from all supplies."

"True enough. And if they run short of supplies, so will we, with this many mouths to feed."

Gaucelm crossed his arms and stared at the flickering torches along the wall walk and lighting the towers, spaced at intervals. "This is indeed a curious way to begin such a crusade. Let us hope that something happens to change the situation."

André was more skeptical. "I cannot think of what that will be."

Into the night the army wagons rolled forward carrying lumber to construct siege towers. A few arrows were hurled at them when soldiers drew too near, but little damage was done. It was simply a matter of both sides settling down to outwait the other. Gaucelm was busy riding about the camp and issuing orders to the various corps. He heard the discontent spoken in low tones behind his back as he rode on.

But Louis followed in his wake, speaking to the men as he went, attempting to rally their pride and explain why they must subdue the stubborn bourgeoisie. It was a battle of wills all the way around.

André rode with Gaucelm, doing his duty, but gazing wistfully at the town. He was an urban man and always liked to sample the delights of new places. Bored with the camp followers, he sadly rued that they could not go inside and find a pleasant wine shop. When they rode back to their own tent, André said, "It is too bad that we cannot find our way in. Do you not think the king needs some spies? I've a keen desire to get in there, disguised as a bargeman. Do you not think we could better assess their strength and their stores if we made ourselves welcome in a tavern and found the company of some wenches who would talk?"

"You dream," was Gaucelm's reply. "You do not speak their language. They would spot you for what you are."

But André's imagination was on fire, as were his loins at the contemplation of some pretty, clean Avignonese women. While Gaucelm had been busy with negotiations, he had gazed into the crowd and had seen some pretty faces. Some had even returned his gaze openly. And he did not believe they would be so prejudiced that he was a Frenchman. These southern troubadours wasted time writing poetry about love to woo their women. André had always found women to be more responsive to direct means of expressing his feelings.

"Hmmm," he said, his mind already conjuring a plan. "I do not speak their language, it is true. But you do."

Seventeen

It took only a moment for André's proposal to take shape in Gaucelm's mind.

"I do not know that we would gain as much going as spies as if we went as envoys."

André stuck a length of reed into his mouth and chewed disconsolately on it. "The king is obstinate. You heard the negotiations. Neither he nor the burghers will give an inch."

"That is true. But perhaps that was because the confrontation was so public. Tempers were high. If both sides have a chance to think on this, they will see the unreasoning behind a lengthy siege. I have not given up hope that a compromise might be reached."

"What do you propose to do?"

Gaucelm glanced behind him at the king's tent, set far enough away so as to be in no danger from the missiles hurled from the city walls.

"Louis will not send us officially. I think, my friend, that we must do as you suggest and go unofficially."

André broke into a smile. "And once we are inside?"

"We will seek out the mayor, Master Wykes, and see if we can arrange a private talk with him."

"I like the idea, of course," said André. "But do you think it will really help?"

Gaucelm shrugged without enthusiasm. The lines in his face that he had worn since the beginning of this venture seemed permanently carved there.

"We must attempt to put sense into the king's head as well as into these Avignonese," he said. Then his mood lightened slightly as he glanced at André. "If it is adventure you want, it seems that the only way to have it will be to do as you suggest and enter the city disguised as bargemen bringing supplies to the beleaguered city."

André lifted curious brows. "Well, now, in that case, I believe I best set about finding us a barge and some clothes. Meet me at the western gate of our camp a quarter of a mile north of the bridge just after sundown."

Gaucelm clapped him on the shoulder. "I've no doubt of your resourcefulness. I will be there."

"There will have to be a distraction to get us past our own forces. Perhaps you can arrange a threat that will distract the men blockading the suburb that sprawls on the other side of the river. If we can get through, and get the attention of the citizens on the walls, they'll help us get in that way, for they'll need the supplies we will bring."

Gaucelm queried with arched brows, "And where will you get such supplies?"

"Leave that to me."

Gaucelm spent the next few hours seeing to the arrangements of the siege. But here and there when no one noticed, he strolled to the line of horses tied behind the baggage wagons at a position just where he and André would have to break through. He didn't think of it as sabotaging his own army; rather, he was taking matters into his own hands and intervening, because if he did not, thousands would eventually sicken and starve and time would be wasted.

Sundown found him in his tent where he disrobed down to the short, loose linen breeches, and his padded gambeson, a tunic worn beneath the mail hauberk. He instructed William to see to the tears in his hauberk and to oil and soap his saddle while he went to bathe in the river.

As the camp settled in for the evening, and the women who followed the camp slipped about preparing food and other comforts for their men, Gaucelm left for his rendezvous at river's edge. Carrying towels and a jar of soap, he appeared to be going to bathe. If one wondered why he also carried short bow and a quiver of arrows, it might be supposed that he took weapons to protect himself from any possible ambush.

He passed through the western opening to the river between the earthworks the men had thrown up and continued upriver for a quarter of a mile. When he clambered down the bank and divested himself of the gambeson, he did indeed walk into the water.

Out of the corner of his eye, he saw a low-floating barge gliding in his direction. Its barrels were stacked high, and it wasn't until it glided up to where he stood that the cloaked bargeman could be seen pushing the barge along with his long pole. As soon as André revealed himself, Gaucelm grinned.

"I won't ask how you came by this vessel and its contents," he said. He tossed in his quiver and bow and then hoisted himself aboard. André nodded toward a bundle, which turned out to be tunic and cloak for disguise.

"It wasn't difficult to persuade the owner to hire me to take his goods inside when I said I had a way to get past the French lines."

Gaucelm gave a knowing chuckle as he donned the merchant's attire that would make them fit in inside the town. What they attempted was quite serious, and his own skills as informer and negotiator just might possibly help lift this siege before time and money were wasted, to say nothing of lives. But he could not help but respond to André's infectious sense of adventure.

He took up a pole and helped steer the barge, which they slowed as soon as they approached the outer limits of the camp. The earthworks stopped just where some of the extra horses were tied up. Now it was time for Gaucelm's diversion.

He strung the bow and aimed at the tree trunk around which wound the rope to which the horses were tied. Little did any of the grooms know that Gaucelm had loosened the halters. The first arrow whacked into the tree, upsetting the horses and causing some of them to rear. The rope came undone, and the animals were loose in the camp. Before the soldiers could identify what had frightened the animals, the barge slipped onward.

The next group of soldiers came down to the bank and Gaucelm stood up, calling out in French and gesturing behind them. "Ambush!" he cried, and sent soldiers running up the bank. Then, with their attention diverted, he aimed again, this time to dislodge a lantern hanging from the front of a wagon. Cries went up as the arrow shaft shattered the lantern and spread fire across the ground.

The return fire landed harmlessly in the water behind the barge, which moved more swiftly now as soldiers ran to the water's edge but turned northward to fend off the attackers they thought came from that direction. André poled swiftly as Gaucelm strung another arrow to fend off any who saw through his trickery and came after them. But by the time the confusion turned in their direction, they were under the bridge and within range of the protection offered by the town militia from their ramparts.

"Do not shoot!" Gaucelm called upward in Provençal. "We are merchants from Orange with supplies."

Their ploy worked, and the militia on the ramparts gave covering fire to the French soldiers gathered on the bridge. The barge came alongside the quay and then slid past the curve to where a gate opened to allow them entrance to the stone-paved dock. The gate closed again, and Gaucelm stepped out and tied the barge to iron rings, while a notary came forward, wax tablet in hand, surprised to see a barge of goods that had slipped past the soldiers. But the man was nevertheless prepared to make an accounting of the goods and collect their tax.

"These goods will serve us well if they are staples to be consumed," said the notary. He was dressed in burnished red tunic with loose sleeves that hung to his thighs. On his head was a purple turban with the end hanging down one side.

"Tell him the barrels contain wine from Vienne," said André in French.

Gaucelm explained and added, "My friend here persuaded the merchant to let us make the run past the soldiers. We are from the French army ourselves, but thought it worth the risk to enter the town and seek audience with your mayor."

The notary stared at them aghast. He glanced from the wine casks back to them. "Are you spies?"

Gaucelm gave him a wry look. "We could be. But since we've made no attempt to slip in unnoticed, no. Consider us unofficial emissaries devoted to preventing the waste of lives and resources."

The notary gazed a little wistfully at the wine. "Is that still for sale?"

"By all means," assured Gaucelm. "My friend André Peloquin was commissioned by the owner of this barge to take full payment."

"Then I'll send word to the mayor that two Frenchmen wish to speak to him. What are your ranks?"

"We are both knights in the service of the king. I am Sir Gaucelm Deluc. Lately lieutenant to Simon de Montfort," he added, thinking to frighten the notary enough to make him realize just who he was dealing with.

The notary scurried off to send word and then returned to offer one of his servants to escort them to the mayor's house. They placed the barge in the care of the notary, though André insisted that they might be cheated if they did not wait for a receipt. The casks accounted for to his satisfaction and the money paid, he then assented to accompanying Gaucelm through the streets of Avignon to do what they had come for.

On their walk, they took notice of the prosperity of the place. Butchers, bakers, and vendors of all kinds seemed well stocked. And from the lack of panic as the townspeople went about moving siege machines in place and stacking up missiles, they were not afraid of defending themselves. The town would not fall easily.

Master Wykes's house was a four-story stone house with steeply pitched shingled roof. They entered the ground floor anteroom, where an open door to the side led to the counting room. The notary's servant went up to say who was calling, and in a moment he returned and sent them up.

Gaucelm and André climbed the steep flight of stairs and came out into the hall. A plump, matronly woman in rich clothing came forward.

"Please come in," she said. "My husband will be here directly. May I get you refreshments while you wait?"

They accepted wine and sat down in sturdy wooden armchairs before the fire. From another door leading to a kitchen on the other side of the chimney came tantalizing smells. The mayor's wife informed them that a meal was being prepared and they were invited to join in.

"What do you think we can accomplish here?" mused André, happier now that he had been given good-tasting wine for his trouble.

Gaucelm shrugged and sipped his wine more slowly. "One never knows, but it is worth a try. This siege will eat up months with both sides so obviously prepared for it."

There were steps on the stairs, and then Master Wykes entered the hall and crossed to them.

"Ahh," he said. "My wife told me I had important visitors and I recognize your faces from this morning. Yet you are not dressed as knights of the king's army now. I am curious as to what brings you here."

He accepted a goblet of wine which his silent wife had brought him and then gestured for her to leave the ewer within their reach as she retired. Then he seated himself with his two unexpected guests and talked softly so that any servants who might happen to be near would not overhear.

"I am surprised to see two French knights walk so boldly into my house. What makes you think I will not summon the militia and keep you hostages?"

"Do not think that we did not come here armed," said Gaucelm, though it was not a threat. "We would not make it easy for your militia to take us hostage. But in any case, we took you to be a man of honor. We are here because we wish to put off a siege in which both sides will suffer. Our lives are not worth so much to Louis that he would humble himself and bow to your wishes merely to save our skins. He has other good knights in his army, in fact, a good number of them. No, we took the risk because we perceived you to be a man of reason."

The serious burgher leaned back in his chair and shook his shaggy head with an expression of complete irony.

"I find my home to be the refuge not only of yourselves but of another august negotiating party here to gain information and offer advice. Is it not strange?"

Gaucelm's skin prickled and he repeated what Master Wykes had said for André's benefit. Then he inquired as to who the other party was.

Their host considered for a moment and then said, "I have offered my protection and promised I would not reveal their presence. I'm afraid I will have to let them decide whether they wish to make their presence known and so converse with you."

Gaucelm watched the mayor carefully. "I take it you have been visited by nobility of the South who have a vested interest in the outcome of this siege."

Wykes lifted a hand in a shrug, but did not comment further. Gaucelm was quick to understand the implications.

"Might not these noblemen be here to influence you against the king?"

There was a trace of wry humor in the corners of the stout

burgher's mouth that Gaucelm had difficulty interpreting. He had the distinct feeling that he was at a disadvantage.

"Perhaps," said Gaucelm, "it would be best for all of us to meet together to see what can be done. Ofttimes enemies have better luck negotiating when it is done by men of middle rank rather than kings and counts who are too stubborn to see sense."

"I do not disagree with you, sir. And for myself, I am glad to listen. But I shall have to consult my guests, who have named themselves honorary advisors."

Gaucelm frowned, irritated that he had been beaten here by someone from the opposing side. He would not leave, however, without making his point.

"It does Avignon little good to hold out against the king. Agreements were reached to let him pass. His argument is not with you."

"True," said Master Wykes. "But he has no authority here. Avignon pays homage to the Holy Roman Empire."

"I would warn you that jurisdictions are often uncertain. Would it not be wise to do as Louis asks and make sure he bears you no grudge? If you open your gates now, I'm sure it will quell his anger and he will do little more than demand a show of apology and perhaps some slight fines. But if you wait it out, you will be sorry. He is determined."

Wykes seemed to listen attentively, but all he would say was, "It is not my decision alone. I will call the council together, though it is late. We will go to the guildhall and you can present your case. I guarantee you will have a fair hearing."

"And will your southern friends join us?"

Master Wykes rose, indicating the interview was ended for the present. "That depends on their wishes. Come. My wife is ready to oversee supper. Sup with us, you will need your strength."

While the trestle tables were being laid and platters and trenchers brought in, Gaucelm quickly translated what had transpired for André's sake. Then the burgher's solemn children joined them and they all took their places. Gaucelm did not miss the trays that were carried from the kitchen up the wide staircase to a third-floor landing. He narrowed his eyes. The mysterious noblemen from the South must be residing in upper rooms and were not ready to make their presence known.

"Who do you think would have traveled this far to spy on the king's army?" Gaucelm said in a low voice to André, who was gnawing on a turkey drumstick.

After wiping his chin with the tablecloth, André turned his mind to the matter. "Someone who considered it very important to know just what kind of threat we pose, no?"

"And many of the southern towns have already surrendered. Many of the great lords are dead."

André's drumstick stopped midair. "I see where you are headed. Only Toulouse now holds out. Whoever is here must be sent from the count of Toulouse."

"The old count is too ill to fight or travel, but there remains the son, who will inherit the title."

"Surely he would not make such a journey himself when he could send informers?"

"Perhaps." Gaucelm ate silently and only took enough wine to clear his palate but not to muddle his thinking. Something niggled at him, and he found himself staring at the upper landing as the servants brought down empty dishes.

After the dishes were cleared and the table taken down, the men donned cloaks and Master Wykes led them through the streets to the guildhall. Gaucelm did not waste the walk, but took a mental accounting of what he saw. As he expected, he found no weakness. An even greater reason to find a way for Avignon and the king to compromise.

In the silversmith's lane, they came to a tall building of post-and-beam construction, rising straight between its older neighbors, which leaned slightly. As they climbed the stairs to the hall, they could hear the din of voices, which ceased one by one as the newcomers' boots sounded on the stairs. They came out in a large room, with fire crackling in an enormous hearth at one end of the room. The men stood in groups around a long table as Master Wykes brought the two unofficial emissaries forward.

"Fellow councilmen," he began, "I have here two knights from the French king who claim they have sneaked into our city more to do a favor for ourselves than to help the king. They fully realize we could keep them hostage and faced that risk. For that reason, I agreed that we would give them a fair hearing."

"Perhaps if we don't like what they have to say we can still keep them as hostages," suggested one of the councilmen.

"We can do that," agreed Master Wykes. "I think that how honorably we behave toward them will depend on how honorably they behave toward us."

The sour little man who was so anxious to make prisoners of them pinned his mouth shut.

"It seems that we have been chosen as arbiters of this unfortunate war," Master Wykes went on. "Earlier today two other respected guests appeared here and I gave them sanctuary. They have agreed to meet these two French knights and offer their views to this assembly as well."

The mayor's provost now came forward, a thin elder with an aristocratic bearing. His fur-lined surcoat was of the finest wool. "If you please, Mister Mayor, introduce us first to these two French knights. What are their credentials?"

Gaucelm and André introduced themselves, though they could see that with all their impeccable northern lineage, the burghers' polite nods did not hide their own pride at being self-made men in trade.

"And who are the other nobles who come from the South?" the provost asked.

Master Wykes's young servant, who had obviously been given prior instructions, now marched to a door that led off the hall and opened it. Two cloaked figures entered the room.

Gaucelm was ready for who he thought it was. And indeed the alert young man with the proud bearing resembled his father, the count of Toulouse, with whom Gaucelm had once parleyed. But he barely heard Master Wykes announce that young Raymond of Toulouse had arrived among them a few days ago, for his usually controlled face lost its pose of neutrality as he stared, stunned beyond belief at the woman who revealed herself from behind Raymond's shoulder.

Allesandra stepped into the room and removed her cloak. She was garbed in a tasteful dark-blue gown with a surcoat of the same color. Her hair was covered by an ivory-colored veil, and a linen wimple covered her throat. But as modestly as she was dressed, her face portrayed her nobility in the lift of her chin and the smoothness of her brow. A thousand thoughts flew through Gaucelm's mind as he stared at her, and he could see at once that she was prepared for this meeting. Her unruffled bearing told him she had known that he was here.

Allesandra slowly lifted her eyes from the floor to meet Gaucelm's intense gaze. He looked astonished. She had braced herself for this moment, but now that they were forced to meet in so public a manner, she struggled to control the thumping behind her ribs. She was aware that the mayor was introducing them now to the other councilmen and to the unexpected emissaries from the North. But for her there was no one else in the room.

Then Raymond was speaking and she re-collected herself. She felt the high color on her cheeks but that would be excused by the tense situation confronting them. She had to look away from Gaucelm, though she felt his eyes boring into her.

The two parties sat down on benches with Master Wykes at the head of the table. "If there is anything to be said here that has not already been said, let us get on with this. I am not pleased that our town has been besieged. Neither do we wish to allow an army to march through our streets. Can a compromise be reached?"

After a look at Allesandra that she interpreted as one of anger, Gaucelm began to speak. Since he had arrived at Master Wykes's house she had listened to his conversation through her partially opened door. She had seen him dine and had watched him converse with his friend, who seemed to regard her now with puzzlement. But it still took all of her fortitude to face him across a table in the midst of strangers. She had wanted to see him again, but not this way. She tried to calm her racing thoughts, for she was no fool. Their situation was dire. Perhaps the seriousness of it only fueled her desire to speak to Gaucelm alone. But she stiffened her spine and paid attention.

"The king wishes to make use of your great stone bridge, which leads from the heart of your city to the other side of the Rhône. He insists on the fulfillment of that promise. He has not said so, but perhaps if you allow only the king's guard to do this, it will satisfy him. The vanguard of the army has already marched across the wooden bridge. I cannot promise it, but perhaps we can persuade him this is a likely solution."

The councilmen began to murmur among themselves and voice various arguments. Beside her, Raymond sat stiffly, a symbol of why the king was marching south. He said nothing, and Allesandra was as conscious of the southerners' desperate plight as she was of the determination on the face of the man across from her.

She stole glances when she could, and each time, Gaucelm looked at her as well. The dark eyes seemed at first accusatory, then questioning. On the next glance she thought she saw regret. She was trembling now and gripped the edge of the table with one hand to hold herself steady. She did not trust herself to speak. Finally, Raymond had his say.

"Gentlemen. You all know that this crusade is abhorrent to me. As a sister city, Avignon has always shown sympathy for Toulouse. I would beg that you do not abandon us now. Do not let the king draw blinders over your eyes. He marches south to quell not only the eastern lands of the Languedoc, many of which are already cowed, but he will then turn westward and assault us once again."

"He already knows your strength, my lord," observed the provost. "Has not Toulouse already thrown his armies off?"

"We have. All the more reason for you to stand firm. The cities form the core of Languedoc resistance. If he can enter your gates, then so will he be able to enter all the others. For your own sakes as well as ours, I beg you, stand firm."

They argued then about Avignon's position outside Louis's domain, but Allesandra's eyes were drawn to Gaucelm again, whose look she now read as his emotions roiled beneath his diplomacy.

And for all she had been traitorously pleased to see him, the old bitterness surfaced as she gave half her mind to what the council was saying. She had spent more than a year telling herself she had forgotten the sudden passion that they had shared when thrown together in her castle. Her castle was back in her hands now, her lands prospering, her people enjoying the right to live their own lives. There was no way to let Gaucelm Deluc back into her life that would not change all that. There was still nothing for them, nor could there ever be. Perhaps that was why, when they turned to speak to each other across the negotiating table in such formal tones, they looked at one another with so much sadness and longing.

But even with the table between them, she felt his eyes graze her face. Felt the blood racing through her veins, felt her mouth go dry, so that she was forced to wet her lips with the wine a servant had set before them.

As she swallowed, the liquid moistened her throat, but the sweet taste on her lips only reminded her of his lips on hers. As she struggled to take jagged breaths, she felt as if at any moment, he would reach slowly across the table to touch her fingers. Of course he would never do that in public, but her mind began to run away with the need she felt for him. Desire flooded her body, and she tried frantically to wish it away.

But with every gesture Gaucelm made with his powerful shoulders, his muscular arms, he sent only one message to her across the distance that separated them. She remembered him as a man who took what he wanted. And she gleaned from the way he studied her without the others knowing, that in spite of being her enemy, he had to know what it would be like to lie with her again.

Eighteen

The voices around her were raised, as suddenly all the councilmen in the room decided to express an opinion. The decorum of negotiation was lost as the hotheaded Avignonese put their pride ahead of all else.

Wealthy burghers despised powerful nobles and kings. The guilds and merchants' communes had grown up out of a need to defend themselves against both secular and ecclesiastical lords. Their fathers and grandfathers had settled in the towns in order to escape feudal duties. Town dwellers had won freedom from the feudal system in exchange from paying annual taxes. No wonder that the bitterness remained.

After translating for André, who did not understand Provençal, Gaucelm was drawn into the argument, still pleading for compromise. But fueled by Raymond's passion, the Avignonese did not give way.

Allesandra watched with dread as Gaucelm lost patience and leapt to his feet. Raymond rose as well, urging the burghers to take the side of the southern towns of Languedoc and stand firm.

Allesandra remained in her seat until to do so would have allowed her to be crushed in the excitement. She felt the swell of guilt that she had done nothing to help Raymond.

However, it appeared he needed little help. At last Master Wykes succeeded in restoring order and then addressed the French contingent with a frown.

"My lords. Go tell King Louis that we will not bow. We feel that if we open our gates to the king and that ecclesiastic who rides with him, it will be tantamount to acknowledging king and pope as our rulers. We have done what we could to allow him to pass, but we cannot bend to royal wishes. Such is not acceptable to us."

The mayor crossed his arms across his chest and set his lips in a firm line. The council erupted again. An angry merchant shook his fist. "Let us keep these two as hostages until the king passes by. That will guarantee our success."

"Here, here," said another.

Then the room was a din as the council insisted on keeping hostages while Raymond argued loudly that if they held hostages to force the king around the town it would do him no good. "That brings the king closer to Toulouse," he shouted, but he was drowned out.

"Quiet, quiet," said Master Wykes, pounding his fist on the table until the voices subsided.

"I gave these men my word that they would be released from our town. I do not go back on my word. Keeping them here would only anger the king further. I do not want to start a war, only to show our strength. The Frenchmen go to tell the king what we have said."

Allesandra was pushed sideways in the crowd. She caught Gaucelm's eye and saw the angry flicker there. She set her jaw. Desires or no, she had no choice. She could do nothing to keep the hated French army from marching toward their lands. A sudden wrenching tore through her heart, and she blinked back moistness. It was a fantasy to think that he wanted to see her again. He had his duty as well as she.

And then she retreated the way that Raymond had cleared a path for her. They went down the stairs and into the street. Master Wykes's servant waited to light their way home with his lantern.

"Come," said Raymond. "Let us go. Now that the French army will know of my presence here, we are not as safe as these Avignonese might think we are. If two French knights can slip into a fortified town and are allowed out again, what is to stop them from assassinating us in our beds? No, I think we have accomplished what we must here. The town will stand. Louis will remain. But as soon as he learns I am here, he will make other offers."

He said no more, knowing that the servant who led the way would repeat all this to his master. But when they reached the house and climbed the stairs to their rooms, Raymond stepped into Allesandra's chamber and shut the door.

"We must depart from here. I have a feeling that our host will be just as glad to see us gone. Then he can tell the king that we have slipped away. He may be keeping his word now. But in weeks to come, he will be sorely tempted to hand us over to the French in return for relief for his town."

"You are right," she said. "We do no good by staying here. Our people need us."

She thought of the dark eyes of the enemy that she would see no more and stifled the feeling of injustice that she carried in her heart. She turned her mind to their plans.

Master Wykes soon joined them and agreed that their presence was now dangerous.

"Is there a way that you can get us past the soldiers?" asked Raymond. "Or are we trapped here?"

His face was set as if he were prepared to face the entire French army by himself and fight his way through. Allesandra knew such a sortie would be foolish, but it was part of the brashness that endeared him to the citizens of Toulouse.

"There is a way, if you will consent to a disguise that might in some circumstances be thought abhorrent."

"What is that?"

"We can get you as far as the wooden bridge in darkness. Disguised as lepers, if you are not afraid, you can face the French camp. They will think we set you out of the town walls on purpose, as a threat."

Allesandra glanced at Raymond, who with a determined face considered the plan. She looked back at Master Wykes. "True, they would draw back in fear when they first saw us," she said. "But they could shoot us with their arrows from a distance."

"No," said Raymond, understanding the ploy. "None among them would even touch our dead bodies for fear of the contagion. They could not kill lepers and leave the diseased carcasses to infect their entire camp. Instead, they will clear a path for us and send us through as fast as we may go, shouting abuses at us, no doubt."

Then his eyes focused squarely on her. "But I would not force you into such a dangerous mission, my lady. Let me go alone. You can remain here under the protection of the town. It is my skin they want, not yours."

She clenched her hands together. "It would be pointless to stay here where I can do no good."

Raymond permitted himself a moment of wry humor. "You are the warrior who killed Simon de Montfort. Perhaps Avignon would like your services in that capacity again. Who knows? This time you might succeed in hitting the king."

And remain behind walls where she would be constantly reminded of the man she could not have who fought on the other side.

"No," she said. "I come with you, my lord. I have duties in my household and my people will need us should this army turn that way."

Raymond set his chin. "Very well. Get us the disguises. We will go tonight as lepers."

Coarse gowns were found for them, and Master Wykes's wife set about adding holes and singeing edges to make it look as if they'd lived in the clothing for some months. In their rooms, both Raymond and Allesandra were stripped to their linen undergarments. Both carried daggers tied to their girdles. Then they were given the tin dishes with metal clappers that rattled a warning to anyone who came near that the two making the sound were carriers of the dread disease.

With cloth to cover their faces, cut with eye, nose, and mouth holes, it could not be seen that their faces were actually whole. Mistress Wykes cleverly cut a different finger off each glove and sewed the material together where the joint would be. By tucking their fingers under, the gloves would fit well enough to make it look as if their extremities had rotted and fallen off. Old leather shoes and leggings would cover legs and feet. After they were dressed, they practiced a halting limp and mumbling speech. The mayor passed judgment on their performance, and after reassurance from his two daring guests, he led them out again and through the streets to a gate that would let them onto the quay.

He held out his hand to them both. "I wish you good luck. We Avignonese do not care much for the nobility, but you have shown great courage in coming here. And I daresay your exit will be a memorable one. We will send up prayers for your safety. Our archers are ready on the ramparts should any trouble befall you immediately you cross the bridge. But once you are out of their range, you will be on your own."

He gave them time to reconsider, but Allesandra pressed his hand, speaking in a muffled tone through her face mask. "Thank you, sir. You have been most kind."

Then Raymond waited for a sign from her that she was ready. Trembling, she nodded once.

The door opened, and the moist breeze from the river bathed them. They slipped through in the shadows and stood beside the solid stone wall as the door shut again and locked behind them.

She felt a tremor as they took their first step. Armed only with short daggers, they were now faced by an army of tens of thousands encamped on the other side of the wooden bridge that Louis refused to use. Their way lay to the south, and thus it was the vanguard they would pass through. The rest of the army still surrounded the town on the north and east on this side of the river.

Her heart rattled, and she felt a sheen of fear dampen brow and palms, but she lifted the dish and began rattling the clapper as she and Raymond started to limp across the bridge. When they reached the middle of the arched structure and could be seen on the other side, Raymond raised his voice and whined out, "Unclean, unclean." Then he rattled his clapper louder. She took a lopsided step and echoed his words in a tinny voice.

Now the sleepy guards on the other side were aroused. They mumbled among themselves and one came forward. "What's this?" he asked. "Lepers?"

There followed curses that indicated their plan was working. The French soldiers thought that the townsmen set the lepers out on purpose, to infect their camp.

"Get back!" the guard shouted. "Those bastards have sent their lepers here. Make a path to send them through as quickly as they can go."

More shouts went up, muffling the cries of the two posing as lepers. Then came the threat they had expected. "Let's kill them" came an angry voice.

Allesandra's heart stopped, and her throat went dry. But she continued on, cowering as anyone would when threatened with death. But Raymond stumbled forward, pretending to lose his balance and fall toward a gathering of soldiers. They hastily sprang out of the way. She saw that he was careful not to fall to the ground, lest his healthy flesh be revealed. She reached out to help steady him as they stood for a moment as if awaiting their fate.

She rattled her dish to cover the sound of her pulse pounding in her ears. At any moment someone might see through their ruse and take the risk of uncovering them.

But the fear of contagion was too great. A scoffing voice replied to the threatening one, "And who would bury them? You can catch leprosy off the dead as well as the living, you fool. Unless you want the sickness, stand clear."

Seizing their chance, Raymond led her slowly forward. How difficult it was not to break into a run and flee down the dark path that opened up before them, as in the distance the shout was carried forward, "Lepers, let them pass."

And so they stumbled slowly, clapping their dishes and calling out in a whine their warning, "Unclean, unclean."

It took a great effort to maintain the gait and the whining voice. And when she bumped into Raymond, she feared that one of them might fall accidentally. But neither must their movements appear too quick and give them away.

They were nearly to the end of the camp when heavy boots came tromping behind them. Her breath stopped as she thought surely the captain of the guard had seen through their ruse and now came after them. She glanced out of the mask to see who was about to capture them. Then in great agitation she saw that it was none other than Gaucelm bearing down on them from the other end of the camp.

They'd almost reached the end. Beyond a line of torches planted in low earthworks was the dark and open plain. Out there, robbers, wild boars, and any number of expected dangers awaited them. But that was preferable to being taken prisoner, stripped of their disguises and then executed, their heads carried on a pike to dissuade their own people from resisting the French king.

"Where did these people come from?" called Gaucelm to the guard who had followed him.

Allesandra felt sure all was lost. She and Raymond continued to mince forward, but stopped calling their warnings as they listened for what Gaucelm would say. She sent up a silent prayer and avoided looking at his face. Surely if anyone would guess their plot, it would be he. He knew they'd been in the town. He knew the townspeople would want to be rid of them. Would he take the next leap of thought and figure out that this was only a disguise?

"They came from the town, sir," the guard was explaining. "No doubt set out to infect our camp with their disease."

She hunched over, giving a pitiful picture indeed. Raymond continued to hobble in the direction of the earthworks and rattled his dish threateningly. For a moment it seemed to be the only sound nearby. Other night sounds, the rustles from within tents, the soft clop of a horse's hoof in the distance, the wind coming from the river, all seemed to fade into the background.

Gaucelm was near enough that she imagined she could hear him breathing. She could feel his eyes penetrating the darkness and knew him to be considering. She only risked glimpsing his feet and the hem of his gown, for he still wore his own disguise, which he had used to get into the town. She dared not raise her eyes for fear he would recognize her even thus dressed.

Then from the distance came another sound. She looked up when she heard it and could not help but see Gaucelm turn his head. He had heard it, too. He turned to stare beyond the torches at the darkened plain.

Allesandra felt a prickling sensation at the back of her neck. There was something out there. What could be moving across the plain in the dark?

A great shout ripped the night, and suddenly an army rushed toward them on foot. A line of archers scrambled up the earthen embankment built by the camp that day. And as they let fly with their arrows into the surprised French camp, lances were thrown by the second line of men-at-arms. A knight on horseback led a charge through the ranks of foot soldiers, who were spaced to allow the horsemen through. Then all was a mêlée of confusion as French soldiers grabbed whatever weapons were to hand. Some of the common soldiers still wore their quilted vests or leather coverings, but many had already shed even those.

The carnage was immediate, and Allesandra froze in horror. She watched Gaucelm draw his sword and defend himself from a knight on horseback. She stopped breathing as the knight thrust toward Gaucelm, who sidestepped and brought his sword down hard to clash with the other knight. Men fought all around her and when she finally turned around, she'd lost sight of Raymond.

She scanned the tangle of fighting men, afraid that he'd been wounded and was being trampled at this moment under the hooves of a horse, or lay with an arrow in his chest. Then a horse moved from in front of her and she saw him some yards off. He had seized a weapon, his face mask was cast aside, and he was thrusting and slashing at the French. All pretense of being a leper was thrown off.

She picked up the hem of her own gown and tried to flee out of the way. It was all she could do to stay out of the way of the blows being delivered all around her. Great thuds and cries filled her ears, and blood ran on the arms of soldiers and splashed on the horses' caparisons, some of which she now recognized as being from Toulouse. She'd been at the site of sieges before, but the horrific din of battle was greater by ten times here on the ground amidst the fight.

Dust flew up to sting her eyes, and in wiping them to try better to see, her face mask came away. She never really knew where she dropped it. Still, her garment must have marked her as a civilian, so no soldier from either side attacked her directly. She was only in danger of flying weapons from every direction, rearing hooves, and those who flung themselves to the ground with a cry.

She scrambled between them toward the embankment, thinking to take refuge there, and retrieved her dagger in case of need. She glanced again to see Raymond holding his ground. His gown was ripped, his hood tossed back, but he slashed and wounded all the Frenchmen who came his way.

Then she found a spot on the rise of embankment just above two fallen southern men-at-arms. Seeing from the stare of their open eyes that they were dead, there was nothing she could do to help them. Her heart in her throat, she looked anxiously at the spot where she'd last seen Gaucelm. He was not hard to find. Having picked up a shield from a fallen soldier, he now cut a wide swath all around him with his ringing, merciless sword.

Her mind stopped working; the rage of battle was too great for anything but trying to survive. Yet she could not leave for fear that something awful would happen either to her overlord Raymond, or to her beloved enemy, Gaucelm Deluc.

As more of the fighting came her way, she clawed farther up the earthworks until she knelt near the top. Some of the southern knights had been unhorsed now and fought on foot. One such suddenly spotted Gaucelm, and with a great growl, charged through the rest on foot to send his sword straight at Gaucelm's throat. But Gaucelm saw him and quickly parried the thrust.

Now the two strong knights engaged in their own battle, metal clashing. Then, gripping each other, they tangled and fell to the ground. Allesandra held her breath as with a grunt, Gaucelm pushed his attacker aside and was first to his knees. But the southern knight brought his sword upward, slicing at Gaucelm's thigh. The attacking knight rolled and then got to his feet again to rush at Gaucelm once more.

Without thinking, Allesandra held her dagger ready, thinking she might throw it at the attacking knight if he were near enough and Gaucelm's life was threatened. Then Gaucelm swung his blade in an arc, the weight of the blow causing the knight to drop his sword. The knight grunted and stumbled forward, but drew a dagger from his belt. He made a lunge, the dagger aimed at Gaucelm's side. But with a blow to the side of the head, Gaucelm knocked the man backward to sprawl senseless on the ground at Allesandra's feet.

Gaucelm drew breath and stood up, his sword at the ready to look behind him for the next attacker. But all around him were engaged in their own battles. He made a full circle to assess the ground around him and then looked down again at the southern lord he had knocked aside, in case the man was about to regain his senses. Finally, inevitably, Gaucelm lifted his eyes and saw her.

Her hair flowed loosely down her back, dirt and blood were splattered on her hem, a fierce gaze on her stunned face, and the dagger ready to stab any man who came near to take advantage.

The dagger made him pause halfway up the slope, and when she saw his glance, she lowered it. Their eyes met again, while behind them the heated battle still raged. Then he was up the slope, reaching for her other hand, and pulling her to her feet.

He said not a word as he sheathed his sword, then led her down the other side of the embankment and pulled her down to huddle low in the grass and brush, protected from the dangers beyond.

"You must get away from here," he said fiercely.

She reached for his face. "Are you all right?"

He grasped her hand, his eyes drinking her in. Then he kissed her palm hastily. She saw the pain in his eyes. Then he was on his feet and strode toward the opening in the embankment back toward the battle. For a moment, she thought he planned to leave her there, and she followed for a few steps to see. Then she saw him grab at the bridle of a frightened horse that had dashed this way. Its rider was somewhere in the mêlée beyond.

He got control of the rearing beast and then brought it her way. As the wild-eyed animal stretched its neck back toward where it had lost its rider, Gaucelm said to Allesandra sternly, "I must get you to safety."

He knelt and indicated that she should use his knee to climb into the stirrup and then into the saddle. Her leper robe was not quite as full as the gowns she normally wore for riding, but her leggings protected her skin from scraping on the leather skirt of the saddle. Once mounted, she extracted her feet from the stirrups, so that he could mount behind.

Still holding the reins, he pulled himself up behind her and then turned the horse away from the battle. Once away from the fighting, the horse did not seem to mind taking them where they wanted to go. There was enough moon now to see the ground, but they could not risk riding very fast. They struck out across the plain, and then turned south when they came to a cart track.

Allesandra did little but hang on and catch her breath. Hugging her with his arms and guiding the horse with the reins, Gaucelm breathed heavily from his own exertion. He said nothing as he concentrated on guiding the horse safely.

When they came to another crossroads, Gaucelm turned east again. He finally spoke. "We will be safer this way in the lands of the empire."

She understood what he meant. If they were discovered together in any of the counties of Languedoc, it would be assumed that he had abducted her, and he would be taken prisoner. And if discovered in French territory, what was to keep Gaucelm from making her identity known and holding her for ransom?

She said nothing, but squeezed the sides of the horse with her thighs to keep balance. She needn't have worried, for as they jostled along, she was secured by his strong arms around her. Her back was against the damp cloth of his merchant's disguise.

As they got farther from the scene of battle and regained their breath, she became more aware of their closeness. His head rested against her ear and she tentatively couched herself against him. He pressed his arms around her and better fit her against him. She closed her eyes, amazed at this twist of fate.

Where they were going she did not care, though silently she wondered about Raymond's fate. She felt a pang of guilt at abandoning him. But he had seemed to be holding his own. And when Gaucelm had swept her away from danger, all her instincts were to go with him.

She fought to still the ever-present conflict that came to her every time she was with Gaucelm. Duty and passion battled within her with as much tempestuousness as the clash of enemies behind them. But as Gaucelm held her closer and guided the horse along the road in the moonlight, there seemed little to do but accept him as her rescuer.

He did not seem satisfied to stop until they had traveled for quite some time. An hour or more had passed and she jerked awake, realizing that she must have dozed against his shoulder. They still traveled carefully, and now all sounds of battle were left behind. She gave a little shiver, for the night air chilled her, and she stared into the darkness where only dim shapes were visible from the road. Brigands and highwaymen might stalk this road, and they had only Gaucelm's sword and her dagger to protect them.

The horse pulled his head forward as if he smelled water, and soon after, she herself caught a moist breeze wafting toward them. Then she heard the rushing of water along a bank and strained to look ahead for river or stream.

The sky to their right seemed to lighten a tinge, and she gave a gasp as she made out a monumental shape that traversed the river they had come to. Great arches stretched from one hilly bank to another, rising grandly in two tall stories, with a smaller set of arches on the top row. It was a Roman aqueduct, the heavy limestone blocks forming a channel across the arches where water had once flowed.

Aqueducts were a familiar sight in these lands, but this one was especially well preserved. They paused near the riverbank and then Gaucelm judged it safe to dismount. He helped her down, then led the horse to drink. After tying the reins to a bush, he turned back to her.

She felt vulnerable standing there in such a disheveled state in the first hint of morning. She ought to feel victorious that she'd drawn him away from battle, thus depriving the French of his abilities. But she knew as well that she was as much his captive as he was hers.

He strode toward her now, and she trembled, not knowing whether to expect anger or pity. He stopped a little ways from her and gazed at her in the shadows, saying nothing.

She could not find her voice for a long time. But in those moments she took in his features. Stronger, more mature, if that were possible. And she was filled with the need to touch his face. She shook her head helplessly and moved toward him just as he reached for her hand.

"Oh, Gaucelm," she breathed. "I never thought to see you again."

"Nor I you, madam," he said. And then he drew her to him and leaned down to kiss her lips gently. He did not crush her against him, but touched her face with his fingers.

Her hands went to his shoulders, and she knew a great need that would not be held back. His face was inches from hers, and he parted his lips to kiss her again. This time his tongue lashed at hers more hungrily, and a runaway desire shook them both with their need.

Nineteen

"We must find shelter," he said when he lifted his head again.

Allesandra was speechless, but struggled to gain control over her emotions as Gaucelm went to retrieve the horse. She saw the sense in his advice. Here, they were in the open and near the river. Until they decided what to do, it would be best to avoid meeting anyone. She looked about at the hilly landscape of the unfamiliar territory as shadows began to recede. But she hadn't any idea where they were or what their course of action should be.

The horse's hooves and the leather on the bottom of Gaucelm's feet crunched on the small pebbles of the riverbank. His chiseled face and the concentration of his dark gaze gave away nothing. He took her arm and led her up the bank. Not far away was a shed at the edge of a field, and as they got closer to it, they could see that fresh hay had been strewn in it, not long ago. But no one was using it now.

Gaucelm scanned the horizon for a moment as he tied the horse. "We'll be safe here for the moment. There are no curls of smoke indicating a peasant cottage nearby. This must be used for herders driving their cattle to market. Come and rest."

He arranged some bales of hay to provide further seclusion and comfort. He unbuckled the belt to which was attached the sheath for his sword, and laid it down. Then he pulled off his surcoat to spread beneath them. His movements were not rushed. He went out again to study the ground for signs that anyone had passed recently, and seeing none, he came in to find Allesandra seated on the hay.

When he removed his tunic, her heart contracted at the sight of his muscular back. Blood had dried along cuts and scratches, and she bent to examine him.

"You are hurt, my lord. Your cuts must be bathed. But we have nothing to dress them with."

He turned around. "They are not deep and do not trouble me."

The hardened muscles of his chest made her draw in her breath, and her hand came up to touch him. She allowed herself a secret smile of pleasure. He was standing in linen breeches tied at the waist by a drawstring, and she could not help but remember when she saw him thus last in the bedroom at the castle so long ago. Her pulse throbbed in her ears, but she was mindful of his wounds and wished to see them cleansed. Something of the same thought was evidently in his mind, as he held out a hand.

"Come, let us bathe in the river before travelers or field hands set upon us here."

She wouldn't have minded lying down with him in the hay just as they were, but she wanted to wash the blood from his scratches and see for herself just how mean they were.

"If I had the proper herbs," she said, with concern in her voice, "I could make a salve."

He pulled her close for just a brief kiss on her forehead. "You will be the balm that heals."

He reached up to untie the lacings at the neck of her coarse gown and then bent to lift the hem over her head. She had no wounds to be careful of; rather she was aware of his hands as they sought to undo the coverings that she had made sure hid her form so that she could pose as one not whole.

He knelt in the hay to hold her shoes while she stepped out of them. Then his hands felt beneath her shift to the girdle where her leggings were tied. She trembled, standing there, holding the shift high to her waist so that he could undo the leggings, and then she dropped the shift modestly as the leggings fell. Still, he caressed her leg as he pulled the coarse cloth from her limbs.

Sharp desire pierced her at his ministrations. Now his gaze freely roamed over her face, his sensual lips curved in anticipation of pleasure. She did not know to what she owed this chance to be with him. But she dared not think about the future. They walked down to the water as the morning broke in earnest. At water's edge, he untied the drawstring that held the breeches and then dropped them unashamedly to the ground. She did not stare, but out of the corner of her eye, she glimpsed the hard thighs, scratched and stained with the blood of battle. He walked into the water waist-deep and then turned to encourage her to come in.

He closed his eyes in a wince as he let the water wash his scratches, but then he opened them again to watch her. She knew that he meant for her to remove the shift before she joined him to bathe, but modesty made her step into the water up to her calves before she reached for the hem to pull the garment free of her head. Then she tossed it to the bank.

She took more steps into the water, and caught his gaze sinking to her fine breasts and then to the dark triangle just before she lowered herself into the cold river. Her skin chilled, but she hardly noticed. For the intimacy of their encounter and escape and now the erotic nature of their refuge here in the open, had already lifted her to an excitement she had not known before. She drank it in.

"How long do we have before we face danger again?" She put a hushed voice to her thoughts.

"I do not know," he replied. "But I do know that I wish to live the present moment to the fullest."

She pushed through the heavy, moving water to where Gaucelm stood. Water gurgled past them at chest height. He took her hand and she lay back to let the water run over her shoulders and her hair stream behind. Then she felt his hand wash her, and she parted her lips in pleasure at his touch.

He bathed her sensuously as if his hands enjoyed forming her shape in every place that he could touch. And then he moved to higher ground so that she could gently dip water to wash over his wounds.

"Ah, I see these are not so deep," she said. "The water will cleanse them, and the fresh air and sunlight will help the healing."

Then Gaucelm swam back into deeper waters, and she smiled to watch him splash about. She, too, waded in deeper, and then he was by her side. His hand came up to cradle her head, and his other arm slid around her back. She opened her mouth to meet his as he hungrily took a kiss. They drank the wetness from each other's mouths, tongues thrusting and probing.

One hand came up to touch her breast, and the sharp throb of desire eddied through her.

"I have waited more than fifteen months for this," he said almost with a growl. "I plan to take my time enjoying you."

"Oh, my lord," she said, resting her body against his as the water drifted around them. "I did not believe you thought of me."

"Hmmm," he murmured. "I did not hold out hopes that you would think on me kindly, either."

"I could never forget you," she said, her chest tightening with emotion. She frowned. "Though I am a traitor to say it."

He caressed her body consolingly as he spoke. "Certain things we cannot help. Our feelings know no politics."

She met his dark gaze with a questioning one of her own, remembering suddenly when she first set eyes on him at Muret. "Yet we fight for what is right on the side of different causes."

He pressed her breasts more tightly against his chest. "Do not ruin the moment, woman. We have left a battle behind. Both our skins are worth a ransom. That is not why I brought you here."

Her lids drooped over her eyes as she drew circles on his shoulder with a finger. "Why did you bring me here?"

"I think you can tell what my intentions are," he said, humor lacing his guttural tone.

And with his words, she felt the intimate thrust of his hardness against the bones that guarded the most private place on her body. She, too, took the time to experience every small aspect of this pleasure. Her heart palpitated. Chills prickled her skin. Her deep hunger and the daring of standing naked in the open thrilled her and made her arch against him. But the sun was well up now, and they might not remain alone for long.

Reflecting her thoughts, he pressed his hand against her side to guide her to shore. They reached for their clothing, but only to cover themselves while they made their way back to the shed. There was still no one about, and once inside, Gaucelm positioned more hay bales so that they would not be seen. She sank onto the bed of clothing that would protect their skin from the hay.

"We'll hear anyone before they can get within yards of this place," he assured her. Then he lowered himself to the nest he had made.

They stretched on their sides, leaning on elbows and gazing at each other with excitement and desire. It was a lover's reunion of the most touching kind. The year had been etched into his face. But she saw there that he had not forgotten her, and it made her yearn for him and thrill at his desire.

He feasted his dark eyes on her body, gently running his hand over her upright nipples and melon-shaped breasts. Then he followed the curve of waist and hip. She felt an inner thrill that her body pleased him and felt her breathing become more shallow as his hand explored the skin of her inner thighs.

She reached out to trace his hard chest, dried now by the sun and breeze. And the throbbing of desire increased within her. Inhibition fled from her as she bent forward to kiss his hard male nipples. Then she brushed her lips and tongue over his skin from chest to waist.

He rested on his back, his hand loosely moving in her hair as she played with him. His deep moan of pleasure urged her on. His masculinity made her feel daring and she felt free to do things she'd never done before, giving pleasure and taking pleasure like the ebb and flow of the water that had swirled about them sensuously outside.

Her hand slid up his thighs and explored on its own as she moved upward, kissing and caressing his skin, dropping gentle kisses on the scratches that already seemed less severe. When she had moved upward far enough, he reached for her, gazing with half lowered lids, his lips parted in desire.

"Lovely, lovely," he murmured. "I waited for this."

She half wondered if he meant that he'd not taken another woman since he'd been with her. It did not matter to her if he had, for there had been no promises and no guarantees that they would ever be with each other again. She found that nothing in the past mattered, only the fullness of the moment and the promise of what they were about to do.

He remained reclined, but moved her upward so that she lay with one leg over his, her breasts within reach of his mouth. Then he took the nipple and gently sucked, causing her to gasp and shiver in pleasure. His hand thrust below, spreading her legs further apart, as her thigh grazed him. She lowered her head, her hair falling over him as they pressed, tasting, exploring, vibrating against each other.

Then he hoisted her astride him, and slipped into her. She pressed her hands against his shoulders. Her hair tangled around his head and his thumbs pressed against her nipples.

"Oh, Gaucelm!" she gasped.

Then they found a rhythm as he thrust upward against her. She squeezed with her knees and held tight to his shoulders with her hands as he bucked under her, finding the spot that deepened her pleasure. Then he lowered her against him so that their mouths joined and his tongue reflected the movements below, and she drank him in.

Then suddenly his movements quickened. He released her mouth and she found her balance on her knees, arching her back as the deep uncontrollable quivering began. He held her waist firm and moaned as his thrusts exploded with even more passion. They gave release to their cries of ecstasy, moaning in unbelievable, intense pleasure such as they had never achieved before.

It lasted for a long moment and they squeezed the last ounce of sensation from the explosion within. Finally, she heaved in great gasps of breath and lay facedown upon him, burying her face in his hair as he cupped her buttocks gently with his hand. She nibbled at his ear as he caressed her hair.

"My love," he breathed. "I love you, Allesandra, my lady. I cannot deny it."

The ecstasy coupled with his words made her heart sing and she turned to smile at him. "I have loved you for a very long time, my lord."

He tucked her in against him.

They waited as their hearts slowly returned to earth. Then she found a position against his side and closed her eyes. In the cocoon of his love, she found badly needed slumber.

* * *

When she awoke, she was alone in the hay, but with some of the clothing neatly covering her. She blinked at sunlight creeping over the bales of hay. For a moment, her heart knocked with fear and she sat up. But then she glimpsed Gaucelm, dressed now in his shirt, tending the horse. So, they had still not been found by anyone. She took a deep breath and lay back, much as she would on a pleasant morning in her own bed after a fulfilling night.

Her heart turned over. Fulfilled she was, but uncertainty was not far away. When Gaucelm's form filled the opening they had made, she looked up at him, and he gazed down, his eyes smiling.

"No, do not move. I want to think of you thus. Your face has a deep contentment on it." Then he came to sit on the ground beside her and held her cheek in his hand.

"I saw you thus once, but you were asleep."

"So seldom—" she began, but he put a finger to her lips to stop her from lamenting how seldom they had found pleasure in each other's arms. "Will it be—" she started to ask, but again he silenced her, gathering her in his arms for a warm, slow kiss.

She held him against her, loving his nearness, wanting it to last forever. But physical needs were calling. He loosened his hold.

"I stopped a peddler," he informed her. "He was on his way to a fair and I managed to buy clothing that is better suited to us."

"With what did you pay?"

"There were coins in the saddlebags. The horse had a prosperous owner."

Her mood sobered. "I wonder who he was."

"Whoever he was, he will have found another horse by now," he said gently. "We must see to our own needs now."

She felt a tremor of anxiousness at what they would do next, but she didn't question him as they rose and bathed again in the river, then dressed in the simple, well-made garments. Gaucelm again resembled the merchant he had posed as to gain entrance to Avignon.

Only the sword in its sheath, which was fixed to the saddle, looked ominous. But it would keep away robbers, who would think twice about bothering them. For even in merchant's clothing, Gaucelm looked like a prince, and a man who was adept at using weapons.

Their first requirement being food, they took to the road and soon came to a village. They obtained bread, cheese, and ale, and set to it on a bench outside the woman's door who fed them. She accepted payment and then spoke of the fair now going on in Aix, where the peddler who had sold them their clothing was bound.

"Aix is not far from Marseilles," Allesandra said when the woman had left them alone. They could not risk being seen together in such a public place as a town for fear they would be recognized and their loyalty questioned.

But Allesandra did not yet know what Gaucelm planned to do. She was not ready to turn her mind to her responsibilities. That time would come. She would lose him again. But for a moment, perhaps a day, he was hers and she refused to let anything mar that happiness.

When they finished their meal and washed it down with ale, they took the horse and walked along a lane that led among trees.

"This is not the way to Aix," she said when they had reached the dappled shade. "Unless you know this country better than I think."

"I do not know the country at all. I merely wished to walk a little."

They walked in silence for a distance, and Allesandra breathed in the fragrances of forest and field nearby. The people this far to the east had been free of the war. Their overlords paid homage to the German emperor. But then she did not know if the French king planned to march this way as well. And she did not care to ask.

Still, there was much that needed to be said between herself and Gaucelm. Now that they'd shared such ecstasy, she felt the tug of longing that would come when he left again.

"I wondered if you hated me," she said at last, stopping by a thick plane tree and running her hand along its flaky bark.

He stopped to consider her but said nothing. Then he looped the horse's reins around a branch and walked a little away, looking off into the distance.

He did not answer, but she realized that she preferred his silence to a lie. He turned back and came to her, leaning his hand against the tree and looking down at her. The troubled look on his face reflected many of her own feelings. Her body still tingled when he was near, and she closed her eyes and leaned her head back against the tree.

"Would that we were simple peasants," she mused. "I feel the weight of my wealth."

He gave a despairing laugh, "Peasants free from duty, tied only to the soil." She opened her eyes again to watch him twist a twig from the branch above them.

"But even the peasants suffer in these times," she said bitterly. She turned her face away from him, the sadness creeping back to mar the joy she had found in his arms.

"You are a heroine among your people," he said.

"I cannot deny the part I play in this war."

"Nor I mine."

"So," she said, lowering her chin to stare at the ground. "There is no hope and no escape for us. You will return to your army."

"I cannot do otherwise. And you?"

"I must help Toulouse. It is our last chance." Then she could bear to look at him no longer. "Gaucelm," she said with sudden feeling and walked away, grasping one of the low branches. "Why could you not have been born in the South?"

"Or you in the North? Ah, but do you really think that if you were a mason's wife as you once pretended to be, that you would find solace in the religion that you seem to hate?"

She flushed. "We tread on dangerous ground, my lord. Why must we speak of religion now?"

"You are right. Let us speak of other things." He changed his tone. "Shall I tell you how I thought about you during the winters in Paris?"

"Did you?" She turned and smiled.

"I wondered if you were angry when you found a collection of your poetry stolen."

"I did not know you had stolen it. But I did see it was missing. I thought only that I had misplaced it or that one of the troubadours took it."

"Ah, yes, your friends, the troubadours."

"What of them?"

"Gallant knights all, ready to serve a damsel in distress. I'm surprised you did not marry one of them."

"How could I?" She was surprised that he could think she could marry anyone else after the passion they had shared.

Still, his tone held a slightly masked resentment. "I see that the younger Raymond travels with you. Does he always escort you on journeys?"

She felt the first touches of anger. "If you mean, is he my lover, no, he is not. Neither are we betrothed."

"I see."

"You see, but you think my affections are fickle."

"I did not say I understand women."

She exhaled a breath, hating the anger that still came between them. It quickly brought tears to sting her eyes. Happiness was not possible. She'd been a fool to imagine it was.

She gave a bitter laugh. "Then our rendezvous is over. We must make our way back to our battles."

"Then you will continue to fight?" he asked.

"Of course. What do you think I am? You can seduce me, my lord. But I am not such a weakling that I will turn traitor and hand you my household. We do not want the French in our lands. I do not want the French in my lands. That much will never change, no matter what happens between us."

He gazed at the passion in her face and believed her. Regret pervaded his heart.

"Perhaps I am the fool. I am still able to imagine the crusade at an end, Louis satisfied with new lands, the South subjugated and you, my lady, in my arms. You hold out foolishly."

She looked away from him. "We do not think so. Toulouse will never bend."

"You cannot win. Already much of the South has given up the fight."

"Toulouse will not give up."

"What do you think you can achieve against the king of France?"

"We will keep our independence."

"I despair of your steadfast loyalty to a way of life that is doomed, my dear. Equally exasperated by your loyalty to friends who seem to mean more to you than one who loves you."

She parted her lips in surprise. "How can you say that? You understand nothing if you do not know, do not see how I feel."

"You may not be a heretic yourself but you will go to great lengths to protect them."

"What would you have me do, turn over their names so those hateful, greedy churchmen can seize their lands?"

"So you have names to turn over, do you?"

"If I did, I would not give them up."

Gaucelm gave up on the argument and shifted to a direct appeal. "Come back to France with me."

"And live in lands where I would be a stranger? Would that I could." She shook her head. "I do love you, Gaucelm. Surely you could tell that much. But I would not be able to forget. Why don't you stay and help us in the South? We need good knights like yourself."

Now it was Gaucelm who had to look away. "My family and our home is in Ile de France. That, too, is inbred. I could not see my name held up as traitor to future generations of the Deluc family. It is a very old and respected name."

Her shoulders slumped. The anger and resentment had not left her, but she knew that there was no end to this siege. Both of them would hold out. He waited a moment until their ire abated. Then he came to her and lifted her chin with his finger.

"I did not bring you away to wage yet another war. We may not have a future, but we have this day. Let us not waste it."

"How so?" she said warily.

"We will go to the fair in Aix. We will pretend to be the simple householders that we are not."

"And then?"

"We will drink at a tavern. Make love at an inn."

"And the next morn?"

"I will ask you whether we should travel to Marseilles and take ship for England."

He loved her that much, was all she could think. She was too choked by emotion to speak. "For England? To a land where we are both strangers? What possible fortunes would we have there?"

"You see? You are as practical as I am, madam. We would have little fortunes. I would serve some lord who had need of my skills as knight. But we would have no land. You would be forced to be a lady-in-waiting to a lady who would decide every minute of your time. Or we could sail to foreign lands."

She shook her head in sadness. If she believed in great adventure, she might be tempted. It would be a pleasant dream to contemplate these possibilities as they spent the day at the fair. But Gaucelm's mind seemed to be on other things again.

He pressed his body against hers for a kiss. Their anger had departed, and in its place the desire and love sprang between them once more. Perhaps it was the notion that they had only one day together that made her reach for him once more. And he began to caress her as if he, too, knew that he must fill himself with her before he had to turn his back again.

"I want you again, my lady," he said in a voice fraught with need.

"And I you."

Their movements became more sensual. He slid his hand under her tunic. Unable to bear their need, he led her deeper into the woods where thick branches and growth covered their lair. He did not even bother to make a bed for them, but leaned her back against a thick oak. He lifted her tunic and deftly played her body as an instrument, hearing it tremble at his touch. Then he loosened his linen until his flesh touched hers. He entered her then and there, supporting her in his strong grasp.

Allesandra wound her legs around him and arched, her breasts aching, her head against the rough bark as he took her wantonly, as she wanted to be taken. Her whole being relished his powerful lovemaking, and his moans of possession only made her want to yield more. His mastery was erotic, bringing them both to a savage climax that merged with their wild surroundings.

"My lord," she gasped when it was over, and her body sated. "I wish it could be so every day."

"By God, we must find a way," he muttered before he opened his lips to plunge his tongue against hers as he still caressed her in the last vestiges of passion.

Twenty

Allesandra felt as if she'd entered an imaginary world as they rode toward the city gates of Aix, following the crowds to the fair. When the lane they followed came to the main highway, they saw that sergeants guarded the road to the fair, protecting traveling merchants and those who were carting goods home.

She rode pillion behind Gaucelm, and he drew up a little distance away to get out of the way of a large hay wagon. But it gave him a chance to observe those in authority.

"We cannot know if they are looking for a French knight and a lady from Toulouse," he said so that only Allesandra could hear.

"We are simple householders going to shop at the fair, are we not?" she replied. For they had planned what to say if questioned. Indeed the packs they had fashioned made it look as if they had traveled some distance to attend and had a few goods to trade in exchange for fabrics, spices, and kitchen utensils they would wish to take home.

"We will meld with the crowd. The peddler's clothes will not give us away," he said.

"Provided your stature and air of command does not seem odd in a simple householder," she spoke warmly into his ear.

He slouched his shoulders and leaned forward, grasping the pommel of the saddle to make it appear he was a less expert rider than he was. The fine battle charger they rode was another problem. But if questioned, they intended to claim that the horse had wandered onto their holding, and that they'd brought it to the fair to seek its owner in order to claim a reward.

But the sergeants were too busy ordering a farmer to keep his herd of pigs to the side of the road out of the way of the carts and barely noticed the genteel householder and his lady as they passed by.

At the city gates they passed by inspectors checking the quality of the goods being brought in and tax collectors examining documents of those going out to make sure taxes had been collected.

Once inside the town, they followed the hubbub through streets filled with jugglers, acrobats, chained bears, and monkeys performing on street corners. Jongleurs sang and strummed on church steps. Even at this hour the taverns they passed thronged with patrons coming and going. At last they came to the big square where stalls and booths were set up between the larger halls for the cloth merchants.

They disembarked at a stable and took their belongings.

"Tell me," Gaucelm asked of the stableboy, a youth of sixteen or so. "Are the inns full? Or is there a place where my lady and I can put up?"

"The inns were full a week ago," he answered. Then he looked them over as if to assess how much they could pay for a place to stay. "You might try the widow behind St. Peter's Church in Cooper's Alley. She has clean rooms."

They thanked the boy and asked directions, then pushed

through the crowds to a small house squeezed between church and a cooper's workshop. There they found the widow. After putting their request to the plump, dimpled woman in white wimple and veil and berry-colored gown, they were invited in.

"The room was used by a spice merchant," she told them. "But he's gone now. How long do you plan to stay?"

"Not long," Gaucelm answered, his eyes scanning the modest house. "Two days at most. Our flocks need tending, and our herder is not well."

They agreed on a price that included their dinner and then the housewife showed them to the upstairs room and left them to unpack.

"I think we'll be safe enough here," he said, stuffing their packs under the bed.

Allesandra smiled at the quaintness of the place and tingled with pleasure at the sight of the clean, comfortable bed. Gaucelm seemed to follow her thoughts.

"I thought a woman of your rank deserved better than a hay byre or a tree tonight."

Her heart turned over as he came to put his arm around her shoulders and pull her next to him. She murmured against his cheek. "I appreciate your consideration for my comfort. But I shall never forget the hay byre, or the tree."

He looked at her with love and already with the regret of parting which they both knew was inevitable. Then he kissed her gently and warmly as if wanting to make the most of their time together here.

But she was too wise to think that Gaucelm had brought her here merely for a romantic escapade. "And after tonight? What do you plan to do then?"

He looked as if he regretted having to say what was in his mind. But then his face drew into serious lines.

"There are many travelers at this fair going east and west, north and south. Even to foreign lands. Should we wish to ally ourselves with some of them it would be possible to make our way to distant lands and never see France again."

She could say nothing for a long moment. She grasped his arms and leaned her head against his shoulder. Finally, she lifted her head and looked up at him again.

"You would do that for me, my lord? Go to a foreign land where as you said earlier we have no lands, no overlords who know our abilities and would respect our ranks?"

He looked off into the distance as if he could see through the shuttered windows to faraway countries. "They might believe our reasons for being there and accord us respect for our ranks. You are a celebrated poet. But beyond our skills, we would have nothing. It would be a risk."

He dropped his eyes to study her again. "But if that is what you wish to do, my lady, I will take you where you want to go."

She lifted a hand to touch his face. Her eyes searched his. "To put our fate in the hands of God and seek our fortune elsewhere. To put this war behind us then?"

He jutted his chin forward as if not capable of speaking.

Tears moistened the corners of her eyes and once again she had difficulty forming her words. "To be with you every day and every night that you were not doing your forty days of feudal service to a new lord? It would be heaven."

Her heart rippled at his love and at the dream he placed before her. But she lowered her eyes, closing them as she leaned against his shoulder again.

"I thank you, my lord, for this dream. But of course it will remain a dream. We cannot do it, can we? For every day we might be filled with our love and ecstasy, but every day we would think of those we abandoned. My lands would suffer if I were not there to defend them. My people would die. I could not live with that."

After a long moment holding her, he spoke again. "No, I did not think you could."

"And you, my lord? Would you not be unhappy knowing you had abandoned family, king, and cause?" She did not mean it to sound bitter, but the truth of how well she knew him could not help but color her words.

He gave a small grunt. "I would try to please you, my lady.

And I would keep my word. But you would see the guilt I suffered. And that would erode our happiness, would it not?"

"It would." With a great sigh, she broke away. "Then we will not travel with merchants to foreign lands. What then?"

"Those same merchants will be going to the lands where we must go instead," he said slowly. "It will not be difficult to find escorts for you as far as your home if that is where you must go."

Her throat clenched with emotion. "And if I must go to Avignon instead?"

"To find out if your overlord Raymond of Toulouse is there?"

She did not miss the jealousy in his voice. "Only because it is my duty to let him know that I am well."

"And what will you tell him?"

"I will say that when we became separated during the battle, that I found a horse, and the horse bolted. That French soldiers gave chase but that I was able to escape. However, I was thrown in the woods and twisted an ankle. Some cottagers took me in until I could walk again. Then I made my way back."

"It is plausible. But it will not be easy to get you back into a city under siege. I think we have exercised every possible ploy in that attempt. Their gates will be firmly closed this time. They will not open them again for fear of yet another trick."

She looked distraught. "Raymond will think me dead."

"If he is still there."

She lifted her chin. "Then I will go to Toulouse. I will need to tell Raymond the elder of how things fare. That is, if God wills that the old count still lives."

The lines around Gaucelm's mouth deepened. "If you must go to Toulouse, then we will find you escort."

Of course she understood that he could not go. For in enemy territory, he would be taken captive. Clearly he would return to his own camp at the siege of Avignon.

"And you, my lord, what will you tell your king?"

"That I was taken captive and held for ransom, but that I over-

came my captors in a moment when their guard was down and
made my way back to the camp."

"Equally plausible. Will you be believed?"

"I will make it so. Now come, we must at least appear to be
purchasing goods for our home."

Her heart contracted at the casual way he uttered words about
their imaginary home. But she straightened her shoulders in order to face the fair without showing the emotions she really felt.

Playing her part as housewife, she went from booth to booth
and examined a vast array of kettles, spoons, pincers, spits, skew-
ers, and long-handled forks. Pretending she was unable to decide,
she moved along to prod and feel linsey-woolsey covers, hemmed
to cover children's beds, even wandering to a furniture maker who
displayed well-crafted chests, chairs, and writing desks.

She made as if to go away and think about the purchases and
found that Gaucelm was engaged in a similar charade near a pen
where stock was kept. She stood in the background and watched
Gaucelm examine cattle hooves as if he did it every day. And his
apparent knowledge of the beasts made her wonder even more
about his life in France and his own family's demesne. She felt
a sudden longing to know his family. How tragic that she never
should. He had sisters. To whom were they married? And what
was the older brother like?

He caught her watching him, and she saw the glint in his eye
as he told the man that he would have to confer with his wife
about their means.

"There she is now," he said. "I must find out if she's spent all
the household money. But your prices are fair. I will consider a
new milk cow before we leave the fair."

He came to lead her away from the stock pen. The mood of
the day made her feel confident enough to tease him.

"What will you do with a milk cow when you return to your
King Louis?" she asked.

"I will take the cow," he said. "We have a large army to feed,
and one more milk cow will be helpful to the steward who must
feed us. And what, pray tell, did you buy?"

She shook her head. "Nothing. I can hardly travel with pots and pans back to Toulouse. It would belie my story about cottagers taking me in after I was chased by soldiers and thrown by a horse. Unless I say that I happened on a fair on the way to Toulouse."

He guided her through the crowds, and she reveled in the simple intimacy of being with her imaginary husband sampling the pleasures of the fair.

"Come," he said. "It is time we returned to the widow's house and took our dinner."

When they entered the tidy, well-organized house, they took their places at a table that included other boarders. She had a moment of panic that she and Gaucelm would be tripped up in their tale. But Gaucelm was adept at mealtime conversation, and she had to do little but smile and nod as he made up a story about their holding as if he had given it great thought.

They retired to their room for a rest after the meal. After he had shut the door on the rest of the world, Allesandra turned and said, "You once told me you did not have the gift of poetry or storytelling, my lord. I think it can be said that you created a story very well, and for an audience, no less."

His face showed amusement and he came to her, letting his hands run up her arms to her shoulders. "Perhaps it is the inspiration of having my . . . woman next to me."

She had no time to respond, for he lowered his head for a kiss. But before they became too involved in passion, he released her mouth and set her away from him.

"However, I have not merely been telling a fantasy. I have learned what we need to know. There is a party of travelers making their way westward as far as Montpellier. I am going to arrange for us to travel with them. That will get you to the other side of the Rhône. Perhaps from there you can send for friends to escort you home."

She let her hand drift to his sleeve. "I appreciate what you are doing, my lord. You know that if you wished it, you could take me hostage and collect ransom for me."

He turned back and gripped her shoulders, looking into her face intently. "Do you wish me to do so? Just say the word and I will take you back to France with me. You would be my hostage, but I would accept no ransom to allow someone to take you from me."

The thought of him taking her back with him held strong appeal, so much so that she had to force herself to look away. She didn't trust herself to words, and he gently released her, accepting her answer.

"I dare only go as far as Montpellier," he said. "You should be safe there. The town has already bowed to the king. From there I will have to make my way northward."

She gave a little nod, understanding the arrangement. All that would be a few days hence. She would not think about it yet.

They returned to the fair and wandered through the crowds. They stopped at the church steps to watch tumblers, musicians, jugglers. As the evening turned to dusk, they wandered out toward the edges of the festivities, saying little, knowing that their time together was dear. Both of them had questions, both had no answers. They stopped in a lane behind a stockade fence, a willow tree dipping its branches to touch their cheeks.

Gaucelm pulled her to him and held her gently, his lips in her hair. She drank in his embrace, but they staved off passion until they were again alone where he could show her the ecstasy she could only know with him. They exchanged soft words, tender endearments, but made no promises.

"Come," he said at last. "We must find supper at a tavern. We will need nourishment to face the morrow."

The taverns were full of revelers, but they squeezed onto a bench in a corner of one busy place. Gaucelm caught the eye of the serving girl who pushed aside the grasping, drunken men who taunted and reached for her as she came to see what Allesandra and Gaucelm would have. The girl was all eyes for Gaucelm's good looks, but with a glance at Allesandra's regal bearing, gave a toss of the head as if to say she knew that the handsome gentleman with the mysterious dark eyes was off limits.

They ordered food and ale, but Allesandra found that she wasn't hungry. Gaucelm glanced idly around the room. He spoke in a low voice to Allesandra.

"Be careful what you say. I feel that we are being watched. Perhaps our common clothing does nothing to hide who we really are. Say nothing that would lead anyone to become too curious. Even though I shall send you with protection, I don't want your party to be set upon by robbers who think you have any valuables."

She heeded his warning and with a glimmer in her eye began a discussion with her would-be husband about the pots and pans she had anguished over at the booth earlier today. He in turn carried on about the cow he wanted to purchase, and before long they were carrying on an argument about which they needed more, kitchen utensils or a cow.

When Allesandra glanced out of the corner of her eye, she saw the men Gaucelm had alluded to. Rough types enjoying their ale, but who might have an ear cocked toward any conversations that would be worth following. She was well aware that such fairs attracted low-class brigands, even though the fair officials tried to keep them out.

But when she and Gaucelm finished their meal and left, she felt confident that they'd done nothing to betray their real purpose at the fair.

Night had fallen, but the streets were lit with lanterns and torches. The booths and halls were locked for the night, but the revelers continued their games and pastimes, the shadows and flickering light giving their faces a garish quality as if they all wore masks.

Gaucelm touched the hilt of his dagger fastened to the belt under his surcoat and kept one arm about Allesandra's shoulders, glancing into alleys to make sure they would not be accosted before they reached their room.

Once inside the widow's house, they latched the door behind

them and retired. Allesandra struck flint to light a lantern, giving a soft pool of light at the edge of the bed. Gaucelm began to toss his clothes aside in a casual manner, as if he did it every night in front of his wife. Allesandra felt her heart give a little lurch as she watched him, and then she did the same.

When she was down to her shift, he came to her and placed his hands on her shoulders.

"Let me do it," he said softly. His eyes grazed her face, making her heart hammer, and the desire sprang suddenly as he lifted the shift over her head and she stood before him nude. He bent to lift the bedcovers and she slid in, resting her back against the pillows. Then he followed.

He wasted no time with words, but pressed himself against her, and then they entangled themselves in fiery passion, more desperate for the fact that they had only a few days left together.

She lay under his strong body, helpless with ecstasy as he worked his magic on her. She squeezed him in a hard embrace, crying out at the pinnacle of his love. His mouth came down to muffle her cries. And then she hazily realized that they mustn't let the household hear too much of their passion, or the other boarders would wonder at the heat of love between two who had said they'd been wed for a decade.

When their passion at last calmed to a deep feeling of satisfaction, Gaucelm extinguished the lantern and nestled in quietly next to her. They listened to the sounds of the town outdoors, the whack of a branch that beat on the shutters of their window when the wind struck. Sometime later, she fell asleep.

The merchant's train for Montpellier formed early in the morning, and Allesandra was introduced to the merchant's wife, one Marie Darbac, with whom she would ride in the wagon. They were pleased to have the couple join them. For Gaucelm's size and strength and his apparent ability with arms would stand them in good stead should any highway brigands be tempted.

There were other armed men in the party, and Allesandra's

only fear was that she and Gaucelm would not be able to maintain their masquerade. Even though the merchant came from a town that had bowed to the king of France, Montpellier had fought on the southern side for many years before that. It would be impossible to tell where the merchant's sympathies lay.

They traveled only on the main roads, stopping at inns and at farm holdings along the way. Though there was an occasional rustle in the trees they passed, suggesting that watchers followed their progress, no one attacked them. With relief, many days later, they passed through the city gates of the town. Already a French garrison was much in evidence. But Gaucelm did not make himself known until he and Allesandra were installed in an inn from which, on the next day, he would have to take his leave.

That evening he returned to her after being gone for a few hours. He bolted the door and then threw himself on the bench beside the hearth. Allesandra sat in the one sturdy wooden chair that graced the plain room. He leaned back against the rough stones of the hearth.

"I have had news," he said.

From the way he said it, she did not think it could be very pleasing news.

"There is still some distance for you to go to your own lands from here, or to the city of Toulouse, if that is where you wish to go. I wanted to make sure you had friends to escort you."

"That is kind of you, my lord."

"Your overlord the count is ill in Toulouse. And you did not know the fate of your friend, the young Raymond."

At the mention of her friend's name, her heart missed a beat in fear that there had been bad news. Her hand flew to her chest and she looked anxiously at Gaucelm.

He rested his head on the stone of the hearth. "He fought with the relief forces, but was not wounded. They say he rode away with the troops that caused the skirmish the night we escaped."

She gave a sigh. "I am relieved." Then she looked guiltily at Gaucelm. "He is a good man," she said in a somber voice. "It is a pity that you cannot know him as anything but an enemy."

"Perhaps." There was a long pause, and then Gaucelm said, "I will be gone from here before the sun rises. You will have friends to escort you home."

She looked at the floor, knowing better than to argue or to complain. They had known this from the start. She had agonized over their inevitable parting for so long that she had almost no feeling left. But somewhere in the recesses of her mind, she did not forget to be grateful for the time they had spent together. She gathered her strength and stood up.

"You must do your duty. So must I."

They spent no more time talking, but prepared for bed. After tender lovemaking, more precious now for being their last time, she lay beside him, thinking, long into the night.

Her sleep was interrupted at dawn by sudden pounding on her door and muffled voices. She sat up with a start, her head clearing. She glanced around the room and knew with certainty that Gaucelm had been gone for hours. His side of the bed was cold. But her heart was in her throat at the sound of the urgent knocking.

"Who is there?" she called, reaching for her gown to throw over her head.

"Lady Allesandra Valtin," a stranger's voice called.

"Yes, yes," she said, going to the door, but she knew better than to open it until her early-morning callers identified themselves to her.

There was a hurried exchange of voices and then the same voice boomed, "Soldiers of the king," he said. "You are wanted at the lord mayor's house."

Her heart all but stopped. Something boded ill. If the lord mayor wished to pay his respects or invite her to call on him, he would hardly send soldiers before the roosters crowed. She didn't have time to crawl out the window the way Gaucelm must have done. She would have to go with them, but she would give herself time to think.

"Please, I am not yet dressed. Wait there a quarter of an hour until I am presentable."

Another voice, perhaps that of the innkeeper, said sleepily, "She can't go anywhere. She's safe enough in there."

"Very well," the louder voice said. "A quarter of an hour to make yourself presentable."

Allesandra flew about the room getting ready. There was water in a ewer, a basin, and chamber pot for her needs. She glanced out the shuttered windows, but only a straight drop to the street offered itself on that side. She spotted horse dung directly below and surmised that Gaucelm had arranged to have a horse left at the window for his own escape.

She would have to face whatever was afoot. She and Gaucelm had not given their real names since they'd made their appearance at the fair in Aix and traveled here. But someone had found them out. And now soldiers wanted to take her to the lord mayor? She didn't know the man. But he must be loyal to the king, for Montpellier had been one of the first cities to submit when Louis started marching south.

Finally garbed in her simple gown, her hair braided and wound about her ears, she fixed a band around her head that held a modest veil in place. Her dagger was hidden beneath her skirt. A pouch tied to the girdle at her waist contained coins she would need for the rest of her travels. She draped her cloak over one arm. It was not needed in the warm spring air. But she did not know if she was coming back here.

She opened the door when she was ready and faced two men-at-arms. The sergeant had long straw-colored hair and a narrow, belligerent jaw. "Lady Valtin?" he inquired.

"Yes."

"Lord Mayor wants to see you."

"At so early an hour?"

He gave a shrug of the shoulder as if the hour were none of his business, he only took orders.

Both soldiers looked unfriendly, either from the nature of their mission or the uncouth hour at which they'd been asked to fetch her. They were armed with swords and daggers, which gave her a chill. This was no formal social visit. She was being taken prisoner, but for what reason, she did not quite understand.

Nevertheless, she held her head high and marched in front of them down the narrow corridor, behind which other guests at the inn must be stirring. No one could have slept through the noise the soldiers had made.

Lamps lit the way where the wooden stairs turned on a landing, but she saw that the main room of the tavern was still in darkness. Fingers of gray light showed around the closed shutters. The innkeeper must have gone back to his bed. She paused, getting her bearings in the darkness, and the belligerent man with the straw-colored hair stepped ahead of her to open the door.

A flicker of movement out of the shadows told her they weren't alone. Then the unmistakable ring of swords being drawn from their sheaths and a grunt from the man still behind her made her dart behind a keg and crouch down to avoid the oncoming blows.

Twenty-one

The two men who had fallen to the floor in a heap rolled toward the door. Another figure leapt forward, crossing his sword with the Frenchman who'd just opened the door. In the spill of gray light, Allesandra saw the swords meet and thrust as if held aloft by ghosts. Then the two on the floor became entangled in the swordsmen's feet. With a great grunt, the second Frenchman was thrown off and his attacker hoisted himself up.

She saw with a gasp of great surprise her own friend, Jean de Batute. His dark hair framed his keen features, and as the swordsmen above his head drew back for another thrust, he got to his knees and made a flourish.

"My lady," he said.

Then he dove forward as the swordsmen danced to the side,

and he grabbed the winded Frenchman crawling to his feet. They fell back onto tables where Jean got the man down on his back and delivered several blows to the jaw.

The other two swordsmen danced in the shadows, knocking into kegs and tables. Allesandra backed out of the way and then into a window, which she unlatched and opened, throwing another square of light onto the scene. To her equal surprise, she saw that Peire Bellot chased his opponent up the staircase. Metal rang. The Frenchman gave a startled cry as his sword dropped to the landing. Peire tossed his own sword aside and lunged for the man, lifting him and tossing him over the wooden railing to crash onto a trestle table below. All was wood and splinters as the man's weight broke through to the floor. His groan died into silence.

Allesandra barely had time to shut her mouth, which had flown open in surprise. But as her rescuers brushed themselves off and came toward her, she fashioned her expression into a smile.

Jean reached her first. "Come, madam. The landlord is bound and gagged. But if too much time passes, the lord mayor will realize something is amiss and send others from the French garrison to investigate."

"I'm glad to see you, but how did you know?" she asked.

"We'll explain after we've gotten outside the city. This way."

And she followed them through the tavern and out the back to the stables. Another face she hadn't seen since before she'd left Toulouse with Raymond, Christian Bernet waited with four saddled horses. He handed her a mount.

"Any sign of more soldiers?" asked Jean.

"Two of them passed, but they didn't pause here. Likely on other business."

"We must fly," said Jean.

He helped Allesandra mount, and then the four figures rode along the alley and turned into the street. They might have been anyone going about their business. The French garrison left to guard the town did nothing to interfere with the life of the town as long as the town government and tax collections were conducted according to the new agreements with the king.

As smoke curled upward from chimneys and servants emerged to throw buckets of water on their masters' stoops, early-morning travelers were not an unusual sight. The knights' long cloaks draped over their swords, so a casual observer would not know they were armed. Yet Allesandra kept alert for any warning that their escape had been noticed. She wondered how long the men sent to fetch her would remain unconscious, for she did not think they were dead.

Jean and Peire in front of her, and Christian behind her, all glanced right and left, even along rooftops for any sign of danger. Just how they knew she was going to be taken hostage was a mystery to her, but there would be time enough to tell in a while.

They rode through the quiet streets, their horses' hooves scraping the cobbles. Only when the gatehouse was in sight did they hear a cry go up. A group of the king's men-at-arms appeared in the streets behind them.

"There!" came the shout.

"Quickly, my lady," said Christian. "Ride for the drawbridge."

She dug in her heels as her friends spurred their horses forward. The sleepy porter at the town gate staggered out of his door.

The kings' soldiers came at a run, but they weren't mounted. "Raise the drawbridge!" shouted their leader. "Stop them."

Allesandra's party galloped through the street, which curved at a slope toward the massive gate. Then they thundered onto the wooden bridge. They heard the creak of rope and gears as the drawbridge on the other side began to be raised.

Peire was within the gatehouse first, then came Jean, then Allesandra followed. Peire turned his horse so quickly, the animal reared, but Allesandra didn't pause. She followed Jean over the bridge, which had raised two feet, but their horses leapt to safety. Christian flew over behind them. She circled her horse to look behind and then realized why Peire had stopped.

With a loud clang, the heavy metal portcullis slithered downward, barely missing Peire's horse as he thundered across. He had stopped to cut the rope and send it downward behind them just in time for his own escape. He crouched for his horse to leap over the gap that had grown wider as the bridge creaked upward above the moat. But the mighty charger landed at a run without missing a pace, and then they all gathered speed to dash along the road, exposed to their confused pursuers.

Arrows whizzed in their direction, but landed harmlessly at their heels. They didn't stop to look back but galloped along the wide, flat road, made light now by the beginnings of the day. They took a curve, putting the town behind them, and Jean led them up a slope and behind some trees. They crashed through the thin forest and over a rise, down again along a lane that the knights seemed to know.

Dew from leaves brushed Allesandra's face when they rode under low branches, but they came to a grassy clearing and still raced across. Trees thinned to scrub, and they drew up at the edge of a lake. There they halted to catch their breaths, and let the horses trot through the water, spraying moisture on their heated bodies.

"We've lost them, I'd say," ventured Christian, who looked back. They were on an open plain and would see anyone emerging from the upward slopes they'd left behind.

"We'd still best make haste," cautioned Jean. "They could follow."

"I doubt they'll follow across the next river without reinforcements. Montpellier might be in the king's hands, but farther west they know they'll need an army to protect them."

Allesandra gasped for breath, still unable to speak. It had all happened so fast, she'd barely had time to think. Finally, she was able to pose her questions.

"How did you know the lord mayor had asked to see me? I did not know my identity was known in that city. Do you think he was going to ransom me?"

"Worse," said Christian. "He would have had to turn you over to the king, who would know that with you as hostage, Raymond would have to cooperate."

"Then you've seen Raymond? He's all right?"

"We met up with him in that skirmish outside Avignon. He told us of your disguises as lepers and was sick with fear that you'd been found out and captured."

"I was discovered, but I managed to escape."

"So we learned later when a message came to us that you'd been brought to Montpellier and needed an escort home."

"A message?" Her already pounding heart fluttered with nervousness that didn't come from the exertion.

Christian looked at her curiously. "The message was anonymous."

"No more time for talk," interrupted Jean. "We must ride. We may be in neutral country, but there was a whole garrison of soldiers back there. If the lord mayor thinks our skins important enough, he'll send them after us. We do not know him. If he is a true southerner, then he will make only a big enough fuss to please the king and say the hunt is impossible because we had enough of a lead to lose them."

Allesandra barely listened. She went over again the story she had told Gaucelm she would use when she was reunited with her kind, and got it ready on her tongue.

But they started off again at a serious clip. The countryside they passed still had not recovered from the damage wrought when Simon de Montfort had been here. Blackened trees, burned fields, abandoned villages. They passed through lands where his swath had been cut. It was a grim reminder of the determination of the king to overrun the South. And it hurt Allesandra to see how the South had suffered in this war.

Much later in the day, when they had put enough small ridges and bluffs behind them, they stopped to rest and refresh themselves. They watered the horses at a stream, and then sat beneath the trees to catch their breath.

The conversation finally came back to her escape and the appearance of her friends out of thin air.

"We are glad to see you well, my lady," said Jean. "The message reached us where we had taken Raymond after retreating from the skirmish. We were worried that something ill had befallen you. Raymond saw you one moment in the thick of battle and then became too busy fending off the French. We looked for you as best we could before we were forced to retreat. We only prayed that if the French had taken you captive, you would be treated as befits a lady."

She shivered appropriately at the memory of the danger and her narrow escape. But she was careful not to meet any inquiring eyes as she told her story.

"Yes, Raymond and I became separated during the battle. I found a horse, whose owner had been pulled from the saddle, and I managed to mount. But the horse bolted, carrying me away from the battle. However, I was thrown when we reached the woods. I twisted an ankle and could not walk far. But some cottagers took me in until I could walk again."

Christian gazed at her pensively, and she had to meet his eyes for a few seconds.

"And your ankle, how is it now?"

"It is well."

Only now did she glance down to see that her loose gown had sprawled about her, revealing the ankle in question. Her shoes came just to the ankles. It was too late to withdraw. Her hose covered no swell or bulge. She felt obligated to explain.

"The cottager's wife applied a salve and wrapped it. You see the swelling has quite gone down."

"That is good," said Peire.

But Christian just looked at her. "We were curious as to the sender of the message. Why an anonymous sender? Why not yourself?"

She tried to keep the warmth out of her cheeks. "I did not know you were so close."

"No," said Jean, smiling a challenge. "But the sender of this note did."

He reached into his pouch and extracted a small strip of parch-

ment on which some writing had been scrawled. It indicated that
the lady Valtin waited at the Black Swan Inn in Montpellier and
needed an immediate escort. She studied the note and then looked
up with blank eyes.

"So they did." She was not ready to reveal Gaucelm's part in
her escape.

Perhaps the three men became aware that she did not wish to
discuss it. As troubadours, they would never press a lady to speak
her thoughts unless she wanted to reveal them. Their manners
made them hold their tongues, and this gave time for Allesandra
to decide what should be said.

In her heart she wanted to share with them her knowledge that
Gaucelm was good and gentle. It was not his fault that he'd been
born a vassal of the king. But she also feared to show her friends
her weakness for one of their foes. A man who would march to
take her lands again, given the chance.

They all turned their attention to munching the dried fruit the
knights carried in their saddlebags. Then Peire suggested they
mount up again.

"This country is so scorched from the fighting," he pointed
out, "that we might have some distance to go yet before we find
a patch of land that has been farmed, an abbey that has not been
destroyed, or a settlement that may provide us with a meal and
a place to rest."

They took his advice and moved on.

They spent that night at a monastery that had been spared by
Simon de Montfort because it already swore fealty to the Mother
Church. They were fed in a guest house and given beds in separate
quarters. They were far from any settlement and so there was no
female servant to assist Allesandra after a monk brought her
several ewers of hot water and a basin from which to bathe. But
she was just as relieved to be left alone to make her toilet and to
sit for a while in a stout chair before a shuttered window as night
drew in.

She pondered for a long time how Gaucelm had been able to
find out where the southern troubadours were and send for her

rescue. Of course it must have been his inquiries that had led someone else to take word to the lord mayor that she was in the town. Perhaps someone had seen him write his message, or perhaps the messenger had read it before delivering it to Maguelone. She was fortunate that it had been delivered at all. She might never know the answer.

They struggled on through impoverished lands that had once been the milk and honey of the Languedoc. Being farther from Toulouse, these lands had been more sorely affected by the years of the crusade. What she saw made Allesandra angry, and she realized how her own lands had been so much more fortunate. Heavily burdened with fines and taxes to the king while Gaucelm had ruled it, she had suffered economically. But her fertile land had continued to produce.

She finally set eyes on her own castle again, and was welcomed with great ceremony. A few days later, the news came that the count of Toulouse lay dying, and they all left immediately to console young Raymond.

In Toulouse, the count's palace was draped in black. The count had passed on to the next life. Young Raymond was now Count Raymond VII.

Everyone grieved, for Raymond VI had been a well-loved man. Allesandra took part in the funeral service and procession that wound around the city for the benefit of the thousands of mourners. The troubadours carried his coffin into the crypt beneath the church, where his bones would rest with his father and ancestors.

The next day Raymond VII received blessings and honors. All the troubadours sang for three days of feasting. Allesandra was emotionally drained by the show of feeling, especially during these dark days when all of Toulouse must band together against the encroachments of king and pope.

In the next weeks, Raymond traveled about the county, surveying the mood of his people and taking an assessment of their resources. At the end of August, he met with Allesandra, who was once again hosting Jean de Batute and Christian Bernet, come to keep her company and cheer her after the sadness of the old count's passing. The troubadours were not blind, either. And several times when Allesandra entered the room, they broke off their low whispers to turn and greet her with curious expressions.

She surmised that they were speculating on her time after the skirmish at Avignon and were full of curiosity about her anonymous protector.

The weather had turned sultry and warm. The summer light lingered long into the evening, and they sat on a balcony off a receiving room that perched in the western tower. Stars twinkled in the evening sky, and scents of honeysuckle wafted from shrubs on the slopes beyond. Raymond spoke his mind among his friends about what he had been thinking.

"Avignon has fallen," he mused. "Both sides have become weary enough to compromise."

They had already received the news about Avignon at Allesandra's castle, but now Raymond explained how it had come about.

"The Avignonese were convinced that Louis would not leave without some satisfaction," he told them. "The siege hurt the town financially, of course. In a few more months they would be ruined. Their pride was not worth that much. A surrender was easily arranged."

"It was terrible, though," said Jean. "Their walls were destroyed, and a fine was paid."

Raymond nodded in disappointment. "The town paid an indemnity of six thousand marks and gave hostages. But there was no killing or looting."

"Thank God for that," commented Christian.

"Yes," continued Raymond. "The king entered the town peacefully."

"And used the stone bridge to cross the Rhône." Jean scowled in irony.

Raymond gave a shrug and shook his head. Allesandra sympathized with his burden, but thought she knew something of what he was about to say next. For he had alluded to it when they'd spoken privately before supper.

"The fall of Avignon is a great achievement for France. Louis will meet no resistance on his march."

"But he cannot rush headlong for Toulouse," said Jean. "He must leave garrisons and establish administration in the lands that have submitted themselves to his rule. This will take time and further reduce the strength of the army that comes this way. He will not attack us this year."

"No," said Raymond. "I do not see how he can." His face looked tired, his shoulders weighted by the length of their fight. "We hold Toulouse and the lands north of Toulouse to Poitou. France can only drive us out at the cost of bloody fighting. But by the end of the fighting season they will hold all the lands east to the Rhône. And there is another thing I fear."

"Our people are tired of the fighting," he explained with a tired look of resignation. "I do not think they will rally again the way they did after the death of Simon de Montfort. They sense the difference between resisting the Capetian king and resisting the hated Montfort greed. What I've heard these last weeks on my travels is that many men are ready to consider a permanent peace on the basis of existing boundaries."

There was silence for a moment as they digested this news. Allesandra feared being trodden under the heels of the French, who would no doubt take harsh financial punishments, or worse. It spelled the end of their independence. She was chilled by what she knew must be promised in any treaty of reconciliation and felt the ominous presence of the hand of the church even from this great distance.

"What will you gain?" asked Christian solemnly.

"I cannot say, unless France will explore the possibility. But if a conference is set and a treaty negotiated, there would be two things I would hope for. Peace for our lands first of all. Recognition as count, so that I may protect our rights as much as I can." He paused. "And reconciliation with the Church."

No one said anything, and Allesandra read the shuttered expressions of her two friends. She found words to try to ease the discomfort of the conversation. "If you are reconciled with the Church," she said slowly, "will the Church leave us alone?"

He lifted a hand. "That I cannot say. I would have to make compromises I am sure . . ." He did not enumerate.

"Is there a council set already?" asked Jean, who knew that Raymond would not have told these things unless he had some indication that they might actually take place.

Raymond leaned back as if preparing his words. "You know my young sister, Jeanne. She would be promised to the king's young brother, Alphonse."

The other three glanced at each other. Then Jean spoke again. "But you might one day have a son."

Raymond shrugged. "I might."

"And Jeanne and Alphonse might have children of their own," said Christian.

Raymond nodded. "There would be hope for the future."

They all considered what he proposed. An end to war, boundaries drawn, compromises made. And hope that future generations would soon forget their obligations to distant cousins in Paris.

They said little after that. Raymond did not know when such a conference would be called, but he had indications that it *would* be called. There would be written negotiations first. But eventually he would have to travel to Paris to ratify a treaty.

Later that night Allesandra was left alone in her chamber to consider all that Raymond had said and all that it might mean. As much as she cherished what now seemed like a faraway fantasy of passion and escape with Gaucelm for a few days, that dreamy time was colored by the realities that would accompany this compromise Raymond was willing to make because he thought it best.

She heard a tap at her door and expected it to be Julian, come with some late-night urgent request. Entertaining the count put a great deal of strain on her capable steward. Instead, she saw that Jean stood at the door, looking apologetic for disturbing her. But also looking as if he wanted to talk.

"Am I disturbing you, my lady?" he asked quietly.

"No, Jean, please come in. I was just contemplating."

She invited him to sit in the wide window seat where the evening breeze helped cool the room.

"You think it wrong that Raymond wishes to fight no more?" he asked.

She shook her head. "Oh, Jean, I'm not sure what I think. No war is good. And yet I dread seeing the Languedoc overcome by the French monarchy. Things will not be the same."

"We have always had war."

"That is true. But times of peace are when the people and the land prosper and grow healthy again. I would wish for that."

"And for yourself?"

She looked at him sharply and then looked out into the darkness. She could feel that he read her thoughts. "What do you mean?"

"I do not mean to pry, my lady. But I have been wondering who your protector was that summoned us to Montpellier."

She paused only for a heartbeat. "Gaucelm Deluc."

He exhaled a breath. "I thought so."

"Do you think I am a traitor?"

He laughed softly. "Your heart is the traitor. But no, my lady. None of us is impervious to love."

She leaned back and rested her hands in her lap. "Is it so apparent?"

"You do not reveal your feelings unless you choose to, madam. But for those of us who know you well, or take the time to observe, there are signs of melancholy that only come when one is affected."

She managed a smile. "You make it sound like a malady."

"Is it not?"

"Then what am I to do, Jean? I thought I would forget him when he was out of my sight. But my malady only grows worse."

"You must sing of it," he said. "Pour forth your feelings in song and poetry. It will help you feel that there is a place for your sadness and longing."

Her lips still curved in amusement. "Spoken like a troubadour." He smiled and lifted his arms in a gesture of acknowledgment.

She looked out again to where a silvery moon cast a dull glow over the trees and capped the purple mountains with its pale glimmer.

"If there is peace, that is only the beginning," she said with a worried expression. "Raymond will be made to compromise. What of the heretics?"

Jean turned more grim. Alone in the castle with no French spies about, they could speak freely of the French crusade.

"We will never be free of the pope's tyrants," he said bitterly. His vision took on an ethereal look as if he were seeing into the distance. "Those who will not bend to the Church will be punished. There will be many penances for those who recant. For those who refuse to give up their faith . . ." He shrugged as if he did not wish to contemplate the consequences.

"Yes," she said sadly. "To live with the French is one thing. To bend the knee to a corrupt church with hypocrites for priests, who deny the scriptures to any but the clergy." She shook her head slowly. "There are many who would rather throw themselves onto the flames than betray their beliefs."

She looked back at Jean, her jaw set, her personal struggles set aside. "We must help them, Jean. There must be a place where the believers can go. A last refuge where they can be left alone."

He frowned. "There might be such a place. Perhaps if Raymond must agree to search out heretics in his lands, those who wish to flee can take refuge at a monastery far out of the way where they will not be considered a danger to the intolerant Church."

She nodded thoughtfully. "Is there such a place?"

"There might be," he said slowly. "A refuge in the Pyrenees where French soldiers would never get to. A place isolated and harsh, all the better for the parfaits, who deny the world in any case and do not need to live in comfort."

"Where would such a place be?" she inquired.

"The château at Montségur," he said. "I have seen it once

myself. It perches on a peak accessible only by a steep winding path, too narrow for any army. It can be well stocked with provisions. The winter there is very cold. In a word, the place is impregnable. I've had word that Lucius Hersend is there now."

A chill suddenly made her tremble, and she hugged herself. "Then if Raymond arranges a peace treaty and the inquisition must come, at least there will be a refuge for the faithful."

Twenty-two

Allesandra accepted Raymond's invitation to accompany him as part of his entourage traveling to Paris to negotiate a treaty. Gaucelm was likely to be in Paris, serving in the same capacity to the king. Then what? Even if a treaty was negotiated, it would be an uneasy peace with much bitterness in Languedoc.

Gaucelm's words echoed in her mind; he wanted them to find a way to be together, but how? She could not abandon her lands. She was tied to them until her overlord decided who she should marry. He might agree to her marrying a Frenchman to help him with his political goals if he was really resigned to compromise. But even if Gaucelm accepted such a political alliance, he would not want to live in Languedoc, where he would be disliked, a symbol of their defeat.

Aside from the passion that existed between them, she did not know what was in his mind. If he married her, he might wish her to remain in Ile de France with his family, while he continued to fight wars for France. She wanted nothing better than to be with him, but given time for reflection, which she now had for many weeks, she knew in her heart that such a life would make her unhappy.

She'd been formed by the South. Her exposure to foreigners from other southern kingdoms and the Far East was too inbred.

She might be able to make concessions to outward appearances demanded by the Catholic Church. But in her heart she was a believer.

And so she entered Ile de France in a somber mood. She took in the impressive sight of Notre-Dame de Paris rising magnificently above the Ile de la Cité. Scaffolds supported skilled workmen putting their artistry on the soaring building, and she remembered how she had pretended to be the wife of one such mason. But Gaucelm had quickly seen through that guise.

Where was Gaucelm now? Would he be waiting in the royal palace that they now approached? The fortified palace sat not far from the quay along the great River Seine, and she could not help but look at its formal gardens and well-guarded towers with some resentment.

King Louis had a dire illness and was not expected to live. His son was just a child. Blanche of Castille would be regent, should the king die and her young son be crowned.

Count Raymond and his entourage were greeted with due respect and formality and shown to chambers where they would stay. French ladies and maids came to help Allesandra make herself presentable, and they seemed to understand her soft-accented French well enough. Perhaps it was her growing anxiety about meeting Gaucelm in such a formal surroundings. She was also very aware of her great responsibility to the people of Languedoc to help Raymond come to the wisest decision they could make.

The ladies in waiting led her to an antechamber where Raymond waited with other advisors who had traveled with them, the count of Foix and the count of LaMarche. Also, there were two other minor barons, accompanied by Jean de Batute and Christian Bernet, who had been brought along to entertain with their songs once the treaty was agreed upon.

Raymond was garbed in a rich green tunic with gold-threaded collar, girdle, and hem. A cloak of matching gold cloth was fastened with a ruby brooch at one shoulder and flung back to reveal one sleeve. His beard was freshly trimmed, his features noble.

She felt gratified that he was every inch the well-loved leader his father had been.

Her own raiments of deep burgundy silk with silver bands at cuffs and hems blended into the other rich colors that their assemblage wore. Her hair was coiled and held in place by the crespine of silk cords woven into a net and studded with jewels at the intersections of the mesh. The crespine was held in place by a fillet worn around her head over the stiffened band of silk that came beneath her chin. Buttressed by her fine dress, she was ready to face the royals. And Gaucelm.

She'd had no word that he would be present, but as soon as the doors opened, and Raymond's party was admitted into the great hall, she saw him at the end of the long, regal room. Her party had to walk down a great length of hall, past great arched openings that gave onto a gallery above on one side. Two stone fireplaces were carved into the thick walls on either side, and the oaken beams that supported the ceiling were far above them, giving the feeling that those who approached the throne were very small in the great space.

Upon a great chair placed on a platform with two steps leading up to it sat the regent, Blanche of Castille.

Raymond approached and made reverences, and Allesandra dropped a curtsy. She was thankful that she was not expected to say anything, for as Raymond and Blanche of Castille exchanged formalities, Allesandra's thoughts were all for the man who stood proudly to one side, gazing at her. She stole a quick glance, but kept her expression veiled. His, on the other hand, lit fires in her veins. For he was staring directly at her, as if not caring who watched.

After a moment he gave his attention to the conversation, and Allesandra heard her name as Raymond introduced her. She curtsied again, and tried to pay attention to what was being said, but she knew that no real negotiations would take place yet. This was just the formal beginning of the conference.

"I speak for the dying king," said Blanche, whose face looked harsh with little beauty. "It is my instruction to negotiate the peace in the manner Louis would have it. My son, who will inherit the throne, must be considered, but we will listen to what Count Raymond has to say."

"I thank you, madam," Raymond replied.

Blanche rose, and they all moved to two heavy, carved high-backed chairs arranged in front of the largest of the hearths. Blanche sat down and arranged that Raymond do so. A smaller, armless chair, little more than a stool with a shield-shaped back, was brought for Allesandra to sit behind and to the left of Raymond. The rest of the men stood as the conference began. One of the retainers handed Blanche a rolled parchment, which she held on her lap without opening it.

"The king has read your missive and taken it under consideration."

Raymond waited.

"You hold Toulouse and lands north of Toulouse. The king acknowledges that you can be driven out only at the cost of bloody fighting."

Finally, Raymond began to talk politely but proudly. But Allesandra still felt most keenly aware of Gaucelm, who stood back a little. When she glanced at him, she thought that he, too, was paying little heed to what Blanche was saying. Perhaps he had heard it all before. Allesandra's attention wandered between the negotiations and the warmth and tingling of her body under Gaucelm's stare. Her face warmed, and her back began to ache from straining to sit rigidly.

After some time, Allesandra again began to hear Blanche's words to Raymond.

"You realize, of course, that if we reach a reconciliation, there will be a public act of penitence. We must act in accordance with the Church on this, but it will not be too harsh."

"I agree," said Raymond.

Allesandra looked at the side of Raymond's face that she could see, and saw the wince he must be trying to hide from Blanche. Although he was prepared to make these concessions, neverthe-less, Allesandra knew it cost him something.

"You will be recognized as count of Toulouse, but you will promise to hunt out and punish heretics. You will offer a reward to anyone who captures a heretic."

"Very well."

"The Church wishes to establish a center of orthodoxy in the heart of your lands. Therefore, the Church wishes you to pay the salaries of professors of theology, canon law, and the arts, who will come to Toulouse to form a university there."

Raymond nodded. Allesandra began to feel the grip of the church descend, and her attention was diverted from Gaucelm. The price of the peace was not going to be pretty. But they had all agreed to go forward with it. She listened as the rest of the agreement was discussed. Raymond promised his sister to the king's brother, Alphonse.

"Even if you should sire other offspring," Blanche said slowly and deliberately, "Jeanne of Toulouse will be your sole heir. On your death, the county of Toulouse will pass to Jeanne and Alphonse and their children."

"To this, I agree," said Raymond with some strain.

Blanche leaned forward slightly. "And if they are childless, Toulouse reverts to the Crown."

Raymond said nothing. Allesandra watched as his face drained of color. He had not considered this. Even she was surprised. Jeanne was to be sole heir, that they knew. But they had not considered that Jeanne herself, who was still very young, might be childless after her marriage.

Allesandra studied the woman who would soon be regent. She felt a bitter anger build within her as she contemplated the Capetian greed. They hoped Jeanne would not bear children. She suddenly wondered how far they would go to prevent her doing so. Allesandra stood up, trembling. The Capetians wished to see the extinction of the House of Toulouse.

She held her words, but all those in the gathering turned their eyes to her. Her pulse pounded in her ears and she opened her eyes wide, certain that her expression was one of agitation. Raymond glanced up at her, but said nothing. Finally, Blanche lifted her chin.

"Does Lady Valtin have something to say?" she said, but in such a way as to suggest that it would be ill considered to disagree with the demands put forth.

Allesandra glanced down at Raymond, who sent her a look of caution. The fire in her eyes blazed forth and she held her chin just as high as that of Blanche.

"I do wish to speak, but perhaps it would be better to speak to Count Raymond in private. He has asked me to come in the capacity as advisor, as my husband served as his father's advisor before his death."

Blanche inhaled a long breath of air through her nostrils. "We are all thirsty. We shall break off our conference until tomorrow. You will want food and drink after your long journey. And we will hear the entertainments of the musicians who traveled with you." She stood up. "Tomorrow is soon enough for these agreements to be concluded."

And she turned her back on them and swept off toward a doorway at the side of the room. No doubt the egress led to where King Louis lay in his bed, waiting for Blanche to tell him how things progressed.

Servants appeared with goblets of wine. Perhaps Blanche thought fraternization would help Raymond accept her terms. Allesandra saw Gaucelm move into her line of vision, but she was too angry to speak to him. Instead, she seized Raymond's elbow.

"Sole heir," she said between clenched teeth. "But don't you see what she is trying to do? What if Jeanne should have no heirs? Then we have lost everything we've fought for."

Raymond glanced over his shoulder and then steered Allesandra away from the others. "You are right. I had not considered it. I might yet beget a son of my own."

"Someone who could claim Toulouse as his inheritance after Jeanne. But if you don't conceive an heir and Jeanne doesn't either . . ."

Raymond tried to calm her. "I cannot imagine that will happen. Allesandra, we have come this far. These terms are bitter to us all. But we already deliberated long and hard. It is the least of all the evils now."

"And let the inquisition loose among us. You yourself are being forced to offer a reward for heretics."

"A few will suffer, yes. I will have to cooperate. I thought you understood that there is no choice."

Her anger began to give way to hopeless resignation and she grasped his hand. "Oh, Raymond, it is so hard to deal with these French. We will never be able to like them."

Raymond glanced behind her and she felt Gaucelm's presence. She turned, but the expression she gave him was not welcoming. Gaucelm bowed to them both, and Raymond acknowledged the other man.

"My lady Valtin is unhappy with the terms," said Raymond since Gaucelm had witnessed the incident. "I value her advice, but after a night's rest, I am in hopes that we can proceed and reach agreement." He gave a vague gesture that included Gaucelm in the conversation.

But Gaucelm was already ignoring Raymond. "Perhaps my lady would like some wine," he suggested, and hailed a servant who brought a goblet. He handed it to Allesandra, who took it this time. Raymond was called away.

"How do you fare?" asked Gaucelm. In such a crowd, he behaved formally.

Allesandra lifted her chin. "It is difficult to stand here and allow your rulers to plan the complete demise of the House of Toulouse."

"Hmmm. Is that what you think? You do not know the future, madam. I believe we are trying to see it as a joining of the House of Toulouse and the Capetians."

"I cannot see it that way."

"Then I will not argue. Instead, why not look forward to the evening's entertainment." In a lower voice, he said, "There are things you can do nothing about, Allesandra. Cease trying. The winds of fate are blowing. Do you not think that the end to this war is best for all concerned?"

She was able to look into his eyes, and she did not miss the fact that his statement held some personal meaning. But she was still too agitated and fearful of the results of this conference.

"I am not ready to think such thoughts, my lord," she said a little more quietly.

He offered her his arm. "You need be ready for nothing except to dine. That is the only thing demanded of you now."

And he gave her a look that began to undo her. She accepted his arm and let him lead her through the passage that led to the chamber where tables were set for a feast.

The French and the southerners were encouraged to mingle, but the atmosphere was stiff. Allesandra sat next to Gaucelm and listened to the music from the musicians' gallery and the low hum of conversation. From time to time, silence reigned except for the sound of fruit being sliced and wine being poured. Blanche spoke to fill the silences.

"I do recommend that our guests take time to visit the cathedral being built on Ile de la Cité. I am most interested in your opinion of the sculpture."

There were a few murmurs, but hardly the revelry of a normal gathering.

After the meal, the guests broke off to wander in the gardens. Allesandra accompanied Gaucelm, but she still brooded over the negotiations. And in spite of her relief at seeing Gaucelm again, and the inner longing that even her anger could not completely quell, she felt more hopeless than hopeful and kept lips pressed together as he walked with her along the rows of herbs and flowers under a blue sky.

"Tell me, madam," said Gaucelm in a tone formal enough to satisfy anyone who might hear their words on the clear air, "have you written any poetry in these last months?"

"I have been too busy for poetry," she said in a sharp voice.

She realized she was beginning to sound like a harpy. But perhaps it was fitting that Gaucelm see a side of her that was not submissive to his charms. If he cared for her, then he would understand her qualms. He did not misunderstand her mood.

"That is too bad," he said. "The greatest unpleasantness is sometimes easier to bear if it is given expression in poetry and song."

"Oh? And did you learn this from the time you spent among us?"

"I learned that and many things."

He stopped, seized her arm and turned her to face him so she could not avoid his gaze. "Allesandra, this treaty may be abhorrent to you, but there will be a day when it is past. You will return to your lands and pay tithes to the Mother Church and taxes to the king. It is the way of the future. I know you dislike it, as do your countrymen. But unifying France is not a bad thing. As one country, all our peoples can prosper. Squabbling between nobles will stop if they all serve the same king. Can you not see it that way?"

She tugged her arm free and looked to the side. "You ask that we stop fighting. Even Raymond wants to do so. But what good are empty displays of faith and loyalty where none exists in the heart?"

"Be careful what you say," he said only for her ears. "What I am suggesting is that you accept the inevitable. You still have your own life to live. I had thought you might wish to live it in my presence."

This forced her to look at him once more, but her expression was still questioning. "How so, my lord? Will you be awarded my lands again? Am I a piece of property to be sold along with my lands?"

He gave an irritated scowl. "Your marriage is up to your overlord, the count. I planned to speak to him."

"Before you spoke to me?" The words snapped out; in her present mood, Allesandra could not stop them.

His lids lowered and he gave her a look that said he had already looked into her soul. "Words were not necessary, my lady. We exchanged all the talk needed when we were at the fair in Aix, did we not?"

Memories of that sensual interlude sent a flush through her, and she glanced down in sudden embarrassment. "Perhaps we did. But that was while we were still at war." Her chin came up. "My people had not yet surrendered."

"But you had surrendered." His words were low, suggestive. There was no doubt of his meaning.

She looked him in the eye for a long moment at last, and could not back away. The bond between them held her there, and in spite of their differences, she knew she was not free of it. But in the late-afternoon sunlight she saw that her love for him was clouded by the other horrors that had always been between them. Even so, she laid a hand upon his arm.

"Gaucelm," she said more quietly, but with feeling. "So much lies between us. I'm not sure we could be happy."

His grip moved up to her shoulders. He did not care who saw them. "You could learn to be happy."

"If we marry," she said, "I will lose all the freedom I now have. I will bow my head to husband, Church, and king all at once."

The muscles in his jaw twitched. "I can see that my love would not be enough. You have forgotten then what we shared at Aix."

Their conversation was interrupted by Jean, who made so much noise, treading on the path and humming a tune as he approached, that Allesandra knew he was intentionally letting them know they were about to be interrupted. They broke apart. Jean gave a flourish and bowed.

"Sir Gaucelm, my lady. The music is about to begin. Perhaps you will join us."

"Of course, Jean," she said. "We will return to the hall in a moment."

He lifted a knowing eyebrow and bowed again, then he turned to retreat. Gaucelm frowned. "You are surrounded by friends. I am surprised that Count Raymond does not marry you himself. Or is that what you've been trying to tell me?"

"No, we . . ."

But Gaucelm would not let her go on. "I can see that in spite of the passion you showed me, your loyalty to your kind is more important. I was the fool, then, to think that we could achieve happiness. Well, madam, perhaps you are right. I release you. You are free to give your hand to a powerful count who can while away the night writing poems to you."

He took a step backward, and then he left her there.

She made her way back to the hall alone, regretting the bitter words between them. A black mood settled over her, and she almost wished she'd not come to Paris at all. In the hall, she joined others of her entourage to listen to the music and watch entertainments.

Later in the evening, a light supper was served. She noticed that Raymond was absent as well as Blanche of Castille. She surmised that they had withdrawn to private chambers to talk alone. Part of Allesandra resented it, but part of her saw why they might do so. The two already knew what they wished to achieve. They might reach agreement in private and then after presenting it to the king, tell the others on the morrow that it was done.

Allesandra retired early to her chamber, prepared for bed and then sat by the window with an oil lamp and tried to read some poetry. But she found the French poets dry and didactic, and longed for Provençal poetry instead. There was a light knock on her door and she put the book aside.

Even before she answered it, she knew it was Gaucelm. He slipped into her chamber and shut the door behind him. Without preamble, he unclasped his surcoat and tossed it aside. His belt followed it.

She stood and watched, trembling at the surprise visit, sure of what he was about to do. When he had removed his shoes and thrown off his tunic, he finally spoke.

"One last time, madam? I want to make sure you will remember what you are giving up."

Then he reached slowly for her and tugged her nightdress upward. She did not protest, but raised her arms so that it came over her head. Her breath escaped raggedly at the sight of him, and her breasts tingled as he removed her shift. He bent to extinguish the lamp and then stood again to reach for her. His lips came to join hers, and his tongue thrust inward as his fingers gently pressed, making her gasp.

Her heart lost control and she trembled violently as his manhood brushed against her thighs. Then he dropped to his knees and let his lips do the work of caressing her skin, his hands and thumbs fondling the mounds of her breasts as he explored.

Her hands were on his shoulders of their own accord as his tongue made the fires burst forth within her. Then he arose again and led her to the bed. He seated her, but remained standing before her so that her hands were on his waist. With deft and unhurried fingers, he unfastened her hair so that it fell about her shoulders and then he gently laid her cheek against his hard abdomen.

In a private rhythm that they had come to understand, she teased with her own mouth and tongue, pleasing him as he moved gently against her. His own grunts and moans of satisfaction let her know that he was full of desire.

Then with his practiced mastery, he lowered himself, his knees against the feathered mattress, and entered her. They joined together, and her own erotic sensations flowed unhindered. Her breath panted to the same rhythms as his thrusts. Then he hunched over her, bracing himself with his hands on the bed in the final moments when his seed spilled into her.

For a few moments they breathed heavily. He leaned down to take one nipple in a moist kiss that sent a bolt of lightning to her womb. Then he pulled himself away and inhaled a long breath. He stood before her in the shadows.

"There, madam, I have given you everything of myself that I can. If you have a child with Count Raymond, who will be able to prove it is not mine?"

His words stunned her, so that she lay, braced on her elbows, her mouth open, but staring at his silhouette in the dim moonlight. Her heart still pounded from their passion, and it took time for her poor mind to arrange the words so that they made sense. By the time she had understood what he'd said, he had replaced his clothing. He sat to put on his shoes.

"You can't mean that," she finally said.

"Oh, but I do."

She sat up, reaching for her nightdress. She had been powerless against his charms, and he had claimed her. She still felt sorry for the bitterness that had passed between them in the garden, but now this. Was this his vengeance?

She stood up, trying to summon words to accuse him. But he was out the door before words would come, and she was left with the shattered feeling that they had come to a terrible end. The slippery wetness trailed down her thighs in ironic witness to what he had done. She had taken no precautions before any of their lovemaking. It was possible that his seed would take root in her.

Perhaps she had not cared before, thinking that if such came to pass, it would only be evidence of the love they bore each other. But now he meant to claim her in a different way. Thinking that she was destined to do her duty and wed Raymond, Gaucelm meant to have the upper hand. If Raymond bedded her very soon, there would always be the possibility that the child was Gaucelm's.

"Fool," she muttered to the door that had closed behind him. And she saw the mistake she had made.

If she were with child, she would be forced to marry Raymond or some other southern lord for appearance' sake. For now that her arguments had offended Gaucelm, it was doubtful that he would come running back to her, even if she humbled herself to him.

Twenty-three

When morning came, Allesandra had to drag herself from bed. The skies were heavy with rain, and the gray mist seemed to penetrate her heart. She let the maids dress her hair and help her dress, but she dreaded another conference.

The moment could not be put off forever. And when it was

time, she went into the hall, half hoping she could make herself somehow invisible, especially to Gaucelm, should he be there.

But he was not there. She broke her fast on bread and cheese with Raymond and their entourage. Then when the tables were broken down, they were instructed to join Blanche of Castille in her private chamber. The musicians stayed behind, only Raymond and the other southern counts went in, along with Allesandra, because of the effect any decision would have on her lands.

But when they assembled around the heavy, square table at which Blanche was seated, Allesandra perceived that all the real negotiating had taken place last night, probably in this room behind closed doors. What Blanche and Raymond said now were mere formalities. When Blanche returned to the point about the marriage between Raymond's young sister and the king's brother, she sent a stinging glance at Allesandra.

But Allesandra had already given her opinions to her overlord and held her tongue. Her head throbbed, and the bread and cheese she'd eaten only sickened her stomach. She wished nothing more than for the formalities to be over with. She wished fervently to be away from Paris and back in her own demesne to let all that was familiar comfort her.

"The king has been informed of these arrangements," Blanche said to Raymond so that all could hear. "And he agrees. If you are prepared to sign the treaty, we will proceed."

Raymond nodded his head. "Let us read over the wording alone," he said. "We will sign the document this afternoon in front of witnesses."

"Very well."

One of Blanche's knights stepped forward to hold her chair while she arose. "My scribes will prepare copies of the treaty. Bishop Frosbier will announce the betrothal of Jeanne and Alphonse. Until that time, the king invites you to make whatever use of the palace and stables you wish."

It was done then, the peace was ratified. But Allesandra carried her forebodings with her from the room as they all retreated into the hall. She and Raymond stopped near a window cut in the thick stone, where a shaft of sunlight brightened the floor.

"So," she said. "It is accomplished at last."

"Yes," he said. His face was set, his lips hardened into a straight line. When he spoke, he gazed out, staring without interest at the rooftops on the Ile de la Cité.

"You think I have betrayed my people," he said without any accusation. It was merely a statement.

Her shoulders sagged. "I see that you had no other choice. We are to be swallowed up by the French monarchy."

"Perhaps it will be for the better in future generations."

"Better for who? Oh, I'm sorry, my lord, I will not irk you by offering barbs at every turn. Indeed, I fear I shall turn into a bitter old woman because I am too attached to a world I thought I would never lose."

She fought the twist of her heart inside her and leaned on the cool stone window seat.

"I could not make our people suffer more bloodshed. Perhaps the French rule will not be too hard to bear."

She gave him a sharp glance and shivered. "We have not seen the end of it, my lord," she said in a hushed voice. "We will be made to submit to the Church. The bishops will descend on us to squeeze out every trace of heresy. Many will suffer."

He glanced about to make sure they were not overheard. "We will try to help them get away before that happens."

Allesandra pushed away from the window opening. "Then may I have permission to return home? I need not stay to witness the treaty. I have given you what advice you needed, my lord. The agreements are made."

He nodded. "As you wish. Take an escort and return to Toulouse. Take the news with you. Have it cried in the town. Meet with the town council and tell what I have done. They will not be so surprised."

"Yes, my lord."

His gaze seemed to return from the difficult place to which

his mind had wandered and he studied her in a more personal way. "And you, my lady? What of your life?"

She remembered Gaucelm's accusations of the night before and stiffened her jaw. "My fate is up to you, sir."

His mouth relaxed into a gentle smile. "We will have to discuss that when I return."

She swallowed. He would no doubt renew his suit for her hand. Perhaps Gaucelm was right; by declaring where her loyalty lay, she was in danger of trapping herself into a marriage out of duty. But then, according to the troubadours, when was marriage ever based on love? Love was a romantic notion to be shared between lovers. Marriage was a political responsibility between nobles.

Tears suddenly threatened at the edges of her eyes and she made a small nod and retreated. She found her way to her chamber and then sent the maid to find Jean de Batute.

When he came to wait on her, she told him what had happened. "I've been given leave to return home. The count must stay here to sign the treaty. Will you escort me?"

"Of course, my lady," replied Jean. "I will make sure we have a good party of men-at-arms to travel with you. When do we ride?"

"At dawn tomorrow."

He left her to make arrangements. Thinking that tomorrow's departure would allow her time to find out what had happened to Gaucelm, she returned to the hall. But Gaucelm was nowhere to be seen at dinner, and foreboding began to fill her. She tried to find a way to ask indirectly and finally had to admit to Raymond what she wanted to know.

He did not give anything away by his expression, but she felt that he must know why she wanted to know what had happened to the knight Gaucelm. After the meal, while the musicians were playing, he came to seek a word with her.

"The knight Gaucelm Deluc has left Paris, so it seems," he told her in a casual manner. "He has been sent to escort the pope's legate on the Church's business."

Allesandra's spine prickled. "So, it begins."

She shook her head bitterly. In all their times together, she never imagined that Gaucelm cared much for religion. His loyalty was to the Capetians and their kingdom. But perhaps his own bitterness had made him engage in service to the Church.

"Thank you, Raymond. I just wanted to know."

She started to turn away, but Raymond laid a hand on her arm. "Allesandra, forget him. I know there was love between you. But I think that you are too noble to bow to love that is so foreign to all you believe in. You would be doing the House of Toulouse a great honor if you would become my wife and sire me a son. The dynasty would continue in spite of treaties and kings."

She trembled at his words, tears glistening in her eyes. "I know, my lord." Her words choked her throat and she looked down. "I will think on the matter."

He released her. "That is all I ask."

At dawn the next day, Allesandra left Paris with Jean de Batute and an escort of their own soldiers. Her heart was heavy, but she was soon distracted from her own trouble as they stopped at inns along their route. Everywhere the gossip was about the peace that had been signed with the count of Toulouse. She overheard comments about the counts of Toulouse being worthy foes. Some expressed pride that France had managed to bring the rich lands of the Languedoc within French boundaries.

Jean tried to keep her from listening to the talk. But when they came to the River Lot and had to wait for the ferry to return from the other side, Allesandra got her first breath of a chill wind.

There was no mistaking a bishop's carriage, and the crosses emblazoned on caparisons and shields of a religious retinue. Allesandra and Jean sat on their mounts, their soldiers stretched in a line behind them as they watched the white horses led from the ferry, pulling the ornate carriage behind. Several long-robed priests followed on foot. The water carried voices across, though the words were indistinct as the party of churchmen, guarded by knights, struggled to form up on the bank.

The figures moved about, small from this distance, but gold glittered off a tall mitre as she saw a bishop descend. Evidently, the embankment was too steep, and even His Holiness was forced to walk. The man turned for a moment, and she almost felt as if he saw her where she sat her horse. She felt a shiver. Then he turned and picked up his robes to climb after the carriage, once the horses reached the top.

Jean was the first to speak. "We will find out in Cahors where they are bound."

"Indeed."

She had not seen Gaucelm among the escort, and again she wondered where he had gone. But there would be many such entourages of religious orthodoxy winding into the southern lands, now that Raymond had promised his help in finding heretics. Having had one such hearing forced upon her at her own castle when Gaucelm had been castellan, she could well imagine the disquieting effect a whole army of inquisitors could bring upon their lands.

At length the ferry crossed to carry them into the town of Cahors. They dismounted at an inn and Jean went inside to make arrangements. Allesandra handed her horse to the groom and then looked to her left along the street. The end of the narrow street became a window on a scene being enacted upon the church steps beyond.

The bishop's coach had halted and the bishop descended. Allesandra slipped along the street to get a better look. Several priests had come out from the impressive church with square towers rising above the houses and buildings crowded along its sides. She couldn't hear the words, but she could see from the gestures that introductions were being made. Two other impressively garbed churchmen had descended from the carriage and stood to one side. Even from across the road, Allesandra could see the haughty expressions on their faces and felt uneasy looking at them.

As the evening fell, lamps were being lit at the church portal and flickered at the stained-glass windows. A religious conference was about to begin. Jean came up the street to join her, and following her glance, he ascertained what she was watching.

"Ah, there they are. I heard at the inn. The pope has wasted no time in sending his inquisitors southward. The iron grip of the church."

His words were bitter and tense, and Allesandra only shook her head. "They will not be popular here, but Raymond has promised his protection."

She turned back in time to see Jean's eyelids close halfway at her last remark, but he said nothing. She wondered if he'd already picked up more gossip at the inn, but her head was aching from the long ride that day, and more than anything else, she wanted to rest.

After refreshing herself from a basin and ewer in her room, she descended to join Jean and the others for a meal. She found the inn strangely quiet. There were knots of patrons who whispered over their ale and their food, but as soon as she passed between them, they guarded their words or looked aside. Some such inns could be rowdy of an evening, but an eerie pall had fallen over the guests here.

Of course Allesandra could surmise that the mood of the town was darkened by the arrival of the inquisitors. For now the trials would start in earnest again, and property would be confiscated. Punishments meted out. Raymond thought he could satisfy his part of the bargain by handing over just a few who openly professed to be heretics. But somehow she felt that he was wrong. And what part was Gaucelm going to play in all of this now?

"Madam, you have hardly touched your food," commented Jean after he had picked his trencher clean and broken off pieces to toss to the dogs.

"The wine was bracing," she said, and sighed heavily. "I saw a small garden at the back of the inn. I feel the need for some fresh air. I think I will walk there before I retire."

Jean glanced about the company and then lowered his voice to speak. "I would advise against going outside tonight, madam."

She looked up sharply at the ominous trace in his words, and suddenly wondered what he knew that he wasn't telling. Nevertheless, she took his advice and retired to her room.

"Have the horses ready at first light, Jean," she said. "And tap on my door when you rise. I doubt I'll oversleep, but I want to be gone as soon as there's a gray light to ride by."

"Very well, my lady. Sleep well. Do not let any of the city sounds disturb you." He glanced over his shoulder and again she did not miss the warning in his words. "And keep your door barred."

The wine and the little food she had eaten did not lull her mind. The quiet evening in the dining room of the tavern with the averted gazes and the pent-up energy held some meaning. And then her mind returned to the sight of the Church's inquisitors, come to disrupt the fabric of a society that now must bow to a king. She shivered but nodded to Jean and closed the door, sliding the bar across it. Then she made ready for bed.

All the hard riding of the last week made it easy to fall into a deep slumber. No cries in the night woke her. No alarms were given to rouse a sleeping town. And she was wide awake as darkness began to lift its curtain the next morning. She was dressed and opened the door when Jean came to knock.

They went down through a silent inn and outside where the morning air refreshed the normal smells of a walled city. And at the city gates, they had to rouse the gatekeeper to let them through. Then their horses trotted briskly out to the road and away. Daylight lay claim to the day, and they slowed to a walk. Jean said little, and it wasn't until they had stopped to water their horses near a stream late in the day, that the news caught up to them. A traveler pressing to reach his home where the Garonne flowed into the Aueyron stopped to exchange a few words.

"We are bound for Toulouse," Jean told the stranger. "We were at Cahors last night."

It was always wise to refrain from telling anyone that Allesandra was a noble lady with vast lands in case strangers decided her party was worth robbing.

But the ruddy stranger, whose clothing was made of good

cloth and whose horse was not just a common nag, eyed them with interest.

"Ah, then, if you came from Cahors, perhaps you left too early to hear the news."

"What news is that, friend?" asked Jean.

The traveler looked over his shoulder, though they stood in a clearing just off the road. And there were no other travelers in sight but themselves. "There was a group of inquisitors arrived there."

Allesandra nodded, and Jean glanced at her before saying, "We saw them."

The traveler lowered his voice so that it wouldn't carry past the trees of the little grove where they watered the horses. "Murdered in their beds last night. The culprits were not caught."

Allesandra's heart missed a beat. Murder! Then she understood the furtive glances and the hushed mood of the tavern. The town had known. Perhaps had planned. But better that she and her party knew nothing of who was behind it.

The traveler went on to share his views. "Perhaps it'll make the pope in Rome think twice about sending his judges here."

None in Allesandra's party spoke. Her own lips were slack, but she didn't have any response. Her men-at-arms, who had heard the traveler's news, looked at each other and then back at the horses they watered. She daren't risk a glance at Jean. If he knew something about this, it was better he didn't speak of it.

"Murder is horrible," she said as the traveler led his horse up from the riverbank. And she shook her head.

"Indeed it is," said Jean. "Let us hope there are no reprisals."

Hopelessness tugged at her already lifeless heart. "So soon after a treaty has been signed. What can this mean? Will there never be any rest?"

"Eventually, the people of the South may learn to live with the people of the North," answered Jean philosophically. "And someday there may be a religion that satisfies all of us. But that day has not yet come."

The breeze came to make the leaves above them sigh. Jean

cupped his hands to give Allesandra a step up to her stirrup. Then they all mounted and rode thoughtfully back to the road.

The rest of the journey was fairly uneventful. Allesandra knew she could never banish thoughts of Gaucelm entirely, but when she reached her home, she bent her mind to the tasks at hand. Her lands were vast and she had been absent a long while. While her steward had been capable, there was still much to attend to. In the evenings, her minstrels, and the troubadours when they paid her a visit, would sing softly. But the entertainments were subdued, melancholy, with gentle melodies that soothed.

And it came to her ears that one by one, certain tenants and vassals had disappeared from their homes of their own accord. Jean brought her the news, and through Jean, Allesandra helped those who wished to leave these lands for places they felt safer, high up in the Pyrenees, where they hoped no one cared about their particular religious practices. There were as yet no French soldiers to stop them and no grand inquisitors to question them.

When Raymond returned from Paris, she went to see him. But she said nothing of what she knew. They only addressed the matter of heresy obliquely.

When she was at her own home, she found she spent more time writing poetry again. The love she still bore Gaucelm found an outlet in the words that flowed and the endless ink that formed the letters upon her parchments. Some she was not pleased with. For though it was an outpouring of her own feelings, she was still an artist and a craftswoman. She threw many pages into the fire. But the better ones she kept.

The months passed, and she had time to give thought to her actions and words and felt sorry that they had parted on such ill terms. She began to write him letters. Epistles that he would never see. But perhaps it was some glimmer, some burning coal in her heart fed by a love that would not die, that made her write the letters as if he would one day lay eyes on them. And perhaps forgive her pride and the duty that stood between them.

And then, one night, when she least expected it, for she knew not where he was, he came. He was not even announced by the servants, but burst into the hall where a great meal was celebrating the harvest.

As soon as she saw him, she had eyes for no one else. The household seemed to melt away as he strode across the hall between the tables. Someone pulled her chair away as she stood up at the head of the table, her heart pounding. Somehow her feet carried her to meet him near the arched passage where stairs led to her private chamber. He stopped a few feet from her and then bowed.

She still said not a word when he lifted his eyes and held hers. It was as if they were the only two in the entire castle. For even though their bodies stood stiffly and distantly, their spirits joined in the middle of the space between them, and everything else was suspended.

A moment later they passed through the passage and to the great chamber where so much had transpired between them. Gaucelm walked to the window seat where shutters opened onto stubbled fields in the distance, bathed by a hunter's moon. There was a crispness in the air, though autumn in these southern lands was gentle.

Allesandra felt unable to stand up any longer and sank into the carved armchair in front of a fireplace where Julian had thoughtfully kindled an evening fire. "I am surprised to see you, my lord."

He grunted. "I come only to let you know what you will hear from others in any case. The pope's legate in Paris, Bishop Frosbier, was displeased by the deaths of several priests at Cahors."

She crossed her arms and hugged herself, leaning forward a bit. "I had heard."

She was not about to tell him that she had been in the city that night. Nor that Jean must have known about it beforehand. "It is terrible," she added.

Gaucelm went on in a leaden voice that showed no emotion.

"As you know, the Church will stop at nothing until all the heretics are destroyed."

There was no need to explain. Evidently after seeing Allesandra the last time, he felt even more than before that the lines were drawn between them.

"I know that is your intention," she said quietly. "We all know it."

He turned finally to look at her, as if staring out the window for a long time had given him the strength to face her. "The royal government has decided to avenge the deaths at Cahors."

Her face twisted before she could compose herself. She looked at her knees. "Why do you tell me this?"

There was a pause of a heartbeat. "Perhaps because I feel I owe it to you."

"Very well. What do you plan to do?"

He let go of the inner window arch. "We march to a place we believe to be the last stronghold of the most determined of the heretics."

Her gaze flew upward, but stopped at his chest level before she allowed herself to give anything away. "Really? And where is that?"

"Montségur."

She felt herself sway, even though she was seated, and she reached for her chair arms. "Montségur?" It was spoken in a level tone, but even Gaucelm understood that she knew of it. "I see."

He paced to the center of the room, and at last she had the courage to stand up and face him. "And why do you tell me this?"

He moved no closer, but his gaze simmered. "I thought you should know."

She turned, uncertain how to react. During the months since she'd seen him, she'd promised herself that if she ever had the chance, she would try to mend the tear that had occurred in Paris. Even if they must remain forever on opposite sides of a bitter disagreement, she wanted to know that they did not hate each other. But now that he was here, treading cautiously himself, she did not know how to begin.

Her throat felt dry, but she managed to moisten her lips and say, "Can you not leave them alone? What harm do they do, isolated in such a refuge?"

"I do not make the decisions, as you know. The king must make an example. He cannot condone murders of Church officials. That was done purposely, a symbol that all the treaties in the world cannot change a people's mind so soon. I have no choice but to carry out the king's orders."

He exhaled a breath as if pleased that he'd succeeded in delivering a difficult message. She might have tried to understand more about why he told her where he was going, but she did not. Instead, all she could do was stare at him. And he at her. And yet neither made a move to touch the other. Perhaps their love was torn now beyond mending. They were too far apart, separated by birth and loyalties that were too deep to change.

"Have you been well?" she asked.

He nodded slowly. "Yes, and you?"

She managed a sad sigh. "Yes.

"Then that is good."

"You still think of me then?"

Now he moved a step closer. "Of course. I always think of you. That will not change."

"No?" She looked up.

"No."

"And I will always think of you, my lord." Her heart beat loudly now in her chest. The pulse trebled in her veins.

He came to her and touched her arms, but with restraint. And somehow she knew that the evening would not end in passion the way it always had before. How terrible that they still loved each other, but could not do anything about it as long as their pride and loyalties kept them apart.

He gazed deeply into her eyes and his look said what she surmised. He held her fondly, just enough to remember earlier times together. She smiled, but she felt a tear slip down her cheek.

"Gaucelm," she said, "I did not want to part the way we did."

"Nor I," he said, lifting a hand to brush the hair back from her temple. "I was cruel the last time I saw you. I wanted to take my revenge in a mean, unspeakable way. I ask your forgiveness."

"You were not cruel," she said. "You claimed me, true, when you thought I would soon belong to another. But it was as I would have wanted you to do. If I carried any man's child, I would have wanted yours."

Then she leaned her cheek against his chin and he folded her into him gently. Still, she could feel him restrain himself from passion. They wanted each other desperately, but just as she knew that there was no future in it, so he must have resolved that he came to speak to her only, nothing more.

They stood together in the soft glow from lamps and fire, swaying slightly, breathing in a well-remembered embrace, wanting it to last, but knowing it could not. At length, he lifted her chin and kissed her forehead and cheeks. She felt him tremble as he placed his hands on her shoulders and set her away from him.

"I cannot stay," he told her. There was pain in his eyes.

"I know."

He stepped back, threw his shoulders back as if on military review. He took one last look and then turned for the door.

After he had gone, she relived every second of the visit, sitting by the fire late into the night. It wasn't until much later that she was able to sort through his words and began to understand why he had come at all.

Twenty-four

Late the next day, Jean de Batute burst into the hall where Allesandra had just finished a conference with her steward, Julian. The accounts approved, the steward withdrew as Jean crossed the hall and handed Allesandra a rolled piece of parchment, whose seal had been broken.

"A message from Lucius Hersend," he said. "It was addressed to me, but you should read it for yourself."

She took the letter anxiously and read Lucius's fine hand. Lucius, who had been in the mountains at the stronghold of Montségur for the last several months, was preparing for a confrontation.

"In spite of the recent treaty," she read out loud, "and Count Raymond's guaranteed cooperation in routing out the last of the heretics, Raymond looked the other way as the most determined Cathars, thrown off of their own parcels of land, have gathered within the protection of the particularly isolated and impregnable walls of the mountain citadel. It is located at the top of a steep mountain peak that is barren of any cover besides the smooth rock face upon which it perches."

She paused to glance at Jean, then continued. "I know," said the letter, "that a French contingent of soldiers is on its way. If they succeed in reaching the citadel, they will mete out reprisals for the murders of the inquisitors at Cahors. The heretics at Montségur cannot be called sheep gone astray for lack of understanding. These are not the congenial Provençals who care little for outward appearances even if they cling to suspicious beliefs.

"These are the remaining parfaits, those who have given up everything to take the *consolamentum,* that statement of faith abhorrent to the Catholic Church. And those with them, those who have chosen such a place to retreat to, will not surrender."

Lucius's own voice echoed in her mind as she read on. "No doubt those who surrender will be given a choice between recanting their unorthodox faith or facing torture and death. But with me here are the believers who would walk through flames and carry their faith to the grave rather than recant."

Allesandra saw at once what this meant, and it would come as a surprise to tell Jean that she already knew who was leading the French soldiers. But she had nothing to hide.

"So, Lucius is getting ready. He is that serious then," she said sorrowfully. "I knew he believed. I saw how he took it when he was excommunicated. He will not abandon the others."

Jean shook his head slowly, worried thoughtfulness on his normally happy face. He gave a great sigh. "How I miss his songs. He had a golden voice, but of course you remember."

"Yes." She smiled softly. "He was a gentle singer. Perhaps he sings now, adding his music to the believers' prayers."

"What do you wish to do, my lady?" asked Jean. He knew her far too well to expect that she would remain here and do nothing.

But before she answered, she arose from her chair and walked a little way across the hall, thinking.

"Perhaps their very position will protect them. I cannot imagine an army assaulting those walls. I have never seen it, but from what I have heard, only a narrow, winding path leads upward, exposed to the elements and to the citadel above."

Irritation suffused her. "Is this not a futile effort on the part of the king?"

Jean shook his head. "It will be difficult. But as to whether they make only a feeble attempt or will carry out their mission, I cannot say. It might be that Lucius and the others are in very real danger." He sighed and paced in a small circle, his hands on his hips. He stopped and turned to her again, shaking his clipped, dark hair.

"I am only one man, but I must offer my help."

"Supposing the soldiers do climb up to them and threaten them. Is there no way of escape from such a place? No other place to hide? Perhaps if the king takes an empty fortress, he will give up."

"This I do not know. I would have to go and ask Lucius. I'm sure he would help those who wish to escape. But there are those who would prefer to be martyred. For them, there is no escape."

She shivered, but she knew his words were true. Some of her own friends were in that mountain fastness. Nobles like herself as well as common villagers who had turned away from the rule of the Catholic Church and embraced a more simple belief that they could understand. Left alone to live communally out of the way of the rest of society, consoled by the parfaits, their lives would be ideal. But they were not soldiers, and they feared the anger of Church and king. An ominous fear told her that this time they would not be treated lightly.

She could almost hear their cries of confusion and desperation if soldiers penetrated their mountain citadel. She felt their fear. Her mind was made up.

"We can leave at once," she told Jean. "I will go with you. I cannot think of our friends facing death or punishment at the hands of the French."

Jean gave her a curious look. "Very well, my lady. But do not tremble so. I can see that great emotion seizes you. Are you all right?"

She steeled her runaway emotions to answer calmly. "Gaucelm Deluc leads these soldiers to Montségur. He was here last night briefly. He did not stay."

She lifted her chin, somehow wanting Jean to know that she had not made love with Gaucelm last night. "But he told me his destination. I suppose I should have told you rather than waiting for this message from Lucius."

"I see. Are you sure you still wish to accompany me? Are you sure you still wish to fight this man?"

"I would not fight Gaucelm if I had a choice. He does not have an evil heart. But he has made his choice. He serves king and Church." She straightened her shoulders even if the pain wrenched in her heart as she did so. "And I made my choice long ago."

Jean nodded slowly, still studying her face anxiously. "Very well. We will have to ride hard and avoid the soldiers. When we get to the mountain, we will have to leave our horses behind. The only way to reach Lucius is by climbing up the back of the mountain. If you have retainers who want to go with us, we can take what provisions we can carry with us."

She nodded. "Julian will have everything ready by the third hour after noon. We will go then."

* * *

Inch by inch Gaucelm led his men up the torturous path of Montségur until the lengthening evening made progress more difficult. Trees sheltered them partway up the mountain, but the lonely splendor of the mountain fortress above them did indeed appear daunting. Nevertheless, Gaucelm knew with certainty that his men would not leave until the fortress castle was handed over to the Church and the French Crown. Just what he himself would do when that occurred depended on several things.

He tried not to think of Allesandra, tried not to speculate as to whether she would be there when they overcame the fortress. As his men climbed upward, sometimes almost straight up cliffs, he reflected on his last visit to her. Surely she had understood his message. Surely she would not stand by as a French army marched to capture the last hundred or so Cathars who had taken refuge here.

Surely those in the fortress knew of the presence of the soldiers. But so far there was not a single sign of defense. Many Cathar believers were opposed to violence, and perhaps none would fight at all, but rely on the strength of those walls to keep the French soldiers out.

He scrambled downward a little way to speak to his sergeant and balanced where Enselm waited on a boulder to direct the men behind him. Enselm had followed Gaucelm on this as on most other campaigns.

"I'll go ahead," Gaucelm said. "There appears to be a way up below the north tower. One of us needs to get closer and see if there are any faults. If they resist, we're too exposed on the face of the mountain. But the wooded hills come closer on that side. We may mine our way in."

"I'll go if you want," said Enselm.

Gaucelm shook his head. "Take charge here." He glanced upward speculatively. "If anything should happen to me, I trust you to carry out the siege successfully. They'll give in at length. Remember the king's order: the survivors must be spared and given a choice between abjuring their faith or death by fire."

Enselm nodded, allowing no expression to cross his steady face. "The soldiers know that. The legate made it clear when we rode south."

Gaucelm reached out his hand, and the two men clasped arms above the wrist. He felt sure that Enselm would carry out his orders.

"If I'm not back by morning, tell the men that I have found a way into the castle to talk to the heretics. If I negotiate a peaceful surrender, it will save us uncomfortable months of siege."

"Godspeed," said Enselm.

Gaucelm turned away, having said everything else privately to Enselm early this morning in order to ensure the success of the mission. Then he clambered up the rocks, leaving the main path where the scrubby trees gave way to gravel and rock.

Once having worked his way around the side of the mountain, he paused beneath a tower. A little farther on he saw a small door, no doubt barred shut now. But from the refuse and dark stains on the rocks, he could tell that this was where some of the garbage was disposed of, to fall down to the woods below to be consumed by wild pigs. Water was evidently thrown after, to wash it from the rocks.

This, then, might be his entrance. If no one opened the door to dispose of any refuse this evening, then he would have to climb the walls. He had ropes and iron hooks, and could attempt that when it was dark enough. At any other fortress, he would face a guard on top who would cut the rope or push him backward to break his skull on the rocks. And it might be so here, he could not tell. The peace-loving Cathars might have knights among them who would deign to fight for their faith.

He scrambled as close to the little door as possible and crouched down to wait. The mountain night was cold, and he pulled the cloak fastened at his throat around him to shield him from the night air and to help obscure him in the darkness.

The creaking of the small door made him jerk out of a doze,

and he readied himself. It opened a little wider, and then water splashed outward from a pail. Gaucelm sprang forward, shoving his foot in the door and grasping the wrist that held the wooden bucket.

His hand was across the girl's mouth before she could scream, and his firm grip held her back against his torso as the bucket flew out the door and rattled down the rocks. He hissed in her ear, speaking in Provençal.

"I'm not going to hurt you. There are French soldiers out there, but if you answer my questions, no harm will come." He waited until she stopped struggling, though her body was tense. "Nod slowly if you understand me."

The girl pushed her head against his hand and nodded. He only relaxed his grip slightly, but spoke into her ear. "I seek a lady by the name of Allesandra Valtin. Do you know her?"

No response. Gaucelm shifted the girl in his grasp, but kept his hand covering her mouth. Even if she attempted to bite him, his thick gloves would prevent injury.

"I am not here to hurt anyone," he said again. "But to help you. I must speak to the lady Allesandra. Can you take me to her?"

The girl must have decided that she'd be better off cooperating. Or perhaps it was the intense determination she saw in his eyes reflected from moonlight coming in the open door. She finally nodded, and he felt her body relax slightly. He removed his hands from her, his face still commanding that she should cooperate.

But first the girl pulled the door to, glancing outside as she did so. Seeing no more threatening soldiers, she pulled it tight and heaved the bar into place. Thus the castle was secured again. She said not a word but led Gaucelm up a twisting set of stairs. She paused on a landing and pushed open a door.

"Wait there," she said.

Gaucelm placed his foot in the door to prevent her locking him into some cell in which he might rot if the girl decided to tell no one. But he found there was no lock, and she scurried off. He lit an oil lamp while he waited. At length the girl returned.

With her was a strapping, ruddy-looking fellow in long tunic. He carried a lighted oil lamp, and he was armed with a sword affixed to a leather-tooled belt. There was something familiar about the blue eyes that lit on Gaucelm curiously, and when the man spoke, he thought he remembered the voice.

"Who are you?"

"Gaucelm Deluc," he answered. "I am seeking the lady Allesandra Valtin, who I suspect is here."

The ruddy man lifted reddish-brown brows. "What makes you think she is here?"

"I am a friend."

"I know who you are. You ruled her lands when I was heard before bishops who accused me of heresy."

"Ah, yes, now I remember. Lucius Hersend. So, you took refuge here." Gaucelm cast his eyes about the walls, carved out of rock at this level of the castle.

"I have."

"Then believe me when I say I only mean to help you. I must see Allesandra."

Lucius relented. "She will see you. She only sent me to make sure it was not a trick. You are alone?"

"Soldiers are just above the treetops on the path. But surely you saw that for yourself earlier."

"Of course. It would be impossible not to. What do the soldiers intend to do here?"

"Take me to her ladyship and I will tell you."

Lucius led Gaucelm upward, the lamp in his hand lighting the way. They passed by an arched doorway, open to reveal a hall. Small pools of light and torches mounted on the walls revealed several groups of people gathered, all wearing long, white tunics, almost luminescent in the firelight. But Lucius led onward.

At the top of a short stairway, he opened a door to a private chamber. Allesandra stood at one end, her hand on an oaken mantel, a poker in the other hand where she straightened from stirring up the fire. Her great violet eyes were troubled. She nodded to Lucius, who retreated and closed the door behind them.

Gaucelm went down on one knee, his head bent. "My lady," he said with great humility. "I came to you before to warn you. I come now to surrender."

His words moved her beyond everything she had imagined and she dropped the poker on the floor and swept forward. She sank to her own knees and reached for him, and they took each other in a desperate embrace. She trembled in his arms. But she saw the love in his eyes now, something she'd been afraid she'd never see again.

"How did you know I would be here?" she said in a shaking voice.

"When I told you where we were going, I felt sure you would join your friends here in their last refuge."

"And now?"

"If I can, I will help you and all of them escape. The soldiers are as yet only on the path that leads here. In the morning they will surround the castle, but that will take time. If your friends are brave, we can tie ropes and lower them over the walls. Those who are fit can surely scramble down the rocks as far as the trees and the woods. When the surrounding army is in place, they will find they've been left with an abandoned fortress."

"They will not go," she said.

He knew she referred to the Cathars who were gathered here. "How many?" he said grimly.

"More than a hundred. I came here for the same reason as you. To try to help them escape to yet another place. But this is the place where they wish to die. They are not afraid. Their faith sustains them."

He narrowed his eyes. "And yourself?"

She turned her head to nestle it against him. "I will go with you, my lord. I have been stubborn and I don't deserve your love or for you to risk your life for me. But these many months I've had time to examine my conscience. I have done all I can for the believers, truly. It is important that some of us escape. There are documents, treasures that must be kept safe. Some of the others are determined to be martyred. I am too weak to die. My strength comes from you, Gaucelm, I know that now. I cannot live without you."

Gaucelm closed his eyes and wept into her hair. "To hear you say those words, my love, means everything to me. I had feared you would reject me again."

"No, no, never. My heart has never rejected you."

He held her for as long as he could and then he kissed her on the lips before helping her to her feet. "Then tell me what to do. Who goes with us and what do we take?"

"The valuables are already packed. Jean de Batute brought me here. He will go with us. And two of the believers. There is an easy way down from the north tower. Once we reach the woods there is a path. I have already made my last good-byes."

"And Lucius Hersend?"

She shook her head, tears moistening her eyes. "He will remain here. It is his choice."

"A pity. He is a good man."

She nodded and allowed herself one more embrace. Then before more tears could escape, she straightened and walked to the doorway. From there she led Gaucelm down the steps and through the hall. The believers were gathered in circles, some holding hands, many with heads bowed in prayer. None looked up as they passed.

He followed Allesandra up the tower stairs and into a chamber near the top where he recognized Jean de Batute and was introduced to a man and woman he'd not seen before.

"Gaucelm goes with us," she told them. "He will lead us to safety."

"We are ready," said Jean. "The way is clear. We need only lower ourselves out this window to the rocks. From there we climb down. I'll go first, then you throw the packs after me."

Allesandra turned to Gaucelm just as she was ready to grasp the ropes and make the descent.

"Go safely," he said to her, laying has hand on her arm. "I don't want any harm coming to my wife-to-be."

Her lips trembled with pent-up emotion. But happiness was there, too, because she would be with Gaucelm at last, though she did not know where.

He squeezed her arm. "I will be right behind you, my lady."

"Yes," she whispered. "And we will never part again."

"Never," he said with a certainty that filled her heart. "Never again."

Epilogue

Allesandra and Gaucelm made their way down the mountain, taking the Cathars' most treasured valuables with them. The party traveled for many days through the mountains and at last reached the Mediterranean Sea. From there they sailed to Genoa, and in later years to Alexandria.

Wherever they went, Allesandra was received as one of the foremost troubadours of her day. Her reputation in the noblest of courts was great. Gaucelm did well as a knight both in tournament and in battle. Their marriage was a happy one, and their love shone in all the exotic ports they set foot in and in all the courts from great to small.

They kept abreast of news from Languedoc, which became firmly entrenched in the French Crown through the marriage of Jeanne of Toulouse and the king's brother, Alphonse. Years passed and Count Raymond VII failed to sire a son.

Allesandra and Gaucelm at last decided to return home and

take up residence once more on the great Valtin demesne. There, they sired sons, who were raised to become great knights.

Allesandra and her husband walked together hand-in-hand, giving strength to the people of Toulouse in a land that once rang with the songs of the troubadours.

ROMANCE FROM HANNAH HOWELL

MY VALIANT KNIGHT   (0-8217-5186-7, $5.50)

ONLY FOR YOU   (0-8217-4993-5, $4.99)

UNCONQUERED   (0-8217-5417-3, $5.99)

WILD ROSES   (0-8217-5677-X, $5.99)

PASSIONATE ROMANCE
FROM BETINA KRAHN!

HIDDEN FIRES   (0-8217-4953-6, $4.99)

LOVE'S BRAZEN FIRE   (0-8217-5691-5, $5.99)

MIDNIGHT MAGIC   (0-8217-4994-3, $4.99)

PASSION'S RANSOM   (0-8217-5130-1, $5.99)

REBEL PASSION   (0-8217-5526-9, $5.99)